THE
SORCERER
HEIR

ALSO BY CINDA WILLIAMS CHIMA

THE
SORCERER
HEIR

CINDA WILLIAMS CHIMA

HYPERION
LOS ANGELES   NEW YORK

Copyright © 2014 by Cinda Williams Chima

All rights reserved. Published by Hyperion, an imprint of Disney Book Group. No part of this book may be reproduced or transmitted in any form or by any means, electronic or mechanical, including photocopying, recording, or by any information storage and retrieval system, without written permission from the publisher. For information address Hyperion, 125 West End Avenue, New York, New York 10023.

Printed in the United States of America
First Hardcover Edition, October 2014
First Paperback Edition, April 2016
10 9 8 7 6 5 4 3 2 1
FAC-025438-16015

Library of Congress Control Number for Hardcover: 2014022039
ISBN 978-1-4231-9475-0
Visit www.hyperionteens.com
www.cindachima.com

For Keith Swift Chima: you look at the world slant.
And that's a good thing.

❧ CHAPTER ONE ❧
CURVE BALLS

"Where are you off to, Alicia?" Aunt Millisandra asked as Leesha Middleton sidled past on her way to the door.

"A party," Leesha said, purposely vague. "I'll be back late."

"Is the party here in town?" Aunt Millie asked. "Will there be drinking? Will you be careful?"

This was unusual. Aunt Millie wasn't a particularly intrusive chaperone, given that she had a very clear memory of what it was like to be young, and a very poor memory of anything that had happened in the past year.

"The party is at Seph McCauley's house," Leesha said. "I don't know about the drinking, but I'm always careful these days."

Aunt Millisandra looked over the rims of her reading glasses. The glasses weren't functional—they had no glass in them. Aunt Millie didn't love the way the glass reflected, but she liked the look otherwise. "You look ravishing, my dear. It must be a very fancy party. I haven't seen you wear that dress before. And the leather goggles—is that a new fashion?"

"It's a costume," Leesha said, brushing at her vampish dress. "For a Halloween party."

"A *costume*," Aunt Millie said, emitting a shower of sparks, signifying delight. "Is it really Halloween?" She looked around wildly. "Is it beggars' night? Should I have candy? Oh, dear." She brightened. "I did make muffins the other day. Maybe we can—"

"No, Aunt Millie," Leesha said, batting out the sparks that landed on the settee. "It's not beggars' night. No worries. I'll, ah, bring home candy." Aunt Millie had many stellar qualities, but she wasn't much of a cook. The muffins could have stood in as hockey pucks. Leesha had diverted them into the trash almost immediately. Living with a wizard who was a few cards short in her mental deck wasn't always easy.

Blessedly, Aunt Millie moved on. "What are you supposed to be?"

"I'm a—a sort of Victorian vampire," Leesha said.

"It's quite fetching, dear," Aunt Millie said. "Especially the décolletage. But . . ." She pressed her lips together in disapproval. "You have such lovely jewelry, Alicia; why is it that you always wear that snake pendant?"

Leesha touched the pendant nestled between her breasts. It was a gold snake eating its tail. A talisman against evil. "It's a reminder to be careful who I partner up with."

It was also a reminder of the cost of betrayal. She'd betrayed Jack Swift to the White Rose warriormaster Jessamine Longbranch. She'd partnered up with the wizard Warren Barber, whom she hated, and betrayed Jason Haley, whom she loved. Now Jason was dead, cut down by the wizard Claude d'Orsay in a battle between the underguilds and their wizard oppressors.

Nearly two years had passed, but there would be no do-overs.

Fortunately, Aunt Millie again meandered onto a new topic. "It makes sense to be choosy, especially if you plan on biting anyone. Or being bitten. The human mouth is one of the most—"

"Not going to happen," Leesha said, cheeks burning. "I'm just hanging out with some friends."

Aunt Millie's face settled into disappointed lines. "I had hopes," she said. "You haven't had a gentleman caller since you misplaced that young man I found for you."

"I didn't misplace him," Leesha said sharply. "I've told you. He disappeared while we were out walking in London. Maybe I'm not as charming as I thought."

"Alicia Ann Middleton, you are the most charming young lady I know. No young man would willingly leave your side."

Unless he was attacked and dismembered by the walking dead. Leesha shuddered.

No! I'm not going to think about that. That never happened. Why can't I develop amnesia like every other victim of trauma?

"His family hasn't seen him since either," Aunt Millie said. "They've been terribly persistent. Why, they've even made some rather nasty accusations about you, dear. I think they should look closer to home for culprits. London can be a dangerous place, what with all those graveyards and barrows and ley lines."

Right. Ley lines, Leesha thought. "Let's not talk about that, Aunt Millie. It doesn't make sense to dwell on things you can't do anything about."

That was her new rule, and it seemed to apply to so much of her past. *I used to be so coldhearted and ruthless. What's happened to me?*

As if she'd overheard Leesha's thoughts, Aunt Millie said, "I'm worried about you, Alicia. You haven't been yourself since you went to London."

I haven't been myself since Jason died, Leesha thought. "I'm fine," she said aloud as she wrapped a black velvet cape around her shoulders. "Don't wait up. I'll be back late."

Trinity, Ohio, was a small town (!), so Leesha walked the few blocks to Seph McCauley's house. The house actually belonged to his mother, the enchanter Linda Downey, but lately his parents, Downey and Leander Hastings, the wizard, had been spending most of their time in Europe. At one time, Leesha would have envied Seph, living on his own, doing as he pleased, but right now she welcomed the distraction of having Aunt Millisandra around. The constant risk of incineration kept her on her toes.

You need something to do, Leesha thought. Something to do besides mope. A quick fling might be just the ticket. Her heart beat faster. Maybe she *would* meet someone at this party. Someone who'd never heard of the pathetic Leesha Middleton. Who wouldn't want to rehash old news or dig up the bodies of the dead.

She needed someone *fresh*.

The McCauley-Downey-Hastings home stood in a lakeside neighborhood of Victorian summer homes, built in an era when the rich birthed cottages like a cat drops kittens.

Cars already lined the narrow streets nearly all the way to Aunt Millie's. Leesha heard the party long before she saw it: usually a good sign.

Leesha's former boyfriend, the warrior Jack Swift, was directing people in the foyer. He was co-hosting the party, along with his soul mate and sparring partner, Ellen Stephenson. Jack wore a leather vest, velvet pantaloons, and tights that showed off his warrior build.

"Looking good, Jack," Leesha said, flouncing her skirts, showing her glamoured fangs. Sliding easily into her usual role. "Care to expose your jugular?"

Jack took a step back and raised his weapon for a two-handed sweep—it was a pear-shaped stringed instrument.

Leesha couldn't help laughing. "What are you supposed to be?"

Jack sighed. "I'm a minstrel," he said glumly. "Not my idea."

Leesha could guess whose it was. "*Hmm*. Well, maybe you're a warrior pretending you're a minstrel," she said. "Maybe that's how you get inside the castle walls."

Jack snorted, but the corners of his mouth twitched. Leesha knew he liked that idea.

She greeted a few Anaweir high school friends who'd either stayed in the area or come home for what promised to be a stellar Halloween party. Scanning the crowd, she saw that it was mostly people she knew, a handful of non-magical Anaweir mixed in with the younger generation of gifted Weir from all over the world. The gifted belonged to one of the five magical guilds: warriors, wizards, sorcerers, seers, and enchanters. They were like five feuding gangs linked together by their dependence on the Dragonheart, the well of power controlled by Madison Moss, a.k.a. the Dragon. She'd been ruling in absentia for the past two years while attending art school in Chicago.

You could give college a try, Leesha thought. Aunt Millie had been pushing that, as an alternative to a grand tour of Europe or a year at an ashram. But could she really hang out with a bunch of freshmen?

Q: You graduated from high school *when*? What have you been *doing* all this time?

A: Preventing power-hungry wizards from taking over the world. Also, betraying nearly everyone I care about. Losing the only boy I ever loved. You?

Leesha wandered out into the conservatory. Guests in elaborate costumes danced to a wide-ranging playlist. In the makeshift stage area, people were dragging power cords around, setting up for a band. One of them was oddly dressed for a roadie, wearing a velvet cape, vest, and cravat.

"Fitch!" Leesha said. "I didn't know you'd be here. They don't have parties in Cambridge?"

"Not like this party," Fitch said, scrambling to his feet from where he'd been fussing with some sort of a connection. They shared an awkward two-handed handshake that evolved into an awkward hug.

"Will's here, too," Fitch said. "He drove up from Columbus for this. I think he's in the kitchen. Jack put him to work, too."

Will Childers and Harmon Fitch were wary of Leesha—and who could blame them? She'd sold off their lifelong friend Jack to magical traffickers. Then there was that kidnapping incident in the UK. But they'd fought on the same side in the Battle of Trinity, and they were keenly aware of Leesha's losses in that war.

Fitch retrieved a top hat from the edge of the stage and clapped it on his head. It was probably a costume, but then again it could have been Fitch being himself.

"The red hair is a good look for you," Leesha said, playing it safe. "And I love that suit. Where did you find that?"

"Thrift shop in Boston," Fitch said. "East-coast thrift is top of the line." He looked her up and down. "You look nice," he said.

"Nice?" Leesha raised an eyebrow.

He recovered quickly. "I meant, you look devastatingly gorgeous."

"That's better," Leesha said. "Are you just here for the weekend?"

Pain flickered across his face. "No, I'm here indefinitely. I'm taking a break from school."

"Taking a break?" Leesha cocked her head. "Now? Aren't you a sophomore? Isn't it the middle of the semester?"

"It is," Fitch said, "but my mom's in the hospital again, and my sibs require their older brother's firm hand and wise counsel right now." Fitch was the oldest of six kids. His mother had an autoimmune disorder and had been in and out of the hospital for years. It made it hard for her to support the family; they always lived hand-to-mouth.

Leesha put her hand on his arm. "That really sucks." She could guess how brutally hard it must be for Fitch to step away from a full-ride scholarship to Harvard.

"It's fine," Fitch said. "I'll go back eventually. I'm back working in IT for Trinity College, and they've arranged for me to continue my research and take a few classes." He stuffed his hands into his pockets. "I thought maybe you'd have left Trinity for someplace a little more exciting by now."

"I'm helping Aunt Millie with some things. That's enough excitement for me these days." She scanned the crowd. "Did Rosie come back for the party, too?"

"No." After a beat or two, he added, "We broke up."

"Oh." Way to put your foot in it, Leesha thought. She cleared her throat. "I'm sorry to hear that."

Fitch shrugged. "She's spending next year at an alternative school in Nepal. She wanted me to apply with her, and when I said no, she said I was choosing to be part of the problem. Things just escalated from there. Or deteriorated, depending on your viewpoint."

A young girl dressed as a black cat rocketed around the corner carrying a massive roll of duct tape. "Fitch? I've got the cord taped down all along the wall. Is there any—" She broke off when she saw Leesha. "Oh! Hi, Leesha."

"Hey, Grace," Leesha said, grinning. "Great costume."

"You think so?" Grace wrapped her tail around her wrist. "It's just something I came up with from stuff I had around."

"Those are the best kinds of costumes," Leesha said. She gave her skirts a twitch. "This is actually my old prom dress."

"They let you wear *that* for prom?" Grace exclaimed, then laughed when she saw that Leesha was kidding.

Leesha couldn't help liking Madison Moss's often-grouchy little sister—maybe because her mood so often mirrored Leesha's. Madison had uprooted twelve-year-old Grace from Nowheresville, Ohio, and brought her up to Trinity to go to school. Then parked her with their cousin and gone off to art school in Chicago. No wonder Grace felt out of place and abandoned.

Kind of like me.

Jack walked past, carrying an amplifier, followed by Ellen, leading some strangers through the crowd, onto the terrace. They were all carrying musical equipment, so Leesha guessed this must be Fault Tolerant, the band Ellen had been raving about since she'd seen them at a club in downtown Cleveland.

The band members were all students at Gabriel Mandrake's "special school" for magical mutants (the PC term was *savant*). Originally members of the mainline magical guilds, they'd survived a mass poisoning at a commune in Brazil that had altered their Weirstones in unique and sometimes dangerous ways. Maybe that's what made their music so exciting. Leesha was looking forward to hearing them.

She drifted closer, watching them set up, and realized that she recognized one of the band members, a tall, broad-shouldered boy with ink-black hair and smoldering blue eyes. A smoking-hot guy, in fact, and she had an excellent memory for that breed. She'd seen him at the sword-fighting demonstration at the Medieval Faire in Trinity. He'd fought Jack and Ellen both at once. He'd lost, but he hadn't embarrassed himself—not at all. In fact, Leesha thought, I'd rather watch him lose than watch a lot of other guys win.

What was his name?

"Jonah!" the drummer called over to him. "I thought you said you sent me the set list!" She peered at a tablet computer mounted next to her kit.

"I did," he called back. "I can send it again if you want."

Jonah. That was it. Jonah Kinlock.

Leesha couldn't say exactly what made him so engaging. He hadn't spent much time on his look: his timeworn T-shirt fit like a second skin and was tucked into battered jeans, the kind that start out indigo blue and then fade to a soft cornflower as they shrink to fit. Over the T-shirt, he wore a flannel shirt with the sleeves half-rolled, black leather gloves, and worn sneakers.

Maybe it was the way he moved, the way he chewed on his lower lip while he adjusted the tuning on his guitar, the interplay of light and shadow created by the planes of his face. There was something savage and elemental and feral in him. The fact that he was a savant only added to the intrigue.

I always go for the dangerous boys, Leesha thought.

"You're staring," Fitch said, nearly in her ear. "And you're not the only one."

Leesha whipped around to face him, and saw that Grace was fixed on Jonah, too, studying him with her usual intensity.

"I've met him before," Leesha said. "At the Medieval Faire in Trinity." She paused, but Fitch said nothing, just looked from Leesha to Jonah with an unreadable expression. "Well," Leesha said briskly, "I'm going to go see if Will needs help in the kitchen." Not that she knew anything about cooking, but she was good at bossing people around.

It turned out there were too many bosses in the kitchen already. When Leesha walked in, Will was busy at the sink. He was making a salad big enough to feed a small army, while pretending to ignore the raised voices leaking from the dining room next door. It was Seph McCauley and his parents.

Leesha greeted Will, slid in beside him, and picked up a paring knife, her ears wide open.

"Seph, you know we're in favor of normalizing relations

among the magical guilds," Linda Downey was saying, "but your father and I think it's risky to bring all of these elements together at this particular time."

"If not now, when?" Seph said. Though she didn't have the visual, Leesha knew he was wearing his trademark stubborn scowl, so much like his father's. "Anyway, it's a little late to be second-guessing me. I sent out the invitations a month ago."

"That was before the council meeting. You heard young DeVries," Leander Hastings said. "He blames you and Madison for his sister's death, and for all of the other Weir killings. He threatened you."

"I understand that," Seph said. "But we're in the Sanctuary, and here of all places it should be safe."

"Since when has the Sanctuary been safe?" Downey's voice was low and strained. "You know better than that."

"You can't expect me to hide from him," Seph said, "especially since I had nothing to do with his sister's death."

"You do know that his father was the deadliest assassin in the Black Rose," Hastings said. "The Sanctuary's not much protection if the boy takes after his father. DeVries Senior never limited himself to magical weapons. He used whatever seemed most suitable to the circumstances: poison, firearms, blades, strangulation, killing charms . . ."

"Maybe Senior's back as a vengeful ghost," Seph said. "Maybe he's the one behind all the murders."

"We're also getting an earful about the Montessori kidnapping," Downey said. "It seems that many of the parents of the children involved believe that Gabriel Mandrake's students had something to do with it."

They were referring to a recent incident in which a group

of gifted Trinity preschoolers on a field trip had somehow ended up trapped atop a lift bridge in industrial Cleveland. The children claimed they'd been attacked by zombies. Since the bridge was close to the Anchorage, Mandrake's school that served savants, some parents blamed the attack on "Mandrake's Monsters." As co-chair of the Interguild Council committee investigating the Montessori incident, Leesha had been getting an earful herself.

"Then we find out that Mandrake's students are going to be here, too," Hastings said.

"Not all of them," Seph retorted. "Maybe five? I think we have them outnumbered." After a pause (just about now he would be rolling his eyes), Seph continued. "I'm not discounting your concerns, but I don't think we should defer to a bunch of bigots with a lynch-mob mentality."

"They are concerned parents," Downey countered. "Though I admit, some of them are bigots."

"And *they're* not invited," Seph said. "This is *our* party. Madison and I think it's time we bring the guilds together in a meaningful way. It's one thing to have an armed standoff. It's another to actually normalize relations. We also need to stop stigmatizing savants as monsters and acknowledge the fact that what happened at Thorn Hill was not their fault."

"We agree," Hastings said, "and you know it."

"If you agree, then you should be supporting what we're doing," Seph said. "The only way to change opinions is to encourage contact between us and them. Anyway, are you suggesting we uninvite our guests? How d'you think *that* would be received?"

"*I'll* uninvite DeVries," Hastings said in that voice that could knock a person flat. "You don't have to be involved."

"This always happens," Seph growled. "Neither of you are on the council anymore, but whenever you're here, people start bypassing the council and going directly to you. It makes it really hard for Madison and me to do our jobs."

"What's making it difficult is that Madison is in Chicago more than she's here," Hastings said. "All of that power brings with it obligations—obligations that she is not meeting."

This was followed by a long, charged silence. Then Seph spoke. "Maddie never asked for this responsibility. She shouldn't need to be here, wielding a club to get people to behave. We're working things out in our own way."

"Yes, but you must understand that—" Hastings began, but Seph cut in.

"My point is, you can't ride in here and take over whenever you happen to be in the country. Either run this thing or don't." The swinging door between the kitchen and the dining room banged open. Seph froze in the doorway when he saw Leesha and Will, then he strode on past them and into the hall.

Whoa, Leesha thought, meeting Will's eyes. Go, Seph.

"He's right, you know," Downey said, her voice carrying from the other room. "If we're going to live in England, we're going to have to stop second-guessing him."

"You don't think a bit of counsel would—"

"You don't offer counsel, Lee," Downey said. "You have a rather unfortunate habit of bulldozing over people. When it comes to our son, you have just run into your first brick wall. Now let's go out and say our good-byes before we completely ruin this party."

Leesha and Will looked at each other, stowed the salad in the refrigerator, and fled.

By now, the dancing had started, though the band wasn't yet on stage. Nothing ventured, Leesha thought, and looked for Jonah. She found him out on the terrace with a tall girl dressed like a thirties club singer, down to the lacy gloves, finger waves, and red gardenia. A girl Leesha didn't recognize.

Something about the intimate way they stood, leaning on the wall, heads together, talking, almost convinced Leesha not to interrupt.

But not quite. She wasn't one to step back from a challenge. Nothing ventured, she repeated. "Jonah?" she said. "It's Jonah, isn't it? Remember me? Leesha Middleton? We met at the Medieval Faire."

Jonah turned away from the wall, and his gaze flicked over her, piercing her skin like icicles. "Right. Good to see you again," he said, as if it really wasn't.

Leesha's head immediately emptied. Finally, she asked, "Where's your costume?"

"I'm with the band."

"I am, too," the girl said when Jonah didn't introduce her. "I'm Emma Lee."

"Ah, I see," Leesha said. "So you're not . . . actually . . . together?"

Emma and Jonah looked at each other. "No," they said simultaneously.

"Wow," Leesha said, not sure she believed it. "I can sure tell you're used to harmonizing."

Brilliant, Leesha thought. Entirely smooth.

"How about you?" Emma asked. "What are you supposed to be?" The sound of the South in her voice was unmistakable. As was the snark.

Leesha pursed her lips. "I'm a Victorian steampunk

vampire, of course. Some people don't approve of cross-dressing, but—"

"Cross-dressing?" Emma did a double take, a look of disbelief on her face.

"You know," Leesha went on, "wizards cross-dressing as vampires. *Some people* think it's really kinky." Leesha grinned at Emma, and Emma, somewhat reluctantly, grinned back. Her smile disappeared when Leesha turned back to Jonah. "Want to dance?"

"No, thanks," Jonah said. "Like I said, I'm working."

Leesha's brain was saying, Shut up! Cut your losses and retreat. But her mouth somehow said, "You're not working now."

"I'm not dancing either." Jonah turned his back and looked out at the lake.

Leesha stared at his back for a moment, then said, "Fine. No problem," and turned and walked away, cheeks burning.

This isn't like you, she thought, this absolutely isn't like you. You're the one who says no, not the other way around.

Well. Until Jason. Jason had said no to her, which she'd totally deserved. And then he'd never had another chance to say yes. Tears blurred her eyes, and she stumbled forward, heading for the powder room. But instead, of course, she ran smack into Harmon Fitch. The lower half of him, at least.

He gripped her elbows to keep her upright. Odd. She was suddenly conscious of the fact that his fingers had no sting to them. No sting at all. Somehow, that was a good thing.

Fitch read her blotchy face; she knew he must have, but he said nothing about it. Instead, he said, "Hey, glad I ran into you, ha-ha. Do you want to dance?"

"What?" Leesha said, like he was speaking Japanese.

"Dance," Fitch repeated. "You know, shuffle around the dance floor, figuring out where to put your chin, music playing the whole time? I didn't get in much dancing in Cambridge."

"You want to dance with *me*?" Leesha squinted at him, trying to guess his agenda.

"Look, I know there's a big height difference, but I think we can overcome that long enough to get through one dance," Fitch said.

He saw me get the stiff-arm, Leesha thought, mortified. He's being kind. And yet, Leesha decided, she would much rather dance than leave the field humiliated.

"I'd be delighted," Leesha said.

They circled the floor in silence for a few minutes. Then Fitch said, "I missed this, you know."

"Dancing with me? And here I thought this was the very first time," Leesha said. It was, and they both knew it.

"No," Fitch said. "I mean being here, where it's happening. I mean the constant adrenaline, the high stakes. Saving the world, sticking up for democracy, and all that. I guess I sort of got used to living on the edge."

"Living on the edge?" Leesha forced a smile. "That'd be me, going to Harvard. No, I think I'd rather live as far away from edges as I can get."

Fitch grimaced, his cheeks pinking with embarrassment. "That was a stupid thing to say to you, and I'm sorry."

"Don't apologize," Leesha said. "You've moved on. Everybody has. I've had two years of boredom, and I kind of like it."

"Still," Fitch persisted, "considering the way it was before, with wizards pushing everyone around, isn't it better? Even though I wasn't a major player, I felt like what we were doing mattered."

"Yes," she said. "It's better." She had to think so—otherwise Jason had died in vain. "But don't diss what you're doing. That's what's important. Going to college, living your life, becoming the educated kind of genius that can make a real difference. Those are the people who save the world. Blowing things up, setting things on fire . . . that's overrated."

His eyes narrowed, focused on her. He seemed to be debating whether to say anything more. "You've changed, since—since everything."

"I'm a late bloomer," Leesha said, recalling that she'd once compared Fitch to a cockroach. Why were *those* the memories that came back to her?

Still, as they danced, Leesha felt her pain and humiliation dwindle. Sometimes life throws you curve balls. As with evil, you never know when you'll be blindsided by kindness. Maybe it was a pity dance, but she'd take it.

ᏊᏊ Chapter Two ᏊᏊ
Day of the Dead

Any sensible girl who finds out that the boy she loves is a mass murderer would have made a plan. That plan would not have been to leave him in a gazebo and then wander around in the dark woods so he could finish the job he'd started.

No. A sensible girl would have run away from Jonah Kinlock as fast as her legs could carry her; as fast as she could go in her bare feet with a sprained and throbbing ankle. A sensible girl would have been looking over her shoulder all the way back up the gravel path, worrying that he would come after her. A sensible girl would not have been crying, grieving for the boy with the magic in his voice and the blues in his eyes, mourning the loss of something that was a lie—a lie—from beginning to end.

A sensible girl would have gone straight back to the house, where there was safety in numbers. For all she knew, Rowan DeVries was still lurking about, too. The wizard's words came back to her: *We're going to go where nobody will ever find us, and this time I'm not going to take no for an answer.*

Now, at long last, she knew the truth. Jonah had been the ski-masked intruder who'd broken into the home she'd shared with her father. He'd left her tied up on the basement floor while he went looking for Tyler. He'd pretty much admitted to killing Tyler and who knows how many others on that terrible night back in the fall.

And tonight? Tonight Jonah had been ready to kill Rowan DeVries so he wouldn't give his game away. She'd seen it in his eyes. What was she supposed to do: get back up on stage with him and play the second set at Seph McCauley's Halloween party as if nothing had happened?

But Emma Greenwood had never been known for being sensible. She did not want to go back up to the house and talk to anyone. She was not good at keeping her feelings off her face. So instead, she hobbled along the lakeshore to where the gravel path ended at a boathouse and a sailboat bobbed alongside a dock.

Just then, her phone pinged. A text from Jonah. She couldn't help herself. She read it.

I won't be there for the second set. I'm not feeling well. I'm so sorry for everything. It went to Emma, Natalie, Rudy, and Alison.

"Why didn't I think of that?" Emma muttered. She could have pled illness and taken the spare van back to the Anchorage. And do what? Pack her bags? To go where? She had money, but that was for opening her guitar workshop. She didn't want to dribble it away on rent and groceries. Who would rent to a sixteen-year-old anyway?

Besides, try as she might, she could not jam these puzzle

pieces into a picture that made sense. Little inconsistencies kept niggling at her.

Why had she survived the night of the murders? Had Jonah been scared away before he could finish the job? Even if that was the case, he'd had plenty of chances to kill her since then. It would have been ridiculously easy to drown her in the lake the night he'd rescued her from Rowan DeVries. No one would have ever known. And why, then, after saving her life, would he bring her back to the Anchorage? Did he want to keep her close by so he could take quick action if she regained her memory?

Well, she had. She had regained her memory. So why was she still alive? Didn't he realize that the only way to keep his secret was to eliminate the last remaining witness?

True, what memory she had was imperfect—a collection of sensations and images, really. What came back most clearly was a vivid memory of Jonah Kinlock kissing her, his lips coming down on hers, the weight of his body, flat-bellied and hard-muscled, the pounding of his heart a counterpoint to her own, her insides melting, fiery-sweet. And then . . . nothing.

Kissing her! How dare he?

Maybe that never happened. Maybe that was a wish, played out in a dream.

Try as she might, she could not surface any memory of Jonah Kinlock killing anyone. And yet, he'd admitted it. Sort of.

I didn't go to your father's house to kill anyone. That was the last thing I wanted to happen.

Oh, really? Well, falling for my father's murderer is the last thing I wanted to happen.

Now what? Should she go to Gabriel? She had no reason to trust him. For all she knew, Gabriel had ordered the murders himself.

Could she go to the police? What kind of evidence did she have? A sort-of confession in the gazebo that could be denied. That was something Emma couldn't understand: why had Jonah said anything at all? He wasn't stupid.

Anyway, Emma was not the sort of person who took her troubles to the police.

Should she have thrown in with Rowan DeVries? DeVries had hoped Emma was the witness who'd help him solve a series of recent wizard murders, including the murder of his sister. He had held Emma captive, threatening to torture her until she gave him the information he wanted. No doubt he'd get right back to it, given the opportunity.

So, no.

But DeVries was the only other person who could verify that a murder had taken place at all. Who'd seen the bodies where they'd fallen. Who'd lost his sister, just as Emma had lost the father she'd only just found. He was the only person besides Jonah who might help her piece this thing together, might help her collect enough evidence to finger the guilty.

But DeVries wouldn't wait for evidence. He had no need to prove what he suspected, since he had no intention of going to the police either. He and the Black Rose assassins would handle this themselves.

A battle of assassins. Why should she care who won? She should just leave the field and let them have at it.

Emma shivered. The wind was picking up, and Tyler's jacket was no longer enough to keep her warm. She could return to the house, or stay and freeze. Her shoes were still in the gazebo, but she wasn't going back there. She'd just have to do without.

She limped back up the hill into the woods, her breath hissing out each time she put weight on her ankle. The trees crowded in close, the branches overhead thrashing. She couldn't shake the feeling that she was being watched. The back of her neck prickled and burned, and she resisted the urge to pull her hair down to cover it up.

Under the sound of the wind, she heard something else— a crunch of gravel, a small pebble rolling down the slope. Soft footfalls behind her that stopped when she did.

She shivered again, maybe more of a shudder, as the realization that she was being stalked seeped through her skin.

Her heart began to thud as panic coursed through her. Without looking back, she staggered forward, zagging off the path and limping up the hill toward the house, cursing her stupid self and her stupid dress, her twisted ankle, and every rock and stick that punished the soles of her stupid bare feet. The footsteps accelerated, and Emma limped faster. Now she could hear somebody breathing, just behind her, and she bolted through the underbrush, desperate to reach the safety of the house. It was like one of those dreams where the monster's in pursuit, but your feet are glued to the ground.

Breaking out of the fringe of trees, she smashed right into somebody, all but knocking her down.

"Hey! Watch where you're going!"

It was the Victorian steampunk vampire, Leesha Middleton. And, with her, the tall, red-haired boy she'd been dancing with earlier.

Leesha gripped Emma's shoulders, steadying her. "Are

you okay?" Her gray eyes narrowed as she looked Emma up and down, taking in her shoeless feet, her disheveled clothing, the hair that had escaped from her updo and was now hanging around her face. "What's wrong?"

"I—uh—thought I heard someone creeping up on me in the woods. So I ran, and I—it was chasing me." Her voice trailed off as she realized how lame this sounded. This was so not a story Emma wanted to share with Leesha.

"Probably kids from the high school, looking to crash the party," Leesha said, squeezing her shoulder. "You know, small towns, Halloween. Speaking of, where's your gorgeous and scowling friend?"

It was like Emma's mind was frozen, along with everything else. "My—who?"

"Your godlike lead singer. The one that gave me the cold shoulder earlier. Isn't it nearly time for your next set?"

"Oh. He—uh—he left. He wasn't feeling well."

"Ah." Leesha held Emma's gaze for a long moment, then changed the subject. Gesturing toward her companion, she said, "Have you met Harmon Fitch?"

Emma shook her head, trying to focus on Harmon Fitch. "I'm Emma Gi—Emma Lee," she said. Leesha glowed—all of the gifted did. Fitch did not—so he was Anaweir. Leesha was small; Fitch was tall. An odd couple for sure.

The red-haired boy doffed his top hat. "Call me Fitch," he said, shooting a look at Leesha, "steampunk vampire victim." He wore a fancy suit along with the top hat, and carried a silver-tipped walking cane. Sweeping his cape from his shoulders, he settled it around Emma's. "It's kind of moth-eaten, but it's warm."

Emma pulled the cape closer around her, but she couldn't seem to stop trembling.

Leesha took her elbow, and turned Emma back toward the house. "Why don't you go on inside and warm up? We'll be up in a minute."

Emma set her feet, resisting. "Where are you going?"

"Seph stored some extra drinks in the boathouse," Leesha said. "We're going to bring them up to the house."

"No!" Emma said. "Don't go off by yourselves. There was—there might be—"

"Hey," Leesha said. "We're in the Sanctuary. There are no monsters in here. Anyway"—she smiled—"we're not exactly defenseless."

Some things can't be defended against, Emma thought. "I wish you wouldn't go out there," she persisted.

Fitch and Leesha exchanged glances, as if they each hoped the other would handle the crazy woman. "We'll be careful," Leesha said. They turned away, heading downslope toward the lake.

Despite her misgivings, Emma hobbled back up to the house, where the heaters on the terrace provided a welcome warmth. Natalie and Rudy were huddled up next to one of them, heads together, talking.

"Emma!" Natalie said, brightening when she spotted her. "Have you seen Jonah? Did you get his text? Do you know what's going on?"

I wish I did, Emma thought, shaking her head. "No idea."

"If he wasn't feeling well, I'm surprised he didn't come to me," Natalie said. "Usually I can handle anything minor. . . ." Her voice trailed off.

"We've texted him back, but no answer," Rudy added.

"I hope he's okay. If he left, he must've taken the other van. What's strange is that he left all his equipment here."

Emma just stared at the two of them. She had no answers, only questions. One thought cycled through her mind: *Were you part of what happened to my father?*

Had she been so blinded by their common love of music that she'd missed important clues?

"Alison isn't answering either." Natalie swiveled, scanning the terrace and the lawn beyond. "I wish she'd get back here. We need to figure out a Plan B for the second set."

Emma licked her lips, her thoughts flopping around like a school of beached fish. "Maybe we should just forget about the second set."

"No," Natalie said, lifting her chin. "Remember the name of the band: Fault Tolerant. We continue to function, even when one part fails. Anyway, we've already been paid, and I don't want to give half the money back."

Feeling a little foolish, Emma removed Fitch's cape, folding it neatly and setting it next to her on the stone wall. Don't say anything to anyone, she thought. Keep your head down, keep your secrets, and you'll be all right. None of this brings Tyler back. You don't even know who your enemies are. Anything you say can't be unsaid. Play it safe, girl. Give yourself time to figure out what to do.

"Hey. What's up?"

Emma flinched, and turned. It was Alison. "Isn't it about time for the second set?" she said, stuffing the last of a slice of pizza into her mouth.

"Where have you been?" Natalie said. "We've been trying to figure out what to do."

"Do? About what?" Alison said, brow furrowed.

Natalie hissed through her teeth, exasperated. "Isn't your phone on?"

Alison pulled her phone from her pocket. "I guess not. I turned it off during the first set and forgot to turn it back on." She scanned the screen, her eyes shifting as she read the text. Then swore violently. "Jonah's *left?*" Alison looked like she'd been smacked in the head. She waved the phone. "That's— that's impossible."

"Never mind," Natalie said. "He's not here, so we need a plan."

Alison flung her phone onto the flagstones. It shattered into pieces.

"Whoa, Alison," Rudy said. "Anger management, you know? If he's sick, he's sick."

"Emma, you'll just have to manage the guitar line on your own," Natalie said. "I'll sing my usuals, and, Rudy, you'll have to step up to lead, I guess, for Jonah. I've come up with a tentative set list that we might—"

She broke off when Madison Moss shouldered her way through the French doors and onto the terrace, followed by Seph and an Anaweir boy with a football-player's build. Madison scanned the patio and the grounds beyond, a furrow of annoyance between her brows. "Has anyone seen Grace?" she asked.

Gooseflesh rose on the back of Emma's neck. "No," she said. "When did you last see her?"

"We listened to your first set together, and then she said she was going out to make sure the pumpkin lamps were still lit," Madison said. "That was a while ago. I told her to come right back. . . ." She trailed off, reading Emma's face. "Is something wrong?"

"I just—it's nothing," Emma said.

"Grace is your little sister?" Rudy said.

Madison nodded. "She's twelve, going on eighteen," Madison said. She extended her hand out in front of her, palm down. "About this tall, with light brown hair. She was wearing a black cat costume."

"Want us to spread out and look for her?" Rudy asked, always eager for action.

Madison wavered, then shook her head. "Seph and I will check the house again before we all fly into a panic. Grace will never forgive me if I send out a posse." She turned to her Anaweir companion. "Will, could you keep looking around outside?"

Will nodded. "Got it."

"Did you try her cell phone?" Rudy asked.

Madison's lips tightened. "Where I come from, we don't give cell phones to twelve-year-old kids." She turned back toward the house, but just then they heard shouting from the direction of the woods, and two figures stumbling up the slope toward them.

"That's Leesha and Fitch," Will said. "I'll go see what's up." He vaulted over the wall at the edge of the terrace without missing a step, and quickly closed the distance between them.

Emma watched with growing foreboding as the three spoke briefly, and then all turned and ran toward the house. Seph and Madison walked forward to meet them, but Emma hung back with her bandmates, not sure she wanted to hear what they had to say.

She heard it anyway. "There's been an attack," Fitch said. "Like—like a stabbing. Or a shooting. We're not sure. But there's at least three bodies in the woods between here and the lake." He stole a quick look at Madison.

Madison went sheet-white, her blue eyes brilliant against her pale skin. "Who?" she demanded, balling her fists and taking a step toward him. "Who's dead?"

"Hang on," Leesha said. "We're not entirely sure of anything."

"I called 911," Fitch said, "and help should be here any minute. Let's wait until they get here."

"Who. Is. It?" Madison repeated, light flaming up under her skin, shining through, her hair snaking around her head.

"I'm a healer," Natalie said, coming to her feet. "Is there anyone—is there anything I can do until EMS gets here?"

Leesha just stared back at her, speechless, tears streaming down her face.

Madison Moss took off running, hair flying, her pirate skirts bunched into her fists, with Seph McCauley right on her heels, pleading with her to wait, to slow down, to at least not go out there on her own. The race ended just inside the edge of the trees. Seph circled Madison with his arms and pulled her back against his body, the magic flaring up within her underlighting the trees, flickering out into the darkness.

Emma and the others, drawn like moths to a flame, came up behind them, huddling silently, waiting.

Slowly then, Seph and Madison walked forward, and Madison dropped to her knees in the leaf litter next to a darker shape among the others. Emma's heart plummeted to her toes. She tasted metal on the back of her tongue, the taste of blood and despair. She could not bear to look, and yet she could not tear her eyes away.

Then Madison Moss began to scream. It seemed to go on and on and on, the thread of Seph McCauley's wizard voice running through it, their bodies merging into one shadow as he pulled her into his arms.

ᏋᎡ Chapter Three ᏋᎡ
Murder in the Midwest

Emma should have left before the police arrived. But it's hard to think clearly when you're trying to not think at all. So, instead, she huddled on the terrace with Alison and Rudy while a fleet of emergency vehicles lined up in the driveway, spilling onto the street. After a while, Natalie returned, close-faced and tight-lipped and grim.

Once the police arrived, they herded everyone into the house and onto the terrace. A nervous-looking young officer commandeered Jonah's voice mike. "Nobody leaves, all right? Everyone stays put until we've secured the crime scene, searched the area, and interviewed all potential witnesses," she barked. "Don't talk amongst yourselves either, or we'll have to split you up. We want clean accounts from everyone. One of you might've seen something that will help us."

Not me, Emma thought. I didn't see anything. I don't know anything.

Sometime during the initial confusion, Hastings and

Downey had returned. Seph and his parents managed to talk Madison back to the house. The mainliners took over the kitchen, forming an impermeable barrier to outsiders.

The police established a command post in the parlor. They used yellow police tape to cordon off an area around the scene. They marked out access routes onto the grounds, and set up huge spotlights that all but turned night into day. When they funneled out into the woods, the officers proceeded cautiously, shining powerful flashlights into every dark crevice and shadow.

Trapped inside the law-enforcement bubble, Emma began packing up her equipment, hoping for a quick getaway. As if eager for something to do, Rudy and Natalie followed suit, breaking down the equipment and casing everything up. Alison just sat on the floor in a corner, arms wrapped around her knees, head tipped back, eyes closed as if pretending she were someplace else.

Emma ran her fingers over the head of Jonah's Stratocaster, standing abandoned in its stand. He must be guilty, she thought. He must have been involved in the murders. Why else would he leave it behind? She settled it lovingly into its case, slid the strap into its compartment, closed the lid, and buckled the catches. Familiar. Automatic. Soothing.

All around them, the mainliners clustered in small groups, remarkably silent. Some stood along the edge of the terrace, watching the police deploy through the woods. Others whispered together, shooting wary looks toward the band.

"Does anybody else have the feeling that whatever good-will might've resulted from the show is gone now?" Rudy said, nodding toward the clusters of partygoers.

"They can't think *we're* responsible," Natalie muttered.

"Yes, they can," Rudy said, rubbing his eyes. "In fact, I think we can count on it. I'll bet nobody ever got murdered in Trinity until we came along. I'll bet nobody even jay-walked before now."

A ripple of excitement out in the woods caught Emma's attention. People shouting, the crackle of radios, a rush of EMS personnel down the cordoned path. Soon, Emma could hear the *thwock-thwock-thwock* of a helicopter. Turning, she saw that a massive yellow chopper was setting down in the park at the end of the block.

"Looks like they've found somebody else," Natalie whispered, her body as rigid as a dog on point. "Somebody who must be still alive, else they wouldn't have sent Life Flight."

She's a healer to the bone, Emma thought. She can't stand hanging back when someone is hurting.

Natalie positioned herself right beside the route they would have to take. Emma eased up beside her. Moments later, a quartet of paramedics loped up the path toward them, carrying a litter. Even Alison roused herself and joined them, looking on as the medical team swept by, one of them holding a bag of fluids high above his head.

It was Rowan DeVries, his face bloodless, lips pale, lashes dark against his skin. The thermal blanket over him was already soaked through with blood. He looked dead, but, as Natalie said, he must be still alive or why the rush?

Natalie gazed at him fixedly, her dark brows drawn together. She even brushed her fingers over his bare arm as he passed by. The nearest paramedic glared at her and shook his head.

"Hey!" she called after them. "Hang on a minute!" They didn't break stride.

"What's up, Natalie?" came a voice behind them. They both turned. It took Emma a moment to remember the woman's name. It was the healer-sorcerer, Mercedes Foster.

"He's got a serious bleed, right upper quadrant," Natalie said, without a scrap of doubt. "Blood vessel, artery, something. If they don't operate immediately, he'll bleed out. But there's no way they're going to listen to me."

Mercedes nodded. "Got it. And if I don't get some Weirsbane into him, the hospital is going to have a lot of questions we don't have answers to." She charged after the paramedics, her thin legs pumping like pistons, her clothes flapping around her limbs like a scarecrow's. "Rowan!" she bellowed. "Wait! I'm coming with you. That's my son!"

Somehow, the sorcerer talked her way onto the helicopter.

Natalie was on the phone with Gabriel, and Emma half-listened to her side of the conversation. "I know, I know . . . I don't know . . . Alison and Rudy and Emma are here with me. . . . Jonah? He sent a text after the first set. Said he wasn't feeling well and was heading back . . . No, I haven't heard from him since. They've searched the house and grounds, and he's not here. I've texted him several times and even called him, but his phone just goes to voice mail. . . . All right. See you soon." Natalie clicked off and returned her phone to her pocket. "Gabriel's on his way. He's bringing his lawyer."

"I hope Jonah's okay," Rudy murmured.

"Just sit down and shut up," Alison hissed. She opened her mouth as if to say something else, but changed her mind.

Emma tucked her hands under her arms, trying to warm them. "I wish we could leave," she muttered, teeth chattering. "I really, really want to get out of here."

And go where? She did not want to go back to the Anchorage, where she no longer knew whom to trust. She did not want to talk to the police. If they asked who she was and where she came from, it wouldn't take long to connect her to Memphis.

Still, three people had been confirmed as dead. Two wizards, attendees at the party. And Madison Moss's little sister. The black cat. Grace.

What was it they said on the cop shows? Jonah Kinlock had means, motive, and opportunity to kill those three people. If Emma had sounded the alarm about Jonah Kinlock sooner, maybe it wouldn't have happened.

And yet, a voice in Emma's head kept saying, *No.* She'd seen something deadly in Jonah Kinlock from the beginning. He *was* dangerous—but he wasn't indiscriminate. He was like a weapon that was exceedingly accurate. She could totally imagine him cutting down wizards. Including Rowan DeVries. But she could not picture him killing a child. Especially one so close to his brother's age.

Emma thought of the scowling young girl in the black cat costume with the blown-out knees. The way she thrust her face up into the music like a cat soaking up sun. The bitten-down nails, and the dreamy way she gazed at Jonah. Why would somebody hurt a girl like that? Could Grace have stumbled on something she shouldn't have?

Beyond the stone wall, flashlights bobbed like fireflies in the dark, clustering together, then exploding apart, silvering the trunks and branches of the trees. Police cars lined both sides of the street, carrying emblems from surrounding communities. The Trinity police force had called in reinforcements.

Would they fingerprint witnesses? Run background checks on them? Panic flared up in her again. Emma turned, scanning the crowd of people waiting until she spotted Fitch and Leesha sitting together at the edge of the terrace.

"I'll be right back." Crossing the stone terrace to where they stood, Emma said, "Hey."

They swiveled to face her. Fitch had his arm around Leesha, and her lashes were clumped up with tears.

Emma groped for words. "I don't mean to bother you."

Leesha blotted at her eyes with the back of her hand.

After a moment's hesitation, Fitch said, "It's just—this brings back a lot of memories for us." He looked at Leesha, as if she might want to say something, but she said nothing. "There was a battle here two years ago," he went on, "between the wizard guild and the other guilds. A number of people close to us were killed."

He knows about the guilds, Emma thought, even though he's not a member. Even though she was gifted, she'd only learned about them a few months ago, when she came to live with Tyler. Sometimes she felt like the only person in the dark.

Fitch was still looking at her expectantly, and Emma lost her courage. "I'm sorry. So sorry. I'll leave you be," she said, and went to turn away, but Fitch said, "Wait!"

Emma turned back toward them.

"Can we help you with something?" Fitch asked.

"Well . . ." Emma looked over her shoulder, to see if anyone was close enough to hear, then turned back to face them. "I really don't want to talk to the police. And, you know, since I didn't actually see anything, I was hoping you could just keep me out of it."

"I'm sorry," Fitch said, shifting his weight. "I think it's too late for that. We already talked to them—you know, briefly. Your name was mentioned."

"Damn." Emma lifted her aching shoulders, then dropped them again.

Leesha and Fitch looked at each other. "Are you in trouble?" Fitch asked softly.

Why, yes, Emma thought of saying. My entire family—my daddy and grandfather—have died in the past six months, and now I'm an orphan and I don't want the county to take custody of me.

But they had their own troubles. She wouldn't pile on more.

"Oh, no," Emma lied. "I just—I just don't want to get involved."

Leesha twisted a lock of hair around her finger. "But what if something you saw or heard might help catch the killer?"

Emma fisted her hands. "I don't know how that could be when I didn't see or hear anything."

"Okay, okay," Fitch said, raising his own hands, palms out. "Just tell them that. You'll be fine."

Leesha kept gazing at Emma, but her expression was less accusatory and suspicious than it was . . . sympathetic. The wizard dug her phone from her tiny pocketbook. "What's your cell number?" she asked briskly, ready to key it in. "I'll call you, so you'll have my number."

"Why?" Emma asked warily. "Why do I want your number?"

"So we can exchange fashion tips," Leesha snapped. Then rubbed the back of her neck like it hurt. "Sorry. Snarkiness

is a habit I'm trying to break." She looked up at Emma, her
smoky eyes haunted. "Sometimes," she said, "you just need
somebody to call. I'm not saying I'm that person, but at least
you'll have the number in case." She paused. "Or if you'd
rather I didn't have your number, just take mine."

Emma surrendered her number.

"Ms. Lee?" The voice came from behind her, startling
Emma so much that she nearly fell over the low wall edging
the terrace. But that was good. Otherwise, she might not
have responded to the unfamiliar name at all.

She spun around to see a stocky, sandy-haired man, hands
stuffed into his pants pockets, wearing a battered leather jacket
and open-collared dress shirt. Despite the casual look, Emma
had been on the street long enough to recognize the law.

"Emma Lee?" The officer stuck out his hand, and Emma
reluctantly shook it. "I'm Ross Childers, chief of police and
head of the Investigative Bureau here in Trinity." He flipped
open a leather case to display an authentic-looking badge.

"You're the *chief*?" Emma blurted out.

Ross Childers shrugged. "Small department. Anyway, I
like to keep my hand in. I wonder if we could sit in my car
a few minutes, so I could ask you some questions about what
happened here tonight."

Emma broadened her stance, as if trying to take root.
"Couldn't you just ask me here?"

Childers rubbed his chin. "I'm just old enough to want
to sit down whenever I can," he said. "Anyway, my laptop's
in the car."

Emma did not want to get into the police car, but couldn't
think of a reason to say no, so she followed Chief Childers

around the side of the house and down the stone walkway to where police cars were lined up in the drive. The ambulances had gone.

Childers yanked open the passenger door of an unmarked car, and invited Emma in with a gesture. She settled into the seat, feeling boxed in by equipment—a bulky radio, a loaded center console. Emma immediately banged her elbow on a laptop on a swivel mount. "Ow!"

"Sorry," Childers said, peering into the interior of the car, an apologetic expression on his face. Fast food wrappers and receipts from ATMs were scattered across the floor mats. "This thing is a mess. I didn't expect to have guests." Stripping off his jacket, he tossed it into the back and slid into the driver's seat. Leaning down, he scooped up the trash, stuffing it into a plastic bag on the inside of his door. He kept fussing, tidying up, like he really was embarrassed.

Emma drew in a shaky breath, and memories flooded back. Police cars always smelled the same: a kind of sweaty, underbelly smell. Police cars were where bad things happen to people like her.

She'd had some brushes with the law back when she lived with her grandfather, Sonny Lee, in Memphis. Before he was killed. Maybe murdered. It seemed like a lifetime ago, and yet it seemed like yesterday that she was sitting in with bands in small clubs off Beale Street. Working in the shop with Sonny Lee, talking blues guitar with musicians and club owners like Mickey Munroe and Scott Somerville.

Childers noticed Emma shivering. "You cold?" He cranked up the heater to full blast, even though sweat dampened the underarms of his dress shirt. He turned down the volume on the police radio, which was chattering like mad, and swung the laptop toward himself.

"Emma Lee, right?" he asked.

When she nodded, he began hunting and pecking, ridiculously fast.

"Address?"

She had no idea. *You should know things like that,* she thought. *I'm new,* she thought of saying, but that would just invite a question about where she'd been before this.

"Um. Well, I live at the Anchorage," she said. "In the dorms. I'm not sure of the address. It's in downtown Cleveland."

He stopped typing and studied her from under bushy brows. "The Anchorage? I've heard of that. Isn't that the school for the arts? The one run by that music promoter—what's his name?"

"Gabriel Mandrake. That's the one."

Hunt and peck. Hunt and peck. "Where's home for you?"

"That's it," Emma said. "My parents died in this chemical accident in South America."

Childers's hands stopped moving and he looked up at her, grimacing. "That's tough, Ms. Lee. I'm sorry to hear that."

"It was a long time ago." She waited, but he didn't say anything, so she went on. "All of the students at the Anchorage lost their parents in that accident. So, you know, we have a lot in common."

She gave up her cell number, age, date of birth. Then added, "I know people are saying I saw something, but I didn't. I feel like you're wasting your time."

Chief Childers shrugged his shoulders. "I'm an old dog, Ms. Lee."

"Emma."

"I'm an old dog, Emma. I always do better when I follow procedures. We have a homicide checklist, and I have to go through it. That's the thing about investigations—you never know what's going to be helpful until it is."

"I guess you don't get many murders around here," Emma said. She bit her lip, wishing she could call back the words. He probably thinks I'm playing the big-city girl. Does he know anything about the magical goings on in his little town?

But Childers seemed unruffled. "Oh, we've had our share of incidents over the years," he said, rolling up his sleeves to expose massive forearms. He was in better shape than he looked. "Especially lately. Now, first off, have you talked to anybody else about what happened? Compared notes, like that?"

"No!" Emma blurted. "Well, I mean, not since the cops—the police officers—told us not to."

"Now, how do you know Seph and Maddie?"

"I don't. Not really." Emma shifted on the seat, yanking at the hem of her dress.

"Who invited you to the party, then?"

"I'm—I'm with the band," Emma said. "I play guitar."

"Really?" Childers looked all interested. "I used to play a little guitar myself."

"Is that so?" Emma said. Everybody used to play a little guitar, she thought.

But Childers kept on. "What kind of music do you play?"

"Blues, rock and roll, like that," Emma said. "A lot of original stuff."

"What's the name of your band? Maybe I've heard of it."

"Fault Tolerant."

Childers thought a minute, then shook his head. "Nope, haven't heard of it, but I bet I'm not the target audience. Who else was here, from the band?"

Emma gave their names.

"How'd you end up playing a gig clear out here?"

"Cleveland isn't that far," she said. "I guess this friend of theirs, Ellen Stephenson, heard us play downtown. So she invited us."

"Ellen did, *hmm*?" Childers said, pecking out some notes. "Do you know her?"

He nodded. "Small town. Now, walk me through what happened. What made you go outside?"

Emma's own guilt made that question sound accusing. "We were on our break. I just—I just needed some fresh air."

"So where'd you go?"

If only she had Jonah's skill with the lie. "I walked down by the lake."

"Did you see anyone else out there? You know, walking around?"

He knows! He must know, somehow. He's just trying to trap me. Emma's cheeks heated, and she licked her lips.

No. How could he know? Stick to your story. You saw nothing, heard nothing, know nothing. She'd learned her lesson. Admitting to anything was like pulling the thread that would unravel her whole life.

"I heard other kids out there," she said. "I could hear people walking around, laughing, talking. But I didn't really want to talk to anybody."

"Why not?"

"I'd been up on stage for an hour," Emma said. "I needed some alone time. So I didn't really see anybody, and I wouldn't have recognized them if I had, since I'm not from around here."

"Where are you from?"

Why'd you go and say that? She floundered for an answer. "I—ah—I'm from Cleveland. Like I said."

Childers rubbed his jaw. "Huh. From your voice, I would've guessed somewhere to the south of here."

"My daddy was from Tennessee," Emma said. "I guess I picked it up from him." Childers waited, as if hoping she might say more, but Emma kept still.

"So. Fitch said something spooked you out there. What was it and where were you?"

"I feel like a fool now," Emma said. When Childers raised an eyebrow, she rushed on. "I thought I heard something, and I panicked. That's all."

"Where were you then?"

"I was on my way back to the house," Emma said.

"And what, exactly, did you hear?" Childers persisted.

"It sounded like somebody was following me." When Childers sat waiting, hands poised above the keyboard, Emma stumbled on. "I heard footsteps, twigs snapping, like that."

"Yet you weren't scared before, when you heard other people out there?"

"No," Emma said. "I guess I—I just realized that I was out there by myself and all."

Hunt, hunt. Peck, peck, peck. "Did you have any reason to believe there was something dangerous out there?"

Emma licked her lips. "Well, it was dark. And—you know—it was Halloween."

"What happened next?"

"Well, I ran into this girl, Leesha Middleton, and her friend. They went on to get some drinks, and I walked back to the house."

"Ms. Middleton says you tried to keep her and Fitch from walking out there alone." The chief paused, and when Emma said nothing, added, "Why?"

"Look, maybe it doesn't make sense now, with the lights on, but I had this creepy feeling," Emma said. "I'm a city girl . . . I guess I'm not used to being in the woods. I thought it might be a bear or something."

"Did you see the bodies?" the detective asked bluntly.

"No, sir, I didn't."

"Did you know Grace Moss?"

"No, sir," Emma said, her heart spasming painfully. "I mean, not really. I met her tonight for the first time."

Childers sighed, the lines on his face deepening. "You know she's dead."

Emma nodded miserably.

"Somebody slashed that little girl right across the throat. At least she died quick." A muscle in the detective's jaw twitched. "I used to see her around town sometimes." He cleared his throat, resting his large hands on the keyboard. "You didn't happen to see her, down by the lake maybe?"

Emma shook her head. "I saw her in the audience when we were up on stage," she said. "That's the last time I saw her." Emma hesitated. "I just can't—" She stopped, looking down at her laced fingers. She was about to say that she couldn't imagine anyone doing such a thing, but what was the point in that? Somebody did.

"What happened to your shoes?" Childers pointed toward the floorboards.

Emma looked down at her stockinged feet. "I kicked them off when I started running," she said. "I don't know where they are."

"Are these them?" Childers held up a plastic bag containing her strappy black shoes. It must have been next to his feet, but Emma hadn't noticed it before.

"You found them!" Emma said, reaching for the bag.

He pulled it back, out of her reach. It was then that she noticed the evidence tag on the bag. "These have been entered into evidence," he said, his eyes searching her face. "See, they're spattered with blood. We found them in the gazebo. There's a lot of blood in there, too, like there was some kind of a fight." He paused, waiting for a response.

"Really?" Emma said, thinking, This is what happens when you lie—you get caught. "I wonder how they got there."

"I wonder," Childers said gently. His eyes narrowed, focusing on her jacket. "What's that all over your jacket?"

Emma looked down. The battered brown leather of Tyler's jacket was spotted with darker red-brown stains. Instantly, she knew what it must be. Rowan's blood. Rowan DeVries had been stabbed. And here she was, looking guilty as could be.

She scraped at one of the stains with her fingernail. "I don't know," she whispered. "This jacket belonged to my father. I guess I never noticed there were spots on it." That, at least, was true.

Childers's expression said he wasn't fooled, not at all, and yet it was somehow kind, as if this whole thing was a problem they would work out together. "I'm going to need to borrow your jacket, Emma, and run some tests. And see if the blood on your shoes matches the stains on your jacket."

"You think it's blood?" Emma whispered.

"That's what it looks like to me," Childers said matter-of-factly.

Wordlessly, Emma shrugged Tyler's jacket off her shoulders and handed it to Childers, who slid it inside a large plastic bag. He scribbled some notes on a tag with a marker, and attached it.

Emma shivered as the cold air hit her bare skin. Or maybe it was the realization that if she didn't tell the truth, she'd be in more trouble than ever. And that little girl, Grace Moss, might never find justice.

Despite the roaring heater, she felt exposed, her skin pebbled with gooseflesh. Childers reached for the dashboard. "Here. Let me turn up the—"

"Can I start over?" she asked, looking down at her hands. "Can I change my story?"

"It's your story, Emma," Childers said. "All I want is the truth." He paused, then continued, "Just so you know, you don't have to talk to me if you don't want to."

"That's all right," Emma said. "I'm not guilty of anything, except for being stupid."

And so she told the truth, or most of it, anyway. About Rowan DeVries cornering her in the gazebo, and her smashing his nose, and Jonah intervening, and then each of them going their separate ways. She didn't mention anything about her father's death, the kidnapping, the rescue, any of that. In fact, she left out all references to murder. If they jumped to conclusions, they could do it on their own. Childers kept quiet through most of it, just asking the occasional question, tapping notes into his computer.

"How do you know DeVries?" the detective asked when Emma wound down.

Here's where she had to lie and make it stick. "I don't."

"You'd never met before tonight?"

She shook her head. "No, sir, not that I recall."

"Any idea why he might—?"

"No, sir." Childers just sat there, looking at her, questions all over his face, so she added, "I'm just guessing here, but, you know, some people make assumptions about a girl in a band. I usually have no problem setting them straight."

"So you're saying that he—?"

"No!" Emma said. "Nothing like that happened. After I hit him in the nose, things went south in a hurry. And then Jonah came."

Emma realized that it sounded very much like Jonah and Rowan were fighting over her. As if that would ever happen.

"How would you describe your relationship with Jonah Kinlock?"

"We're in a band together. We both go to the same school."

"Did DeVries hurt you at all?" Childers leaned forward. "If so, it's really important that we get it on record."

Emma thought about it. *He tried to hex me, but his hex didn't work.* "Not really. I did fall and twist my ankle."

"He didn't push you?"

"I don't really remember," Emma said. "I was just trying to get out of the way."

"No other bumps, bruises, injuries we should make a note of?"

"No."

"So DeVries was the first to leave?"

Emma nodded.

"And nobody had stabbed anybody up to that point?"

"No," she whispered. "As far as I know, he wasn't hurt, except for . . . except for his nose."

"Where you hit him." Emma saw the chief's gaze drop to her hands, looking for damage.

"I hit him with my head," she said.

"What did you and Kinlock do then?"

"I left," Emma said.

"You didn't talk?"

"To tell you the truth, I was pretty mad at both of them, so I walked back up to the house alone. That's when I thought I heard someone following me."

"Did either of them seem angry enough to—to want to finish the fight later? At the end, I mean?"

Jonah had been ready to kill Rowan DeVries, until Emma talked him out of it. At least, she thought she had.

Emma shrugged, extending her hands into the airflow from the heater. "I can't say. I guess I'm not a very good judge of people."

"Emma? There you are!"

This time the voice came from outside the car. Emma looked up to find Gabriel Mandrake, flanked by Natalie and a man Emma didn't know.

"What the hell is going on here?" Gabriel yanked open the passenger door, motioning to Emma to get out. She complied.

Ross Childers opened the driver's side door, unfolding out of the car to his full height. He spoke across the roof of the car to Gabriel. "I'm Ross Childers, chief of police, Mr.—"

"I'm Gabriel Mandrake, head of school, and Ms. Lee's guardian," Gabriel said, the words sliding easily off his tongue. "This is my lawyer, Matt Green."

"You always travel around with a lawyer?" Childers rubbed the back of his neck as if it pained him.

"Do you always interrogate minors without benefit of counsel or parental involvement?" Green snapped back.

"It's not an interrogation, Mr. Green," Childers said. "Emma—Ms. Lee—is a possible witness to a crime, and I'm asking her some questions is all."

"And you had to drag her out here to your car to do that?" Gabriel said. "You don't think there's an element of intimidation in that?"

Childers seemed uncowed by Gabriel's aggressive posture. "It's standard procedure, Mr. Mandrake, to remove a witness to a private area without distraction, where he or she can speak without worrying about being overheard. We also like to collect witness accounts individually so they are uncontaminated by what other people say. Anyway, she came willingly. The point is, we have three young people dead and one critically injured, and not a lot to go on so far. She seemed willing to help."

"I hope you can appreciate that Ms. Lee is one of the young people *I* am responsible for protecting," Gabriel said. "I don't know how much you know about my work with the Thorn Hill Foundation and the Anchorage, but these children are fragile."

"Fragile?"

"Many of our students have been physically and emotionally traumatized," Gabriel said.

"Is that so?" Childers took another look at Emma. "I didn't know that."

"You would know if you had gone through proper channels," Gabriel said.

I'm not some kind of invalid, Emma wanted to shout, but since Gabriel seemed bent on yanking her out of this web of lies she was snagged in, she could hardly complain. She rubbed her arms, missing the warmth of the jacket.

"I take your point, Mr. Mandrake, but the sooner we can gather some preliminary information, the closer we'll be to solving this thing," Childers said, leaning his arms on the top of the car.

"It seems to me your time would be better spent conducting a thorough search of the area and collecting forensic evidence than by browbeating a vulnerable young woman," Green said.

"I've got people searching the grounds," Childers said. He shifted his gaze to Emma. "You feeling browbeaten, Emma?"

"I just want to go home," she whispered, tears leaking from her eyes.

Childers nodded. "Ms. Lee, I appreciate your talking to me. I have your contact information, and once we get all the analysis done, I'll probably want to have you back down to the station to answer a few more questions and sign a statement."

Emma just nodded.

Childers groped in his pocket and came up with a battered card case. He fished out a card and handed it to Emma.

"If you think of anything else—anything that might be helpful—will you call me?"

"Sure," Emma said. "Okay."

Emma watched him walk away. The Trinity, Ohio, chief of police seemed to be the kind of person you'd want to have on your side if you got into a jam: solid, methodical, and thorough. He was *not* the kind of person you'd want on the case if you were trying to hide something. Or if you just wanted to be left alone.

⊛ CHAPTER FOUR ⊛
DAMAGE MANAGEMENT

When Jonah Kinlock woke up covered in blood in Seph McCauley's backyard, he suspected that he'd been set up. Maybe it was the bodies scattered all around him or the bloody daggers that lay half-buried in leaves next to each hand. Anyone who happened upon this little scene would name him the prime suspect. He needed to exit the stage.

First and foremost, Jonah thought, I have to get out of these bloody clothes. He wasn't sure whose blood was on them, but he knew it wasn't his own.

It wasn't easy to think strategically with his head swimming. Whatever drug they'd used on him was still in his system. He was staggering, stumbling, shambling more than running. It was unlikely he could outrun anybody in his present state. His vision swam and blurred, like he was looking through a rain-streaked window. Was he safe to drive? He hoped so, because he didn't see that he had any other options.

The van was parked where Jonah had left it, a block away

from Seph McCauley's house. He reached for the door handle with his gloved hand, then stopped. His gloves were smeared with blood, too. He pulled them off. He'd have to go glove-less for the time being.

Jonah knew the worst thing he could do was leave a trail. He had studied forensics as a recruit to Nightshade, Gabriel Mandrake's network of savant assassins. Known as shadeslayers, they were tasked with putting to rest the undead survivors of the Thorn Hill poisoning. Even though those they killed were *technically* already dead, the authorities might not see it that way. The last thing shadeslayers needed was to be hauled in for questioning by the police. It could cause Gabriel's whole empire to unravel.

So. It was best if these clothes didn't come anywhere near the Anchorage. Also, it would really help if he wasn't carrying around two bloody knives. He'd brought them with him on instinct, suspecting that if he left them at the murder scene, they would somehow lead to him.

The furniture pads Fault Tolerant used to protect their equipment in transit were piled in the back of the van. Jonah spread one over the driver's seat and one on the backseat. He laid the knives on the pad in the backseat, dropped his bloody gloves on top, then wrapped them in the padding.

Jonah wished he could somehow leap the distance between Trinity and Cleveland, get off the road, and into hiding. He forced himself to stick close to the speed limit all the way. He made two stops between Trinity and Cleveland: first, to drop the knives into Sandusky Bay. And again, after he threw up all over himself.

For once in his life, Jonah guessed he looked totally unappealing.

He thought of texting Kenzie to warn him, give him a heads up, but didn't dare. Cell phone records could be traced. Fortunately, it was his long-standing habit to keep location services turned off on his phone. By the time he got back on the road, his cell phone was pinging. He glanced down at the screen. Natalie. Rudy. Natalie. He powered it off.

He might have a little time before they zeroed in on him. They would be searching the woods, looking for more bodies (how many were there?) and questioning witnesses (what would Emma say?) and wondering if Jonah himself were a victim. But sooner or later, when they couldn't locate him, they'd be calling the Anchorage to find out if he'd returned. He needed to account for where *he'd* been.

Being the prime suspect was different from being one of many. He had to assume he could get away with exactly nothing.

As Jonah was passing the buff brick buildings of St. Francis High School, just off the Shoreway, he made a split-second decision. It would take a little time, but it would put some evidence out of reach. Exiting the highway, he parked in a convenience store's lot next to the school. It was an easy matter to break into the field house. Who knew his Nightshade skills were so transferable?

Not long after, he emerged, freshly showered, wearing sweatpants and a generic sweatshirt from the lost and found. His soiled clothing and the furniture pads and gloves had been burned to ash in the school incinerator. If he was lucky (when had he ever been lucky?), nobody would ask what had happened to the clothes he wore to the concert.

When he arrived back at school, he parked the van on a side street, rather than in its usual parking spot behind the

Keep (too many surveillance cameras there). Pulling up the hood of his sweatshirt, he walked briskly to Oxbow. He was reaching for the keypad when he realized that he would be leaving tracks. Tracks that Gabriel could follow. What if they subpoenaed records? Gabriel would cover for him, right?

Would he? Jonah's gut iced within him, heavy and cold. What if Gabriel truly thought he was guilty of murdering mainliners? Which he might, since they'd been arguing about strategy for a couple of years now. An argument that had led directly to Jonah's dismissal from Nightshade. Gabriel might see this as the ultimate act of rebellion. He had opportunity; he had motive; he had the skills.

Worse, was it possible he'd actually done it? Most savants experienced a gradual mental and physical decline, the process known as *fading*. But Jonah himself had been responsible for chasing down savants who'd decompensated suddenly and violently. Who'd gone rogue and needed to be hunted down before they hurt anyone else. Was it possible he'd had a psychotic episode?

No. It must've been Lilith Greaves and her army of rogue shades—the undead survivors of Thorn Hill. The ones who'd been murdering the gifted for years. Lilith's words came back to him, from when they sparred over the kidnapping of children from Trinity.

We will destroy you. Whether you join us or not, you'll be blamed for the deaths of mainliners. See what kind of justice you'll get from them.

Still. If he *hadn't* done it, then he'd been convincingly framed. Meaning he could trust no one. Well. Almost no one.

Jonah backed away from the side door, turned, and headed for Safe Harbor. He was halfway there before he remembered that Kenzie and the other residents of the skilled facility had been moved to the Steel Wool building. Right. There'd been an explosion—an attack by vigilantes who wanted Gabriel and his mutants out of their backyard. Vigilantes who likely came straight from Trinity.

Get it together, Kinlock, or you might as well turn yourself in.

To Jonah's surprise, Kenzie's lights were out, the door closed, and it took him several minutes to respond to Jonah's knock. Finally, he heard his brother call, "Come *in*, already!"

When Jonah entered, Kenzie was in bed, hair tousled from sleep. His laptop lay open beside him on top of the covers.

"Were you sleeping? It's still early." Jonah crossed to Kenzie's bedside. His brother looked pale, dark circles under his eyes. Instantly concerned, Jonah leaned close. "Hey. Are you all right?"

"I'm fine," Kenzie mumbled, yawning. "Don't be such a worrywart. I figured you wouldn't be by tonight since you had that concert. I thought I'd read in bed. I must've fallen asleep." Kenzie focused in on Jonah. "Look who's talking. You look terrible. Did you party too hard or what?" Pulling the laptop toward him, Kenzie murmured, "Harry, wake up." Kenzie glanced at the screen, then did a double take. "Um. Shouldn't you still be there?"

"I should," Jonah said. "But something's happened. I hate to involve you in this, but there's nobody else I can trust." He paused. "I need an alibi."

"You don't have to ask. You know I'm in," Kenzie said, propping up with some effort. "Bring my chariot."

Jonah rummaged in Kenzie's closet and found an old pair of suede gloves. He felt more secure once he'd yanked them on. Maneuvering Kenzie's wheelchair to the side of the bed, he helped Kenzie into it. His brother was sweating, tremoring a little. It seemed that he hadn't totally recovered from the trauma of the explosion.

Getting a fresh, close-up look at Jonah, Kenzie said, "I'm serious. You look half-dead. Should I call Natalie?"

"No. She's still back in Trinity." Once Kenzie was in position, Jonah collapsed into a chair. "First of all, I need to know—has anyone called you to ask if I'm here?" It was all over if Kenzie had talked to anyone.

"Nope. I've been asleep, remember?" Kenzie checked his phone. "Missed call from Natalie, and voice mail, an hour ago. Harry, read voice mail message."

Natalie sounded half-frantic, something Jonah had never associated with his best friend. *"Kenzie? Are you there? Pick up. Have you seen Jonah? It's important."* She paused, waited. *"Call me back when you get this."* She clicked off.

"All right," Jonah said, "They'll call back, and when they do, I've been here since"—Jonah checked the time—"since nine thirty, all right? I came in, all upset, because Emma and I had a big fight."

"You did?" Kenzie raised an eyebrow. "Just so you know, I'm on her side."

"You should be," Jonah said wearily. "You definitely should be."

"And if you've hurt her, we are history." Kenzie seemed to be reviving, regaining his usual snarky attitude.

"No!" Jonah said. "I didn't hurt her! I just—I don't think I did . . ." His voice trailed off.

"Stop it!" Kenzie snarled. "I was joking. You know you didn't hurt her. You wouldn't."

You're wrong, Jonah thought. I already have.

"Have you been back to your room?" Kenzie asked, with that distracted expression that said he was already working the problem.

Jonah shook his head. "No. I didn't want to be time stamped when I went in."

"Actually, I think you do want to be time stamped. You *have* been back to your room. Before you came here. When do you want to be there?"

"You can do that?"

"Have a little faith, bro," Kenzie said. "Rudy and I designed most of the architecture when Gabriel upgraded a few years ago. He didn't want to go outside to have that work done."

"Don't you want to know what happened before you become a coconspirator?" Jonah asked dryly.

Kenzie shook his head. "Let's take care of the alibi first. I assume Gabriel's on the outside in this?"

"Yeah," Jonah said. "He is." As he said it, he couldn't help wondering: when was it that he'd stopped trusting Gabriel?

"Then we need to keep him out of the system until I get things set up. Which means I need to do this sooner rather than later, so he doesn't get suspicious." Kenzie turned back to his workstation. "Harry, go to Facilities Systems."

"Is there anything I can do?" Jonah asked.

"Get us both something to drink and turn on some tunes. There's drugs in the lav if you want."

Jonah swallowed two ibuprofen, then grabbed drinks from the refrigerator. He handed a bottle of fruit juice to Kenzie and settled back into his chair as Kenzie murmured orders and code to Harry.

"Harry. Access Building Security Systems. Oxbow number 457." Kenzie's eyes scanned the screen. "So if the first set was over at nine, and you came straight back . . . we'll put you in your room about nine thirty, right? And you came here about ten, and you've been here since."

"What about the surveillance cameras in the corridor?" Jonah said.

"Damn cameras!" Kenzie said, slapping his hands on his desk. "They went down this morning and haven't worked since." He raised his eyebrows at Jonah.

"Will anyone be able to tell you've been into the system?" Jonah asked. "I don't want you to get into trouble."

"Gabriel's smart about using technology to do the things he wants, but his knowledge of these kinds of systems is superficial at best."

"What about Rudy?"

"I don't think so." Kenzie eyed Jonah. "Is Rudy in or out?"

"Everybody's out right now," Jonah said.

Jonah's phone pinged again. He scanned the screen. Text from Gabriel. *Jonah. Call me right now. Urgent.*

"Gabriel's on the case," Jonah said. "Won't be long now."

Two more texts from Gabriel, and then his phone rang. Jonah allowed voice mail to pick it up.

Kenzie's eyes narrowed at some activity on the screen. "Gabriel's trying to log into the system right now, but he's off-campus. I've put a few roadblocks in his way."

Finally, Kenzie sat back. "We're good. I can pretty it up later, but this should do the job. Gabriel's in, but he's seeing what we want him to see." Using both hands to steady the bottle, he took a long swallow of juice. "So. What's going on?"

"I don't *know* what's going on. I passed out and woke up covered in blood." When Kenzie raised his eyebrows, Jonah added, hastily, "It wasn't mine."

"Where did this happen?"

"Outside McCauley's house in Trinity. I believe at least three people are dead. There may be more." Jonah quickly explained what happened.

"It sounds to me like somebody framed you," Kenzie murmured.

Jonah hesitated. "I had a—a confrontation with Rowan DeVries earlier tonight. Out on the grounds. So there's a chance he's involved somehow, though it's hard to imagine he would murder his own kind in order to get back at me."

"Don't wizards do that a lot?" Kenzie said. "Murder each other, I mean?"

Just then, Kenzie's cell phone rang. The Kinlock brothers looked at each other. Kenzie said, "Harry, answer the phone. Use speakerphone."

Gabriel's voice came through the speaker, husky and strained. "Kenzie? Is that you?"

"Hi, Gabriel," Kenzie said, still watching Jonah. "'Sup?"

"Tell me—have you seen Jonah tonight?"

"Sure," Kenzie said. "He's right here. Want to speak with him?"

Dead silence. Then Gabriel sucked in a quick breath and said, "Yes. Put him on."

"Hey, Gabriel," Jonah said in a thready, weak voice. "Did Natalie call you?"

"Natalie? Why would she call me?" Gabriel snapped.

"I think I caught some kind of virus," Jonah said. "I couldn't stay for the second set at McCauley's. How'd it go?"

"You *left?*" Gabriel's voice cracked.

"Well," Jonah said, "I didn't want to puke all over the equipment. I already slimed my clothes. I had to pitch them."

Another long silence from Gabriel.

"He looks *awful,*" Kenzie put in. "I can vouch for that."

"How long have you been there?" Gabriel said finally. "When did you leave Trinity?"

"I left right after the first set," Jonah said, figuring it was best to stick as close to the truth as he could. "Emma and I . . . we had kind of a fight. And then I was feeling so crappy, I ditched. I'm sorry to let you down. I know the concert was important." Jonah could hear voices in the background, the crackle of a police radio. "What's all the noise?" he asked. "Are you in the club?"

"I'm in Trinity," Gabriel said. "Three people have been murdered. Guests at the party."

"Murdered?" Jonah said, pushing horror and astonishment. The horrified part was totally real. "In Trinity? *Who? Not*—not anyone I know. Not Nat or—or—"

"No," Gabriel said impatiently. "Not Alison or Natalie or Rudy. Three teens, two of them wizards. Rowan DeVries was badly wounded. He may not make it."

"Rowan DeVries!" Jonah had no need to act surprised—he was stunned. "*DeVries* was one of the victims?"

"Apparently so."

"That's convenient," Jonah said, mind racing. "That totally takes him off the list of suspects." And puts me on it.

"Do you think he stabbed *himself?*" Gabriel growled. "If so, he did a remarkably good job."

"They were stabbed?" Jonah asked.

"Same as in the other killings. Stabbed and slashed to

death, nightshade scattered at the site. I haven't even told
you the worst part. One of the victims was Madison Moss's
younger sister."

"Grace?" Jonah said, his heart sinking. "That young girl?
Somebody murdered *her?*"

Gabriel sighed heavily. "I cannot tell you what a disaster this is. Whatever happens, it's going to cause a world of
trouble for us."

And for me in particular, Jonah thought. It was as if he
could feel the jaws of a trap closing around him. "Is there
anything I can do? Should I come?" Jonah asked.

"I thought you were sick," Gabriel said.

"I am. But, if you need me, I'll be there."

"No," Gabriel said. "Stay right where you are—at
Kenzie's. We'll come to you." He paused, lowered his voice.
"Is there anything you want to tell me in confidence? Anything I should know before we get there?"

"No," Jonah said, faking confusion. "I mean, if you have
any specific questions, I'll be glad to answer them. Anyway,
who's 'we'? Who's coming?"

"Me and the police and my lawyer. I get the impression
that you are a prime suspect."

⌘ CHAPTER FIVE ⌘
PRIME SUSPECT

The detective from Trinity, Ross Childers, was like one of those small-town cops out of a novel, the kind that *seemed* homespun until they outsmarted the big-city criminal.

It was good that he and Kenzie had worked out a story ahead of time, because Jonah was marched down the hall to the family conference room and questioned separately. Matt Green stayed with Kenzie. Gabriel came along with Jonah.

Jonah's physical state was a double-edged sword. On the one hand, it probably helped that he was pale and sweating, still half-sick from whatever had knocked him out. It supported the story he had to tell. On the other, it was harder to think, to strategize, and to make the best use of his enchanter's charm.

Jonah had to assume that Emma had told the police at least some of what happened in the gazebo. What he didn't know was how much she had left out. For instance, had she offered any explanation for DeVries's attack on her? Had she told police that Jonah was a mass murderer?

He guessed not, or he'd be in custody already. Was he really going to benefit from Emma's distrust of the police? Or was she just biding her time? Jonah preferred to be master of his own fate. He did not like waiting for the other shoe to drop.

All he could do was stick as close to his own truth as possible, trying to anticipate the traps that Childers might set for him. The detective typed notes into a tiny computer that seemed to disappear into his lap. Once he'd collected basic information from Jonah, he got down to business.

"I understand you were out on the grounds during the party," Childers said. "Did you see or hear anything unusual?"

"I was passing the gazebo, and I heard raised voices, like people fighting," Jonah said. "I went to see what was up."

"And what was up?" Childers asked.

"Rowan DeVries had my friend Emma up against the wall, and seemed to be threatening her. So I pulled him off her and asked him what the hell he was doing." Anger boiled up in Jonah once again at the memory, but he fought it down. You killed his sister, he reminded himself. You have no standing.

Out of the corner of his eye, Jonah saw Gabriel react to *that* revelation. He looked like he'd been punched in the gut.

"So you knew both of them?" Childers continued.

"Emma and I are in a band together. DeVries—I don't . . . we haven't really met officially, but I've seen him at least once before. In Trinity."

"You come to Trinity often?"

"No," Jonah said, massaging his forehead. "I think tonight was my . . . third visit."

"You must have a good memory, then," Childers said. "Since you recognized DeVries."

"He made an impression."

"What kind of impression?"

"He seemed like a very angry person," Jonah said truthfully. "Both times I met him."

"What were they fighting about?"

"We didn't really get into that. I figured if they wanted me to know, they would tell me. And they didn't."

"What happened after you separated them?"

"DeVries left."

Childers raised an eyebrow. "Really?"

"I told him to leave, and he did," Jonah said evenly.

"Where did all the blood come from, then?"

"Blood? Was there blood?" Jonah racked his brain. He hadn't left any blood in the gazebo. Had he? "Oh. I think maybe Emma punched him in the nose or something before I got there. His nose was bleeding, anyway."

"So it was Emma?"

"So it was Emma *what*?" Jonah growled. "If she punched him in the nose, he deserved it. She was defending herself."

"She didn't have a knife or other weapon?"

"Why would she have a *knife*? She was there to play a gig, not to slaughter the audience during the break." He snorted. "Way not to be asked back."

"It's just that some things aren't adding up," Childers said. "Her clothes were covered in blood. Yours look absolutely clean."

"I puked on myself," Jonah said. "So I changed clothes.

Trust me, you should be glad I did that." Out of the corner of his eye, he saw that Gabriel was glaring at him.

Charm, Kinlock, not sarcasm, Jonah thought. It was hard to keep that front of mind.

"Where are they now?" Childers asked. When Jonah frowned, puzzled, he added, "Your clothes, I mean."

"I tossed them," Jonah said. "Some cleanup jobs just aren't worth doing."

"Where did you toss them?" Childers persisted.

"I threw them in the incinerator," Jonah said. "Trash pickup isn't until Thursday, and I didn't want to live with them until then." He paused, then asked, "Are you collecting clothes from everyone at the party, or am I getting special attention?"

"I had the same question," Gabriel interjected. He'd remained silent up till then. "If Jonah is a suspect, then we need to proceed differently. I'll fetch Matt, and we can begin again."

Childers shook his head. "I'm just, you know, being thorough in collecting evidence. Why did you leave the party? Didn't you have another set to play?"

"I was sick, like I said."

"Did you tell anyone you were sick? Or that you were leaving?"

"I texted the other band members to tell them I was ditching," Jonah said. "They're the only ones who would care."

"Did anyone see you leave? Or notice that you were sick?"

"I figured nobody wanted to see that," Jonah said. "It wasn't something I wanted to share with anyone."

"Had you been drinking?"

Jonah shook his head. "I'm underage," he said, as if he

were puzzled by the suggestion. "I was drinking pop. I did eat some quesadillas."

Childers gestured toward Jonah's hands. "What's with the gloves?"

"Jonah has an extremely painful nerve problem in his hands, caused by exposure to a deadly toxin when he was a child," Gabriel said. "He wears the gloves all the time. Has since he was little."

"You have a nerve problem in your hands?" Childers looked down at his screen. "But it says here that you're a guitar player. How does that work?"

"I have a high tolerance for pain," Jonah said, thinking, It's a skill you develop when you kill everything you touch.

Childers's eyes flicked to Gabriel, then back to Jonah. "How did you get back here from Trinity?"

"We took two vans," Jonah said. "I drove one of them back."

"Where is it now?"

"It's a couple blocks away," Jonah said. He felt the pressure of Gabriel's eyes, and guessed his mentor was wondering why Jonah hadn't parked in his usual spot.

"I'll need the make, model, license, and all that," Childers said. "We'll want to take a look at it."

"Don't you need a warrant for that?" Jonah asked.

"Not if you give us permission," Childers said.

"He's not giving permission," Gabriel put in. "You'll have to show probable cause."

"That shouldn't be a problem," Childers said genially.

The door slammed open, and Matt Green entered, followed by the uniformed officers who'd been interviewing Kenzie.

"All done?" Childers asked, surprised.

"Yeah, pretty much," one of the officers said. "Anyway, all our equipment went down. Some kind of electrical thing. We weren't getting much anyway; it was obvious the kid was in pain, so we decided to pack it in and let him go to bed."

Maybe Kenzie's right, Jonah thought. Maybe I should start setting fire to things.

At the end of it, Jonah thought he'd done reasonably well, given what he had to work with. He was still on the list of suspects, but he hadn't incriminated himself, at least, and he'd bought a little time.

After the others finally left, Gabriel rose and paced back and forth. "I hope you realize that you've put us into an impossible situation," he said. "I cannot believe that you would get into a fight with a mainliner while you were there as a guest. Especially someone on the Interguild Council. Especially someone who ended up nearly stabbed to death."

"If you're talking about DeVries, that was a rescue," Jonah retorted. "It seemed like the right thing to do. Would you have preferred that I let him carry Emma off to his lair?"

"What possible reason would Rowan DeVries have for kidnapping Emma?" Gabriel asked wearily.

"Why don't you ask him?" Jonah said, knowing that Gabriel never would, even if Rowan survived. Counting on it, in fact. "Probably, he was just doing the usual wizard thing—taking what he can't get any other way. If I'd known he was going to get stabbed, I would've been more circumspect. Anyway, whose idea was it for us to sign on to play at this party, Gabriel? It wasn't mine, I'll tell you that. I fought it tooth and nail."

"Still, you agreed to go. I used to be able to rely on your

good judgment when it came to interacting with mainliners. Now—I don't know what to think."

"Well, I don't know what to think either," Jonah shot back. "Sometimes I get a vibe from you, like you hate mainliners. Absolutely despise them. Other times, it's like you're more worried about them than you are about us."

"I can't believe what I'm hearing," Gabriel said, radiating white-hot fury. "After I've spent a lifetime trying to undo what happened at Thorn Hill, you think I favor *mainliners*?"

Jonah had no answer for that. "I'm sorry, Gabriel," he said. "That was out of line. If not for you, Kenzie and I would be dead."

Gabriel searched Jonah's face, then nodded. "Apology accepted." He hesitated, as if trying to choose the right words. "You know I have to ask this, Jonah—were you involved in any way in the killings at McCauley's?"

"No," Jonah said without flinching.

Gabriel finally sat down across from Jonah and leaned forward. "All I'm saying is, if you were, we would put all of our resources behind you—the best legal representation, the best expert witnesses—whatever it takes. It certainly complicates things that one of the victims was Moss's younger sister, but—"

"I said *no*, Gabriel. Who do you think I am? Do you really think I would murder a little girl?"

Gabriel rubbed his chin. "Well. We can hope that DeVries survives. Maybe he'll be able to shed some light on this."

Jonah was reading something odd in Gabriel. Was it doubt? Suspicion? Disappointment? That was it. Disappointment. Did it mean that Gabriel didn't believe him? That he didn't trust him? That he thought that Jonah had actually done the murders?

Change the subject. "Where are Natalie and the others?"

"I told them to go home and go to bed," Gabriel said. "I'm concerned about PTSD, what with the bombing at Safe Harbor, and now this." He raked his hand over his close-cropped hair.

"The bombing's still unsolved, right?" Jonah said. "I wonder if the police ever questioned anyone in Trinity about that." He paused, but Gabriel didn't take the bait. Jonah had pushed Gabriel to act on those suspicions, but Gabriel never seemed to want to engage.

"Is Emma all right?" Jonah tried not to sound too interested. "I mean, Childers seemed to suspect her of something."

"He's just a small-town cop," Gabriel said dismissively. "He's probably bigoted against outsiders. And people of color."

"That's not the way I read him," Jonah said. "I think he just wants to solve this. To find out what really happened."

Gabriel snorted skeptically, then swung round to face Jonah. "I need to know the truth, Jonah: this thing with DeVries and Emma. Is this some kind of love triangle? Is something going on among the three of you?"

"Remember who you're talking to," Jonah said, raising his gloved hands, wiggling his fingers. "No love. Not for me. Not ever. It didn't look like there was any love lost between Emma and DeVries either."

"What about Emma?" Gabriel said. "Has *she* fallen for you, Jonah?" It was a familiar question. They'd had to navigate a number of infatuations over the years. He and Gabriel had worked out strategies for defusing them, for redirecting crushes. They'd become damned efficient at keeping love away from Jonah's door.

Jonah shook his head, the memory of the confrontation in the gazebo knifing through him. "Right now, if I had to guess, I'd say she hates me."

"Natalie said you were dancing with her."

"This is exactly why I usually refuse to dance with anyone. I say yes to any girl in a moment of weakness, and Natalie has me fathering her children. Though how I'd manage that, I have no clue. It was just a dance." The words burned in his memory.

Gabriel fingered his earring, his eyes troubled. "I understand your caution, believe me, but you may be exaggerating the risk."

"I don't have any reason to believe that anything has changed," Jonah said. "And I don't care to risk somebody's life to find out. I've killed enough people already."

Gabriel sighed. "I wish you would let go of the notion that Nightshade is in the business of killing. Shades are remnants of savants who have died. That's all. They are not viable as human beings." His eyes searched Jonah's face. "Back to Emma. We don't know much about her, except for her relationship to Sonny Lee Greenwood. Is it too much of a coincidence that she showed up here and insinuated herself into our operation, and the next thing we know she's having a fight with DeVries? Can you get a read on her? Is there a possibility she's involved somehow?"

"No," Jonah said.

Gabriel held Jonah's gaze a moment longer, then shifted away. "Well, then. What happened tonight should convince you that we're on the right course. If none of us is responsible for the murders tonight, then Lilith must be. She's doing exactly what she threatened to do—continuing her killing spree while ensuring that we get the blame."

On that count, Jonah had to admit that Gabriel was probably right.

Lilith Greaves was the charismatic shade who had organized the undead survivors of the massacre at Thorn Hill into an army; a force dedicated to taking revenge on the mainline guilds, especially wizards. Killing the gifted produced blood magic, something that strengthened the ability of shades to possess new bodies. Lilith had been trying to recruit the living members of Nightshade to her cause. "So," Gabriel said, when Jonah didn't respond. "Are you going to continue to defend her to me?"

"I've never defended her," Jonah said. "You know I've riffed more shades than anyone else by a long shot. I only suggested we talk to her." He paused, took a breath. "But now I'm beginning to see your point. We can't win this thing as long as Lilith is killing mainliners indiscriminately. I need to do something about that."

He couldn't allow Lilith and her army to go on killing the Grace Mosses of the world.

"*We* need to do something about that," Gabriel said. "Nightshade is a team effort, remember?"

Right, Jonah thought. But at the end of the day, I'm the one that usually does the killing.

⊛ CHAPTER SIX ⊛
MEMORIAL SERVICE

Everyone seemed to find a way to take the blame for Grace Moss's murder. Madison, because she'd brought her sister to Trinity against her wishes. Grace would still be alive, at least, if she'd stayed at home. Also, Madison had neglected her role as the Dragon, because she'd never wanted it in the first place, and maybe if she'd done a better job, none of this would have happened.

Seph McCauley, because it happened at his house, and he'd been the one to stir the pot by inviting a volatile mixture of guests. Bring people together, and see what happens.

Leander Hastings and Linda Downey, because they'd let him have his way about the party.

Leesha Middleton, because accepting blame was becoming a habit. All through the funeral service, Leesha felt smothered, weighed down by guilt, deafened by the voices of her accusers, even though they were only in her head.

The services were held in St. Catherine's Church, though

there was not a whiff of Catholicism about anybody in Madison's family. Leesha had assumed that they might hold the services down in southern Ohio, where Grace was born and raised.

Maybe this church was appropriate, since it had been the scene of so much triumph and tragedy already. Down in the crypts, Jason had stored the magical objects he'd stolen from Dragon's Ghyll. Here, in the sanctuary, Madison Moss had absorbed the Dragonheart and become the source of magic for all of the guilds. From the bell tower, she'd confronted the wizards of the Red and White Roses, and demonstrated the consequences of bad behavior.

In this churchyard, Leesha had betrayed Jason Haley to Warren Barber and lost Jason's trust forever.

Madison's and Grace's mother, Carlene, and little brother, John Robert, had come up from southern Ohio, escorted by a lawyer, Ray McCartney, who seemed to be a family friend. The other attendees represented a whole range of agendas. Everyone on the Interguild Council came, of course, with the exception of Rowan DeVries, who was still hospitalized in critical condition. Apparently, the trauma surgeons had discovered and sutured a major internal bleed in the nick of time.

There'd been no word on whether he'd identified his attacker.

Nearly everyone who'd survived the party, Weir and Anaweir, were there. A few of Madison's Art Institute friends made the trip, too.

The Terrible Trio of preschool parents—Scavuzzo, Morrison, and Hudson—occupied an entire pew, wearing mournful and self-righteous expressions. Leesha couldn't help thinking that Madison should have made the service invitation-only. But then maybe Leesha herself wouldn't have made Madison's list. They'd had their ups and downs over the years.

The media were there, of course, national as well as local. A mass murder on Halloween in a small town—this was a story with legs. They camped out all over the town green, tramping through flower beds in order to get that perfect photograph.

When had Leesha begun to care about the town flower beds?

Jack, Ellen, Will, and Fitch were stationed by the doors to keep the media at bay, looking odd and uncomfortable in their somber suits. Leesha guessed that the suit Fitch was wearing was borrowed, since he swam in it. A pair of suspenders was the only thing that stood between him and disaster. He'd also gone back to blond.

Just before the service started, Leesha saw someone slip into the sanctuary, exchange a few words with Jack, and slide into the back pew. It was Emma Lee, wearing a black sweater, an ill-fitting straight skirt, and sunglasses.

Surprised, Leesha scanned the mourners again. Just as she'd thought. Nobody else from the Anchorage. Just Emma.

Carlene Moss sobbed so loudly throughout the service that a few warrior ghosts wandered in to see what was going on. John Robert held tightly to Madison's hand, looking solemn and sad. He'd inherited his mother's blond good looks, but maybe that was all. Though he was only seven, he seemed more grown-up than his mother did.

Leesha knew from experience that when parents don't parent, kids grow up fast.

Carlene drew all the attention, but Madison was the one

Leesha watched. The Dragon sat still, jaw set, her eyes like blue flames against her pale skin. Like all the power within her blazed out through the windows of her eyes. Her hair was pulled back into a knot at the base of her neck, and she'd set aside her usual riotous color for dead black. An old term came to mind: widow's weeds.

Seph watched her, too, dark brows drawn together, sometimes leaning in to murmur something in her ear. Holding on to her hand as if she might fly apart otherwise.

Now and then, Leesha stole a look at Emma, who sat, stick straight, hands gripping the back of the pew in front of her, eyes narrowed as she studied everyone in the church. She seemed to be on some kind of a mission.

After the service, there was a reception at the house Jack shared with his mother, Becka, since Seph's house was still cordoned off. Besides, the setting was too fraught, too recently the scene of tragedy.

It had been a while since Leesha had been in Jack's house. It still resembled a library run by a second-generation hippie hoarder. It was an ecumenical and untidy clutter of books, bulging research folders, half-finished remodeling projects, folk art, and paperwork. The front parlor, which served as Becka's office, had been cleaned out for the occasion. Leesha suspected that if she opened any closet, the contents would tumble out on her head.

The Moss family received guests in the front parlor. Madison and John Robert stood on one side of Carlene, Ray McCartney on the other, as she received condolences from the attendees.

The contrast between mother and daughter was astounding. Madison seemed likely to burn the house down at any moment, while Carlene was the most delicately beautiful mourner Leesha had ever seen, as frail and dewy as a flower in the moonlight. Now and then, she dabbed her eyes with a tissue. Waterproof mascara, Leesha thought. Then hated herself for noticing.

Linda Downey and Leander Hastings held court across the center hall, in the dining room, receiving the gifted, mostly. Seph moved back and forth between.

Leesha drifted into the kitchen, where an array of food was laid out, but nothing seemed appealing. Dispiritedly, she chose three olives and two pieces of pineapple, a chocolate-covered strawberry for dessert.

"Leesha?"

Leesha spun around. It was Emma.

"Could I talk to you a minute? In private?"

"Sure," Leesha said. "Um . . . let's go in here." Leesha led the way into the service pantry, tucked between the kitchen and the dining room. Setting her plate down on the counter, she leaned back against the warming oven. "What's up?"

"I need a place to stay," Emma said. "Here in Trinity, if possible. I wondered if you know of a place. I can pay rent, though not very much."

"Aren't you at the Anchorage?" Leesha asked.

Emma nodded.

"Isn't that a boarding school?" Leesha said.

"It is," Emma said. "But I'm thinking of making a change. They have schools here, don't they?"

"Well, yes, but . . . are you sure you want to switch schools this far into the school year? Trinity High School is okay, but, well, maybe you've never lived in a small town."

Leesha couldn't think of Trinity High School without wincing. There were still plenty of people that hadn't forgotten her tenure there.

"I'm just . . ." Emma looked around, like she might find an answer taped to the wall. "I'm just trying to figure some things out. Get both sides of the story."

"Do you have a way to get back and forth? There's no public transportation between here and anywhere. If you want to get anywhere else, you'll have to drive."

"I have a car," Emma said. "It's old, but it's been reliable."

Leesha eyed Emma appraisingly. "Look, this is a college town, and it's hard to find housing during the school year," she said. "Especially in the fall, before anybody's dropped out. But if you want, you can stay at my place. It's actually my aunt's house."

"Oh, no," Emma said, taking a quick step back and coming up against the cooler. "I'm not looking for a handout. I don't want to be anybody's project."

"Here's the thing," Leesha said. "I could use some help with my aunt. Aunt Millie is a sweetheart, but she's not playing with a full deck these days, so I hate to leave her alone for very long. She's a wizard, though, and that makes it hard to keep help. It's what you might call a high-risk situation."

"I'm not sure I—?"

"She sets fire to things now and then, okay?" Leesha said, thinking that being honest wasn't nearly as easy as everyone made out. "And blows things up."

"On purpose?"

"Oh, no," Leesha said. "She wouldn't hurt a fly. It's just . . . Trying to get Aunt Millie to give up conjury is like getting any older person to give up driving. She can't resist trying some spellwork, even though the results are unpredictable. Also, her cooking is appalling."

"I can cook some," Emma said, hesitantly. "Mostly plain things: scrambled eggs, grits, fried potatoes, and grilled cheese. I used to cook for my grandfather sometimes. Probably not anything you all would like."

"Who doesn't like grilled cheese?" Leesha said. "The most important thing is whether you'd be able to deal with my aunt."

Emma shifted her eyes away, as if debating whether to speak or not. Then she leaned in a little closer, lowering her voice. "One thing a lot of mainliners don't know: savants are resistant to conjured magic. So, um, I guess she could set fire to me, but if she tried to change me into a frog, it wouldn't work."

Leesha gaped for a moment, rendered speechless by Emma's matter-of-fact delivery. This was huge. Huge. Savants were resistant to conjury. Why would that be?

She couldn't quite smother the voice that said, *If savants are responsible for the attacks on the gifted, it might explain why they've been so successful.*

Leesha was already learning something about savants that she didn't know before.

She looked up at Emma, who seemed to be waiting for a response.

"That's *perfect*," Leesha said, gripping Emma's hands. Better not seem overenthusiastic and scare her off. "I mean, it sounds good to me. If you want to give it a try. Trial basis. No obligation." Money-back guarantee, she added silently.

Just then, Leesha became aware of raised voices in the parlor. Some kind of an argument.

"Hang on," she said, and moved to the door so she could see what was going on.

There was a crowd in the room, including Seph, Linda, and Leander, but the voices belonged to Madison and her mother.

"No, Mama, we are *not* going to hold a news conference," Madison said. "I don't care how many reporters are camped outside."

"Come on, now, baby; the media, they're just trying to do their job," Carlene pleaded. "Don't you think it makes sense for them to get the straight story direct from us?"

"No!" Madison practically shouted. "You are *not* going out there and air our dirty laundry to the *Star* or the *Squealer* or whoever."

"It's not the *Squealer*," Carlene argued. "*People* magazine is out there. Real journalists."

"This is a mess," Emma muttered over Leesha's shoulder. "This is a sorry mess."

Just then, Madison looked up and spotted the two of them standing there in the doorway.

"You! What are *you* doing here?" She strode toward them, pointing a shaking finger at Emma.

"Me? I'm—I just, you know, wanted to come to the service and pay my respects," Emma said faintly. "I'm so sorry for your loss."

"Well, you don't belong here," Madison said, trembling, tears glittering on her cheeks. "I never should have—I'm sorry, but I just—I can't believe that you turned up covered in blood, but you didn't see *anything*. That you don't remember *anything*."

"Well, I—I talked to the cops," Emma said. "I told them what I—"

"This is not over," Madison said. "I'm going to stay here and get to the bottom of this. We are not going to count on the police. We are going to conduct our own investigation, hold our own hearings, and make sure whoever was responsible for this is punished."

Emma kept her mouth shut this time, but she kept shaking her head.

"Hey, Maddie," Seph McCauley said gently, sliding an arm around her. "Let's go in the kitchen and get you something to eat. It's been a long day, and you haven't eaten a bite."

Madison allowed Seph to lead her away. Emma watched them go, biting her lip.

"What was that all about?" Leesha murmured.

For a long moment, Emma said nothing. "I guess she's been talking to the police. I actually stopped in at the police station before I came here, to sign a statement. Chief Childers asked me some more questions, but I told him everything the last time. They seem to think I know more about the murders than I'm letting on."

"*Hmm,*" Leesha said. "Chief Childers is probably just being thorough. There's a lot of pressure on the department, what with all the media attention."

"There's still some test results that need to come back, I guess." Emma took a deep breath, releasing it in a sigh. "Look, maybe staying in Trinity isn't such a good idea. I don't want to make Madison any more miserable than she already is."

"I don't think your presence or absence will make that much of a difference to her," Leesha said. "I think it's more up to you—whether you can deal with that kind of reaction from some people."

Emma straightened and her chin came up. "I don't scare easy, if that's what you mean."

Good, Leesha thought. That will help when you meet Aunt Millie.

ᚘ CHAPTER SEVEN ᚙ
EXIT INTERVIEW

It was beginning to get light when Emma parked in the lot behind the Keep, but it would be another hour before the sun found its way into the canyons between the buildings downtown. About the only time Emma was up at this hour was when she'd never gone to bed. But this way maybe she wouldn't run into anyone else. She planned to wait for Gabriel outside of his offices, state her case, and be gone before the campus was stirring.

If she'd had a choice, she'd have moved out in the middle of the night without a word to anyone. But that would close the door to the Anchorage, and she needed to keep that door open. She needed to keep in contact with the people who might answer the questions she needed to ask. Once she knew what those were.

Most of all, she needed Gabriel Mandrake to not contact the authorities in Memphis. She'd run away from there after her grandfather died to avoid going into foster care. She needed Mandrake for cover, which meant she needed his blessing.

To Emma's surprise, the lights were on in Gabriel's reception area, though Gabriel's assistant, Patrick, was not yet at his desk. Emma could hear a murmur of voices from Gabriel's inner office. He keeps early hours, Emma thought. Surprising, for a music promoter.

She sat down in one of the chairs and leafed through a magazine, but she didn't read a word. She was trying not to listen, but the voices in Gabriel's office got louder and louder so that pretty soon she could make out who was in there, and bits and pieces of what was being said.

Gabriel. And Alison. Maybe Alison was facing away, because Emma couldn't hear much of what she was saying.

"And I am telling you that you will get through this, Alison," Gabriel was saying. "As you always have done. I realize that you're going through a difficult time, but I need you to keep moving forward. You do know how important you are to me, and to our continued survival."

Emma gripped the arms of her chair. It was hard to resist going over and putting her ear to the door. This was Alison's private business.

Alison said something else Emma couldn't make out.

"No!" Gabriel said sharply. "The risk is too great. We'll just have to sit tight. There is nothing more to be done right now."

Again, she heard Alison's muffled voice.

"Very well," Gabriel said. "Meet me at the infirmary at six this evening, and we'll see what we can do. But right now, I need to prepare for a meeting, and you need to get ready for class."

Emma heard a scraping as chairs were pushed back. She buried her nose in her magazine as the door to Gabriel's office slammed open. She heard a quick intake of breath as they spotted her there.

"What are *you* doing here?" Alison demanded. "Eavesdropping?"

Emma looked up, and saw that Alison's face was fishbelly pale.

"N-no," Emma said. It wasn't like she was *trying* to eavesdrop. "I was hoping to talk to Gabriel."

"I was, too," Alison said. "In *private*." And she stomped out.

Gabriel stared after her for a long moment, eyes narrowed, then turned his attention to Emma. "I'm sorry about that, Emma. Was there something you needed?"

"I wanted to talk to you about making a change. But it looks like you're in a hurry?"

"No worries," Gabriel said. "I have a few minutes. I just needed to end that last conversation." He gestured to a chair. "Please. Sit."

So Emma explained what she intended to do, while Gabriel looked more and more annoyed.

"I still don't understand why you would choose to live in Trinity," Gabriel Mandrake said, snapping shut his laptop. "It seems to me that the Anchorage is ideal for someone in your situation. You've only been here for, what, three months?"

Emma picked at a scab on her arm. She could guess what he was thinking. *You're living in your own apartment for free. Meals and healthcare and tuition are provided. You're attending a school that is designed to meet your peculiar needs. Why would you want to go somewhere you had to pay your own way? Are you crazy?*

Since Gabriel still seemed to be waiting for an answer,

she said, "I'm not saying I don't like it. It's amazing, and I feel lucky to be here. The woodshop and the music program are—I appreciate everything you've done for me. I just need a little different experience."

"You're not likely to be well-received in Trinity. Mainliners in general are not very accepting of our students. This most recent catastrophe has just added fuel to the fire."

Emma recalled Madison's reaction to her being at Grace's funeral. Still, she'd never in her life been sheltered, and she didn't intend to start now. "I know. But I have a—a sort of sponsor there. Who has offered me a job and a place to stay."

"A sponsor?" Gabriel looked surprised. "Who?"

"Alicia Middleton," Emma said. "A wizard."

"And also one of those investigating the bridge incident," Gabriel murmured.

"Bridge incident?"

Gabriel waved off the question. "What kind of job?"

"I'm going to help with her aunt," Emma said. "Do light housekeeping and cooking."

Gabriel slammed both hands down on his desk, making Emma jump. "So . . . let me get this straight. You are leaving the Anchorage in order to become a domestic servant for mainliners." Something about the way he said *mainliners* hit Emma's ears like the aftertaste of a bitter medicine on the back of her tongue.

He *hates* mainliners, Emma realized, even though he tries to act like he doesn't.

Emma's ironwood spine stiffened. Lifting her chin, looking Gabriel Mandrake straight in the eye, she said, "I guess that's one way of putting it. I would call it honest work."

Gabriel released an exasperated breath. "I just hate to see

someone with your talents being underutilized. If it's a job you're looking for, we've talked about your working with the music program here, and teaching woodworking skills to some of the students."

"I just need a change of scenery," Emma said.

"If you leave the Anchorage, do note I'll have to report that you're no longer under my supervision." Gabriel's voice was back to clipped and businesslike. And pissed. With her.

This was what she'd feared: that he'd turn her over to Child Services. One thing would lead to another, and it would turn into a tangle.

She collected her thoughts. "I'm not out to burn any bridges. It's just . . . a lot of the students here have health problems. Well, I don't. I mean, I've got problems, but I'm not sick. I need to get ready for a life after here."

Gabriel's eyes narrowed. Pulling the laptop toward him, he popped it open, then keyed something in. He scanned the screen, frowning. "I don't see any evidence of an admission health assessment." He looked up at Emma. "Did you ever have one?"

Emma shook her head, fear snaking through her middle. "I don't need one. I'm fine."

"Even if you feel fine," Gabriel said, "an assessment would alert us to any potential problems that might appear later on." He tapped his fingers on the keyboard. "Did something happen with one of the other students? With Jonah Kinlock, perhaps?" Gabriel's seemingly lashless eyes lasered in on her.

Emma's cheeks burned.

"Emma," Gabriel said gently, "there's something you should know about Jonah that he will not tell you himself."

"I don't really want to talk about Jonah behind his back," Emma said.

Liar, she thought.

"Hear me out," Gabriel said. "You will have noticed that Jonah is extraordinarily attractive physically, and irresistibly charismatic."

Emma had the sense that this wasn't the first time Gabriel'd had this conversation. "Well," Emma said, "that about sums it up."

Gabriel sighed. "Actually, it doesn't. There's a lot more to Jonah Kinlock than meets the eye. He was born an enchanter, you know."

"I did know that," Emma said. "My father told me to stay away from them—that they can talk you into anything."

"Your father?" Gabriel raised an eyebrow. "I thought you lived with your grandfather."

"I did," Emma said quickly. "But I used to see my father now and then—before he died. A long time ago." Less talking, more listening, she scolded herself.

"Well, your father was right," Gabriel said. "Enchanters *are* persuasive. Jonah has special challenges, though, because of his history. His Weirstone is damaged."

Any pretended reluctance about talking about Jonah behind his back flew out the window. Emma leaned forward, her hands gripping her knees. "What do you mean? What's wrong with him?"

"As you've probably noted, he is physically gifted: extremely strong, quick and agile, with acute sensory perception, and, of course, an empath's ability to read emotions." Gabriel spoke about Jonah like he was a collection of abilities and features, strengths and weaknesses, and not a person. It hit Emma's ears wrong.

"So . . . that's all good, right?"

"Unfortunately, his touch is deadly."

"What?" Emma folded over like she'd been punched.

"You've probably wondered why he wears gloves all the time."

"He told me his hands were disfigured," Emma whispered. "But then I—then I saw them, and they were as beautiful as the rest of him." So many puzzle pieces were falling into place now, forming a pattern that even she could figure out. "Why wouldn't he tell me? It would have made everything so much easier."

Gabriel's gaze met Emma's. He's reading me like a book, she thought. "Jonah prefers not to disclose it," the sorcerer said, "because he can't take the emotional reverberation."

"The what?"

"People are attracted to Jonah, then repelled when they discover his—his gift or disability or whatever you want to call it. Attracted, then repelled. It's as if he has a contagious disease. Embarrassing for both parties, and Jonah feels every bit of it. Jonah would rather keep everyone at a distance, than to take that hit every time. Still, despite all of his efforts to be . . . disagreeable . . . people fall hard for Jonah and everyone gets hurt."

"Is it—" Emma's cheeks heated. How to phrase her next question?

"You're wondering if every part of him is equally dangerous," Gabriel said. "I've proposed doing some testing to determine exactly what his situation is, but he wants nothing to do with that. He doesn't want to risk killing anyone else."

Emma looked up. "Anyone *else?*" She could barely force the words between her dry lips.

"Jonah holds himself responsible for the death of his little sister back at Thorn Hill, before we were aware of the danger. She was a toddler at the time. He was just seven years old. He carries tremendous emotional baggage and guilt related to that."

Gabriel studied his hands. "Since then, Jonah's gone to a great deal of effort to keep from killing anyone accidentally," he said. "In addition to the gloves, he covers up as much as possible. He wears leather whenever weather permits it, even though fabric seems to provide an adequate barrier to the toxin. He's extremely uncomfortable being touched, even through clothing. As you can imagine, skin-to-skin contact is terrifying for him."

Emma instantly recalled Jonah's reaction that day they went back to Tyler's, when Emma was crying and Jonah was trying to soothe her. He'd wrapped his arms around her and held her close, but he'd been stiff as a board, like he couldn't wait to get away. Emma had assumed that it had to do with how he felt about *her.*

At the party at McCauley's, when they'd danced, he'd insisted that she keep her face turned away, had pressed her head against his shoulder.

He was afraid I might try to kiss him, Emma thought. And that's why he had told her that they could never be together.

As if Gabriel had overheard her thoughts, he said, "Jonah has resigned himself to being . . . solitary. I guess what I'm saying is, don't fall in love with him. It's so easy to do, but he will break your heart, and I'd hate to see that happen.

If putting a little distance between you helps, then take a break and move to Trinity. But I hope you'll consider coming back."

Emma felt like she'd swallowed a stone of despair, and it had settled in the pit of her stomach. "And there's nothing you can do? No way to treat him?"

"I wish there were," Gabriel said. "If we knew exactly what kind of poison was used, it would be easier to devise a treatment. I've devoted my life to trying to undo what was done to these children at Thorn Hill. Failing that, to provide a permanent home and meaningful work."

"What's going to happen to him?" Emma whispered.

"Well," Gabriel said, "I thought Jonah would be a good candidate to succeed me as director of the foundation and the music promotion business. Aside from his . . . problem, he's physically healthier than most of his peers, and his talents make him suitable to the job."

Emma got the message. *Cross Jonah Kinlock off your list.*

But it wasn't as if you could call it a list when there was only one person on it.

Well, at least that had stopped the questions about why she was leaving—Gabriel assumed it was because Jonah had broken her heart. So she didn't have to tell Gabriel the truth, that Jonah Kinlock was maybe a murderer, a murderer who could get in and out of any building whenever he pleased, who had all kinds of reasons for killing Rowan DeVries at the Halloween party and probably had tried.

Gabriel sighed wearily. "Give Trinity a try if you like. I can get you some help moving your things. We'll keep your room open for you, so feel free to leave anything heavy or bulky there. I would ask you to keep details about the

Anchorage and what we do here confidential. Sometimes, the less the mainliners know, the better off we are."

"Thank you," Emma said, relief washing over her. "Thank you so much."

Somehow, she'd pulled it off. She couldn't help feeling sorry for this man who'd devoted the last ten years of his life to helping the survivors of Thorn Hill. And now someone— probably Jonah Kinlock—was doing everything possible to destroy what he'd built.

For a moment, she was tempted to tell Gabriel Mandrake everything—about Rowan DeVries and her father and the fact that his protégé, Jonah, was probably behind the murders of mainliners.

Why shouldn't she? She could give over the responsibility for handling it to someone else. Someone who wasn't in love with a murderer.

Except for this one thing: she still couldn't bring her self to believe that Jonah had killed Grace Moss. And if he didn't commit those murders, maybe he wasn't responsible for Tyler's either.

I need more information, she told herself, before I begin accusing Jonah Kinlock of anything. She tried to dismiss the notion that she was just postponing the inevitable.

But then, just as she turned toward the door, Gabriel called after her. "One more thing. We still need to get you evaluated."

Emma shook her head. "No. I don't go to doctors. They just find things that are wrong with you."

"Did someone tell you to avoid doctors sometime in the past?" Gabriel asked.

"No!" Emma blurted. "It's just—my grandfather Sonny

Lee—he never went to doctors. If you don't have insurance, you're better off not knowing you're sick."

Gabriel entered a few notes into the computer. "I'm not talking about seeing a doctor. Natalie will do the evaluation. It's nonnegotiable, if you want to maintain a connection here at the Anchorage. I'm responsible for you, whether you're here or in Trinity."

As he had five nights previously, the physically gifted, quick, and agile Jonah Kinlock prepped for the hunt. T-shirt, jeans, leathers overtop, Nightshade amulet—the amulet that enabled him to see unhosted shades. He missed the reassuring weight of Fragarach between his shoulder blades. But it couldn't be helped. On these hunts, he was serving as bait, and a massive sword would send the wrong message.

Charlie, Mike, Thérèse, and Alison were gearing up, too, only, unlike Jonah, they were armed to the teeth. All carried the shiv-launchers Jonah had first seen during the sweep of the Flats. They made Jonah uneasy. In the hands of a trigger-happy slayer, they could give the game away. If Lilith showed up hosted in a physical body, they wouldn't do any good until the cadaver was out of the way.

He hoped that Lilith would once again leave the cadaver at home. Then she'd be vulnerable to a quick strike from Jonah. And he could avoid the blowback pain of a shiv kill.

Alison still seemed moody and withdrawn, even pricklier than usual.

As if to compensate, the other three were joking around with a kind of forced cheerfulness, as if to say, *This is serious work, but we shadeslayers, we're full of camaraderie. And we love you, Jonah, even though you went a little crazy for a while and called us murderers.*

Jonah guessed they all had a little bit of that old bloodlust. Each of them longed to put the Lilith Greaves notch in their belts. Once she was out of the way, they hoped the shade army would disperse, and the slayers of Nightshade could go back to business as usual.

Jonah wasn't so sure. The murders had opened a wound in Trinity that wouldn't heal up any time soon. Whoever set off the bomb at Safe Harbor would be incentivized to try again. Jonah could sense trouble brewing, but had no idea how to put a stop to it.

You've kept too many secrets, Gabriel, Jonah thought. If mainliners knew what we were up against, if we'd told them the truth, if we'd partnered with them back in the day, we'd have some credit to draw upon. Maybe even allies going forward.

Thérèse put her hand on Jonah's shoulder, squeezing it through the leather. "I know this is hard, to go out there unarmed. But we're glad to have you back on the team, Jonah." She smiled, the light illuminating her faded brown eyes.

"Should we try a different part of town?" Mike said. "Maybe they've moved their headquarters elsewhere."

Charlie shook his head. "The Flats and the Warehouse District are still the hotspots for shade activity. We've been pushing pretty hard in downtown, and yet they keep hanging around. Maybe it's because there are so many people on the street late at night."

"Should we try somebody else as bait?" Thérèse said. "Maybe they don't want to tangle with Jonah again."

"No," Jonah said, "I don't like playing this part, but I'm the only one who can talk to them. They don't target savants as a rule. They avoid us, in fact, but they need to go through me to get to Gabriel. Remember, even if we make contact, you may not actually get a kill tonight. You don't make a move unless you have a clean shot, because I can't play this same card twice. And I want you to hang back until I've had a chance to talk to Lilith."

The other four exchanged glances. He knew what they were thinking: (1) It didn't take long for Jonah to start bossing them around. And (2) Gabriel had said not to give Lilith a chance to talk them into anything.

She's a sorcerer, Jonah thought. Or was. Not an enchanter. What's Gabriel afraid of?

"That seems risky," Charlie said finally. "They've tried to kill you a couple of times already."

"If Lilith wanted to kill me, I'd be dead," Jonah said. "She obviously wants to have a conversation. I want to know why." He shrugged into his jacket. "Let's go."

It was just after two in the morning time for the bars to let out, yet the streets were unusually empty. A cold rain was whipping in off the lake, a rain that hit Jonah's face like needles of ice. It might just turn to ice before dawn, he thought. He had to keep moving or freeze.

Their routine was that Jonah would descend into the Flats by himself, with the rest of the slayers following at a safe distance. He'd stride along, trying to look like he was headed somewhere, which is amazingly hard to do when you're not. Sometimes he'd walk down one side of the river, cross on one of the old iron bridges, and walk up the other side like he was lost. On a mission, going nowhere.

He probably looked like some kind of idiot tourist, ripe to get his wallet lifted. He almost hoped that would happen. An attempted mugging would at least give him something to do.

He'd walk the Warehouse District, too, though he was too young to get into some places. Sometimes, as he passed the open doorway of a crowded club, he caught a whiff of mischief, that mingling of rotting flesh and magic that meant hosted shades were nearby. He'd either lurk around the entrance, getting harassed by bouncers, or talk his way in, only to get harassed by the other patrons. He'd repeat over and over, "No, I don't want a drink. I'm looking for a friend. No, I don't mean I want to *make* friends; I'm looking for a friend I already *have.*"

Now and then, he heard a sound, or saw a flicker of movement that told him his shadows were nearby.

After hanging around by the river for a while, Jonah climbed the hill. He was just passing a jazz club when a voice spoke inside his head. *Jonah.* He caught a strong scent of magic, untainted by the scent of decay.

He turned, and a thirtyish stranger beckoned to Jonah and disappeared into the club. Jonah followed, pushing his way through the crowd, growling at those who tried to speak with him.

The stranger sat down at a table in the back and motioned

for Jonah to join him. Warily, Jonah took a seat with his back to the wall and took a good, long look at his companion, a slickly handsome man with back-combed hair and a huge diamond ring on his pinkie. Hopefully, it wasn't just another person hitting on him.

Then, on closer inspection, Jonah noticed that the stranger's nose had been broken several times, and his skin was just a bit too sallow to be healthy.

You'll have to order for us, Jonah, the stranger said, mind-to-mind. *Speech is still complicated when you're in a borrowed body. I sound like film dialogue being run at the wrong speed.*

The silent voice, the rush of mingled resentment, disappointment, yearning, and hope—it was familiar.

"Brendan?" Jonah whispered, incredulous.

That's me, Brendan said.

It was Brendan Wu, Kenzie's friend who'd died at Safe Harbor four years ago. Now he seemed to be Lilith's right-hand shade.

Brendan struck a pose. *What do you think?*

"I think you don't look like yourself."

Thank God, Brendan said, shuddering. *Nobody wanted to be in my body, there at the end. Not even me.*

"Whose body is that?"

I don't know the specifics, Brendan said, *but he was kind of a thug. I was high on drugs for the first week, and it seems to have an addiction to nicotine. But, otherwise, it's in great shape, and it seems to have retained some street-fighting moves.*

But Jonah was hung up on something Brendan had said. "For the first week? How long have you been . . . occupying this body?"

Brendan furrowed his brow, thinking. *Going on a month.*

"A month!" Jonah breathed in deeply. "And still fresh? How is that possible?"

That's the advantage of blood magic, Brendan said. *We believe that it might be an effective therapy for the living survivors of Thorn Hill as well as the dead.* He leaned across the table. *Imagine what it would be like if Kenzie was healthy, Jonah. For good.*

Just for a moment that image pinwheeled through Jonah's mind, a searing explosion of hope. With some effort, he forced it away.

Imagine what it would be like for you to be able to kiss a girl, Brendan whispered. *To caress her skin. To—*

Jonah raised his gloved hands. "I get the picture. I'm curious, though. How good is your sense of smell, of touch, of hearing? How well does a shade connect with a stolen body?"

Brendan shrugged. *Not perfectly.* He looked down at his hands. *My skin feels numb. I have to be careful not to injure myself without realizing. Hearing and vision are probably the best.*

"Can you eat?" Jonah said.

Brendan rocked his hand back and forth. *If it's the right consistency. Eating, like talking, is complex. It still sometimes goes down the wrong way, and tastes like sawdust.*

As if on cue, the server drifted up. Jonah ordered for both of them.

We're constantly learning more about how this all works, Brendan said, *developing new methods to occupy a body with all systems intact. Now that we're no longer bumbling around, we're making faster progress. Lilith is a genius.*

"That's why I'm here. I want to meet with Lilith."

This was met by a jab of bitter mirth. *Oh, Jonah,* Brendan said. *That is so not going to happen. Why is it that you slayers always assume that we're stupid? Is it the shambling? Or the stench? Hasn't anyone ever told you that it's what's inside that counts?*

Jonah opened his mouth to respond, but Jonah Kinlock, master of pretty speech, had nothing to say.

The sandwiches came, but neither one of them ate much. Jonah suspected that Brendan didn't want to eat in front of him.

I used to envy you, Brendan said. *You had such a perfect body, so strong and graceful. Sometimes, when I was younger, I'd go with Kenzie to the gym just to see what you could do. I envied Kenzie, too, because you were his brother, and you were devoted to him. But the one thing savants have never understood about shades is that we are survivors, too. I was ignorant before, but I was never arrogant. You, Jonah Kinlock, are arrogant.*

That's when it struck Jonah—an epiphany. This person across the table looked nothing like the Brendan Wu Jonah had known back at Safe Harbor—the frail Brendan, racked with intolerable pain, the one who yearned for the soothing cold of Antarctica. And yet, this man had Brendan's moves, his way of tilting his head and peering at you from under his eyebrows. Jonah had been stung by Brendan's sense of humor often enough to recognize it. This was Brendan Wu in all ways save for the body that had failed him. This was Brendan in every way that mattered.

He'd always sort of known it—it had been the basis of countless ethical debates with Gabriel. He'd argued that the shades they were riffing were real souls, and that riffing was real murder, no matter how hard you tried to pretty it up with a new name.

But he'd known it in a dispassionate, intellectual way. Was this why Gabriel wanted to avoid communication between shades and slayers? Was there too much of a risk that slayers would lose their taste for virtual blood?

Was this why the Safe Passage program, the preemptive riffing of dying savants, had been established? So these kinds of encounters wouldn't happen? This way Jonah would never run into Mose Butterfield, their late great guitarist, and realize that everything that he loved about Mose was still there.

"You're right," Jonah said. "I am arrogant, and I'm probably guilty of whatever charge you want to lay on me. But where do we go from here? How do we resolve this? It's not fair to kill innocent people so you can go on living."

Is any mainliner really innocent? Brendan said. *Don't they all share responsibility for what happened at Thorn Hill, before and after the disaster?*

"No," Jonah said, thinking of Grace Moss. "They don't."

Fine, Brendan said. *Whatever. With what we're learning, maybe one day that will no longer be necessary. We won't have to rely on cadavers—we'll be able to possess a living body. Permanently.*

"It seems to me like you're trying to start a war. Us against you, mainliners against us, wizards against everyone who isn't a wizard. How does that help you?"

Brendan said nothing for a long moment. Just looked at him, dead on.

And then it dawned on Jonah. "That's the point, isn't it? A major magical battle will release enough blood magic to fuel a shade army for years."

Brendan shook his head. *A major magical battle will release enough blood magic to carry out the research that is needed to end this. That's what we're hoping for, anyway. And who better to pay a price than the ones who tried to murder us in the first place? And who now despise and discriminate against the survivors.*

"So what do you need us for? Why not go it alone?" The subtext was, *If you knew this was a trap, why did you show up?*

First and foremost, we need Gabriel's cooperation to pull this off, Brendan said. *Second of all, we want to save you, too.*

"Gabriel will never agree," Jonah said. "Don't expect us to sign on. There's been too much bloodshed already."

Says the deadliest assassin in Nightshade.

"Well, you're catching up quick. Your kills aren't exactly kind. A few more attacks like the one on Halloween, and maybe you'll get the war you want."

Jonah read genuine confusion in Brendan. *What are you talking about? I don't know anything about Halloween.*

He doesn't know, Jonah thought. Maybe Lilith's keeping secrets, too.

"No? Well, maybe you'd better have a talk with Lilith, then, and get caught up. She told me flat-out she was going to keep killing mainliners and casting suspicion on us until we give in and join you."

Brendan shifted in his seat. *If somebody gets killed, it's not necessarily our fault. We can't take responsibility for all shades everywhere. Word is spreading about the benefits of blood magic. We're seeing a lot of freelancers joining in.*

"Well, we'll get the blame, whether we like it or not, as the only visible representatives of our unlucky little tribe. On Halloween, the killers left the same clues behind as you do: nightshade flowers."

It must be mainliners, killing one another and trying to blame us for it.

"Really?" Jonah said dryly. "That's a shame, but it doesn't seem like you have much room to complain." Their eyes met, and held. "I'll tell you one thing—killing Madison Moss's little sister was a major tactical mistake, even if you have no problem with it otherwise."

More confusion from Brendan. *Who's Madison Moss?*

Jonah blinked at him. Of course, Brendan wouldn't know—how could he? He'd died at least a year before Madison Moss came on the scene. Besides, Gabriel shared very little about the mainline guilds with students at the Anchorage.

Knowledge is power. In the wrong hands, knowledge means trouble.

Even those who died at Thorn Hill—like Lilith—would have limited knowledge of what had happened to the mainline guilds in the past ten years, since Jonah was the only one whose gift of empathy allied him to communicate with shades.

And Jonah never did much talking during a riff.

He guessed that, as they became more and more at home in their borrowed bodies, they would have more options.

Brendan was still looking at him expectantly.

"Madison Moss is the power source for mainliners," Jonah said.

Power source? Brendan blinked. *What do you mean?*

Jonah cast about for a simple explanation. "Originally, she was an elicitor—someone who draws magic. Two years ago, she absorbed the Dragonheart stone, which powers Weirstones everywhere. So now they call her the Dragon. She's leading the mainliners, or trying to. It's like herding cats."

Mmm. Brendan seemed lost in thought. *Let me—let me talk to Lilith about it.* He got to his feet. He did it gracefully, capably. Clearly, he was mastering the use of his borrowed body.

"Could we set up a meeting?" Jonah asked. "The three of us? After you've talked to her, I mean?"

Brendan grinned. *Why is it I feel like we'd be walking into a trap? I'll be back in touch. It's easier now that I can move about in polite society.* He took a step toward the door, then turned back toward Jonah, digging into the inside pocket of his coat.

Wary of weapons, Jonah faded back, raising both hands in defense.

Brendan held out a bottle to Jonah—an elaborate glass bottle, stoppered with silver, the kind that might hold expensive perfume. It glowed, illuminating Brendan's face. Jonah took it, weighing it in his hand. It was relatively light, but it appeared to be full of a red pearlescent substance that swirled and swam as Jonah tilted the bottle.

"What is this?" Jonah asked, though he already knew.

Blood magic, Brendan said softly.

Jonah tried to hand it back to him, but Brendan put his hands behind his back.

"I don't want this," Jonah said.

It's for Kenzie, not for you, Brendan said. *Can I trust you to give it to him?*

"You can trust me to throw it in the lake," Jonah said contemptuously. "Or smash it on the street. We want nothing to do with that."

We? Brendan cocked his head. *Have you talked it over with Kenzie?*

Jonah just stared at Brendan.

I thought not. You're used to making decisions for him, aren't you? You ought to ask him about it at least.

That one hit home.

Well, keep it or smash it or whatever you want to do with it,

Brendan said. *I hope it will do somebody some good. I mean, the donors are already dead, after all. Oh, and by the way—unlike you, we're not focused on killing fellow savants. But let the slayers tagging after you know that we will defend ourselves. And our bodies can be replaced.* Threading his way between the tables without a hint of a shamble, Brendan walked out the door.

Jonah was tempted to follow him, but he recalled what Brendan had said about arrogance. Lilith might have spies stationed all around. He'd have to be patient, something he wasn't very good at.

He rolled the bottle between his hands, watching the layers shift, combine, and separate with an awful fascination. Was it possible? Could this really help his brother? What if it did? What then?

Jonah deferred any decision, sliding the bottle into his jacket pocket. He texted the others. *We're done for the night.*

He exited the club, and headed back toward Oxbow. The others were waiting in the mailroom, away from spying eyes on the street.

"Well?" Charlie said. "Who was that guy you were talking to?"

"That was Brendan Wu," Jonah said wearily. "Formerly a student at the Anchorage. Now a hosted shade. Serving as a kind of emissary for Lilith."

"That was *Brendan*?" Alison looked astounded. "But he looked—he looked—"

"Normal. I know," Jonah said. "No stink of decay either. I could smell magic on him, though."

"Are you—are you *sure* that was Brendan?" Thérèse said. "I mean, I've only seen him a few times, but he looked—"

"It was Brendan," Jonah said.

"Then we should have followed him," Mike said. "Maybe he'd have led us back to Lilith."

Jonah shook his head. "They're not stupid. They know it's a trap. Brendan said to tell you that they didn't want to kill savants, but they would defend themselves."

Mike asked the obvious question. "If he knew it was a trap, then why'd he show up?"

"He wants something from us," Jonah said.

"What?" Alison asked.

"Lilith wants to talk to Gabriel."

"Who won't agree to meet with her," Alison predicted.

"He must have said *something*," Charlie said. "You two talked long enough."

Jonah shook his head, feeling a twinge of guilt. You're just like Gabriel, he thought. Keeping secrets.

"Well," Thérèse said brightly. "Try again tomorrow night?"

"I don't see much point," Jonah said. "Lilith isn't going to show up to any party we're planning."

"So you're giving *up*?" Alison's face was all thunderclouds.

"I'm saying I'm going to try and come up with a smarter plan," Jonah said. "I'll let you know when I do."

Jonah walked back to Oxbow alone. He was just unlocking the door to his room when he got a text from Natalie. *Call me. Emma's leaving the Anchorage.*

CHAPTER NINE
RECONSIDER, BABY

Jonah was tempted to take the coward's way out: leave the guitar outside of Emma's room, ring the bell, and run. But that would only leave mute testimony to his guilt—and convince her that she needed to leave for sure.

He put his ear to the door, hoping to get another hit of her musical magic, but heard nothing, not even breathing.

Jonah typed his code into the display on the wall in the hallway, then stood and waited for the scanner to verify. As he waited, he repeated his personal oath to himself.

You will not use your gift to convince her of your innocence. You will only use it to convince her to stay.

No response. Not that he guessed she would open the door to him, but he should be able to detect a rush of emotion that would tell him she was inside.

She was not.

Where else would she be? In the end, it wasn't hard to figure out. She'd be packing up the workshop, her second home.

After a moment's debate, he took the guitar with him, wanting to put it directly into her hands.

As soon as he entered the woodshop building, he heard the whine of a saw. Following the sound, he found Emma bent over the band saw, guiding a thin plate of pale wood through the machine, cutting the graceful curves that would become the back of a guitar. The sound rose to a shrill scream as the blade encountered resistance, then died as the wood submitted.

As Jonah watched, Emma reached up, adjusting a setting, lips tight against flying wood chips, safety glasses pinning her hair to her head.

The shop had been cleaned up since he'd last been there, Emma's hand tools and fittings put away and her wood stacked neatly against the wall, a small sign mounted on the wall above, PROPERTY OF EMMA LEE, DO NOT THROW AWAY.

It was the first time he'd seen her in the weeks since Halloween, and now she was leaving.

He ghosted closer, wanting to breathe in her scent. And there it was: a mingling of sweat and sawdust and whatever it was she put into her hair. She'd stripped off her flannel shirt. Underneath, she wore one of those old-fashioned ribbed undershirts that exposed her muscular arms and capable hands. Sweat glistened on her face, dampened her hair, and ran into the hollow of her throat. When the saw stopped, he heard her humming the tune of some old blues song under her breath.

It was like all of his other senses were conspiring to taunt him with what he could never, ever touch. His own palms sweated inside his gloves. His heart thumped painfully, high in his throat.

That's what happens when you let a little hope leak in, Jonah thought. It's even harder when you have to come down.

And then she saw him, and the humming stopped abruptly. She crossed the room in three long strides, grabbing up a wicked-looking knife along the way. She held it, point down, close to her side.

Her eyes roamed over Jonah, from his gloved hands, to his lips, to his leather jacket and his jeans. Her reaction to him—the mingling of fear and fascination—was familiar. She knew.

"So," Jonah said. "Who told you about my . . . condition? Natalie?"

She shook her head. "Gabriel." She paused. "You should have told me yourself."

"I should have told you a lot of things," Jonah said. "But I was brought up to keep secrets." Swinging the guitar case up, he set it on the workbench between them. "I want to return this."

Emma looked from Jonah to the guitar and back again. "Where did you get that?"

"I took it from your basement, the night your father was killed."

Emma rocked back on her heels. "Are you here to confess? If so, you're a little late."

"I'm here to tell the truth," Jonah said, "as far as I know it."

Emma brushed sawdust from her hair and stripped off the safety glasses, dropping them onto the workbench. "It's a waste of time. I don't want to hear anything you have to say."

"I understand you're leaving," Jonah said. "I'm hoping you'll change your mind."

"You're the reason I'm leaving," Emma said. "So I guess you're not exactly the person to persuade me to stay."

"Give me ten minutes," Jonah said, allowing a bit of enchantment to honey his voice. "Then I'll go."

She straightened, resting her free hand on the workbench. "Clock is running."

"Don't stay because I ask you to," Jonah said. "Do it for selfish reasons."

"Such as—?"

"If you stay, you'll have a place to live and to work, and you can graduate from high school. You can keep building guitars and save up money so you can open your own shop."

"I have a place to stay," Emma blurted out, then pressed her lips together like she was sorry she'd said it.

"Where?"

"I'd rather you didn't know," Emma said. "Please do take it personally."

"What about school? You know the program here has worked well for you." He paused. "Everyone here wants you to succeed. Are you planning to quit, or do you want to go through the same old, same old over again?"

That hit a nerve. Jonah felt Emma's anger drain away, displaced by a rush of despair.

She had a comeback though. "All those other schools have a big advantage—*you're not there*. Maybe I can't prove what you did, but I'm not going to look at you every day and wonder what you're gonna do next."

"Then I'll leave," Jonah said. "I'll leave school and move out of Oxbow. Tomorrow."

"Right," Emma said, snorting. "You know you can't leave Kenzie. And you can't take him with you."

"I won't go far," Jonah said. "I'll see Kenzie every day. But you'll never see me, I promise."

"Don't make promises you can't keep," Emma snapped.

"You can always leave if I break that promise."

"Do you think that makes me feel safe, the idea you'll be creeping around campus, that you might be right around the next corner?"

"I can't leave Kenzie," Jonah said. "My point is, do what's in *your* best interest. That's all I'm saying."

"How do you know that leaving isn't in my best interest?"

"I can't predict the future, but I'm guessing it's not. I'll do whatever I can to make it work for you."

"You've made your point," Emma said. Her tears spilled over, leaving tracks through the dust on her face. "Now, I'm really busy here." Her voice trembled.

"Don't you want to ask me any questions?" Jonah said.

"I do," Emma said. "Why are you still here?"

"You say you hate a liar," Jonah said. "I'm here to tell the truth. It's a limited-time offer. Once it's over, I go straight back to lying."

Their eyes met across the workbench, emotion reverberating between them as if they were connected by a steel-wound string tuned to a high pitch.

Finally, Emma gave in, curiosity overwhelming bitterness. Leaning forward a little, hands fisted, she asked, "Fine. We'll start with an easy one. Did you kill my father?"

"Maybe. I don't really know. It was a melee, everyone fighting with each other."

"Who's everyone?"

"Me, Tyler, you, a half dozen wizards."

"Why were you there?"

"I hoped your father might know something about Thorn Hill—who was behind it, what kind of poison was used."

"*Tyler?*" Once the dam broke, the questions came, one after another. "Why would Tyler know about that?"

"I don't know that he did," Jonah said. "We were looking for people who were at Thorn Hill but who left before the massacre, and we found Tyler. See, the problem is, everyone there died, except for the kids, and we were too young to know what was going on. Gabriel thinks it must've been sorcerers who made the poison, since wizards are no good at that kind of thing."

Emma flinched a little at that, shifting her eyes away.

She feels guilty for some reason, Jonah thought. Why? Does she know something I don't?

"Gabriel's always said that if we knew exactly what was used, we might be able to help the savant survivors."

"So Gabriel sent you?"

"No. It was me. Just me."

"How did you find Tyler after all these years?"

"Should I start from the beginning?" Pushing his luck, he eased himself onto a stool.

"I think you'd better." Emma leaned back against the workbench, still holding the knife, as if Jonah might attack at any moment. As if a knife would do any good. "All I remember is bits and pieces."

Which bits? Which pieces? Jonah wondered. "We did some research online," he said.

"Who's we?"

Jonah didn't want to implicate Kenzie in any of this, especially since Kenzie and Emma were friends. "Me," he repeated. "Just me."

"You mean you and Kenzie. I thought you were going to tell me the truth."

Jonah sighed. "Me and Kenzie. But it was my idea. And he didn't know what I was going to do with the information. We searched some work records from Thorn Hill, and found out that Tyler had been there not long before the massacre, but didn't show up on any survivor or casualty lists."

"He came there to take me home," Emma said, her voice low and tight. "That's why he came and went so quick."

"Well," Jonah said. "Anyway. We had him as Greenwood, and that's how we were able to tie him to Sonny Lee. Once we found out that his business had relocated to this area, we—"

Emma held up a hand to stop him. "How did you find that out?"

"Um." Jonah struggled to remember. It had been a late night, and Kenzie had done most of the heavy lifting. "We found a Web page. We assumed it was Tyler's business, since Sonny Lee was dead. I sent an e-mail."

Emma's eyes widened in horror. "That was *my* Web site. Tyler stayed safe for all these years until I led you right to him." Her shoulders slumped. "Probably the wizards, too. It was all my fault." Now her guilt washed over Jonah in waves.

This was going all wrong. This was supposed to be Jonah's confession. Not Emma's. "It's not your fault," he said sharply. "Why would you think somebody would be looking for Tyler?"

"Tyler told me," Emma said. "He seemed worried that somebody would track me up there. He told me that Sonny Lee didn't want any contact between us, that it would be too dangerous. Maybe it was just an excuse for why he hadn't visited, but I believed him. I had put up the Web page before all this happened, but I didn't have an address on it or anything . . ." She blotted at her eyes with the backs of her hands. "But then, when I got that e-mail . . ."

Jonah recalled Tyler's high-tech security system, the fact that he kept a gun at hand, even in his own home. "Maybe Tyler was worried for reasons that had nothing to do with Thorn Hill," he said gently. "There are lots of ways to make enemies."

Emma's face was gray as ash. She wasn't buying it.

She's got secrets of her own, Jonah thought. Maybe he could distract her by continuing his litany of sins. "Since he'd changed his name and all, I was pretty sure he wouldn't talk to me willingly. So I broke into your house through a basement window. I was wearing a ski mask, because I didn't want to have to kill anyone. I found you in your workshop and tied you up." He paused. "Does any of this sound familiar?"

She shook her head. "Keep talking."

"I went upstairs. Tyler never heard me—he was practicing. Making a lot of noise. When he saw me, he pulled a gun. He was marching me into the conservatory when the wizards broke in."

Jonah told the story matter-of-factly, trying hard not to sell anything to Emma.

Emma seemed to be struggling to focus back on the conversation. "You didn't come to kill the wizards? Or Tyler?"

"No. I . . . ah . . . was there for information."

"So . . . what did the wizards want?"

"Same as me," Jonah said. "They seemed to think that Tyler might know something about how Thorn Hill went down, what poison was used. He said he was just a musician, that he didn't know anything about that."

"He *was* a musician," Emma said. "Why *would* he know anything? So this whole thing was a case of mistaken identity."

"Maybe. Anyway. They began . . . they tried to force us to talk." Emma didn't need to know they'd tortured Tyler. "When that didn't work, they called Rowan DeVries. They planned to take us somewhere else to question us more thoroughly."

"Who's 'they'? Who was there?"

"Do you remember the night we first met? Club Catastrophe? The pool-playing wizards? It was mostly them. Including Rowan's sister. Rachel DeVries. Eight wizards in all."

"Why did they care what poison was used?"

Jonah shrugged. "You'll have to ask them."

"They're dead."

"Ask DeVries."

"He's nearly dead."

Jonah had nothing to say to that, so he didn't try. "Anyway, that's when you showed up with the gun."

Emma frowned. "Me?"

"I guess I hadn't done that good of a job tying you up." Jonah rubbed his chin. "You told them to let Tyler go or you'd shoot them. The wizards stalled, knowing help was on the way. Tyler knew it, too, so he made a break for it, trying to give you a chance to escape. You shot one of the wizards."

"Rowan said one of the wizards had been shot," Emma whispered. "I did that?"

Jonah nodded. "Then it was chaos. You fell and hit your head. The fight went on, and . . . and at the end, the only people alive were you and me."

"And Tyler . . . how did he . . . ?"

"There was a big gash in his thigh, and he'd lost a lot of blood. I don't know if that killed him, or it was me or one of the wizards. The important part was he died trying to save you." Jonah didn't have many gifts to give, but he could offer that at least.

"What about Rowan's sister? How did she die?"

"I killed her," Jonah said. "With a sword."

"You came to question my father with a sword." The storm clouds began gathering again.

"He had a gun," Jonah pointed out.

"He was in his own damn house," Emma said. "Anyway, who brings a sword to a gunfight?"

It was Jonah's turn to flinch. He saw so much of Tyler in Emma, even though they apparently hadn't spent much time together. "Tyler asked me that same question."

"So, if we were both alive at the end of the fight, then how did I end up at Rowan's?"

Jonah felt the blood rush into his face. Honesty was a lot harder than he'd thought. "I—uh—I thought you were dead. I didn't have time to make sure, because DeVries arrived. So I left. I didn't realize you'd survived until Natalie told me."

"You didn't take the time to see if I was alive, but you took the time to steal my guitar."

"I thought you were dead," Jonah repeated, a little desperately. "After I heard you play, I—I just took it. I can't explain it. I'd never heard music like that. It's magic. You have no idea how it . . . anyway. That's no excuse. I'm not a thief. I'm so sorry."

Emma was still frowning, going over some kind of mental file. "Wasn't there something else? When I fell in the gazebo and you came to help, it brought back a memory. It wasn't the wizards or the fight or the gun. It was you. Unless it was a dream. . . ."

She seemed determined to rip every secret out of him.

"There was something else," Jonah said, swallowing hard. "After the fight, you were still alive. Groggy. Semiconscious. I picked you up to carry you out of the house. And then . . . we kissed." Anguish came up in his throat like bile. "You were the only survivor, and I killed you. Or so I thought."

Emma's head came up, her eyes narrowed. "You kissed me? Or I kissed you?"

Jonah avoided her eyes. "Does it matter? It happened."

"Yes," Emma said, "it matters. And you said you would tell me the truth." She sliced off each word precisely, as she might a piece of wood.

"You kissed me," Jonah said, licking his lips like he could recapture the taste.

"I thought so," Emma said, a muscle working in her jaw.

"But it wasn't your fault. I should have anticipated that it might happen. The last thing I wanted to do was hurt you."

"You're talking about your sister," Emma said.

Jonah felt a stab of betrayal. "Gabriel told you that, too?"

"Guess he had to, since you didn't."

"It happened a long time ago. Anyway, it's not something I like to talk about."

"The things you don't want to talk about would fill a library."

"That's the kind of life I've had, all right?"

"Really? Well, I had a pretty good life, up to when Sonny Lee died." Suspicion clouded her face. "You said you connected Tyler to Sonny Lee. Are you sure you didn't go to

Memphis first? Are you sure you didn't go see Sonny Lee in his shop last summer?"

Jonah shook his head. "I told you. I've never been to Memphis. By the time we started looking into this, Sonny Lee was already dead. In fact, it was his obituary that made us realize that Tyler was his son. Only it said Tyler had predeceased him."

"That's what Sonny Lee always told everyone. That when Tyler died, I came to live with him." She closed her eyes, and tears leaked out at the corners. "Can you see why I can't stand a lie? People have been lying to me all my life. Even the people I loved most in the world."

"Sometimes people lie for good reasons," Jonah said. "To keep you safe, or to avoid breaking your heart, or to make it possible for you to go on living."

"And sometimes they lie to protect themselves," Emma snapped.

"I know." He paused. "Do you have any other questions for me?"

"Are you the one killing mainliners?"

"No," Jonah said.

"What about the night of the Halloween party?"

"I didn't murder anyone that night," Jonah said, with as much confidence as he could muster. "Someone is trying to make it look like savants are responsible."

"Who? Who would do that?"

That was a question Jonah didn't want to answer. It would be like falling into a well that he couldn't climb back out of.

See, we're fighting an army of the undead. They want us to join them in a war on mainliners.

So he just shrugged. "Whoever's been killing mainliners

all along. If you use a knife or a sword, the prohibition against attack magic in the Sanctuary is no protection."

To his relief, she didn't press him on it.

When no more questions came, he said, "Well? Will you stay?"

Emma seemed to be debating at least, which was better than before. "Do you promise to always tell me the truth after this?"

"I can't promise that," Jonah said. "Remember what I said—limited-time offer." He bit back the temptation to ask her to keep his secrets.

Emma mulled this over, the muscle in her jaw working. She sighed. Then said, "Self-interest, huh?"

"Self-interest," Jonah said.

"Here's what I'll do, if Gabriel will go along with it. I'm not living in the same building with you. I'll still move to Trinity, but I'll stay in school here at the Anchorage and drive back and forth. I don't think I can deal with changing schools again."

"What about the band?" Jonah knew he was being greedy, but he couldn't help himself. Of all the drugs to be addicted to, why did it have to be Emma's music? And why would she ever agree to this?

And yet she did. After struggling with it for what seemed like an eternity, she said, "Fine. I'll stay in the band if you want to try to keep that going."

Jonah felt a spark of hope, mingled with relief. "Thank you, Emma."

"Oh, I'm not doing it for you," she said, her brown eyes like agates. "I'm doing it for me. We'll see how it goes."

⟨ℛ CHAPTER TEN ℛ⟩
INFIRMARY BLUES

Emma perched on the edge of an overstuffed chair, breathing in the scent of vanilla and sage from the candles burning in the corners. This was like no health clinic she'd ever seen.

Not that she'd seen that many. She'd been vaccinated, of course—they wouldn't let her into school otherwise. She'd gone to the Memphis Health Department for that. A couple of times, when her tonsils swelled up so much she could hardly breathe or swallow soup, Sonny Lee had taken her in to the health clinics. They'd all been cold and sterile-looking.

This waiting room was furnished with handloomed rugs and futons, tapestries and music posters softening the walls. Lamps with paper shades cast a whiskey glow over everything, like the lighting in some after-hours club. Music played softly in the background, a cutting-edge playlist.

It was wasted on Emma. She wouldn't be relaxed until this thing was over with. But if it was the price she had to pay to keep out of county custody, she'd pay it.

It hadn't taken long to pack up her possessions. Maybe she was getting good at it. She stuffed her few articles of clothing into the suitcase she'd brought from Tyler's and loaded her backpack with her laptop. Emma had limited herself to four guitars—her two Studio Greenwoods, the ones she'd built herself; the Stratocaster (which Jonah had insisted she take), and a vintage Martin. Plus assorted sound equipment and other gear. Three acoustics, one electric, though one of the SGs had a pickup. She guessed she could get another electric out of storage if she wanted to, but the Strat always felt just right in her hands when she wanted to make a big noise. She'd put Sonny Lee's guitars into storage, too, where they'd be safe if she had to make a quick getaway. When you're on the run, you have to travel light.

The rest of her tools, supplies, and equipment she'd leave behind. If she couldn't make this work, having one foot in each place, well, those things would be gone for good.

A constant stream of people went in and out of the dispensary—checking in using a screen outside. All seemed to be students.

Finally, Natalie came out of the bodywork room. "Emma," she said, nodding briskly, her face like a blank page. "I'll be doing your evaluation."

"I still don't think I need one," Emma said, even though she knew there was no point. "I don't think I was poisoned at all."

"That's easy enough to figure out," Natalie said. "It's this way." She stood aside so Emma could enter the bodywork room ahead of her.

The coziness continued inside, with more music and

fluffy white robes. Natalie directed Emma to change into a robe and a pair of sheepskin slippers, then she weighed and measured her, and took her blood pressure, pulse, and temperature, all like a regular clinic visit. Emma answered a bunch of questions about her health, while Natalie typed the answers into a tablet computer. She produced a silver conelike device similar to a stethoscope, pressed it to Emma's chest, then slid it around, still watching the screen display. She frowned, chewing on her lower lip, apparently dissatisfied with whatever she was getting.

I told you I was different, Emma thought of saying, but was afraid to speak.

Finally, Natalie set the device aside. "I'm going to try a direct scan, okay?"

Emma nodded, though she wasn't sure what she was signing on for. Natalie dipped some cream out of a jar. It smelled like vanilla and brown sugar. She spread it over Emma's chest, then pressed her fingers into Emma's skin, sliding them around over the surface, eyes closed, a furrow of concentration between her brows.

Finally, Natalie wiped Emma's skin clean with a soft terry-cloth towel, and washed her own hands. "You can get dressed now," she said, "and then we'll talk."

After she dressed, Emma joined Natalie in a small, cozy room that resembled a library, with its shelves of books and black walnut paneling. It looked like the kind of room you might use to deliver bad news to a person.

Natalie motioned Emma to the chair across from her. "I have to say, you do have me a little stumped," she said. "Anybody doing a quick read on your Weirstone would say it's a savant stone. It's definitely not your run-of-the-mill main-liner stone. But it's clear, and most savant stones are pretty obviously damaged."

"When you say 'damaged,' what do you mean?" Emma said. The one thing she'd always been was healthy, despite her random, raggedy-assed life.

Natalie hesitated. "The truth about savants is, we're dying. All of us, all of the so-called survivors of Thorn Hill. We all know it, whether we're willing to admit it or not. Even though Gabriel won't even let us bring it up, it's true."

"Dying?" Emma shifted her shoulders. This was the last thing she expected to hear. "But . . . it's been ten years. I know a lot of you—of us—have health problems. But if you were going to die, shouldn't it have happened by now?"

"Many of us have. There were four thousand children at Thorn Hill. About six hundred survived the massacre. The younger you were at the time of the poisoning, the more likely you were to survive. But now we're dying, day by day and year by year. There's a different time line for every person. Jonah, Alison, Rudy, and me—we're among the oldest ones left. Everyone else is gone or incapacitated."

Emma hadn't known what would happen in the future—but at least it was a future. Now it was like somebody had dragged an eraser across it. "But how do they die? What happens to them?"

Natalie stared down at her hands. "It's like the older we get, the more susceptible we are to the poison. All of the adults died immediately, remember? Maybe it has to do with age. Or that the damage done back then finally catches up with us. Or maybe the toxin is lodged in our bones, like a heavy metal, and gradually poisons us to death."

"What are the symptoms? Do people go down quick or just kind of decline?"

"Before we die, some of us begin to behave erratically, lose our judgment, and grow violent. To be blunt, we lose our minds. We call it fading. You can imagine how dangerous that is among the gifted."

Emma stared, horrified. "But . . . isn't there anything—any treatment?"

"Gabriel has hired the best researchers and healers money can buy. That's our primary focus: research and treatment. That's why so many of us are on medications and other therapies." Natalie smiled faintly. "The good news is you say you weren't there to be poisoned. But if that's the case, I'd expect you to have a mainliner stone. See, someone who builds magical guitars—or any other kind of magical tool—I'd expect that person to be a sorcerer. But your stone doesn't read that way. And the way you play . . . it's almost like there's magic in that, too. But there's no mainline guild for musicians."

"Well," Emma said, feeling puny and low-talent, magic-wise, "I might be able to build other instruments, you know, like violins or dulcimers. I've only ever tried to build guitars. Same with playing. Guitars are the only instrument I . . ." Her voice trailed off as a memory elbowed in. From Thorn Hill.

Emma sat at the piano, on a bench so high her feet couldn't touch the floor. A breeze stirred the curtains at the windows, and she could hear children laughing outside. She wanted to be outside with them. But she stayed, and she played, and her mother listened, eyes closed, a dreamy expression on her face, her fists gradually unclenching. Emma's music made her mother happy when nothing else could. Emma would do just about anything to make her mother happy. She was sad so much of the time.

"I do play a little piano," Emma said. She cleared her throat. "Or I did when I was little."

Natalie's eyes narrowed. "Is it all right if I ask Rudy to come over?"

Mystified, Emma nodded.

Pulling out her phone, Natalie thumbed in a message. When she saw Emma looking at her, she explained, "I texted Rudy and asked him to bring over his portable keyboard."

"Oh!" Emma said, feeling her cheeks heat. "I don't believe I've touched a keyboard since I left Thorn Hill."

Natalie rolled her eyes. "This isn't a recital. Just an experiment."

Emma raised both hands, palms out. "Keep in mind, I'm the person who knows the least about all this. I shouldn't even open my mouth. But . . . isn't it odd that people ended up so different, though? With such particular gifts? I mean, you can see illness through a person's skin, and then heal them by touching them, and Rudy's a genius at digital systems, and Jonah . . . Jonah . . ." Her voice trailed off, and she dropped her hands into her lap.

"Jonah's touch will kill you," Natalie said, looking Emma directly in the eyes, "and it's so damn sweet, you'll wish you could die all over again."

"How do you know?" Emma demanded. "How do you know it's such a great experience, if nobody's ever lived to tell about it?"

"Because Jonah can't stand to cause anybody pain," Natalie snapped back. "Being an empath, the backwash is terribly painful."

"Really? Well, he must be pretty miserable right now," Emma said, "because he sure messed up with me."

"If he's hurt you, he knows it," Natalie said. "He knows it better than anyone."

"Except me," Emma said.

"Except you," Natalie agreed, nodding.

Eager to change the subject, Emma said, "What if people at Thorn Hill had special stones—even before they were poisoned? Me included. But because I left before the massacre, I didn't get damaged."

Natalie stared at Emma. "But I just don't see how that would be," she said, frowning. "The people at Thorn Hill were all members of the mainline guilds to begin with. For instance, my parents were both sorcerers."

"But what I'm driving at is that it's almost like you've been shaped to a purpose."

"I'm not following," Natalie said.

Emma cast about for a comparison. "Let's say I take a piece of rosewood, and I want to make a fingerboard. Do I smack it with a hammer?"

"I'm guessing the answer is no," Natalie said, rolling her eyes.

"Correct. I don't, unless I want it to end up a pile of splinters. If I want it to be useful, I have to use the right tools, and I have to know how to shape it. If I just take a whack at it, there's no chance it'll turn out like I want."

"Go on," Natalie said.

"So if somebody whacks your Weirstone with poison, seems to me it would either destroy it completely, or you'd end up with a stone that does pretty much what it did before, only not as well."

"But—a lot of people's stones *were* destroyed," Natalie said. "Thousands of people died. Those of us who survived ended up with random gifts, some that aren't gifts at all."

Emma was already beginning to doubt her theory. But, ironwood spine and all that, she forged on. "Still, it doesn't seem like you'd end up with someone like you, who can see disease through a person's skin, and heal them. Or someone like Rudy, who can create electrical circuits out of the air. Or Mose, who could see death coming ahead of time. Were there other people who had real specific gifts?"

Natalie shrugged. "I remember there was a girl who could talk plants into growing. If she'd lived on a farm, she could've raised three crops a year. But she died a couple of years ago. And Marlis Adams can communicate mind-to-mind with animals."

Natalie's cell phone sounded. She glanced down at the screen, then crossed to the door and yanked it open. Rudy was outside, a small keyboard cradled in his arms. "Delivery for a Ms. Natalie Diaz?"

Natalie flashed him a quick, grateful grin. "Can you plug in? We don't need a stellar sound system. I just want to try something."

When Rudy had set up, Natalie pointed Emma at the keyboard. "Play something."

Emma edged up to the Roland like it might bite. "What do you want to hear?"

"Musician's choice," Natalie said.

Emma brushed her fingers over the keys. Something awakened within her, a sense of familiarity, like she was meeting up with an old friend who hadn't changed a bit. Closing her eyes, Emma began to play.

It was a work she couldn't have named, a complicated classical piece that buzzed through her fingers with a sense of release, like it had been dammed up inside of her for years. Layer upon layer of notes, a summer storm of music that carried her along in its wake.

At the end, she forced her fingers off the keys and sat back, sweat pouring down her spine. When she looked up at Rudy and Natalie, they stared at her with stunned faces.

"Maybe you should play all by yourself, and we'll just listen," Rudy muttered, looking a bit stricken. "You could have your own one girl band."

"Aw, honey," Natalie said, patting his shoulder, "any band worth its salt is more than the sum of its parts. And you add a lot of sex appeal, too."

Rudy made a face at her. "Play something else?" he urged, as if hoping Emma might be a one-trick pony.

"Everything that wants to come out of me seems to be classical," Emma said. Finally, she improvised, playing the melody line of "I'll Sit In."

By the time she finished, Rudy and Nat were blotting at their eyes and clearing their throats.

"All right, then," Natalie said, "I think we've identified two of your gifts: musical performance and instrument making."

Emma had to admit, even if those were the only gifts she had, they suited her. Sonny Lee always said that the key to happiness was to find something you really love doing and get good enough to make a living at it.

Eager to get off the subject of her gifts, Emma said, "Going back to what we were talking about before . . . Do you know anyone else who was at Thorn Hill, and left before the poisoning? Anyone like me. What's their stone like?"

Natalie and Rudy looked at each other.

"Hmm," Rudy said, frowning. "After what happened, I think anyone who escaped the massacre went underground."

"There's Gabriel," Natalie said. "He spent time there, off and on, but he was away at the time of the massacre. I don't know if there was anyone else." She studied on it a moment, then pulled out her cell phone and punched in a number. Someone picked up on the other end, and Emma soon figured out it was Gabriel, though she could only hear Natalie's side of the conversation.

"I just sent you the—you already got that? What do you think?" Pause. "That's what I think, too, but it doesn't make sense." She listened a while longer. "Well, she says she wasn't there that night, that she left beforehand. . . . Listen, we were talking, and wondered if it was possible people had different kinds of Weirstones even before the poisoning. You know, like they were different to begin with, and then damaged. . . ." Emma could hear Gabriel's voice, sharp as plucked notes. After a few more minutes of conversation, Natalie hung up.

"Well," Natalie said, "he had a lot to say, but the bottom line is no, that's just not possible."

ℭ Chapter Eleven ℘
Sanctuary

Leesha Middleton lived in a mansion on the lakefront. It might have brought back Emma's nasty memories of being held captive by Rowan DeVries, but the atmosphere was totally different. For one thing, the house was pink stucco in a wood-siding kind of town, which made it seem like it had a built-in sense of humor.

Emma liked Leesha's Aunt Millisandra from the start, even though she was dangerous to be around and often said things that everybody else was thinking, but nobody else said out loud. Things that made people cringe.

Aunt Millie always told the truth, even when it wasn't polite. And she was totally nonjudgmental. When Leesha first introduced them, Millisandra surveyed Emma with narrowed eyes. "My dear, I want to hear all about you. Were you the product of a mixed marriage?"

Leesha's smile froze on her face. "Aunt Millie, I don't think we—"

"I am, I guess," Emma said. "My grandfather was black, my father biracial, my mother was white. I even heard there's some Cherokee in the—"

"Oh!" Millisandra's elegant hands fluttered. "My dear girl, I'm not talking about race. I meant, a marriage across guild lines. Like a sorcerer and a seer. Usually that results in one or the other, but Alicia says you are a mongrel."

"I didn't say *mongrel*, Aunt Millie," Leesha said, her face as pink as the stucco. "I said *savant*. That's someone whose Weirstone has been modified, who has different gifts than the standard guilds."

"Maybe I'm old-fashioned, but I don't approve of all this tampering with Weirstones," Millie said. "Swapping them from person to person, creating designer Weir, and all that. You never know what you're going to get. Though I must say, that Jack Swift is a very well-endowed young man. I wonder, though, if he'll be able to reproduce."

Leesha interrupted this with a fit of coughing. "Why don't I show Emma to her room, Aunt Millie? You can get to know each other—"

"You began life as a sorcerer?" Millie persisted. "Sorcerers are good with their hands, I understand."

"Well. I guess so. I'm a luthier. And a musician."

Aunt Millisandra clasped her jeweled hands in delight. "A luthier? Do you build violins, then?"

Emma shook her head. "Guitars."

Millisandra's delight seemed undimmed. "I'm something of a musician myself."

"Used to be," Leesha muttered. "She's hard on her instruments."

"Don't mutter, Alicia," Aunt Millie said. "Speak clearly."

"What do you play?" Emma asked.

"Violin and cello. Cowbell, when it's called for. Which it almost never is. What do *you* play?"

"I play a little guitar," Emma said, then dared to add, "and piano."

"Well, then," Aunt Millie said. "Perhaps we can have a recital after dinner."

"Well, I—"

Leesha took Emma's elbow, tugging her away. "We'll see, Aunt Millie."

They walked down a marble-floored hallway, trimmed in pink and purple. It resembled a bubblegum cathedral.

"Look, I'm sorry about my aunt," Leesha said, her cheeks still flaming. "She has no filter."

"At least you always know what she's thinking," Emma said. "I'm a little tired of secrets, to tell you the truth."

Leesha rolled her eyes. "You've heard the expression *TMI?* Sometimes you don't need to know." But she said it in the way you talk about a vintage guitar that's always going out of tune, but you love it anyway.

"Maybe I should get a look at the kitchen and see what kind of food is on hand," Emma said, to change the subject. "I was thinking I should plan on making dinner mostly, since it's going to be hard for me to make breakfast or lunch. If it's all right, I'll make a list, and you can look it over."

"Don't worry about it," Leesha said casually. "Barbara's off on the weekends, so we'll order takeout."

"Who's Barbara?"

"The cook and housekeeper."

"But I thought you—"

"We're looking for more of a companion than a cook,"

Leesha said. "It will take all three of us to keep an eye on Aunt Millie."

Emma mulled this over, trying to decide whether she'd been offered charity in the guise of a job. Beggars can't be choosers, she thought.

Leesha's house was so big that Emma guessed they never had to see each other if they didn't want to. Emma practically had a wing to herself. It even had its own small kitchen area and a private entrance.

"When the house was first built, this was meant to be a guest suite or servants' quarters," Leesha said.

Am I a servant or a guest? Emma thought, but didn't say aloud.

She and Leesha carried in the rest of her things, which didn't take long. She arranged her meager wardrobe in the closet and put Tyler's notebook on the empty bookshelf by its lonely self.

"What's that?" Leesha pointed.

"Oh. My father wrote out tablature—guitar music and lyrics—for a lot of old blues songs and ballads," Emma said, realizing that she hadn't really looked at it since she'd brought it back from Tyler's. She'd been so busy learning the Fault Tolerant playlist that she'd nearly forgotten about it.

"So he was a musician, too?" Leesha said, running a polished fingernail over the binding.

"Yes," Emma said. "He was." The room got a little gloomier, as if a cloud had passed over the sun.

Now it was Leesha's turn to change the subject. "So you decided to commute to the Anchorage for school after all?"

"If the weather's too nasty, I just won't go," Emma said,

pulling stacks of T-shirts out of her duffel and layering them into the dresser drawer. "But I need to stay there for school. With my track record, it won't help to be changing schools again." Unpacking her backpack, she plunked her math textbook onto the desk. "I wouldn't mind dropping this class, though," she muttered. "Which reminds me. I've got homework to do for tomorrow."

"Oh!" Leesha said. "I'm sorry if I put you behind with—"

"Don't worry," Emma said. "You're not the problem. I mean, I could work on it all night and I still won't figure it out."

As far as Emma was concerned, the conversation was over, but Leesha made no move to leave. Instead, she sat down on the edge of the bed. "I was hoping I could ask you some questions about savants."

"Oh," Emma said, embarrassed. "I probably know the least of anybody."

"Don't assume that," Leesha said. "Most gifted just don't know much about Thorn Hill. It's like the whole thing was buried. I lived in the UK at the time it happened, but still. I heard nothing about it until I came here."

"What do you want to know?" Emma said.

"Okay. A preschool class from Trinity was kidnapped in downtown Cleveland. The kids say it was zombies. So, I'm wondering . . . if you've ever heard anything about zombies at the Anchorage. You know   corpses up and running around. The walking dead, like that."

"Zombies?"

"Just bear with me," Leesha said, picking at the bedspread. "I have reason to think they're telling the truth."

"You think the poison turned us into *zombies*? That's what people are saying?" Emma's voice was rising, and she struggled to bring it back under control.

"That's what *some* people are saying. There's two versions. Some of the kids said that the zombies were led by a boy dressed in black with a sword. Others said the boy with the sword was fighting the zombies and protecting the kids."

Emma glared at Leesha long enough to suggest just how crazy that was. "Okay, now, remember, I haven't been there that long. But I've never seen any zombies at the Anchorage. I've just seen a lot of kids who were badly hurt by whatever happened at Thorn Hill. And some that could pass for normal at any regular school. And some who are really, really gifted in different ways."

"You don't have to convince me," Leesha said, backtracking. "I've heard the band, remember? I've met Jonah Kinlock and Natalie Diaz. Still, as soon as the kidnapping happened, some of the gifted here in Trinity were ready to blame it on the Anchorage—because it happened close by."

"Is that why they blew up one of the buildings?"

Leesha's eyes widened. "I heard about that on the news. Are you sure it was someone from here?" she asked, leaning forward, hands on knees.

She sure isn't afraid of the truth, Emma thought, with grudging admiration. "We can't prove it. But that's what we suspect."

"See?" Leesha rolled her eyes. "Both sides are doing it. Jumping to conclusions. Somehow, we have to break that cycle."

Giving up on putting clothes away, Emma leaned her hips back against the dresser, arms folded, lips pressed together to keep herself from saying something like, *When did I turn into we?*

"So. Leaving off zombies, is there anything else you want to know?"

Leesha seemed to be casting about for a less tricky subject. "You're a savant. If you were originally a sorcerer, then . . . what's your gift now?"

"Music, I guess," Emma said. "And woodworking. It's the only thing I know, the only thing I've ever been good at. Any other magical thing I had going on must've been turned off."

"What if you could choose what gifts you had?" Leesha said, a wistful look in her eyes. "What would you pick?"

"I'd still pick music," Emma said. "No point in thinking about anything else." She hesitated. She wasn't used to prying in other people's business. "What gift would you choose?"

"I'd like to be able to go back in time and change the past," Leesha said. "So if you mess up, you can fix it." Just for a moment, the shutters opened, revealing pain and guilt.

"If you used to live in the UK, then how did you end up here?" Emma asked, thinking she should change the subject.

"Back in the day, the wizard houses used these brutal tournaments between warriors to allocate power. Warriors died in droves, and the few warriors left were in hiding. Word got out that there was a warrior hidden in Trinity. I came here to find him."

"Jack Swift?"

Leesha nodded. "He was, like, a junior in high school, and this was all news to him. So. I betrayed him to some people who planned to auction him off to the highest bidder."

"What?" Emma stared at Leesha. "But—but—but—"

"Full disclosure: I am a terrible person. I guess I should have told you before you moved in here."

Emma figured it was safest not to say anything.

"I didn't learn my lesson," Leesha said. "After running around Europe for a while, I got involved in another nasty scheme. I came back here, and that's when I fell in love with Jason Haley. He was a wizard, another banged-up survivor— we had a lot in common." She cleared her throat. "It was the best thing that ever happened to me. But I was in a bind, and I betrayed him. And when he found out, he dumped me. Which he totally should have." Leesha looked up at Emma, and cleared her throat. "Then he was killed in the Battle of Trinity. That was a big battle between wizards and a coalition of the other guilds two years ago."

"I'm so sorry," Emma said, wishing she knew what to say. She wasn't used to these heart-to-hearts. The only conversations she had were the practical kind that got you from A to B.

"I never got to say I'm sorry. Not really." Leesha touched a pendant that hung from a chain around her neck. "Words can hurt," she said, "but sometimes it's the words you never got to say that hurt the most."

"Well," Emma said, "there's nothing you can do to change the past."

"You're right," Leesha said. "But there might be something I can do about the future. More and more, I'm thinking that what happened at Thorn Hill needs to be talked about. That it's still affecting us now. That it might be destroying whatever hopes we have of peace. It's kind of like when they whitewash history in school, and so you make the same mistakes all over again."

"What do you care about savants?" Emma hunched her shoulders, trying to recall when she'd begun feeling like a part of that group. "I mean, nobody else around here seems to."

"I *don't* care about savants," Leesha said. "Not savants in particular. I just don't think I can stand any more bloodshed. See, I've already survived one magical battle. The boy I loved gave his life to end it. That was supposed to be his legacy— permanent peace among the Weirguilds." She sucked in a quick, shuddery breath. "Well, guess what? It's two years later, and we're going down that same road again unless somebody does something. And if we go to war again, it'll mean that Jason died for nothing. I won't have it. I just won't."

✿ CHAPTER TWELVE ✿
SLOW HAND

Ever since Halloween, Emma had been both longing for and dreading the next practice session with Fault Tolerant. Now that it was here, she was ricocheting between anticipation and worry.

It wouldn't be on neutral ground. Most bands practice at the drummer's house or wherever the drum kit lives. In this case, it lived in Oxbow, in the practice room that Natalie had claimed as her own. Just downstairs from where Emma's apartment still stood vacant. Downstairs from Jonah Kinlock's suite.

And yet, despite everything, Emma's return to that practice room on the ground floor produced a stomach swoop of nostalgia. Though Emma hadn't even been a part of the band for all that long, this was her musical home in Cleveland— the only place she'd recaptured even a sliver of what she had in Memphis. It was one thing to be in a classroom with Jonah, where he made himself as invisible as an enchanter could be. But music—good music—was by its nature an intimate act. And intimacy with Jonah Kinlock was dangerous in every way.

"I'm doing this for me," she told herself, several times, on her way from her last class to Oxbow. Self-interest—wasn't that what Jonah had said? They'd scheduled their practice right after school, so Emma could get home in time to help with dinner. That was the excuse she offered, anyway.

When she walked into the practice room, Natalie was crouched next to her drum kit, fussing with her bass pedal. Rudy was set up already. He'd draped his long body over a couch in the corner, oblivious to his surroundings, cocooned within the music coming through his headphones.

Alison's appearance came as something of a shock. It hadn't been that long since Emma had seen her, but she looked pounds thinner, her hair hanging in lank strands, purple shadows under her eyes.

She recalled what Natalie had said about fading. Was that what was happening to Alison? If so, didn't anyone else notice? Or was there nothing to be done?

Alison was at full strength when it came to one thing: attitude. She did a deliberate double-take when Emma thunked down her guitar case.

"Well, well. Look who's here. Thought you'd ditched us for sure."

"I might have," Emma said, kneeling next to her guitar and flicking open the catches with her thumbs. "Lord knows I tried, but I couldn't find a better band to be in."

A thin smile broke onto Alison's face, like the way the sun pokes through cloud. "All right, then," she said, nodding. "Glad we got that cleared up."

"Did Jonah send you the new stuff?" Natalie asked, as usual all business. Or maybe just eager to get past an awkward moment.

If he had, Emma hadn't opened it. She shook her head. "I haven't seen it."

"Jonah and Kenzie have been on a songwriting spree," Natalie said. "They've been writing some of their best stuff ever." She paused, a shadow flickering over her face. "I'll have him run through some of it when he gets here."

They say you call the devil by naming him. And so, here he was, shouldering through the door, carrying a guitar in either hand. He was using the same strategy as he did in class: last to arrive and first to leave. He'd wait until the scene was blocked, every other player in position before he took his place at his mark. He seemed to think he could come and go unnoticed that way, but Emma noticed. Jonah was like a splinter in your finger—there was no way not to notice him.

His cheeks were pinked up from the cold—it was nearly Thanksgiving after all. He wore a heavy barn coat, a muffler, jeans, and boots.

"Sorry I'm late," he said, setting the guitars down. He unwound the muffler and shed the coat, tossing them over the back of a chair. He stripped off his heavy outdoor gloves, switching them out for a pair of his trademark gloves. His heavy cotton sweater covered up the landscape of his body, making it just a bit less distracting. His jeans, though. His jeans . . .

Emma didn't do drugs, but if there were a drug that would stop her wanting Jonah Kinlock, she'd gladly take it. At least he was careful never to make eye contact with Emma, as if knowing the touch of his eyes might cause her pain.

"I was telling Emma about your new material," Natalie said. "She can't wait to hear it." Which was putting words in Emma's mouth, even though they were true.

"I sent the files to everyone," Jonah said, lifting out the DragonFly and cradling it in his arms. "I was hoping you'd all get a chance to check them out and see if they're worth practice time."

"Just finished," Rudy said, having emerged from his fog of music to join the rest of them. "I'm on board. Let's do it."

"I think 'Untouchable' is the strongest of the new work, Jonah," Natalie said. "Why don't you run through it once so Emma can hear it, and we can begin putting this thing together."

Jonah shifted his weight from foot to foot, his long fingers caressing the frets, his other hand flat against the strings to keep them from sounding. "Maybe she could just listen to the MP3 file first? And then we could—"

"Oh, don't be a baby, Kinlock," Alison said, swinging her guitar into position. "You don't have to go it alone. I've been working on the bass line, and I'm sure Nat has worked out the percussion three different ways."

"Alison's right. We're all going to sit here until you do," Natalie added. "I've got"—she looked at her tablet—"two hours before I have to be in clinic."

Jonah must've known he was outnumbered. With a sigh, he flipped the guitar strap over his shoulder and looped it over the pin. "Open G," he said to Alison and Emma. He plugged into the amp, checked the tuning, and, then, with a rush of chords, he began to sing.

Imagine what it's like to be (untouchable)
Better not take a chance on me (untouchable)
I'm the bad boy your mama told you about
I'm dangerous, without a doubt
Even coming off a ten-year drought
Untouchable.

By the end of the first stanza, Alison had added in a simple bass line and Natalie was working her brushes. Emma didn't even try on this first round. She felt flattened by the music and the message.

I'm the rose with hidden thorns (untouchable)
Don't tell me that you haven't been warned (untouchable)
I'm pretty poison under the skin,
The bite of the apple that's a mortal sin
In a game of love you'll never win
Untouchable.

My reputation's fairly earned (untouchable)
If you play with fire, you will get burned (untouchable)
Stay out of the kitchen if you can't take the heat,
My kisses are deadly as they are sweet,
I'm a runaway bus on a dead-end street
Untouchable.

Fools rush in, that's what they say (untouchable)
But angels fall, too, most every day (untouchable)
I'm the snake in the garden, the siren on the reef
I have the face of a saint and the heart of a thief
I'll promise you love, and bring you nothing but grief
Untouchable.

Hearing Jonah sing this was like watching him slice himself open and show off his insides. Why would he do that? Why would he write such a song?

And then Emma answered her own question. Because good music always tells the truth, no matter how much it hurts.

Emma couldn't be the only one who felt the bite of the blade, but everyone else seemed to take it in stride. Did they know? Did they all know about Jonah?

Of course they did. They were there when it happened. They'd allowed Jonah to keep the secrets that were most important to him. She knew she shouldn't resent that, but she still did. They must have known she was falling for him. They must have.

Emma forced herself back to the present, to the critique that was already in progress.

"The third stanza is weakest, I think, when it comes to lyrics," Alison said. " 'Stay out of the kitchen if you can't take the heat'? That's lame."

"Since when are you a lyricist, Shaw?" Rudy scoffed. "I think it's genius. Anyway, you're not the one who has to sing it."

"I'm not a lyricist, but I do recognize lame when I hear it. And I don't want to hear it when I'm up on stage."

Jonah didn't seem offended. "Originally it was 'Keep away from the flame if you can't stand the heat,' but I had the reference to fire in the line before, so . . ."

"Better a soft repeat than lame," Alison said.

"How about 'Keep clear of me if you can't stand the heat'?" Rudy suggested.

They continued to argue back and forth, polishing and

revising, until Emma said abruptly, "Run through it again, and I'll join in this time."

At first, Emma simply pulled licks out of Jonah's chords, but she gradually worked up a countervailing melody line for the lead guitar. She set her feet and faced off with him, blazing away with the Strat, forcing him back, back, back, twining in and around his guitar work, pinning him down until he had little room to maneuver in. Finally, Jonah found his musical footing and stood his ground. He used his voice, his very best weapon, to push back while Rudy did his best to layer in a harmony.

By the time it was over, Emma was dripping with sweat, and Jonah was, too.

"Whoa," Rudy said, stepping back from his Roland. "Talk about hot! You incinerated it."

"Yeah, well," Emma said, voice shaking. "It needed incinerating."

Jonah just stood, his guitar loose in his hands, his eyes fixed on Emma.

"Let's go over some of the older material before I have to leave," Natalie said, quickly.

"No, I'm done for the day," Emma said. And she was— mentally and physically exhausted. "I've got it down. I'll get in some practice on my own."

CHAPTER THIRTEEN
NEED A LITTLE HELP HERE

Corcoran's was a diner near downtown Trinity, clearly popular with the locals. Midafternoon on a Saturday, it was swarming with teens wearing Trinity sweatshirts, and kids still in soccer shin guards. In one corner, a table of old men hunched over spread-out newspapers and empty plates.

Leesha had asked Emma to meet her there after yet another study session at the library. Leesha was coming from yet *another* meeting.

Leesha ordered a sandwich, and Emma ordered a hot fudge sundae. It had been a good long time since she'd had one.

When she finished her sundae, she dropped her spoon in the empty dish with a satisfying clatter. "Sometimes you forget just how good a sundae is until you have one, and then you think of all those times you could've had one and didn't." Emma reached for the bill, but Leesha covered it with her own hand.

"My treat, remember?" Leesha dropped her credit card

on top of the bill and said, "Emma, I've been meaning to talk to you about something." From her expression, she wasn't looking forward to it. "The council has set up a new task force to investigate the mainliner murders."

"How many task forces do you all need?" Emma said.

"Madison Moss is spearheading this one," Leesha said. "They've been holding a series of hearings, and they want you to come and tell them what you know. Especially about the Halloween party."

"I've already talked to the cops," Emma said. "I've made a statement, answered their questions. They seem satisfied with that." Well, she didn't know that for a fact, but at least they hadn't called her back in.

"The task force will ask different questions," Leesha said. She cleared her throat. "Chief Childers is an excellent detective, and he already knows about the magical guilds, but—"

"He does?" Emma remembered wondering whether the police in Trinity knew that their little town was seething with magic and magical people.

Leesha nodded. "He really helped us out a lot two years ago during the Battle of Trinity. Still, he just doesn't know what questions he should be asking."

The back of Emma's neck prickled. She thought of her encounter with Madison Moss at Grace's memorial service. She didn't care to repeat it. "It sounds like a witch hunt to me," she said. "It doesn't seem right to have Madison running an investigation of her sister's murder."

"Oh, she's not *on* the task force," Leesha said. "The council chose the members, and Maddie chose the chair— Mercedes Foster." Leesha paused, then rushed on with the sales pitch. "Mercedes is tough and fair, and she'll be looking for the truth, wherever that leads. She has a connection with savants through Natalie, and she's not afraid of anything. The fact that Madison chose her tells me that she really does want a thorough, unbiased investigation."

"What if I say no?"

"You could," Leesha said, drawing out the word, her smoky eyes troubled, "but I hope you'll at least consider it. And I hope you'll encourage some of the other savants to testify as well."

"Who? Jonah?"

"Well, him and anyone else who might know something. The committee isn't perfect, but I think it's the best chance to dig out the truth. It's the only group that's working with all the information."

No, they're not, Emma thought. They are *not* working with all the information.

"Tell me this," she said. "Are there any savants on the task force?"

"Savants?" Leesha's cheeks pinked up. "Um, not that I know of."

"What? You think there might be some secret savants on there?"

"Well, no." From Leesha's expression, she knew she'd messed up but couldn't figure out a way to backtrack.

Emma stood. "Get back to me when there's a savant on the committee." She tried to force a smile, to prove there were no hard feelings, but wasn't sure if it actually made it onto her face. "See you back at home."

But the ordeal wasn't over yet. As soon as she got out on the street, Emma's phone sounded. She looked down at the screen. *Private.* She answered.

"H-hello?"

"Ms. Lee?" It was a man's voice. Familiar.

"Um. Yes. That's me."

"This is Ross Childers. Trinity PD."

"Oh. Hi." Spooky how he was calling her just when she thought she was out of the woods.

"Are you here in town?" Childers sounded surprised, and Emma had the feeling he knew the answer to that already. He must've had some way of locating her phone.

"I'm living here now," Emma said. "Up on Lake Street. I'm downtown, heading home."

"Is that so? Well, then, could you stop by the police station? It's right on your way. I promise I won't take too much of your time."

Ross Childers's office was about as neat as his car was messy. His computer system looked to be state-of-the-art, and he had photographs of the town posted on his walls, along with some framed training certificates and award plaques. He was on the phone when she arrived, but he waved her to a seat across the desk from him while he finished up.

After he put the phone down, he walked around the desk to shake her hand. "How *are* you, Ms. Lee?"

"Emma," she said, thinking, At least he hasn't figured out who I really am.

"Emma," he said. "Would you like anything? Some water or coffee?"

"No, sir," Emma said. "I just came from Corcoran's."

"Corcoran's, huh?" Childers patted his midsection. "I gotta stay out of that place or I won't pass my physical. Have you tried their peanut banana bowl?"

"No, sir." She hesitated, then said, "To tell you the truth, that sounds awful."

Childers pretended to be shocked, then said, "More for me, then, huh?" He went back around his desk and sat down. "I didn't know you'd moved here to town. That's a nice area up there by the lake."

"I'm staying with Leesha Middleton and her aunt," Emma said. "I'm helping out with Aunt Millie."

"Ah, Millisandra Middleton," Childers said. "I used to cut her grass when I was a kid. She's a great lady. I'm sorry to hear that she's in bad health."

"She's doing all right," Emma said. She looked down at her hands.

"So. How come you moved here? You get tired of the big-city life?" The question sounded casual, but Emma knew better.

"I'm still going to school in Cleveland," Emma said. "I just—I like it here, and Leesha offered me a job."

"It's not because you didn't feel safe there?" The chief's face was open, kind, and just a bit worried.

"Why wouldn't I feel safe there?" Emma snapped.

"Nobody's pressuring you?"

"Nobody but you."

"Okay," he said, smiling ruefully. "I deserved that. But it'd be no wonder if you felt skittish after what happened." He sighed. "I've been doing some research into the history of the Anchorage. That was a real shame, what happened in Brazil."

"Yes, sir, it was."

"I guess I heard about it at the time, but I didn't connect it to here. That's a great thing Mr. Mandrake is doing, setting up the school and all. I understand that a lot of the survivors are in poor health? Some have special needs?"

"Some do," Emma said. "I'm fine, though." Why did she think she had to keep repeating that?

"Good to hear," Childers said. He paused, chewing on his lip, as if he wasn't sure how to ask the next question. "I've been talking to people here in town, and some of them seem to think that some of the students might—might have serious problems. They seem worried that they had something to do with—"

"If you have questions about my school or any of the students there, you really need to talk to Mr. Mandrake," Emma said. She made as if to get up. "Is that it? Because I—"

"I'm sorry," Childers said, raising both hands. "You are absolutely right. I am talking to the wrong person. I'll get hold of Mr. Mandrake." As if eager to change the subject, he hit his keyboard and his screen lit up. He turned it toward Emma. "I wanted to let you know that we got some of the forensics back. The blood on your shoes matches the blood on your jacket, and they both seem to match with Rowan DeVries."

"I could've told you that up front," Emma said, crossing and uncrossing her legs.

"I wondered if you remembered anything else that might be of help to us."

"No, sir. Nothing comes to mind."

"Have you talked to Kinlock at all since Halloween?"

"Well, yeah, I've talked to him. I see him at school, and, you know, at practices. We haven't talked about the killings, if that's what you mean. You said not to discuss it with anyone. Besides, I think we'd both like to forget about it."

"What about DeVries? Have you had any contact with him?"

"No, sir. Like I said, I don't really know him." And then, because she thought she should ask, "Does that mean he's better? Has he been able to talk? Has he—has he said anything about what happened?"

"No, he hasn't," Childers said heavily. "The thing is, he's disappeared."

"Disappeared? How could that be?" Emma leaned forward, planting both hands on his desk. "I thought he was in the intensive care."

The detective was watching her closely, taking in her reaction. "He *was* improving," Childers said. "He'd moved out of the ICU, and his vital signs were good. He was down to one IV, but he still seemed confused, too groggy for questioning. Then, this morning, he was gone without a word to anybody."

Emma thought of Burroughs. Of Hackleford. And, finally, of Jonah. She cleared her throat. "You don't—you don't think something could have happened to him, do you? I mean, whoever attacked him might want to keep him from talking."

And then she thought, That was stupid; of course he's already thought of that. It's probably why he'd brought her in.

"It's possible," Childers said. "It seems farfetched that somebody could kidnap him and sneak him out of the hospital without anyone seeing him. If you were the killer, and if you didn't want him talking, it would be a lot easier to just finish the job you started."

"Oh," Emma said. "I guess so."

"So right now, we're treating it like he left AMA. Against

medical advice. Maybe he'll get in touch when he's ready. But if he tries to contact you, it's important that you let us know."

"Sure," Emma said, nodding. "Okay."

She thought maybe they were done, but Childers just kept looking at her, his forehead furrowed.

"What?" she said, getting prickly again.

"Promise me you'll be careful," he said, flipping a pen, catching it. He drew a breath, released it slowly. "I can tell that you're not used to trusting the police to help you. But something's going on, something you don't feel comfortable talking about. If there's anything you think we should know that would help us look out for you, I hope you'll tell me. We can't do our best job if we don't have all the information."

He believes me, Emma thought, amazed and touched. Even if he doesn't think I've told him everything, he is worried about me. But would he believe me if he knew I was a runaway from Memphis?

It's just hard to get out of the habit of looking out for myself.

Emma stood. "Thank you," she said. "I appreciate that."

The next night, Jonah arrived at Kenzie's door carrying an ice cream cake. There hadn't been time to custom order one, but this one said AWESOME! in caramel icing over chocolate, so he thought it would do. Kenzie was a total fool for ice cream. Balancing the cake in one hand, he knocked with the other.

No answer.

He knocked again.

No answer.

Setting the cake on the floor, he pounded.

Nothing.

Entering the pass code to the display outside Kenzie's room, he scanned his brother's schedule. Nothing, not at this time of night. Was he asleep? That was unheard of at this hour. Then again, Jonah had scarcely seen him since Halloween, when he woke Kenzie up and his brother helped craft him an alibi.

Fear slithered through Jonah, an icy snake of panic. Pulling out his cell phone, he called his brother. He could hear the phone going off inside. It went on and on and on.

He was ready to force the door, when he heard Kenzie's voice, thick with sleep. "Harry. Answer the phone."

"Kenzie? It's me."

Brief silence. "Come back tomorrow. I'm in bed."

"What are you doing in bed?"

A little of the usual snark returned to Kenzie's voice. "I *was* sleeping."

Jonah double-checked the time. "At this hour?"

"It's after midnight."

"So? This is your new normal?"

"I thought I was getting in a rut, staying up all night."

"I brought an ice cream cake," Jonah said.

Nothing.

"It's melting," Jonah called out. "Open up or I'll have to take down the door, and that will set off all kinds of alarms."

This time, he heard the soft snick of the lock.

Kenzie was, indeed, in bed, and looked like he'd been there a while. Jonah shoved the cake into the freezer to harden up a little and crossed to his brother's bedside. "'Sup? You feel okay?" Jonah sat on the side of the bed and leaned closer. He couldn't tell much, since Kenzie hadn't bothered to turn on the light.

"Quit hovering, okay? I'm tired is all. You know, most people, if they came to visit and found a person in bed, they'd take that as a hint," Kenzie said. "Emma already woke me up once."

Jonah's heart did its usual backflip at her name. "She did? She's already been here?"

"Been and gone," Kenzie said. "This has turned into a high-traffic area."

"So. Has Emma—" Jonah stopped, swallowed. "Has she been coming to visit often?"

Jonah felt oddly envious that Emma would talk to Kenzie, maybe confiding her greatest fears, and seeking his advice. "I was wondering . . . Has she said anything about—"

"One thing we never talk about is you," Kenzie interrupted. "And yet somehow we manage to have a conversation." He paused. "So what did happen between the two of you? Tell Dr. Kinlock."

"She knows I was there the night her father died," Jonah said. "She blames me for his death. She's moved out of Oxbow because of me, though I managed to persuade her to stay in school here." He massaged his forehead with the heel of his hand.

"I knew something bad had happened," Kenzie said, puffing out his cheeks. "I thought maybe she'd found out about your death-dealing touch. That sucks, man."

Eager for a distraction, Jonah returned to the refrigerator, retrieved the cake, pulled back the lid, and displayed it to Kenzie, who signified his approval with a thumbs-up.

Jonah cut two huge slabs. He handed one to his brother, then switched on the bedside light and pulled Kenzie's high-tech desk chair up close.

"You know that you're reinforcing bad behavior," Kenzie said, talking with his mouth full. As he turned back toward Jonah, Jonah spotted a purple bruise on one cheekbone and a scabbed-over cut on his chin.

Jonah's heart stuttered. No doubt that accounted for the romantic lighting. Kenzie didn't want Jonah to get a good look at him.

"McKenzie Kinlock, have you been fighting again?"

"Okay, I confess. I got into it with a biker. *Again*. You should see the other guy, ha-ha." Kenzie stuffed another bite of cake into his mouth. "Now, what was it you—?"

"No, really," Jonah persisted. "What happened?" Then he noticed that the floor around Kenzie's bed was charred black. "Did you have an accident or something?"

"I just fell," Kenzie said. "No big deal." He looked sideways at Jonah to see how that was being received. "You didn't like the more interesting story."

"Does Gabriel know?" Jonah asked. "Or Natalie?"

"Look, the aides picked me up and dusted me off, and I talked them out of reporting it. Every time it happens, they start talking restraints and side rails and all that. Or they have a conference, and decide to send me back to the torture chamber and build up my muscle strength so I bounce next time." He sighed. "What's the point?"

Now Jonah noticed that Kenzie's eyes seemed sunken into his skull. They were murky with fatigue, like windows coated in dust. His collarbone stood out, the flesh melted away, so he had the look of a refugee in one of those disaster photos.

"You've lost weight," Jonah said, almost accusingly.

"Do you really think so?" Kenzie made a sour face. "I'm on a new diet plan—I throw up everything I eat."

"What? Why haven't you told me?" Jonah reached for the cake. "Maybe this isn't such a—"

Kenzie jerked the cake back, out of danger. "It still tastes good going down," he said.

"What was your last weight?" Rolling to the foot of Kenzie's bed, Jonah woke his chart and brought up his vitals.

"Have you not heard of patient confidentiality?" Kenzie muttered.

Jonah scanned his weights. "These all look good," he said, frowning. "And your blood work's—" He looked up at his brother in time to catch the guilt flickering across his face. Understanding dawned. "You've hacked the system," he said. "Haven't you?"

"What happens in Safe Harbor stays in Safe Harbor," Kenzie said. "Kenzie Kinlock is looking good."

"Kenzie. If you're . . . losing ground, we need to do something."

"*We?* It's not like I'm on the team. I'm just the tackling dummy, getting hit over and over again. I'm on maximum everything, and I've been through every one of Gabriel's experimental interventions. I'm the go-to person for clinical trials, because I have nothing to lose and nowhere else to go."

And for the first time, Jonah caught a note of discouragement in his brother's voice. Even Harry caught it, because a new screen appeared—it was WHINING with a slash across it.

"How can I help?" Jonah said simply.

"Promise me something."

Jonah knew better than to say *Anything*. So he said, "Promise you what?"

"I don't want to go to Safe Passage," Kenzie said.

"Nobody's said anything about Safe Passage," Jonah growled. "Stop talking like that."

"Will you shut up and listen to me?" Kenzie paused, and when Jonah said nothing, continued. "I've looked at the aggregate clinical data, and I've looked at my own data, and I have a much more accurate idea than you do about who goes to Safe Passage, all right?"

Jonah met his brother's eyes. "I'm sure you do. So?"

"I'm not going to put you through that," Kenzie said.

"Through what?"

"Do you really think you can keep anything secret from me? Any digital bit at the Anchorage is at my beck and call. I know what your role is there. I'm not going to have you free me or riff me or help me on to heaven. I don't care what Gabriel calls it. You have been through enough shit already."

"You know what happens when a savant dies," Jonah said. "I'm not going to have you turn into a zombie."

"Listen to yourself. You won't *have* it? What about what I want? Do I get a vote?"

"But . . . you can't imagine what that means," Jonah said.

"Oh, yes, I can," Kenzie said. "I have a very good imagination—everyone says so. At least I won't be stuck in one place. And, at least now and then, I might inhabit a body that works."

⊗ CHAPTER FIFTEEN ⊗
HOW LONG, HOW LONG BLUES

"**K**enzie? It's Jonah."

It was the day after the night of the ice cream cake.

Jonah heard furtive movement through the door. "What are you doing here at this time of day?" Kenzie sounded both annoyed and suspicious.

"I'm visiting outside of the box," Jonah said, glancing at Natalie. "Open up."

"Harry. Display corridor view." A moment of silence, then, "Why is Natalie with you?"

Jonah was stumped for a moment, then pointed to the tiny camera mounted over the door. Kenzie had the hallway under video surveillance.

"We want to talk to you."

"I'm busy right now," Kenzie said.

"Busy doing what?"

"Taking a dump."

"No, you're not," Jonah said. "But, just in case you are, get ready for company."

Kenzie was totally uncooperative, glaring daggers at Jonah for his betrayal and shorting out every instrument Natalie brought near him, including the bed scale. He gave evasive, smartass answers to all her questions. She finally dug up an old blood pressure cuff that inflated manually, checked his pulse by gripping his wrist, and examined his Weirstone with an ancient and totally non-digital silver cone inscribed with runes. She took notes with pen and paper.

Kenzie fell asleep before she was finished writing. It was apparent he'd been working hard to keep his body under tight control. Now his thin body was racked with continual tremors, like the engine inside him was badly out of tune. His skin swarmed with blue flame. Jonah brushed his hair off his damp forehead, feeling the sting of power.

"Well?" Jonah asked, when Natalie looked up from her notes. "What can we do? What's the next step?"

Natalie cleared her throat. "The antiseizure therapies are pretty much maximized. I'm worried that if we go with a higher dosage, it may compromise his breathing. We can try some interventions to control the nausea and make him more comfortable. That might help with his hydration status."

"What about his nutrition? I can tell he's lost a lot of weight. If you build him back up, it might help him fight this thing off."

"Well"—Natalie's eyes were troubled—"we could start a tube feeding, but it depends on what he wants—how aggressive we want to be."

"What do you mean by that?" Jonah flared. "He has value, Nat. Of course we want to be aggressive."

"Jonah." Natalie put her hand on his arm. "No one is saying that Kenzie doesn't have value. But his Weirstone is failing. The poison is destroying what little functionality it has left."

Jonah recalled what Kenzie had said about the aggregate data. *I have a much more accurate idea than you do about who goes to Safe Passage, all right?*

"Let's take it out, then," Jonah suggested. "The Anaweir do perfectly well without stones."

"He's Weirflesh," Natalie said. "You know he can't survive without a stone."

And Jonah did know that. "It's unfair," he said. "Kenzie's gift has never done him any good—just destroyed his quality of life. It's his mind and his wit and that snarky sense of humor that— Can't we do a—a transplant or something? Replace his stone with a healthy one?"

"Even if we could find a healthy stone, there's no guarantee the toxin wouldn't destroy that one, too."

"Maybe, but it would buy him some time," Jonah said. "Time for me to figure out how to fix this."

"Jonah. You can't fix this, given what we know now. If I could fix Kenzie, I would, and so would Gabriel." She paused, and because she believed in being honest, said, "It's time to consider moving him to Safe Passage."

"No." Jonah shook his head. "He told me—he doesn't want that."

"How did he . . ." Natalie began, but then decided not to ask that question. "What do you mean, he doesn't want that? Because it means we're coming to the end of this journey?"

"Don't ply me with hospice-speech," Jonah snapped. "And don't call it a journey, like it's just part of the great mandala of life. There's nothing natural about a fifteen-year-old dying."

"Don't you think I know that?" Tears streamed down Natalie's face. "Do you think I want to give up? But all the choices are bad. Do you really want Kenzie wandering the streets, looking for a corpse to claim?"

"I'm just saying that I'm not ready to throw him under the bus," Jonah said. "Whatever we do, it should be what Kenzie wants, not whatever suits us."

Jonah knew he was being totally unfair, that Natalie had been fighting this discouraging battle longer than anyone but Gabriel, with no complaints. It was her example that had persuaded him to cooperate with the Safe Passage program, to cut off the spigot of shades so this terrible job might be done before the last of the shadeslayers went down.

"I'm sorry, Nat," Jonah said. "It's all unfair, but there's no reason for me to come down on you. I know you love Kenzie, and you're looking out for him."

"Well," Natalie said, looking over her scribbled notes, "I don't think the situation is so dire that we have to decide it now. We'll do what we can to help with the symptoms and try to hold the line against further decline. Now, let's let him rest, all right?"

She crossed to the door, opened it, then turned back toward Jonah to fire a parting shot. "Just think this over," she said. "If Kenzie says he doesn't want Safe Passage, ask yourself—is he looking out for himself, or is he looking out for you?"

★ ★ ★

Back in his room, Jonah unlocked his armory, swinging the doors wide, displaying an array of cutting weapons and shivs. His fingers found a catch by the hinge, and he swung open a smaller, inner cabinet. Entering the combination code into the lock, he opened the compartment and pulled out the bottle of blood magic Brendan Wu had given him. It was warm to the touch and somehow full of promises.

It could be anything, Jonah thought. It could be a deadly poison. Strategically, it might benefit Lilith to add Kenzie to her shade army. But Kenzie and Brendan had always been close. Jonah couldn't imagine Brendan cooperating with such a scheme. If he knew about it.

But if Jonah gave it to Kenzie, and it hurt his brother in any way, Jonah'd never forgive himself.

Cautiously, carefully, he worked free the silver stopper, prying it out without damaging it. Lowering his nose to the bottle, he took a whiff.

Energy rocketed through him, penetrating all the way to his core, then rising in him like tree sap in the spring, extending into his fingers and toes. His skin tingled, every nerve alert.

This must be what snorting a line of cocaine is like, Jonah thought.

Taking a deep breath, he raised the bottle to his lips and sipped.

Well-being gushed through him. Aches and pains and discomforts he wasn't even aware of faded away. His wrist had bothered him for three years ever since he took an awkward fall off a building. Now he tested it: no sign of trouble at all. It was as if somebody had been poking him in the eye and stopped. It wasn't that he was high—he was just so extraordinarily *right*, so totally *in synch* that it couldn't help lifting his spirits. It was like he'd been detoxified.

He waited. Tried to distract himself by running through some lyrics he was working on. The sense of wellness persisted.

Finally, reluctantly, Jonah recorked the bottle and returned it to the cabinet and shut the door. If he were still alive tomorrow—if he hadn't grown horns or developed scales or murdered anybody he wasn't supposed to murder—maybe he would see if Kenzie was willing to give it a try.

⊂⊃ CHAPTER SIXTEEN ⊂⊃
BLOOD MAGIC

Kenzie worked harder at being asleep than anyone Jonah had ever seen—twitching, moaning, twisting his bedsheets into knots. His breathing was wet and irregular. He couldn't be getting much rest.

Worse, even in sleep, Jonah could feel Kenzie's pain, a white-hot burning that left him faintly nauseous. It made it hard for him to be in the same room with his brother.

Still, it wasn't easy to wake him up. Jonah felt bad about doing it, but he had to have this conversation sooner rather than later.

"Kenzie?" he said softly. And then, *"Kenzie!"*

Finally, he reached out and shook him.

Kenzie grimaced, and his bluish eyelids twitched. "Is there something about my being asleep that's annoying to you?" he said without opening his eyes.

"I've got a present for you from Brendan Wu."

Kenzie frowned. "Dead Brendan Wu?"

"Undead Brendan Wu," Jonah said.

Kenzie finally opened his eyes. "You saw him?"

Jonah nodded.

Kenzie's pain-dulled eyes showed a spark of interest. His hands moved restlessly on his coverlet. "Recently?"

"He seems to be Lilith's right-hand person." He extended the bottle toward Kenzie. "He wanted you to have this."

Kenzie eyed the bottle suspiciously. "What the hell is that? Looks like a beet-juice milk shake in a genie bottle."

"It's just—it's something that might be worth trying."

"Stipulated, Counselor." Kenzie squinted at the bottle in Jonah's hand. "But if you want me to drink it, you're going to have to tell me what it is."

"It's blood magic," Jonah said, meeting Kenzie's gaze directly.

Kenzie's eyes widened fractionally. "You mean, like—like—"

"Yes," Jonah said. "Like what shades are using to preserve their borrowed bodies."

"The stuff that's released when the gifted are murdered."

"Yes."

"And the idea is that it might work on me."

"That's the idea, yes."

"But I'm not dead yet."

"No."

"In other words, why wait for me to die to try and bring me back to life?"

"Basically."

Kenzie closed his eyes. "No. Not interested."

"Kenzie."

"You don't even know what that shit is. It might turn me into a lizard."

"I already tried it on myself," Jonah said. "It was . . ." He blew out a quick breath. "I think it might really help."

"That's messed up, Jonah, and you know it. You are not my taster. Keep taking risks, and we can have a double funeral. Together in life, together forever in death." Kenzie opened his eyes. "I want my own grave. Not sharing."

"Please, Kenzie."

Kenzie said nothing, just rolled onto his side, his back to Jonah, and pretended to snore.

Jonah spoke to Kenzie's back. "Look, I know we're on shaky moral ground, here, but throwing it out isn't going to bring anyone back to life. We might as well use it."

For what seemed like forever, Kenzie didn't say anything at all. Then he rolled onto his back, staring up at the ceiling. "Don't you get it? What if it works? What then?"

Jonah wasn't sure what he was supposed to say. "We . . . celebrate?"

"Sooner or later, we'll need more. How do you intend to go about getting it? Have you ever heard the term *slippery slope*?"

"Let me worry about that."

"Don't tell me what I can and can't worry about."

"Don't you get it?" Jonah grabbed a fistful of Kenzie's T-shirt. "I'm trying to save you."

"You're the one who doesn't get it," Kenzie said. "This time, *I'm* trying to save *you*. Has it occurred to you that this"—he pointed at the bottle—"that this is a trap Lilith and Brendan have laid for you? What was it Brendan wanted you to do on the bridge? He wanted you to help him kill gifted preschoolers in order to extract blood magic."

"If you're trying to save my soul, you're a little late," Jonah said. "I'm an assassin. I've lost count of the kills I've made, and most of those shades were innocent. I destroy everything I touch. There's nothing here, Kenzie, nothing worth saving."

Kenzie's cheeks were wet. "I disagree," he whispered, swallowing hard, grinding the heels of his hands against his face.

"At least *some* wizards and *some* mainliners are guilty," Jonah said. "The only part of me that's worth saving is the part that loves you. Please, Kenzie, let me buy some time at least. That's all I ask. I'm going to meet with Lilith and see if there's—if there's anything we've overlooked. I wish I could let you go, but I just . . . can't. Not when everything else is going to hell." It took everything Jonah had to keep from smacking his brother down with persuasion and pouring the potion down his throat.

Kenzie shuddered, as if watching his brother beg made him uncomfortable. "What if I drink this and keel over dead? What then?"

I'll kill Brendan Wu, Jonah thought. What he said was, "At least you'll be out of your misery. It's pretty hard to take, tell you the truth."

"Give it here, then." Kenzie stuck out his hand, but it trembled so badly that Jonah didn't want to risk his spilling it. Plus it was entirely possible that Kenzie would dump it out on purpose to end the argument.

"Here," Jonah said. "Let me help." Pulling the stopper from the bottle, he closed Kenzie's hands around it, his own guiding the bottle to Kenzie's lips. Kenzie tilted his head back and drank, throat jumping, continuing until the bottle was empty. He even licked the residue off his lips.

Jonah set the bottle on the side table. It retained a pearly luminescence.

"Well?" Jonah watched his brother warily for any signs of a reaction. "What do you think?"

Kenzie ran his tongue over his teeth. "Flamboyant yet unctuous, a bit chewy yet flabby, with notes of oak and old cigar boxes." He paused. "Distinct aftertaste of barnyard, yet still callipygian."

"What?"

"Nose reminds me of kerosene and charcoal." Kenzie shrugged. "Maybe it needs to be cellared a little longer."

"I mean, how do you *feel?*" Jonah said, weak with relief. "Any different? Better or worse?"

"It's kind of like that time I got into the brandy," Kenzie said. "My insides are on fire, but somehow I have this incredible sense of well-being. Like I could do anything—anything at all I set my mind to." He grimaced. "I hope this doesn't come with a hangover, too."

"The pain is gone," Jonah murmured, as if voicing it might bring it roaring back.

Kenzie's attention turned inward. "You're right," he said, wonder in his voice. "How about that." He extended his hands, and the tremor had nearly disappeared. "Harry," he said. "Display vitals."

Kenzie's data came up. They weren't anywhere close to normal, but his blood pressure had increased almost to standard, and his pulse rate had slowed and strengthened.

"So far, so good," Kenzie said. He raised his hands, patted

around on the top of his head, connecting on the first try. "No horns either."

Jonah smiled. "Not yet, anyway," he said, his voice thick with emotion. Kenzie's eyes seemed clearer than before—maybe it was just the absence of pain. Whatever. Jonah would take it.

Kenzie relaxed back against his pillows, eyes closed, his body still for the first time in a long time. Jonah looked him over carefully. He'd thought that the flaming seizures might return as soon as his brother had a little more juice to work with. But that didn't seem to be the case. He wished he could ask Natalie about it. But this would have to be a secret between the Kinlock brothers.

"If you're going to stay here," Kenzie said, "make yourself useful."

"I'm sure you have a suggestion," Jonah said.

"Order us a large deluxe pizza from Fourth Street Pies," Kenzie said. "My treat."

"Why? You hungry?" Jonah asked, another spark of hope kindling inside him.

"Ravenous," Kenzie said. "And get me something cold to drink from the fridge so I can wash this taste away."

Drunk with relief, Jonah obliged. Maybe it was wrong, maybe it was a slippery slope, but he had bought a little time. And tomorrow—maybe tomorrow was the day he'd finally get to meet up with Lilith and get the answers he needed.

CHAPTER SEVENTEEN
BLACK MAGIC WOMAN

"Rudy and I are going out to Homebrew tonight," Natalie said. "Ghastly is opening for Dreamboat. Want to come?"

Jonah looked up from his laptop. "No, thanks. I'm kind of in the middle of something."

"It's Wednesday night," Natalie persisted. "It's almost the weekend. And you don't have to work on the weekend."

"I didn't say I was working; I said I was in the middle of something. Maybe I'll come out later."

"Alison is meeting us there," Natalie said. "And Charlie and Mike and Thérèse might stop by."

Jonah knew exactly why they would be there. They'd come packing shivs, hoping that if Jonah was out and about, Lilith or Brendan might make contact.

"Sounds like you've got a full table already," he said.

"You're turning back into a hermit," Rudy said.

"I've been a hermit all along," Jonah said. "It's my natural state. I've got some new songs I want to have ready by tomorrow. And I want to hash a few things out with Kenzie."

Natalie and Rudy exchanged a meaningful look.

Jonah was not a fan of meaningful looks. He'd been getting a lot of them since Natalie's in-person evaluation of Kenzie. There'd been no more talk of moving him to Safe Passage, but Jonah knew it was just a matter of time before it came up again. Depending on how long the effects of the blood magic lasted.

"Kenzie goes to bed early these days," Natalie said softly. "Don't keep him up too late."

"It's Wednesday night, Nat," Jonah said, returning to his screen. "Almost the weekend. Nobody goes to bed early on Wednesday night. Anyway, I saw him last night, and I thought he looked much better. If he's in bed, I'll just hang out with him."

He waited a good half hour after they left, to make sure they weren't still lurking about, hoping to change his mind or put a tail on him. He stowed his notebook in his room, pulled on his jacket, then slipped out the back door of Oxbow, taking the crooked stairs that snaked all the way down the hill to the Flats. He carried no weapons save his own hands. If he was going to draw Lilith out of hiding, he'd have to go without an escort. If he was going to save his brother's life, he needed to take a few risks.

Fortunately, the wind from the northwest brought with it the icy bite that suggested snow before morning. The only people who'd be out on the streets tonight would be those with an agenda. He walked down to the park, to the fountain at the river's edge, and sat.

The wind ruffled his hair, and sent cold fingers down his

neck. A freighter churned under the Shoreway and into the river proper. Its passage sent waves slapping against the shoreline wall. A bell clanged as the Center Street swing bridge responded to the oncoming ship.

Come here often?

Startled, Jonah looked up to see that a woman had joined him on the fountain bench. A woman in a flesh and blood body who looked to be not much older than Jonah.

"Often enough," Jonah said, drawing in a breath, testing the air. Nothing.

The woman watched him, amused. *Not the way to make new friends, Jonah,* she said, speaking mind-to-mind. *Sniffing at them like a dog. You could at least be subtle about it.*

"I'm not here to make friends," Jonah said. "You seem to know who I am. That means you have the advantage over me."

I'm Lilith Greaves, she said simply. *It's good to finally meet you in person.* She made a show of scanning their surroundings. *For once, it seems, you didn't bring your bodyguards.*

"They aren't my idea," Jonah said. "I'd guess you'd say it's more of a posse."

He studied her. She wore blue jeans, a hoodie, and sneakers, which somehow made her look less threatening. She was tall, slight of build, with flaking purple nail polish on her bitten off nails, and short, spiky hair the color of butterscotch.

This tells me nothing, Jonah reminded himself. Still, it was hard to lose the human instinct to judge people by appearance. He didn't have much else to go on, after all. He'd always found hosted shades incredibly difficult to read. Maybe because a measure of Jonah's gift stemmed from his ability to sense and interpret the physical indicators of emotion. And Lilith's communication with her physical body was tenuous still.

Lilith endured his scrutiny, then raked back the sleeve of her hoodie, exposing a long, ragged gash that ran from wrist to elbow. It was oddly devoid of blood. *She killed herself,* Lilith explained.

"Is that supposed to get you points?" Jonah said. "The fact you didn't kill her?"

Lilith sighed. *You were always so charming when you were a little boy. Everybody loved you. And now you're rude. And a murderer.*

"Hard times change a person," he said, shrugging. "At least I'm not out murdering preschoolers."

There were preschoolers at Thorn Hill, Lilith said. *Surely you've finished off a few.*

"Maybe," Jonah shot back. "It's hard to tell when they're hidden inside a decaying corpse."

If I had my way, they wouldn't have to be.

"That's one thing we agree on, then," Jonah said. "It's just that I'm not willing to get there by killing mainliners."

Are you sure, Jonah? Lilith leaned in, trying to look him in the eye. *What if you could save someone you loved?*

Jonah said nothing, just stared out at the river.

Lilith tried again. *What if you could get revenge for your mother and father and little sister?*

"The people you're targeting had nothing to do with Thorn Hill," Jonah said. "You murdered a twelve-year-old girl at a Halloween party. How does that make you the good guys?"

Lilith shook her head. *Brendan told me about that. I asked around. It wasn't anyone in my Nightshade army.*

"You are *not* the Nightshade army," Jonah said through gritted teeth.

That's where you're wrong, Lilith said. *We are* all *the Nightshade army.* She brushed her forearm with her fingers. *You do have a Nightshade tattoo.*

Jonah was instantly suspicious. "Why is that important?"

It verifies that you are who you say you are.

"And how, exactly, do I know that you are who you say you are? You might be Brendan tricked out in a brand-new body."

My tattoo is long gone, along with my body, Lilith said, kicking her sneakered feet against the stones. *Guess you'll have to trust me.*

"Don't get your hopes up," Jonah said. "Anyway, if all mainliners have to take the blame for Thorn Hill, then you'll have to take the blame for the mainliner murders."

If I'm not mistaken, you're going to take the blame for the mainliner murders.

There was nothing to say to that, so Jonah didn't even try.

I'm curious about your abilities, Lilith said. *From what Brendan says, you're kind of a superman. You leap tall buildings with a single bound, you have the old X-ray vision, that kind of thing. Is that true?*

"Brendan wouldn't lie to you."

What else? Can you still read emotions?

Still? "Why should I tell you?"

We're trading information, Lilith said. *Clearly, you want something from me, or you wouldn't be here.*

She did have a point. "Fine. Yes, I can read emotions. I have super-acute senses as well: hearing, sight, smell, taste. I'm unusually strong, and I have a tremendously toxic touch.

So toxic I can kill someone who's already dead. That's every-thing that comes to mind at the moment."

Lilith nodded, as if this confirmed something.

"So," Jonah said, eager to move things along. "I hear you want to talk to me."

I hear you want to talk to me, Lilith countered.

"You wanted to talk to me first," Jonah said.

It's Gabriel I really need to speak with. Lilith stared straight ahead, chin raised, her jaw set.

"So you said."

Up to now, the only way to do that was through you. But that is changing. She spoke with conviction.

"Is it?"

As we're able to use bodies for longer periods, we develop more and more skill and control. More integration. With the help of blood magic, it won't be long before I'm able to speak mind-to-mind loudly enough for anyone to hear. Even someone without your abilities.

"How many mainliners do you have to kill to get there?"

Lilith's anger gushed over him. *The point is, I will speak with Gabriel, one way or another, whether you like it or not. It's just easier if we have a go-between.*

It took Jonah a moment to process that one. "Hang on; I'm not the problem," he said. "I've already talked to Gabriel."

Lilith leaned toward Jonah eagerly, hands on her denimed knees. *Really? You asked him? How did he react? What did he say?*

"He said no."

What? This time, Jonah had no trouble reading her disap-pointment and confusion. *You're sure you told him who it was?*

"I told him it was Lilith Greaves," Jonah said.

And he said . . . ?

"He said he remembered someone by that name, but that you couldn't be the same person. He said it was a hoax or a trap."

A hoax? A trap? Lilith stood, and paced back and forth. *Why would he think that? Why wouldn't he want to talk to me?* She whirled around to face Jonah. *What exactly did you tell him?*

"The truth," Jonah said. "I told him about your plans to kill mainliners, and to use blood magic to help Thorn Hill survivors. Don't you think that would be a little . . . off-putting?"

Lilith snorted. *To Gabriel Mandrake? You've got to be kidding. You really don't know him very well, do you?*

"Maybe not," Jonah said. "But I know him a hell of a lot better than I know you." He scrubbed both hands through his hair. "Like I said, I'm not the obstacle you think I am. At least I'm willing to listen. But maybe Gabriel's the smart one. He knows a lot more about you—and about Thorn Hill— than I do."

Oh, yes, Lilith said, her voice rich with bitter amusement. *He knows a lot more than you do. Clearly.*

"That's why I'm here. To learn. That's what I want from you."

Does Gabriel know you're here? Talking to me?

Jonah shook his head. "No. In fact, he really, really wants to prevent this. He'd rather see you dead. He has an entire team of slayers hunting you down."

Lilith flinched, as if she'd been struck. *Including you?*

Jonah shrugged, not wanting to get into it.

Did he say why?

"Not in so many words. I sort of assumed it was because

he's unhappy about the fact that you're murdering mainliners and we're getting the blame."

Lilith settled back onto the bench, shedding her agitation like a worn-out coat, replacing it with calculation. *Fine. What is it you want to know? Maybe we can make a deal.*

Jonah didn't want to bring Kenzie into the conversation. He didn't want Lilith to know just how desperate he was. "We're all dying," he said simply. "It's like our bodies are mortally wounded, and we're just killing time until we go down. I want to find a way to fix this, but I get the impression that Gabriel has given up on finding a cure. He just wants to do what he can to ease the pain while we go quietly into the night."

Of course he's given up on finding a cure, Lilith said, *because he has no idea where to start.*

"How could he? He wasn't there when it happened. And everyone who was there is dead, except for us—those who were children at the time. I have to think that there's a shade out there somewhere who knows the truth about Thorn Hill."

Unless you've killed him, Lilith said.

"Unless I've killed him." Jonah flexed his hands. "That's why I resigned as a slayer."

You resigned?

Misery rose into Jonah's throat like bile. "Well, I tried. I'm finding it's not that easy to stay out of the business."

Lilith hunched her shoulders. *Gabriel's probably on the wrong track.*

"You think *you're* on the right track? Using blood magic in order to possess hosts permanently?"

I don't have any other options, Lilith said, *being a shade, drift-ing from cadaver to cadaver, having no lab to work in.*

Jonah blinked at her. "Lab?"

I'm a sorcerer, Lilith said, *or at least I was. One of the best sorcerers of my time, if I say so myself.*

For some reason, that phrase rang in Jonah's ears. Famil-iar. It was something Jessamine Longbranch had said about Thorn Hill: *The best sorcerers of the age flocked there, because they knew they could source any botanicals they needed without the risk of anyone coming after them in Brazil.*

I'm a better sorcerer than Gabriel Mandrake will ever be, Lilith continued. *That's why he hired me.*

"He *hired* you? For what?"

But this was Lilith's story, and she wouldn't take direc-tion. *At least it started out as a business relationship,* she said, as if she were turning over memory stones, one at a time.

"It started as a business relationship," Jonah repeated "And turned into . . . ?" He stopped, then answered his own question. "You and Gabriel were more than partners. You were—"

We were lovers. Lilith stared out at the river. *Gabriel Mandrake was one of the most intensely charismatic men I've ever met. And there we were, in the steamy tropics, both devoted to the same cause. You can see how a girl might lose her head.* She rolled her eyes.

She rolled her eyes, Jonah thought. She actually rolled her eyes. It's true—they are getting damn good at steering these bodies around. Just for a moment, he allowed himself to imagine Kenzie in a new body, one that worked. For good.

Gabriel made it easy to make a bad decision.

Jonah wasn't particularly surprised. Women (and men) still obsessed about Gabriel Mandrake, even though he was a little frayed at the edges these days.

And so—wouldn't you think he'd be eager to see me again? Lilith said, as if to ask *Am I crazy?*

"You'd think," Jonah said. "Unless . . . did you have . . . some sort of a breakup?"

Lilith laughed. *You could say so. I died. He didn't.* She pointed a warning finger at Jonah. *I'm not conceding any ground, mind you. I'm still saying we shades are alive.*

Jonah turned this over in his mind. "Do you think Gabriel felt guilty because you died and he lived?"

No one saw it coming, Lilith said. *It was a bolt from the blue. Gabriel wasn't there a lot, anyway. He had a business to run on the outside. I don't know how he can blame himself for that.* She seemed distracted, though, talking to herself, trying to sort things out.

"We're not always logical when it comes to guilt and regret," Jonah said.

You're not the cold-blooded killer I took you for, she said, studying him.

"We're not here to talk about me," Jonah said. "Or at least I'm not. If you're such a great sorcerer, maybe you have a theory about what poisoned us. If we knew what was used, then maybe we could come up with a treatment. Gabriel's been trying for ten years."

Gabriel? He was all ink magic and tools. I was the expert when it came to . . . to . . . She sucked in a quick breath and looked up at Jonah, eyes wide and stricken. *He must think—he has to assume—oh my God. Look. I have to talk to him.* She pointed a shaking finger at Jonah. *You need to make that happen.*

"Why should I do that? If Gabriel doesn't want it?"

Because all this time he's been blaming me for what happened at Thorn Hill, Lilith said.

Jonah stared at her. "No, he doesn't. He blames wizards, just like everyone else. Except for wizards, who blame us."

He's wrong, Lilith whispered, as if she hadn't heard. *He is all kinds of wrong. It's no wonder he's been unable to develop any kind of treatment. The only thing worse than not knowing is thinking you know when you don't.*

Jonah decided to attack from a different angle. "You still haven't told me—what did Gabriel hire you for? Why did he need the best sorcerer of the age?"

I hate talking about Gabriel behind his back like this, Lilith said. *I want to speak with him face-to-face. That's my price.* She frowned. *You'd have to be there, of course, to interpret. Then you'll have the information you need to make a judgment about me and him and Thorn Hill. Can you make that happen?*

"I can make it happen," Jonah said. He had no doubt that he could. Somehow. "But how do I know you're not setting a trap?"

Lilith laughed. *A trap for whom? I've been trying to arrange a collaboration, or at least a truce. I assumed it was a lack of communication. And now I come to find out that Gabriel has been trying to kill me ever since he learned I existed. I'm the one who should be worried.* Then, maybe reading the suspicion on Jonah's face, she said, *Look, if I wanted the two of you dead, you would already be dead. You're a lot more valuable to me alive. Right now, you're the only means I have of communicating with the world, at least until I master physical speech.* She said this as though it was only a matter of time.

And maybe it was. That meant Jonah needed to make

this meeting happen sooner rather than later if he wanted to sit in.

"So. How do I get back in touch with you?" Jonah said.

Lilith thought a moment. *Remember the bridge where we first met?*

Jonah nodded. "The road bridge?"

Lilith shook her head. *The railroad bridge. Leave a message underneath, taped to the pillar, where nobody will see it. Tell me when and where you want to meet, and I will be there. It has to be on neutral ground. I can't risk coming onto Gabriel's turf.* She paused. *You think you can pull this off?*

"No problem," Jonah said, his mind working furiously. "But it may take a while to make it happen. In the meantime, I'll be spending a lot of time on the streets, walking around, acting as bait. Don't make contact unless I message you first. I've got to convince Gabriel that you've lost interest in me in order to break him out of his fortress." He stood. "I'll be in touch."

All right. She hesitated, as if debating whether to go on. *Just . . . be careful, Jonah.*

Jonah swung back to face her. "What do you mean by that?"

For one thing, I don't speak for all shades. Herding feral cats is easy compared to this. Many of them have been on the streets for ten years, doing their own thing, surviving any way they can. There's a lot of hostility out there toward Gabriel and his slayers. They can't understand why you're targeting us and not mainliners. She paused. *And you must know that it's not just shades that you need to worry about.*

"I know that," Jonah said, thinking of Rowan DeVries.

I don't know if you realize just how at risk you are, Lilith said. *Think about it. Whoever was behind Thorn Hill, anyone with secrets to protect—they don't want this meeting. I've proven hard to catch. So, what's the next best thing to having me dead?* She waited, and when Jonah shook his head, continued, *Having you dead, since you're the only one who can speak for us. You're the only one who hears our screams when we die.*

⊛ Chapter Eighteen ⊛
A Rock and a Hard Place

Nobody was home when Emma returned from practice. Leesha had driven Aunt Millisandra to her weekly mah-jong party. Emma felt mingled guilt and relief. She should be helping out more with Aunt Millie, and earning her keep. But it seemed like a good chance to think things through in blessed solitude.

Emma thought better on her feet, so she found herself prowling around the pink mansion. Worries prowled through her mind as well. Either Rowan DeVries was out there somewhere and might show up on her doorstep any time. Or he was dead, which raised a whole new set of questions. She liked Chief Childers; she was close to trusting him, but she couldn't help thinking that she was going to end up being blamed for crimes she never committed.

Eventually, her feet found their way back to her room, with nothing resolved. She spied Tyler's notebook on the bookshelf and pulled it down, settling onto the broad window seat. A piece of lined notebook paper was shoved into the front pocket. She pulled it out. On the outside was written *Open when I'm dead.*

This must have been here all along, and she hadn't noticed it. She unfolded it.

Emma—

Sonny Lee always said that good music always tells the truth. He was right about that. He was right about a lot of things, but I never listened. I haven't been the father or the man I should've been. I wasn't there when you needed me to be, but now that I know you, I realize that I was the one who lost out.

When you were a little girl, I thought I loved you, but I didn't even know what love was. You taught me, Emma Claire, when you came to stay with me. Not that I deserved it, but I thank you for that.

And now here you are, almost grown. I'm in your life when you least need me to be, when all I can do is bring trouble your way. I have a feeling that trouble will come, since there is no way I deserve to be your father.

I like to think that there's a little bit of me in you. a love of music and a stubborn streak a mile wide. But we're different, you and me, and I don't forget it. You're strong and you're tough and you tell the truth. You're a good person, Emma. I'm none of those things. I used to think that I was tough, but now I know that I'm the biggest coward that ever lived.

So. I am so very sorry. The truth is hard, but I'm going to tell it, now that I'm dead. You'll find it here if you want to look for it.

—Your father, Tyler.

Her mind spinning, Emma leafed through pages in plastic protectors, all written in Tyler's surprisingly neat hand. She recognized many of the songs; others were unfamiliar. A few of them seemed to be way outside Tyler's usual genre—bluegrass and ballads along with the blues.

But then, Tyler had been in and out of a lot of bands. It was no wonder he had a mixed playlist.

Music. Lyrics. Guitar tablature. Fetching the SG from its stand, she began working her way through the notebook, looking for the truth.

Some of these songs she'd been playing nearly all her life. "Ball and Chain." "I Just Wanna Make Love to You." "Parchman Farm Blues." "Malted Milk." On those, she didn't pay much attention to Tyler's notation, just went with her own style. But that allowed her mind to wander where she didn't want it to go.

When Emma looked for songs that were new to her, she found a divider that was labeled *No Lies: A Special Collection*. First in line, "Emma (Emmaline)," an old song by Hot Chocolate. Some, like "Stagger Lee" and "Frankie and Johnnie" and "In the Pines," she'd heard. Others were unfamiliar: "Rose Connelly." "The Daemon Lover." "The Banks of the Ohio." "Pretty Polly." "Lord Randall." "Silver Dagger." They weren't alphabetical. There was no logic to the order that Emma could see.

Another divider was labeled *Go On Back to Memphis*. It seemed to be a collection of songs with Memphis in their titles, or that referred to Memphis in the lyrics. "One Hundred Miles from Memphis." "Eighteen Miles from Memphis." "Mile Out of Memphis." "Back to Memphis." "That's How

I Got to Memphis." "Walking in Memphis." "Beale Street Blues." "Low Down Dirty Mean."

"What are you up to, Tyler?" Emma murmured. "You said you would tell me the truth. So, what is it? What are you trying to tell me? What is it about these songs?"

At least, working that problem took her mind off her worries.

She wished she could show it to Sonny Lee. Even though he couldn't read music, he was a genius when it came to guitar riffs, and he had forgotten more songs than Emma'd ever learned.

Who else could she talk to? And then she thought of someone.

Emma parked the van in a lot on Fourth Street, so nobody would see it and wonder where she was and what she was doing back at school so late at night.

She'd already pretty much decided that this was a stupid plan. Kenzie likely wouldn't even be able to talk to her. If she wanted to keep her mind off Thorn Hill, she shouldn't be going to visit him.

But sometimes you know you're working a stupid plan, but you just keep on keeping on. Lifting the SG in one hand, cradling Tyler's notebook in her other arm, she threaded her way down alleys and brick-paved streets, jogging past the busy restaurants on West Sixth. It was after ten, but there was still a line outside of the Keep. She hurried past Oxbow, her former home, and turned down St. Clair to the Steel Wool Building on West Tenth.

She buzzed up to Kenzie, and his voice came through

the speaker, sharp and anxious. "Emma? What happened? Is everything all right?"

He sounds wide-awake, she thought. "Um. Yeah, everything's fine. I—ah—I just wondered if you had a few minutes to look at some songs."

After a silence that sounded like surprise, Kenzie said, "You know my door is always open to you." Emma could hear the smile in his voice. "Harry, open the east door, ground level." There was a soft click as the lock disengaged.

Emma climbed the battered wooden stairs to the fourth floor and tiptoed down the dimly lit hallway to Kenzie's door. "I'm here," she said to the display outside.

"Harry, open the door."

Kenzie was sitting at his desk, headphones slid down around his neck, wearing jeans and a sweatshirt. Clearly, he was still up working. In fact, he looked better than he ever had, since Emma had come to the Anchorage.

"Emma?"

That was when she realized she'd been standing there, guitar case in one hand, staring at him. "Oh! I'm—I thought you might already be in bed."

"You thought I might be in bed, so you dropped in?" Kenzie grinned.

Emma took a step back, her face heating with embarrassment. "Well, not exactly, I mean, I heard you were going to bed earlier and earlier. . . ."

"Clearly, my reputation is in tatters, if you expected me to be in bed at"—Kenzie glanced at the display—"at ten fifteen." He waved her forward. "It's all right, even if I had been in bed, you are among the few people I am always willing to wake up for. As opposed to the legions of people I pretend to be asleep for."

She crossed to the desk, set the guitar on the floor, and pulled up a chair while Kenzie finished whatever he was working on. "I'm sorry, Kenzie, it's rude to just show up like you have nothing better to be—" She sucked in a breath of surprise. "You're using the keyboard!" she blurted.

Kenzie looked down at his hands and did a double-take. "It appears that I am." Lifting his hands, he examined them in mock amazement. "It's—it's like magic." There was new color in his cheeks, and his eyes were clear and focused.

"Don't you make fun of me," Emma said. "It's just—you look amazing."

"I *am* amazing," Kenzie said. Then he grew serious. "We tried a new medicine, and it seems to be working. For now, anyway." He paused a little awkwardly. "I'm glad you came. It's been a while since I've seen you."

It *had* been a while, she realized, and despite his bright-eyed appearance, there had been negative changes as well. Kenzie'd lost weight. The wall behind his bed was covered with padding, the floor with a thick rubber mat. A notebook computer was bolted to a desk designed to swing over the bed.

Kenzie followed her gaze. "Always knew I'd end up in a padded room sooner or later. It's to keep me from banging my head against the wall if I have a seizure. The price I pay for refusing to wear one of those helmets."

"They want you to wear a helmet?"

He snorted. "I refused. Interferes with the headphones. Anyway, have you ever had to deal with helmet hair? It's not pretty."

"I'm sorry I haven't been here lately. Now that I'm living in Trinity, it's just harder to get back here."

"Sounds inconvenient. I still don't get it. Were you tired of the shabby digs at Oxbow?"

"What? It's not—no," Emma said. "That's not it."

"Or were you tired of living under Gabriel's thumb?" Kenzie shook his head, answering his own question. "No. Wait, don't tell me—could it have to do with my brother?"

"I can't talk about Jonah," Emma said. "I'm sorry. I just—"

"That's the problem, isn't it?" Kenzie said briskly. "People aren't talking to each other. Keeping secrets. Could you get me a bottle of tea from the fridge? If there's anything there you want, help yourself. There's some chips and like that in the cabinet."

Emma returned with the bottle of tea, an orange soda, and a large bag of barbecue chips. When she handed him the bag, he ripped it open and shook a few into his hand.

"Looks like you're off your special diet."

"Yeah," Kenzie said. "People don't much care what I eat these days. It's great." He paused. "Where are you staying in Trinity?"

"I'm staying with this girl. Leesha Middleton. She's a wizard."

"How'd you meet her?"

Emma tried to remember. "I think I first met her at that gig we did at McCauley's. She was flirting with your brother."

"As one does," Kenzie said.

"I ran into her again at Grace Moss's memorial service. I told her I wanted to try living in Trinity. Leesha offered to let me stay with her and help out with her aunt. I—to be honest,

I wanted to spend some time with mainliners and see what they're like."

"So what did you learn?" Kenzie took a swig of tea. "Are they the low-down scum you imagined?"

"Worse than that, some of them." Emma rolled her eyes. "But Leesha's one of the good ones, I think. She lost someone she loved the last time mainliners went to war against each other. She really, really wants to prevent that from happening again. She's involved in the investigation into the murders at McCauley's, and I think that's a good thing. I think she really wants to get at the truth, whatever it is."

"Interesting," Kenzie said, as if filing that information away. "Now. You said you had some songs you wanted me to look over? Let's see what you got."

"My father left me this notebook full of songs, with lyrics, music, and guitar tablature. He really went to a lot of trouble to handwrite everything out. But the time signatures are messed up. Maybe he did it in a hurry, and it's just mistakes." She opened the binder to the *No Lies* section, pulled out "In the Pines," and held it out it to Kenzie. "Like this one. He knows how to read music—and write it, I guess. I just can't figure this thing out. It's a real mix of genres, everything from Delta blues—which I would expect—to traditional folk ballads to rock and roll."

Kenzie took the sheet and snapped it into a clipboard next to his monitor. "Harry," Kenzie said. "Task lighting." The light over his desk gradually brightened. He scanned the page, eyes moving rapidly. "Well, that's cheerful," he said. "*Hmm*. It would be easier for me to look for patterns if I scan it in. It doesn't have to be digitally readable. It's just easier for me to analyze that way. Harry can help."

"I guess I can do that," Emma said. "If I can find a scanner that will—"

"My aide can do it," Kenzie said, "if you're willing to leave it here for a few days. No charge. It'll give him something to do."

Emma fingered the cover of the binder. "Okay. Thanks."

"In the meantime, let's have us some music. Sing me some songs from the special collection."

"All right. What are you in the mood for?"

"Player's choice," Kenzie said. "Play me something you wouldn't expect to be in your father's repertoire."

"All right." Emma pulled her guitar onto her lap and riffled through the binder. "Um. This is called 'Lord Randall.'" Quickly, she scanned down through the lyrics. "Oh. Not this one."

"Why not?"

"It's a cheerful little ballad about this guy, Lord Randall, whose true love poisons him."

"Sing it," Kenzie said. "I don't mind. I've grown a really thick skin since Thorn Hill. To go with my scaly tail."

Emma blew out her breath and adjusted her capo.

"O, where ha' you been, Lord Randall, my son?
And where ha' you been, my handsome young man?"
"I have been at the greenwood; Mother, make my bed soon,
For I'm wearied wi' hunting, and fain wad lie down."

She sang it through to the end, then quieted the strings with her hand. "So, why would Tyler leave me a song like that? One that isn't even on his usual playlist. He even wrote me this note to go with it, like he didn't plan to be there to explain. But the note was really confusing, too. Was he trying to torment me or what?"

"Was he the type who would do that?"

"I would have said no," Emma said slowly. Tyler had wanted her to stay there, he'd seemed happy to have this second chance to be a father. During their brief time together, she'd genuinely come to like him, and she'd thought the feeling was mutual. "But then, I don't really know. I just met him back in the summer, and he was dead by October."

"Are they all about poisonings?"

Emma shook her head. "Here's one that's more up Tyler's alley—it's a blues song called 'Stagger Lee.'"

Stagger Lee was a bully man, and everybody knowed
When they saw Stagger Lee coming to give Stagger Lee the road.
Oh, that man, bad man, Stagger Lee.
Stagger Lee started out, he gave his wife his hand,
Good-bye, darlin', I'm going to kill a man.
Oh, that man, bad man, Stagger Lee.

"So," Kenzie said, when she'd finished, "are they all about murder or good love gone bad?"

"In case you haven't noticed, just about *every* song is about love gone bad," Emma said. "Every popular song, that is. Even the unpopular ones."

"Why do you suppose that is?" Kenzie said. "Doesn't true love ever win out?"

Emma shrugged. "Guess that's why they call it the blues. Here's another one that's not on Tyler's usual playlist. It's a variation on a traditional ballad." Propping the binder against Kenzie's knee, she began to sing.

"Oh, Polly, Pretty Polly, come go along with me
Polly, Pretty Polly, come go along with me
Before we get married some pleasures to see."

"Oh, Willie, Little Willie, I'm afraid of your ways
Willie, Little Willie, I'm afraid of your ways
The way you've been rambling you'll lead me astray."

"Oh, Polly, Pretty Polly, your guess is about right
Polly, Pretty Polly, your guess is about right
I dug on your grave the biggest part of last night."

Emma stopped singing when she noticed that Kenzie was in the throes of a silent laughter convulsion.

"Hey! Stop that!" Emma said, her voice edged with exasperation. "Have a little respect."

Kenzie could scarcely speak, incapacitated with mirth. "His name is 'Little Willie'? Or is that just Polly's nickname for him? Does that go to motive?"

And then Emma was laughing, too. "Cut them some slack, okay?" she said, when she could manage it. "This is a *traditional* ballad."

"Well, no wonder he's got the blues," Kenzie gasped. "Not only is he a jerk and a murderer, but—he has serious self-esteem problems."

"Well, she's not so bright either." When Kenzie looked puzzled, she rushed on, "Come on, now, you have to admit, that was a boneheaded move—to go off with him like that."

"She was in love, all right? People who are in love sometimes do foolish things."

"She was *not* in love," Emma said. "He broke her heart
once, so why should she give him a second chance?"

After a brief silence, Kenzie said, "Don't you believe in
second chances?"

The room seemed a little colder, a little darker, as if a
shadow had passed over the sun.

"Sonny Lee always said, 'Fool me once, shame on you;
fool me twice, shame on me.' "

"Mmm," Kenzie said. He closed his eyes, as if thinking.
"All of the songs you've shared so far are about murder. Did
your father leave you a whole collection of murder ballads?"

"No, of course not!" Emma said, without thinking much
about it. Then she thought about it. "I mean, I don't think he
did." Scooping up the notebook, she began flipping through
it. "There's all kinds of songs in here—the songs, lyrics, and
tablature." She slowed down when she got to the *No Lies* section. "Except here. In this one place. The special collection.
There's all kinds of songs in different genres, but what they
have in common is . . . they all seem to be about murder."
She half whispered that last part, suddenly reminded of the
terrible burden of secrets she was carrying around. Had Tyler
intended it to be a jab about her mother? He'd once told her
that she made poisons for a syndicate of assassins known as
the Black Rose, run by Rowan DeVries's father.

And yet . . . he'd also defended her mother, said she had
no choice but to work for the powerful wizards. Was this
what he meant when he said he was a coward?

Just then, there was a knock at the door and Kenzie's

computer awoke, displaying a view of the corridor outside.

It was Jonah, head down, hands shoved into his jacket pockets. Emma's heart did its usual Jonah Kinlock shimmy.

"Harry, open the door," Kenzie said, as Emma said, "It's getting late, I'd better go."

The door opened, and there he was, in blue jeans, sweat-shirt, leather jacket on top, cheeks pinked up from the cold.

"Oh!" Jonah said, his eyes flicking from her to Kenzie. "Sorry I didn't call. I didn't know you had company." He took a step back, toward the door.

"I'd better go," Emma said, right as Kenzie said, "Harry, lock the door."

◌ CHAPTER NINETEEN ◌
SECRET LIVES

Emma shot to her feet, nearly banging her head on the IV pole next to Kenzie's bed. She stood there like *she* was the guilty person, her guitar dangling from one hand. Jonah breathed in her scent, breathing out with regret. The last thing he wanted to do was break up this jam session or whatever it was. Kenzie was lit up, more animated than he'd been in a long while. The fact that he was awake, completely dressed, and out of bed at his desk at this hour spoke volumes.

Emma and Kenzie looked like musical coconspirators of the very best kind.

"I was just going," Emma said, turning, squatting, and settling the SG back into its case.

"Don't leave on my account," Jonah said. "I'll come back another time if my being here makes you uncomfortable."

"No, it's not that," Emma said. "It's just that I've got to drive back to Trinity, and then get up early, and—"

"You don't have to drive back, you know," Kenzie said. When they both turned to look at him, he added, "Just trying to help. Like in the movies, where the magical disabled brother helps the main characters see that they were right for each other all along."

Jonah glared at his brother. There was a sarcasm price to be paid for a healthier Kenzie Kinlock. "Look, I can tell there's no talking to you tonight. I have a killer headache. If it's all right, I'll just help myself to some drugs and go on home."

Jonah went into Kenzie's bathroom and examined himself in the mirror. He looked like hell. He sluiced water over his face and was rummaging in the medicine cabinet when he heard Emma say in a whisper, "Drugs? I didn't think he—?"

"Ibuprofen," Kenzie said. "If it's really bad, he might do a cocktail of naproxen, ibuprofen, and acetaminophen."

Emma snorted with laughter.

"He has a high pain threshold. I've seen him come in here covered in contusions, with wounds and broken bones, and he's like, 'Could you give me *three* ibuprofen this time?'"

"Wounds?" Emma said, her voice low and strained. "Broken bones? What are you talking about?"

"Ow!" Jonah banged his head on the door of the medicine cabinet.

Kenzie made no attempt to lower his voice. "You don't know? Jonah has a secret life. See, he's a paranormal assassin, called a shadeslayer, and he hunts the undead for an organization known as Nightshade. Ask him. He'll tell you all about it."

"Kenzie! Shut up!" Jonah charged back out of the bathroom to confront his brother.

"Shhh." Kenzie flapped his hands in a shushing gesture. "Don't shout. Fragile people are trying to sleep all around us, you know."

"What's wrong with you?" Jonah said, desperate to dam up the flood of revelations. "Why are you talking like that?"

Please, Kenzie, Jonah thought. Please, please, please back off from this. His life wasn't much, but it was all he had, this small safe space, walled in by secrets.

"Emma despises lies," Kenzie said. "I think it's time to tell her the truth, don't you?" He turned back to Emma. "See, the thing about Thorn Hill is that when people die they—"

"Kenzie!" Jonah pulled out his cell phone, pointing it at his brother like a weapon. "I think you're reacting to that new medication. You want me to call Natalie? She could give you something to calm you down and help you sleep."

"I don't need help sleeping," Kenzie snapped. "I've been sleeping too much lately. I don't want to spend what's left of my life sleeping. Either you tell Emma, or I will. If people would just talk to each other, maybe we could get at the truth."

Jonah and Kenzie glared at each other, the tension in the room thick enough to slice for a sandwich.

"You guys work it out," Emma said, looking as if she couldn't get out of there fast enough. "You let me know what you decide. Meanwhile, Kenzie, I'll leave the notebook with you. Let me know what you come up with." Sliding on her jacket, and scooping up her guitar, she headed for the door. "Good night, Kinlocks."

Jonah heard the *click* as his brother unlocked the door.

"Natalie's in on it, too," Kenzie called after her. "And Rudy. And Alison. It's a worldwide network. They're like vigilante heroes, fighting demons, and nobody knows."

Not heroes, Jonah thought, as Emma walked out the door. We're anything but heroes.

"Go after her," Kenzie growled. "Tell her the truth. My work is done here. I'm going to bed."

For a moment, Jonah wavered, shifting from foot to foot. Then he charged out the door after her.

Emma was halfway to the elevator. When she heard Jonah coming, she spun to face him, her guitar a barrier between them.

Jonah became acutely aware that he and Emma were, effectively, alone. Even here, in a public hallway, their aloneness crouched like a feral beast, ready to spring.

Emma must have felt it, too, because she backed up another step. "I'm sorry I kept your brother up so late," she said. "He's been a lot of help to me already. He's—he's just such a genius with music."

"I know," Jonah said.

"He looks great," Emma said. "Like a different person. When I got here he was using his keyboard!"

Jonah blinked at her. "He was? But—"

"And me, I'm thinking, whatever this new medicine is, it's working." Emma swallowed hard. "But, then, at the end there, what was that all about?"

All at once, it seemed like too much of a betrayal to continue to pretend that his brother was delirious, hallucinating, not in his right mind. Lying when he was telling the truth. Maybe Kenzie was right—maybe secrets were more the problem than a solution. Maybe Kenzie was the only clearheaded person in the room.

And yet—he couldn't suppress a twinge of fear that if he told the truth, he'd never see Emma again. Never hear her music again. Their musical connection was the closest he'd ever come to slaking his thirst for a human touch.

"Kenzie isn't confused," Jonah said before he thought too much on it. "I shouldn't have said that. He's telling the truth. He always does, whether I like it or not."

"He's telling the truth?" Emma said. "What do you mean? About what?"

"My secret life." And then, in a rush, he added, "I can't really talk about it, okay? That's why it's secret."

Emma's eyes narrowed. "Does it have to do with why my father died? Or what happened on Halloween?"

Jonah considered this, then shook his head. "No, not . . . not directly, anyway."

"You shouldn't have to study on it that long if you're telling the truth." Her eyes narrowed. "Is what you're doing illegal? Is the Anchorage a cover for a—a criminal enterprise?"

"I told you. I can't talk about it. Whether it's illegal or not is a matter of perspective. That's all I can say."

"Hmph," Emma said, sending a clear message: *I don't trust you.* "Well, you keep your secrets, I'll keep mine. Like I said, I've got to go now."

"I'll walk you to your car," Jonah said.

Emma shook her head. "No, thank you," she said. "I think I'm safer on my own."

As Jonah watched her walk away, he couldn't help thinking she was probably right.

☙ CHAPTER TWENTY ☙
STREET-WALKING MAN

"We know they're out there," Alison said, her voice low and frustrated. "It's like I can smell them."

"Really?" Jonah said. "I used to be able to smell them, and now I can't."

"So you say." Alison slumped down in her chair, resting her boots on the table, arms folded across her chest. She studied Jonah through narrowed eyes. "Why aren't they hitting on you? What's wrong with you?"

"Let up on Jonah, Al," Natalie said. "He doesn't work for you. You sound like he's your streetwalker and you're his pimp."

"Well, if he's not going to riff shades anymore, then he has to pitch in somehow," Alison said.

"Oh, I don't know," Charlie said, gazing up at the ceiling. "Seems like Jonah's earned a rest, based on his lifetime kill count. And when you look at his shiv-to-kill ratio, I think you'll find that—"

"Shut up, Charlie," Alison said, flushing. Charlie was referring to an old point of competition between them: the magical daggers known as shivs were complicated and time-consuming to make, and so it was important to make them count when it came to riffs. It was a number that Alison tracked closely. Or used to.

It was yet another debriefing after yet another unsuccessful hunt for Lilith. Finding and killing the leader of the shades had become a kind of obsession for Gabriel. He'd pulled in slayers from around the world to play this cat and mouse game with his ex. Meanwhile, it seemed shades everywhere else could do as they pleased. So much for protecting the public.

Jonah's role as bait had pulled him back into the fold of operations. Maybe not a full-fledged role—he suspected that there were meetings he was not invited to. But he attended the debriefings at least, where their failure to find Lilith was somehow Jonah's fault. At least Alison seemed to think so.

Gabriel had been watching this exchange, his lashless brown eyes flicking from one person to another. Now they fastened on Jonah. "What do you think, Jonah? Do we need to change strategies?"

Jonah covered his surprise. Gabriel hadn't been interested in Jonah's opinion on anything lately. But he was ready with an answer. He'd been working on a plan for several days.

"If you mean would I like to stop walking around downtown all night, the answer is yes," Jonah said. "I'm on a first-name basis with every mugger, sex worker, and homeless person in the city of Cleveland. I've met every police officer on the night shift, too—did you know there's a curfew for under-eighteens?" Jonah lifted an eyebrow.

"We all appreciate the effort you've put forth," Gabriel

said, dismissing it with a flick of his hand. "Any theory as to why Lilith hasn't made contact?"

"Two things come to mind," Jonah said. "First, we need to quit treating shades like they're stupid. Brendan Wu was always a smart kid—that's why he and Kenzie got along so well. He's just as smart now as he was then. He's the *same* person." Jonah paused to make sure Gabriel felt the hit. "Only now he can change appearances whenever he wants by commandeering another body. If you saw him, you'd never recognize him as Brendan or as a hosted shade. They're not going to have bones poking through flesh the way they have in the past—a lot of their hosts are in good condition. They credit blood magic. So when you go trailing me through the Flats, they'll see you coming. Why would they show up when they know it's a trap?"

"It seems like you know an awful lot about shades," Alison said, running a hand through her limp hair.

"What's the second thing?" Gabriel asked.

"You're the one they really want to talk to," Jonah said. "Not me. Oh, they'll want me there to serve as go-between, but it's not worth it for them to take the risk if you're not part of the conversation. The bottom line is, nobody's coming if you're not there, too."

"You expect *Gabriel* to serve as bait?" Mike said.

"Only if you want to catch Lilith," Jonah said, shrugging. "Otherwise, any warm body will do."

"That's too dangerous," Natalie said. "How do we know it isn't a trap? They may be out to kill him, not have a conversation."

"That may be," Jonah said. "We just have to be smarter than them. It's not like Gabriel can just walk around in the

Flats all night either, hoping to get noticed. We're going to have to plan a meeting on their turf." He kept his eyes on Gabriel as he said this, watching for a tell. "It's your call, Gabriel," he said. "But you asked for my opinion."

Gabriel picked up his cell phone, put it down again. Something he did when he was nervous.

"So—the idea is, we'll follow you," Mike said.

Jonah shook his head. "Like I said, they'll spot you. We have to set up a place ahead of time, a place that can be protected."

"And we'll be there waiting," Alison said, with a wicked smile.

Jonah nodded. "You'll be there waiting. And so, probably, will some of Lilith's people. But—here's the thing. If it collapses into a brawl, anything can happen. That puts Gabriel at risk, and it may not even result in a kill. So my idea is that you set up a perimeter, a kind of no-man's land, around the meeting place. No shades, no slayers inside the perimeter. Just Gabriel, Lilith, and me."

At this, panic flickered across Gabriel's face, chased by guilt and anger. Jonah wouldn't have seen it if he hadn't been watching him closely, if he couldn't sense his emotions across the distance between them.

"I told you, Jonah," Gabriel said. "I can't imagine that a meeting with this person—whoever she is—would serve any purpose. I want this put to rest. Now." His voice shook.

"That's the idea," Jonah said. "As soon as we're all together, I'll make the kill. You know that's what I'm good at." He extended his gloved hands and smiled into Gabriel's eyes, mustering all of the persuasive power at his command.

Alison's voice broke in. "Why do *you* get to make the

kill? I thought you were out of operations. All of a sudden you've grown a spine?"

"Do you think I *want* this?" Jonah looked around the circle, his gaze lingering on every face. "I tried to retire, remember? But it has to be me. I have to be at the meeting, to serve as go-between, since I'm the only one who can communicate with them. If we try and bring anyone else, we'll spook them. Or Lilith will insist on bringing her army, and it turns into a melee." He paused. "Do you want this to be over or not?"

"Maybe the rest of us should retire," Alison muttered. "It's always down to Jonah anyway."

"Alison." Gabriel tilted his head forward, looking at her. She subsided back into her chair.

"Or," Jonah said, shrugging, "Gabriel can always handle the riff himself if he prefers." He wasn't entirely successful at keeping the snark out of his voice.

Gabriel locked eyes with Jonah for what seemed to be a long time. Somehow, it was like crossing swords in a sparring match. His gaze dropped to Jonah's hands. Stayed there. "Even if we wanted to arrange a meeting, how could we if they won't make contact?"

This was the tricky part. Jonah couldn't very well tell Gabriel he'd known how to contact Lilith all along.

"Maybe Jonah can walk around with a sandwich board, announcing the place and time," Alison said, unsmiling. "Just kidding," she added when Gabriel glared at her.

"I'll go hunting on my own," Jonah said. "I'll find someone who can pass the word along."

"Do you have a meeting place in mind?" Charlie asked. "Somewhere near here?"

"Are you familiar with the old railroad terminal?" Jonah asked. "It's that stone-and-brick building close by the Carter Road Bridge."

Heads nodded all around.

"Nobody's using it right now," Jonah said. "It's boarded up. It's kind of creepy inside, but it's more or less on neutral ground."

Gabriel sighed, seeming resigned to the plan. "Let's do it," he said to Jonah. "Set it up."

When the meeting broke up, Alison fled the room like an uncaged bird through an open door. Jonah still managed to intercept her.

"What?" she growled, when he appeared in front of her.

"I . . . just wanted to say I'm sorry," Jonah said. "I feel like we're always at cross-purposes, and we shouldn't be. Whatever I do, I seem to get in your way."

"Don't waste the enchanter bit on me," Alison said, flicking her hand as if swatting a fly. "I am so over all of that."

This was going all wrong. "I wasn't—I didn't mean—"

"Aren't you supposed to be the smooth talker?" Alison laughed hoarsely. "That's pretty pathetic, to tell the truth."

Now Jonah looked at Alison. Really looked.

Like everyone else at the Anchorage, except maybe for Natalie, Jonah had developed the blinders that allowed him to dance on. That prevented him from seeing the gradual decline of everyone around him; that allowed him to pretend that they weren't all heading for the same tragic end. The band played on as the ship sank beneath them. Distracted by the magic of music, they would keep dancing until the waves closed over their heads.

Now he noticed that Alison's eyes were dull, her hair lank, her arms wrapped in gauze. That likely meant that her skin was blistering. That sometimes happened, but usually only toward the end.

She was skin and bones, wiry muscle and anger. But anger only takes you so far.

She's fading, Jonah thought, before his inner censor could intercept the thought. She's dying. And his heart broke, just a little. *I'm sorry, Alison. None of my gifts have done anybody any good.*

"Look," Jonah said, "we have so much history between us. We've been friends since—since before Thorn Hill. Nobody else knows me as well as you do."

"That's exactly right." Alison's smile twisted. "I knew everything about you, and I loved you anyway. Just as you were: the beautiful boy with the deadly touch, the assassin who carries his wounds on the inside. I was willing to take a chance on you. But you—you weren't willing to take a chance on me."

"It's not a matter of taking a chance on you. It's a matter of risk I'm not willing to take. I'm just trying to get through life without killing anyone else. And not lose all my friends in the process."

"Too late," Alison said. "You're a damn good singer and a decent guitarist, and you write kick-ass lyrics. I'm glad to have you in my band. Otherwise, there is absolutely nothing between us." And she walked away.

How loud did the music have to be to drown out her thoughts? So loud the bass line rattled around inside Emma's rib cage, buzzing in her breastbone. Adjusting her headphones, she stripped out the guitar, then stepped in with her own, layering sound on sound, resting the SG on her hipbone, foot tapping, Blind Lemon Jefferson's scratchy voice shouting in her ear.

The lights flickered, and Emma looked up to find Leesha standing in the doorway, her hand on the switch. Emma slid the headphones from her ears, letting them rest around her neck.

"I thought you had to study," Leesha said.

"I . . . ah . . . I *am* studying," Emma said lamely. "I study better with a guitar in my hand."

The fact was her mind had been occupied with Kenzie and Jonah, and Jonah's so-called secret life. When she'd asked if he was involved in something illegal, he'd said, *Whether it's illegal or not is a matter of perspective.*

What the hell did that mean? Last she'd looked, murder was illegal, right?

"What's the matter?" Leesha said in her usual blunt way. "You look like somebody died."

"I—I just realized that I wouldn't have heard Aunt Millie if she woke up," Emma said, with a twinge of guilt. "I made her a snack after I got home from school, and took her to work out. She's still napping, right?"

Leesha nodded. "Don't worry. She's fine." She wore a leather miniskirt, a heavy sweater, and a pair of expensive-looking red boots, and she'd spent time on her makeup. "Listen," she said, "Fitch and I are going to Cleveland to hear a band. Come with us."

"What about Aunt Millie?"

"I called Cathy, and she said she could come." Cathy was one of the aides who helped out with Millie. "And Barb will be here. She'll make dinner and keep an eye out."

Emma chewed on her lower lip. She had no business going out on the town with everything she had to do. On the other hand, all work and no play . . . Everybody needs a break sometimes. "What band?"

"I don't know," Leesha said vaguely. "We'll walk around until we find one we like."

"Where in Cleveland?"

"Do you want a written contract?" Leesha said, rolling her eyes. "Music samples before we go?"

Embarrassed, Emma returned her guitar to the stand and killed the power to the electronics. "Thanks for inviting me. I'd love to come. Only . . . I'll never get into most places unless it's an under-eighteen night. I don't want to hold you two up."

"Oh, honey," Leesha said, grinning. "You've never been clubbing with a wizard, have you? We'll get in, I guarantee it."

The band was called Rust Belt Chic, a local group Emma had heard about, but not seen in person before. The club, called Tonks, was small, and usually hard to get into on weekends. Leesha chatted up the bouncer, who introduced her to the manager, and in no time they were threading their way forward to some prime seats near the stage.

That's a useful gift to have, Emma thought, especially if you don't know anybody. She could get into most clubs in Memphis, those she wanted to get into anyway, but it was usually through the back door, with the band.

"Maybe we'll see some of your friends here," Leesha suggested as they settled into seats.

"They won't come here," Emma replied. That's why I picked this place, she thought.

It was a good pick. The place was loud enough so you didn't have to talk if you didn't want to. Leesha's gift had been enough to get them in, but Emma ordered soda, so that's what all three of them were having.

The band was easy to listen to at least, playing a mix of covers and original music. It was an older crowd, people who likely lived in the city, not tourists from the suburbs. That was what she was used to back in Memphis. For the first time, Emma's flannel shirt and jeans felt like camouflage.

Emma was glad to be with people who had nothing to do with Thorn Hill or the Black Rose or Nightshade. Leesha and Fitch got up to dance a few times. Fitch asked Emma to dance, too, but she shook her head, knowing he was just being kind.

"Want some more fries?" Leesha asked, pushing the basket toward Emma. Emma groped for fries without taking her eyes off the band. She could feel the pressure of Leesha's eyes on her.

The check arrived, and Leesha grabbed it.

"Here, let me," Fitch said, attempting to snatch it out of her hand.

"Let's split it," Emma said, digging in her jeans for her walking-around money.

"My treat," Leesha said. "The difference between me and you is that you two are earning the money you spend."

"I pay my own way," Emma said.

"You can get the next check if you want to support the vapid idleness of trust-fund youth."

"What?" It was like Leesha had started speaking a whole different language.

"Bottom line is, she's rich and she *wants* to do it," Fitch said. "*Go with it* is my advice. Otherwise, we'll be here all night. Speaking of, the band's going on break. Do you want to try to go somewhere else before closing time?"

"There's a place down in the Flats that's under new management," Emma said. "I hear they showcase a lot of local indie bands, and there's no cover. We've been thinking about pitching them a show. If we go down the hill and toward the Superior Bridge, I think it's right there. Want to try it?"

"This is your turf," Leesha said, shrugging. "Lead the way."

When they emerged onto the sidewalk, it was still snowing, and it was beginning to stick. Emma zipped up her thrift-shop coat and stuffed her hands in the side pockets.

Leesha struggled to navigate the icy pavement in her high-heeled boots. On the slope down into the Flats, Fitch grabbed her arm once to steady her when she almost went down on her butt.

Swearing, Leesha extended her hand and sprayed flame along the pavement, clearing it of ice. Winding her scarf tighter around her neck, she glowed brightly, giving off heat like a woodstove.

It's not like *your* shoes are all that practical, Emma thought, looking down at her sneakers. Only Fitch seemed ready for bad weather. He wore military-style lace-ups with heavy soles.

There were lots of people on the streets up in the Warehouse District, but not so many down in the Flats, especially on this side of the river, where there weren't many restaurants and bars. At the foot of the hill, they turned left onto a walkway through a little park in the elbow of the river.

"Where was the Montessori incident?" Fitch asked. "Wasn't it close to here?"

Leesha pointed. "The high-level bridges are blocking the view, but it's over that way."

"You're not worried that this might be a zombie hang-out?" Fitch asked, grinning.

Leesha shook snow from her hair, tightening her lips in annoyance. "Lightning doesn't strike twice in the same place."

"Actually, it does," Fitch said. "Studies show that a place that has seen one lightning strike—"

"Shut up, Harvard," Leesha said, scowling. "Anyway, it's been a long time since I was in preschool." She seemed nervous, though, hunching her shoulders and shivering, or maybe she was just cold. When the alarm clanged on the Carter Road lift bridge, Leesha nearly jumped into the river.

"That's just the lift bridge alarm," Emma said. "That's to let drivers know the bridge is being raised to let a boat through." Taking a breath, she rushed on. "Look, we don't have to go down there if you don't want to. Let's just go back up to the district and call it a night. I don't mean to drag you around to every biker dive in downtown."

"Who says I don't want to?" Leesha said, trudging on. "A biker bar sounds like the perfect end to a perfect evening. And I'm totally dressed for it."

Leesha's nerves were catching, though. Emma slid her hand inside her T-shirt, and closed it over her mother's amulet. She didn't want to admit that the hairs on the back of her neck were already standing at attention, and her heart was thudding in her chest. She was used to walking the streets of Memphis, where you'd be all right if you knew where not to go and just used common sense. The magical world was a lot scarier.

Leaving the park, they turned down another street, passing under the Superior Bridge. Emma hadn't really walked down this way before. The area seemed desolate, deserted, lined with parking lots, marine businesses, and one or two skanky-looking clubs. The kind you didn't walk into without knowing who was there waiting.

When Emma looked back at the bridge, she thought she saw movement underneath, between the bridge pillars and the river.

Leesha gripped Emma's arm, and Emma felt the sting of power through her jacket. "Did you see something? I thought I saw something moving."

"Probably just somebody settling in for the night," Emma said. "The bridge pillars can be good shelter when you don't have a place to stay."

"Oh," Leesha said, with forced humor, "I thought maybe it was trolls."

Emma was rapidly losing confidence in her sense of direction. If there were a club near there, they should be seeing people on the street or hearing some music.

But something about it didn't smell right. In fact, something smelled like rotting flesh.

"Emma!"

Emma swung around.

"You know what, this is creeping me out," Leesha said, her teeth chattering. "Let's get out of here."

Emma heard a sound, like dragging footsteps, coming from the direction of the Superior Bridge. She turned in time to see a mob of people pouring out from under the bridge, coming straight for them. As they got closer, the stench of decay washed over her, and she could see their pallid skin, ragged clothes, and uneven gait. Some had bones poking through their flesh. Others were actually missing parts.

Emma stood frozen, one hand covering her mouth, her breath coming in gasps.

"Emma!" Leesha gripped her arm, which broke the spell. "What are they? I—I've seen them before. In London."

"You think *I* know what they are?" Emma growled.

Leesha set her feet, as if she planned to take them on, but Fitch grabbed hold of her arm. "Come on! We've had too many dead heroes. Being a coward increases your odds of survival—that's my motto. I'm counting on being faster than them."

And so they all ran, away from the underpass. Fortunately, they *were* faster than those chasing them, and they opened a little distance between them.

"They're still coming," Emma gasped. "We have to get back across the river. There's no place to go over here."

So they took their first right, back toward the water. That's when Emma became aware of the bridge alarm, clanging in her ears.

"Damn!" Fitch said, losing some speed. "The bridge is open."

This street crossed the river here on a red metal swing bridge. But the freighter they'd seen earlier had just passed through the channel, and the bridge had swung open to allow it through. Lights were flashing, and a wooden arm blocked the road.

"I guess we're going into the river," Leesha said, looking down at her leather skirt regretfully.

"Not me," Emma said. "I'll take my chances with them." She jerked a thumb over her shoulder.

"Don't worry," Fitch said. "The water's actually pretty clean these days. The last time it caught fire was way before I was born."

"That's not the problem," Emma said. "I can't swim."

"How'd you like to learn?" Fitch said grimly as they reached the end of the pavement. "Now would be a good time."

Instead, Emma stepped forward, waving her arms at the oncoming horde. "Go back!" she yelled. "We don't want to hurt you."

"Not the message to send to zombies," Fitch muttered. "Don't listen to her!" he shouted. "We *will* hurt you if you come any closer!" He looked around for possible weapons.

An old wooden pallet leaned up against a nearby building. Fitch grabbed it and smashed it against a telephone pole, ripping free several jagged wooden pieces. He charged forward, swinging, hitting the corpse in the lead in the side of the head. It was a hard blow. It splintered Fitch's weapon, and made a visible dent in the creature's skull. It still came on.

"They're not going to stop," Emma whispered in disbelief.

Emma bent and scooped up several chunks of broken brick. She aimed, threw hard. She had strong arms from years of sanding and hauling wood around. She winged one of the creatures, nearly spinning him around. His arm dangled, useless at his side. But it was as if he didn't feel it. She shouldn't have worried about hurting them—she'd be lucky to get their attention, let alone stop them.

"It's like they don't feel pain," Fitch said.

"Get back," Leesha said. "I'm on this." Stripping off her high-heeled boots, she stepped in front of them. Planting her feet, she sent flames rocketing into the leading edge of the small army. They didn't even break stride. She extended her hand and spoke some kind of charm. Nothing. They kept coming, the smell of decay and charred flesh growing stronger and stronger. One of them was carrying something that glittered under the streetlights. A knife?

No. A broken bottle.

By then, they were nearly on top of Leesha, reaching for her with eager hands. Fitch barreled into the nearest shade, bowling him over, but then one of his companions swung a baseball bat, sending Fitch flying.

Howling with rage, Leesha blasted a crater in the roadway ahead of them. The ones in the lead managed to stumble to a stop, but the ones behind ran into them, toppling into the hole. Blessedly, that slowed them up long enough for Fitch to get back on his feet.

Already, though, Emma could see heads appear on the near side of the pothole, fingers clutching at the pavement as they boosted themselves up and over.

"The bridge is swinging back," Emma said, pointing.

And, indeed, with a screech of metal on metal, the bridge was swinging back into place. But the zombie posse would be on top of them before it reached the shore.

"Get behind me," Leesha said, facing the onrushing cadavers. "I'll keep them from coming any closer." She sent blast after blast of flame at them.

Emma breathed in the stench of burning flesh, but Leesha's magic just seemed to spur them forward.

Leesha went back to blowing holes in the pavement, which at least slowed them down. They toppled in, climbed out, came on. She hardened the air into a shimmering barrier, but they crashed right through.

"Come on, Leesha!" Fitch shouted. "Give it up. Into the river."

Emma backed away from the edge, worried that Fitch would just toss her in. Then a flicker of movement caught her eye, high up on the Superior Bridge.

"Look out! Now they're coming down from the high bridge!" she shouted.

A tall, black-clad figure dropped to the ground just in front of them. Fitch waded in, swinging his makeshift weapon, but the newcomer sliced it off with a wicked-looking sword, leaving Fitch holding nothing but a stub of wood in his fist. The swordsman threw up a leather-clad arm to block a blow from Fitch's spare club.

"Stop it!" he hissed. "I'm on your side. Sort of." He pointed at Emma. "Her side, anyway." When Fitch kept gaping at him, he added, impatiently, "I'm Jonah Kinlock. We met on Halloween, remember?"

It *was* Jonah, leather-clad as usual, but bareheaded, his hair tumbled by the wind off the lake.

He looked around, ripped an iron bar from the bridge chassis, and thrust it at Fitch. "This will work better for you. If you're going to swing at them, use this, and aim for their legs. They don't feel pain, but break their legs, and they'll stay put."

Fitch weighed the iron bar in his hands, stared at the place Jonah had ripped it from, then back at Jonah. Adjusting his grip on the weapon, he nodded.

Emma stuck out her hand, palm up. "Where's mine?"

Jonah hesitated, then ripped off another jagged piece. Their eyes met, and Emma could see the pain in his eyes, a kind of bleak defiance on his beautiful face. "These are strictly for defense," he said. "Let me handle this. This is what I do."

"Jonah!" Emma pointed to where the shades had all but surrounded Leesha. She was standing on an island, ringed by cratered pavement.

Jonah swore. "She's the one they want. She shouldn't have come down here." Planting a hand on Emma's shoulder, he turned her back toward the river. "Stay here, wait for the bridge, and get across when you can. Don't wait for us."

Moving impossibly fast, he plunged into the crowd of shades, mowing them down like a scythe through a wheat field, wielding his massive sword like a surgeon, miraculously managing to avoid beheading Leesha in the process. Bones and body parts went flying, pinging against the bridge supports, splashing into the river.

Emma was horrified and transfixed at the same time. She was watching Jonah Kinlock doing what he did best. There was a certain macabre beauty in watching form and function wedded together. In Jonah's case, a dance of beauty and death.

Emma sagged against the bridge pillar, her makeshift dinner threatening to come back up. *This is what I do*, he'd said. This is his life, she thought. But were the walking dead his allies or enemies?

Tearing her eyes away from Jonah Kinlock, she looked up, away from the massacre on the riverbank. And that's when Emma saw them—something like angels emerging from some of the splintered corpses. They were shimmering, beautiful. Creatures of light.

"Oh," she breathed, reaching a hand out as if she could touch them.

Jonah paid no attention to them as they fled. He had his hands full as it was. Somehow he managed to extract Leesha from the melee, giving her a hard push toward the riverbank. She was stumbling, bleeding, obviously injured. Emma ran forward, and she and Fitch each took an arm, practically carrying her to the water's edge.

Emma looked back.

It seemed that more and more of the walking dead were appearing, as if springing out of the ground, closing in on Jonah from all directions.

"Jonah!" Fitch shouted. Emma looked up in time to see Jonah disappear under a pile of bodies. Then Fitch streaked past Emma, howling and swinging his iron bar like a Scottish warrior in mismatched plaid.

Fitch took directions well. His weapon swept through the edge of the zombie mob at knee-level, toppling them like bowling pins. Emma followed close on his heels, unsure if she could do what needed doing but unable to stand and watch.

Then, as if by magic, Jonah reappeared, forcing his way through the crowd, a blur of motion and glittering steel.

"I told you to get across the river!" he shouted, herding Emma and Fitch ahead of him, just as the bridge deck finally snapped into place and pavement met pavement.

Jonah waited until Fitch and Emma had crossed onto the bridge deck, supporting Leesha between them.

Once they'd crossed over, Jonah slammed into the near end of the bridge. At first, Emma thought he'd somehow run into it by accident, but, no, he hit it with such force that it broke connection with the land and swung back out into the river, tethered only to the pivot on the far side. All at once, there were ten yards of rippling black water between the shades and them.

"How did he do that?" Fitch whispered.

Shades spilled into the gap, splashing into the river. Jonah lay on his back on the deck of the bridge, gasping.

Emma recalled what Kenzie had said: *I've seen him come in here covered in contusions, with wounds and broken bones, and he's like, "Could you give me three ibuprofen this time?"*

"What is he—Superman?" Fitch whispered, looking down at Jonah. "Zombie-hunter?"

Emma shook her head. "I don't know," she said. "But it's time I found out."

☙ CHAPTER TWENTY-TWO ❧
THE COOL THING ABOUT SUPERHEROES

The cool thing about actual superheroes, Jonah thought, is that they can just disappear after the big action scene. They aren't accountable to the public. They answer no questions, they tell no lies, they offer no excuses.

He'd walked back down to the old railroad bridge to leave a message for Lilith, taking a circuitous route. He'd come armed, up to and including Fragarach. He wasn't looking for trouble, but he wasn't stupid.

He was heading back to Oxbow, crossing the Superior Bridge, taking his usual path along the abandoned trolley level. He'd scanned the flats below, hoping not to spot any trouble.

That's when he'd seen Emma and the others clustered at the edge of the river, besieged by hosted shades.

Well, Emma, he thought, you said you wanted to know about my secret life. There you go.

Would he even have intervened if Emma hadn't been

there? Maybe. Probably. He didn't want the Anchorage to take the blame for more Weir murders. But now he had a situation.

Jonah disapproved of Gabriel's policy of secrecy, but he didn't especially want to explain Nightshade to the wizard investigating the preschool kidnapping and an Anawcir Harvard dropout. Jonah couldn't help wishing he had that wizard ability to wipe the mind clean. He could nudge, persuade, talk people into and out of trouble. But he didn't think he could make Leesha and Fitch forget being attacked by zombies.

Was this what Gabriel had been afraid of? He was such a control freak—did he fear losing control of this story, having somebody else rewrite the ending?

Now Leesha was hurt, Emma and Fitch looked shell-shocked, and once again, Jonah had left a major mess in the Flats. When they reached the other side of the river, he pulled on his gloves again.

Leesha was only half-conscious, bleeding in several places, in obvious pain, snarling at everyone who tried to help her. Not a good patient. Not a good patient at all.

Fitch had his phone in his hand. "I'll call 911," he said. He looked around, getting his bearings. "What do you call this—?"

"No!" Emma and Jonah said in unison.

Jonah stared at Emma. He was glad to have her support, but he was surprised just the same.

"I'll call Natalie," she said, pulling out her own phone. "She'll know what to do," she told Fitch, holding the phone up to her ear.

Jonah put his hands on Leesha's shoulders, leaning down

so he was looking into her face. The wizard's eyes were hazy with pain, and it radiated from her like a fever.

"I'm going to pick you up," he said. "We can go faster that way." Fighting down apprehension, he scooped her up. She cried out in pain as he put pressure on her battered body.

Fitch took a step toward them, his eyes meeting Jonah's. Jonah could read the warning and mistrust there. "Careful," he said.

"Fitch!" Leesha cried, looking around wildly. "Fitch! Is he—?"

"I'm here," he said, putting his hand on her arm. "Right here."

Jonah cradled Leesha close, using all of his soothing power, while keeping an iron grip around her to prevent any magical attacks. Or, God forbid, kissing. "You're all right," he said. "Everything is going to be all right. We're going to go see somebody who can help."

Leesha relaxed, smiled dreamily, and snuggled closer, even though they were both covered in blood and gore and who knows what.

Fitch scowled.

Emma put her phone away. "Natalie says to meet her at Oxbow, to come to the clinic on the first floor."

"Let's go," Jonah said, and started walking, back toward the Anchorage, passing under the high-level bridge. He didn't look back to see if the others were following—he knew that they would be.

Jonah knew Fitch didn't trust him, knew he must be spilling over with questions, but remarkably, the Anaweir boy bit them back and played vigilant wingman, his eyes searching the deserted streets around them, slapping his iron bar against his palm. Emma walked on Jonah's other side, as they passed back through the park and climbed the hill. She said nothing at all.

It was closing time, and as soon as they reached higher ground they encountered a policeman on foot patrol, keeping an eye on the action on the street as the bars closed. Fitch took a step forward, as if to complete the 911 call in person, but Jonah blocked his way.

Fortunately, the officer was focused on Leesha. "What the hell is going on here?" he asked, looking up at Jonah. "Is she all right?"

"*Shh,*" Jonah said, freeing one hand and putting his finger to his lips. "Please don't wake her up. She'll be better once she gets a little sleep. She should know by now that she can't stay out this late when she works Saturday mornings. One or two drinks, and she's done for the night."

"One or two drinks?" the officer said.

"Well," Jonah admitted, "I wasn't exactly counting. But she is a small person, as you can see."

"You're really taking her home?" the officer asked, directing the question at Emma.

"I'm her roommate," Emma said. "I'll make sure she gets home all right."

The officer still hesitated. Obviously, he wanted to make sure Leesha was in safe hands. "You got any ID?"

Great, Jonah thought. Now I'm going to get nabbed for curfew violation.

"Don't worry," he said, smiling at the officer, charm rolling off him like a stupefying vapor. "There's no problem here. No need for that. We just want to get her home, okay?"

Message: we may be covered with blood and gore, but we're not the kind of trouble you're looking for.

"Well, it seems to me that you kids—" The cop seemed to lose his train of thought as he basked in Jonah's sunshine. He hitched up his uniform trousers and cleared his throat. "See that you take her right home," the officer said. "I have kids of my own. You may think you're indestructible, but there are bad guys who hang out around here, waiting for nice kids like you."

"We'll remember that, sir," Jonah said. "Thank you." He watched the police officer until he turned at the corner and passed out of sight.

Fitch couldn't hold back any longer. "What the hell did you do to him? It was like he didn't even notice that you're covered in blood and—and—it reminded me of that scene in Star Wars, when Obi-Wan Kenobi—"

"He's an enchanter, remember?" Emma said. "At least he was to begin with. Before Thorn Hill."

So Fitch must know some history, Jonah thought. Even though he's Anaweir.

Fitch processed this as they walked along. "So, you're saying you're like a warrior crossed with an enchanter? Kind of like Jack is—"

"I'm a savant," Jonah said. "I'm not anything crossed with anything."

It was a few more minutes before Fitch spoke again.

"Do you want me to carry Leesha for a while?" Fitch asked. "Aren't you getting tired?"

Jonah shook his head. "I'm fine."

"I'll go get the car, then." Jonah could tell Fitch's engine was running, and he so wanted to shift into drive.

Jonah shook his head. "This will be faster, I promise."

Natalie was waiting for them in the clinic. Emma must have given her part of the story, because she was prepped and ready, wearing her bedside face. But her expression dissolved into surprise and irritation when Jonah showed up with Leesha and Fitch.

"What are they doing here?" she demanded, turning on Emma. "When you said someone was hurt, I thought you meant someone from—from the Anchorage. Not a—a—"

"You've treated wizards before," Jonah said. "You worked a whole summer in Trinity." He laid Leesha down on a gurney, feeling filthy in the pristine environment of the clinic. "They were attacked in the Flats, not far from here."

"But . . . why did you bring her *here?*" Natalie asked, making angry eyes at Jonah. "This is a trauma case. Why didn't you call 911, or take her over to Metro or Lutheran?"

"Because we know you'll do a better job," Jonah said. "And you won't tell anyone."

Natalie's lips tightened. "When you say 'anyone,' who exactly do you mean?"

"You know what," Fitch said, "it's a good thing for you I'm totally deaf, because otherwise my feelings would be hurt."

Natalie's expression said *I'll deal with you later, Jonah Kinlock.* Then she shifted into order-giving mode. "All three of you, wash up, over there. All the way to the elbows. On second thought, change out of those clothes. There are scrubs in the closet."

Jonah peeled off his jacket, wiped it off as best he could, then laid it out on the table in the linen room. Methodically, he pulled knives, shivs, daggers, and other weapons out of their hiding places. The clean weapons he dropped onto the jacket. The soiled ones he rinsed quickly in the laundry tub, toweling them off before adding them to the pile. Once he was finished, he rolled everything up in his jacket.

He felt the pressure of Emma's eyes as he pulled off his sweatshirt and T-shirt, stripping to the waist. He washed off as well as he could and pulled a scrub shirt over his head. This wasn't the first time he and Natalie had been in this situation. He was used to the drill.

Emma was the least slimed, so she was the first to return to Leesha's bedside. Natalie slapped a pair of scissors into her hand. "Cut away her clothing so we can see what's what."

Emma gingerly cut into Leesha's jacket, all the while looking like she'd rather be anywhere else. "You—you're not going to operate on her, are you?"

"That shouldn't be necessary," Natalie said briskly. "It's just a flesh wound, after all." She shot a look at Jonah. He rolled his eyes. It was an old joke between them. Anything less than a beheading was a "flesh wound."

Things moved quickly after that. Natalie started an IV, and she must have given Leesha something for the pain, because she relaxed under Natalie's hands and allowed her to work her magic. One sign that Leesha was feeling better was that she started in on Fitch.

"What were you thinking, Harvard, wading into that mob with nothing but an iron bar?" she said. "You could have been killed."

"I was testing a theory," Fitch said.

"*What?*"

"It's well known that creatures of faerie are sensitive to iron," Fitch said. "So I thought I'd see if the same applied to the walking dead." He paused, rubbed at a scratch on his face with the back of his hand. "Based on the data so far, I'm thinking no. Though a better research plan would've been to have some people with iron bars and others with—"

"Know this," Leesha said. "If you risk your life like that again, I will kill you."

Fitch considered this, brow furrowed. "Okay," he said at last. He cleared his throat. "Did you notice that magic doesn't seem to work on them either?"

"That's impossible," Leesha snapped. "Magic works on everyone."

Natalie and Jonah exchanged glances. Typical wizard arrogance, Jonah thought. No wonder Lilith and her crew have found them so easy to kill.

Jonah considered leaving. Natalie wouldn't be happy. But now the questions would be coming, thick and fast. He couldn't answer them if he wasn't here, right?

"Those—those things," Leesha said. "That's what attacked the Trinity Montessori kids. They were telling the truth, weren't they, when they said they were taken by zombies."

I so hate being right all the time, Jonah thought. "I have no idea what happened to those kids," he said. "I wasn't there."

Leesha ignored this. She was paler than Jonah remembered, but her gray eyes were bright and focused. "What are they? Where did they come from?"

"I hoped maybe you could tell me. I hate finishing fights that other people start."

"Don't try and tell me this is the first time you've encountered them," Leesha said.

"Leesha's right," Fitch said. "You seemed really familiar

with how to fight them. In fact, you kicked ass." Jonah heard notes of admiration and gratitude in his voice.

"He saved our lives," Emma said. "Give him a break." She was sitting on the window ledge, knees drawn up, her arms wrapped around them.

"He *did* save our lives," Leesha said, turning toward Emma. "But he knows more about those—about what attacked us—than he's telling." She refocused on Jonah. "What's your connection to them?"

"Don't make me sorry I intervened," Jonah said. "The proper response when somebody saves your butt is to say, 'Thank you.' And 'Is there any way I can repay you?' But that's mainliners for you."

"Mainliners?" Fitch repeated, raising an eyebrow.

"Not you," Jonah said. He pointed at Leesha. "Her. Look, I am not going to make up a story for your entertainment. You're just going to have to live with being rescued by a savant. End of story."

"You're not going to even try to explain this?" Fitch said.

"Nope. The best way to thank me is to be more careful in the future. You're not in Trinity anymore. Big cities can be dangerous." Jonah pulled out his phone, his usual means of escape. He scanned the screen. "Whoa! Look what time it is. I have to be somewhere."

"Hold on," Natalie said, storm clouds gathering. "You're not meaning to leave me here with—with—"

"My work is done," Jonah said. "I'm about the furthest thing from a healer there is." Scooping up his bundled weapons, he went out the door.

❧ CHAPTER TWENTY-THREE ❧
AIN'T SUPERSTITIOUS

Jonah should have known that Emma wouldn't let this slide one more time.

He was bone-weary and discouraged by the time he finally reached his room, his gut twisted into a knot. He wanted nothing more than to fling himself down on his bed and lose himself in sleep. He was so distracted that he was already unlocking his door when he realized that he wasn't alone. Hearing breathing behind him, tasting a familiar scent, he spun around and saw Emma sitting on the floor against the opposite wall, her arms wrapped around her knees, eyes glittering in the light from the ceiling fixture.

"Emma!" he said. "What are you doing here? I thought you'd gone back to Trinity."

"No," Emma said. "We need to talk." There was a hard resolve to her voice that said she wouldn't take no for an answer.

Jonah's stomach clenched tighter. "Look, it's been a long day, you've been through a lot, and we're both tired. I think we should—"

"We need to talk *right* now." Emma lifted her chin. "I'm going to dog you until you talk to me."

Reflexively, Jonah reverted to his usual prickly style. "Good luck keeping up with me, then," he said.

"I may be slower than you, but I'm persistent," she said. "I'll catch up with you eventually. And then you will talk to me."

Jonah snorted. "This always happens when I try and help somebody. Next time, I'll walk away."

Emma didn't budge.

Jonah eyed her, taking in her white-knuckled fists, the rigidity in her shoulders and arms, the stubborn set to her jaw, the anger smoldering deep within her. It would be easy enough to back into his room and shut the door on her. He was in no mood for a heart-to-heart. He'd kept these secrets so long that they seemed welded to his soul. And yet, at the same time, he was too tired to carry them around any longer.

So he took a step back, shouldering the door open wider. "Would you like to come in?"

Now she studied him, head tilted, suspicion clouding her eyes.

"Truth be told, I'm just as dangerous here in the hallway as I am in my room," Jonah said. "But it's your call."

"Is that supposed to make me feel better?" Emma said as she limped forward across the threshold.

"You're hurt," Jonah said. "You didn't say anything at Natalie's."

"She had a lot more important things to contend with,"

Emma said. Two steps into the room, she stopped dead. She swiveled, taking in the view. "Whoa," she muttered. "I thought my place was fancy."

Jonah followed her gaze. "You've really never been here?" he said.

She'd never been here, and they both knew it. It was the kind of thing neither one of them would have forgotten.

"I've never been invited," she said.

"I don't entertain much," Jonah said. He looked around himself, trying to see it through her eyes. The furnishings were simple, almost plain. Wood floors, a couch and two chairs around the fireplace, a flat-screen television, an unmade bed.

Once he'd noticed the bed, it couldn't be unnoticed. He wished he could make it disappear. It looked big and lonely, the setting for dreams that wouldn't come true. And the nightmares that Jonah lived all day long.

There walls were bare, with only the beautiful view to decorate the room. Nothing on the kitchen counter except a cradle for an MP3 player. The most important clues to who he was were the high-tech sound system and the wall-mounted speakers. If he moved out, there wouldn't be much to pack.

"The studio's through here, if you want to see it," Jonah said, crossing the room to the doorway on the far wall, then standing aside to let her precede him into the room.

Where the first room had been plain, nearly empty, this room was where he did most of his living. Guitars stood in stands everywhere—Jonah's idea of decorating. Also amplifiers, banjos, recording equipment, a piano, a workstation with a computer, cords snaking everywhere. Half-filled glasses and dirty plates spoke of late nights alone.

Emma closed her eyes, breathing in through her nose,

as if tasting the air. Then swayed a little, as if she'd taken a long, intoxicating drink of Jonah Kinlock and it had gone to her head. Or maybe it was the scent of wood and shellac and music in the air.

Jonah crossed to his weapons cabinet and keyed in a code to unlock the doors. He swung them wide, revealing his personal armory—a glittering array of knives, battle-axes, and swords of various sizes.

Jonah unrolled his bundle of weapons and plunked them down on a side table. Standing in front of the open doors of the armory, Jonah stowed his weapons as he had a hundred times before. It seemed oddly intimate, having her watching.

Shedding his baldric, he lifted Fragarach onto its stand. He ran a rag along the blade to remove any last vestiges of gore, then followed with an oiled cloth. He did the same with each weapon, carefully returning it to the rack, meaning to give them a more thorough cleaning when Emma wasn't standing there. Finally, he opened a small drawer, chose a clean pair of leather gloves, and pulled them on.

He sensed Emma at his elbow. She'd come up beside him and was looking over the array of weaponry.

Show, don't tell, Jonah thought. Isn't that what they always say?

"No assault rifles?" Emma said.

"They aren't as useful as you'd think," Jonah said. "Especially in the city. There's too much danger of hitting civilians who stray into the line of fire. I have used them in rural areas, because—"

"I'm kidding," she said. "You know that, right?"

Jonah cleared his throat. Emma always seemed to put him off balance. "I guess that's way too much information."

Shrugging, Emma reached out and tested Fragarach's edge with her thumb. Too late, Jonah gripped her wrist and yanked her hand back. Her thumb came away bloody.

"Well," Emma said, sucking at her thumb. "It sure keeps an edge."

"It has to be sharp," Jonah said, "to cut through flesh and bone." Closing the cabinet, he turned and put his back to it. Stand-up conversations were always briefer. "So," he said, "you wanted to talk?"

"Let's sit." Emma stalked back into the main living area, crossing to the gathering of furniture around the fireplace. She perched on the edge of the couch and waited, looking like someone who meant to wring him dry before she left.

Reluctantly, Jonah eased into one of the chairs. He felt vulnerable, defensive, on edge.

"I want to know exactly what happened earlier tonight, in the Flats," Emma said. "I want to know what you have to do with those—those—" She shuddered. "Are you fighting them or are you, like, allies?"

Jonah swallowed hard, as if he could swallow down the secrets he was about to spill. He was already second-guessing his decision to tell the truth. It didn't come easily to him. And once you tell the truth, the consequences roll out and there's no way to untell it.

"Just—just hear me out, Emma, before you react," Jonah said. "This might sound crazy." Maybe it would sound so crazy that she wouldn't believe him.

"Crazy like magical guilds, savants, and murderous wizards? That kind of crazy?"

Jonah considered this. "Maybe a little more crazy than that." Still . . . once you were able to entertain the notion of murderous wizards, that was kind of a gateway, right? Could a belief in shades be that far out of reach?

"It's got to do with the massacre at Thorn Hill," Jonah said. "As you know, thousands of people died, including all of the adults. Those who weren't killed right away were damaged magically. Many of those have died since. The thing is, the victims of Thorn Hill don't really die. They're immortal, in their way."

Immortal. He hadn't really thought of it like that before. Immortal sounded like a blessing instead of a curse. Like something you might wish for. Plan for. Hope for.

Emma took a deep breath, let it out slowly. Drummed her long fingers on the surface of the table between them. Emma's hands were restless, always moving, as if looking for something to do. Jonah loved Emma's hands. You could tell a lot about a person from their hands.

"What do you mean, immortal?" she said finally.

"After their bodies die, they persist as shades. Spirits without bodies. They wander around, trying to find a body to take shelter in."

"You mean—they possess people?"

"In a manner of speaking. They aren't strong enough to possess a live person. So. They look for corpses."

"And if they find one, they—"

"They occupy it for a while, until it decays so much that it's no good to them anymore. Then they look for another one, the fresher the better, because it will last longer, see. Or they kill someone, in which case the corpse is super fresh."

"So . . . you're saying those zombies—"

"Like I said, we call them shades," Jonah said, "because they are remnants of the people they used to be."

"Those *shades* we saw by the river—they died at Thorn Hill? They're like ghosts? Ghosts that can kill?"

Jonah shook his head. "Not exactly. Unhosted, they don't have any mass. They can't wield a weapon. Sometimes they can startle someone into falling, and like that. Shades are most dangerous when they have a host body, when they're physically capable of overpowering and killing their next host. That's their preference—because a new kill is going to last longer. If we deprive them of a body, they are forced to find a cadaver to inhabit—someone who's already dead."

"Why?" Emma blurted. Then added, "I mean, why do they want a body?"

"Having a body allows them to interact with the world," Jonah said, looking down at his hands. "I guess—I guess they miss that. And a body serves as a kind of armor, protecting them from people like me."

Emma rubbed her eyes with her thumb and forefinger, as if she'd heard one too many revelations. "Why do they need protection from you? Is that what Kenzie meant when he said you had a secret life?"

"Shades hunt humans, both mainliners and the Anaweir. I hunt shades—me and a few dozen other slayers."

"A few other what?"

"Shadeslayers. We're all Thorn Hill survivors. Gabriel established the Anchorage to serve the survivors of Thorn Hill—the magical mutants we call savants. He takes a broad view of survivors—he includes the living dead—the hundreds of shades still walking around. That's where Nightshade comes in." Jonah pushed back his sleeve, exposing the flower tattoo. "We're named after the flower. Or the poison."

Emma stared at Jonah's tattoo. "I do remember that.

Nearly everyone at Thorn Hill had those," she murmured, her face clouded with memory. "Except me. I always wondered why I was left out. But . . . that means you've had those tattoos since way before the massacre, right?"

Jonah shrugged. "I guess so. Everyone at the Anchorage has them, whether they're a part of Nightshade or not." When Emma opened her mouth to ask another question, Jonah hurried on. "Our mission is to protect survivors and the public and to put the shades to rest for good. So one thing we do is locate hosted shades and evict them from their bodies. Basically, by cutting the bodies into bits. That renders them less dangerous to the public. Temporarily, anyway."

"Why is that your job?"

"It's the only grace we can offer the undead. And at least it gives us a purpose other than waiting around to go crazy and die. It's an outlet for our most frustrated—and therefore dangerous—savants."

"And if they kill one of you—?"

"We become shades as well." Jonah paused, clearing his throat. "Don't get me wrong. We're all savants, but we're not all slayers. Everyone contributes what they can—healers, metalsmiths, tech experts."

"Is Natalie a part of this? Is that why she seemed so—so matter-of-fact about treating Leesha?"

Jonah gritted his teeth. "I'm not going to tell you who's in and out, besides me. But our metal shop forges most of the weapons we use, and our compounding pharmacy produces the medications we use in the dispensary. Much of our funding comes from our iron and gemstone mines in Brazil, plus what we raise through the annual auction and concert. This way, Gabriel doesn't have to submit to the kind of scrutiny charitable foundations require."

Emma's face sharpened again as she refocused on Jonah. "If they are really immortal spirits," she said, "then what's the point? If you destroy their bodies, don't they just hunt up a new one?"

"They *are* hard to kill," Jonah admitted. He extended his gloved hands, resting them palm-up on his knees, and looked Emma in the eyes. "For everyone but me."

Emma stared at his gloved hands as if fascinated and horrified at the same time. "You're the only one who can kill them?" she said, finally. "What does everybody else do, then—carry your bags? Sharpen your sword?"

"I'm the only one who can kill them painlessly," Jonah said. "The others use magicked blades called *shivs* on free shades." He licked his lips. "That death is extremely painful."

"What do you mean, 'free shades'?"

"Shades without bodies. See, it's impossible to kill a hosted shade. Like you said, they just go hunt up a new body. So, first we need to evict the shade from his host body. Then kill it with a shiv—or my hands."

Emma thought for a moment. "Why would the Wizard Guild use a poison that would kill some people and make others immortal?"

"You'll have to ask them. Maybe they messed up. Gabriel says that wizards aren't very good at poisons. I've been trying to answer those kinds of questions for years." He couldn't resist adding, "That's why I went to Tyler's. We'd figured out that he had a connection to Thorn Hill."

Emma's lips tightened. Clearly, she was not in the mood

to entertain excuses. "So . . . you're saying that if you and I . . . if we die, that's the way we end *up*?" Her voice cracked.

"I have to assume that's the case," Jonah said, "based on what's happened to the other Thorn Hill victims."

"How come nobody knows about these shades?" Emma demanded. "How come this isn't all over the newspapers?"

"Free shades can move easily from place to place, without being seen. Most operate in remote areas of the world, where killing goes on all the time anyway. What's one more murder during a civil war in a far-off country? And because they work alone, the killing is scattered and sporadic. Until recently. About six months ago, we found out that shades have been organizing under the command of a shade named Lilith Greaves. Now they're hunting in packs. That makes it harder for us to fight them, because there are a lot more of them than there are of us. We've lost several slayers because of that. And it's only going to get worse."

Emma sat very still, just looking at him, her emotions a chaotic jumble. Jonah couldn't tell whether she believed him or not, though what she'd witnessed in the Flats should go a long way toward convincing her. "Why haven't you at least told the other magical guilds about this so they can defend themselves? Or help you."

"Some of us would like to see that happen," Jonah said. "Myself included. What's stopped us is history. If mainliners found out about this, do you really think they'd partner with us? I don't. They've killed enough of us as it is."

"What are you talking about?"

"Just after Thorn Hill, mainliners slaughtered the most severely injured survivors. Some of us were visibly damaged, and we were all viewed as potentially dangerous mutants. They told themselves it was the merciful thing to do. It was also the expedient thing. If not for Gabriel"—Jonah took a quick breath—"if not for Gabriel, Kenzie would have been one of them. Gabriel has devoted his life to protecting us, to providing a haven where we can live, can go to school, can make a living. The last thing he wants is to have people know that savants turn into vengeful spirits when we die. And yet, he can't allow shades to prey on the unsuspecting public who had nothing to do with Thorn Hill. So we're committed to putting them to rest in the kindest way possible."

Jonah sighed. He was spouting canon again like a recruiting poster for slayers. How much of what he'd just said did he believe?

It's hard to lose ten years of indoctrination, he thought.

Emma's skeptical demeanor was fading. "Can they make more shades? You know, like vampires, spreading the infection by biting people?"

"I don't think anybody wants to make more of us," Jonah said. "And, no, it's not contagious. But each time a survivor dies, their numbers increase. We can't keep up."

"Won't you run out sooner or later?" she asked. "Then at least you wouldn't have to—"

"We won't run out until I'm dead, too," Jonah said. "And Nat and Rudy and Alison—everyone I care about. If I'm not the last to die, I guess someone will do the honors for me. If I am . . ." He shrugged. "Think about who these people are. My parents. My friends. My little sister. I put myself in their shoes because I have to. Isn't there anyone you loved—and lost—at Thorn Hill?"

Emma stared at him, understanding kindling in her brown eyes. She took a quick breath, then let it out slowly. Jonah felt the sharp rush of pain and guilt.

"Who?" Jonah asked.

"My mother," Emma whispered. "My mother died at Thorn Hill."

Jonah looked down at his hands. "Well, then. When you see these hosted shades, and you're thinking 'monster,' imagine your mother wandering the earth, desperate for a body, knowing she'll never breathe in the scent of a summer day, or hear music, or feel a human touch or a breeze on her skin."

"She loved music," Emma whispered. "It was the only thing that could raise her spirits when she was down." She paused. "And so—you're saying my mother is out there somewhere?"

Jonah inclined his head. "If she died at Thorn Hill, yes, I'm guessing she's out there somewhere. Or was, anyway."

⊛ CHAPTER TWENTY-FOUR ⊛
HARD LUCK BLUES

Emma felt like her head might explode, like there was too much new information getting stuffed in there — information that crowded up against what she'd always known to be true. And none of it matched up.

Images elbowed forward. Her mother working in the garden, dirt smudged on her nose. Smiling as Emma ripped away wrapping paper to find music recordings and sheet music. Waving good-bye in her white coat as she turned toward her lab, and Emma walked to school. Coming home late at night, tiptoeing into Emma's room, kissing her, and tucking in her covers.

Lying in bed, a cold rag on her forehead, the lights dimmed, while Emma played the piano.

And it hit her—maybe she *wasn't* an orphan. Not exactly. In the space of one conversation, Emma's mother had gone from dead to undead to maybe even alive. Maybe.

"If my mother is out there, then I could find her, right?"

she said eagerly, leaning toward Jonah. "Maybe the other shades could help me."

"That's just not possible," Jonah said. "It's not like they can look her up in a directory."

"But . . . maybe if I talked to them, they would remember something that would help." Jonah was still shaking his head, so Emma lifted her chin and said, "I want you to take me to meet them."

"You already met them," Jonah said. "You saw what happened. You don't want to go through that again. It's too risky. They're unpredictable. They're angry—and who can blame them?"

"I have to find a way," Emma said.

"Look," Jonah said. "My parents died at Thorn Hill, too, and my little sister. But I've been doing this job for seven years, and I've not heard a word about them. Shades are scattered all over the world, and they don't want to be found."

"Have you even *asked*? Have you even *looked*?"

Jonah shifted his gaze, and Emma knew—he hadn't asked. He hadn't looked.

"Why wouldn't you?"

Pain flickered across Jonah's face. "I was afraid of what I'd find."

"Well, I'm not like you. I'm not afraid."

"If you're not afraid, you should be."

It was like Jonah had given her back her mother, and then snatched her away again. "Maybe you've already killed her. Is that it? You've already killed her and you don't want me to find that out."

"It's possible," Jonah said, clenching and unclenching his fists. "Me or somebody else. But I just can't think about that."

"You just can't think about it." Fury boiled up inside Emma. "Who do you think you are? God? What gives you the right to decide whether my mother—whether all these people—should live or die? You criticize the mainliners for the same damn thing." Glaring up at the ceiling, she scrubbed her hands through her hair, trying to swallow the huge lump in her throat. Leaping from the couch, she kicked the wall, hard, leaving a major dent in the wallboard.

"Emma," Jonah said, his voice as sweet and potent as Southern Comfort. "Please. I have to hope that if I have riffed them, that means they're at peace now."

"What do you mean, 'riffed'?"

"It's our word for—for—"

"Murder?" Emma snorted. "Just because you use another word, that doesn't make it okay."

"I never said it was okay."

"Don't you realize that you may have killed the only person who might have the answers you need?"

Jonah stared at her, looking confused. "You mean your mother, or—"

"No!" she shouted, tears spilling over, streaking down her face. "Nobody in particular, just—just in general. And would you stop that *soothing* bullshit?"

"I'm sorry," Jonah said, stiff-backed. "I'm an empath. When I know you're in pain, it's just really hard for me not to try to make you feel better."

"I don't *want* to feel better! Which you'd know if you asked me." She took a breath. "As for the shades, maybe you should ask them what *they* want."

Jonah flinched. "I have," he said. "I'm the only one who can communicate with them mind-to-mind. They want to live, just like the rest of us, all right? They want to touch and taste and feel—to participate. But it comes at a cost. It was one thing when they stuck to possessing corpses. But now they're killing people, especially the gifted."

He paused. "When the gifted die, they release an energy called blood magic. It's like a tonic to shades. It makes it possible for them to possess a body for long periods of time. It—it also seems to be helpful to living savants. They justify it because of what was done to them. Should we stand by and let them slaughter a preschool class so they can go on living?"

"Of course not." Emma blotted at her eyes with the backs of her hands, her mind working furiously. "What about when they—when they don't have a body? They can't hurt me then, right?"

Jonah sighed. "Are you still talking about going looking for your mother?"

"You don't understand. She's all I have left."

"You'd never find her. An unhosted shade is nearly impossible to see, if you don't know what you're looking for. . . ."

"Why? What do they look like?"

Jonah sighed, sounding sad or frustrated or both. "Like a vapor, or—or a thickening of the air. Kind of the way a jellyfish looks in the ocean. Something you don't notice until it stings you."

"Oh," she said. "Right. I already saw some."

"Saw some what?"

"Free shades."

"That's unlikely," Jonah said. He took a quick breath, like he had more to say but thought better of it.

"I saw them," Emma said stubbornly. "Tonight. When

you—when you cut up the corpses, they'd float up. But I wouldn't call them jellyfish. They were like shimmering spirits. Or—or angels."

Jonah stared at her. "I don't know what you saw, but—anyway." He waved the argument away, seeming reluctant to get into it.

"If they're so hard to see, then how do you kill them? Do you just grope around blindly until you catch one?"

"Slayers have sefas that allow us to see them."

"What's a sefa?"

"It's a magical object. An amulet—in this case, a pendant. Gabriel provides them to members of Nightshade."

"Let me borrow yours, then."

"No," Jonah said, his voice dropping into the exasperated range. "I've already told you too much as it is. You can't go walking around looking for shades on your own. It's too dangerous."

"Isn't it dangerous for you, too?"

"I have some advantages that you don't," Jonah said.

"Can I at least see it?"

"See what?"

"Your amulet."

"What's the point?"

"Does everything have to have a point?" Emma was practically shouting.

Scowling, Jonah thrust a hand under his scrubs and pulled out a pendant, holding it up so she could see. It glittered in the overhead lights.

It was identical to the one Tyler had given her. The one that had belonged to her mother.

"Oh! I have one of those!" Emma reached into her neck-line and pulled out the pendant her mother had left for her. "I don't need yours after all."

Jonah stared at the amulet, the blood draining from his face. "Where did you get that?" he asked, his voice hoarse and strained.

Emma ran her fingers over it, caressing the metal. "It was my mother's. She left it to me."

"Your mother—that died at Thorn Hill?"

Emma nodded.

"But these—they weren't even made until after the mas-sacre . . . at least, that's what I was told." He trailed off. "Why would your mother have one?"

"How would I know? She died when I was six."

"What was your mother's name again?"

"Gwyneth Hart. Or Gwen. I guess she kept her own last name when she married." She shrugged. "She was always 'Mama' to me."

Jonah cocked his head, frowning.

"What?"

"That name's familiar for some reason."

"That's not surprising," Emma said. "She was at Thorn Hill."

He looked up, the confusion in his eyes clearing. "That's just it. She wasn't."

"Yes, she was."

"No. Kenzie and I—we came across the name when we were looking for Tyler Greenwood, your father. We looked for it in the records at Thorn Hill, but it wasn't there. Tyler Greenwood showed up briefly, right before the disaster. Then disappeared. But Gwyneth Hart was never there."

"Yes, she was." Emma's backbone straightened. "I know we weren't on the casualty or survivor lists, but Gabriel didn't seem to think that was a big deal." She paused, and when Jonah said nothing, added, "I'd know, wouldn't I?"

"I'd think so. But she wasn't in the work records either."

"How do you know? What work records?"

"They kept a record of everyone and the work they did for the commune. Kenzie and I searched them when we were trying to track down somebody who might've left Thorn Hill soon before the massacre." Jonah hesitated. "We thought an adult survivor might be able to tell us something that would help us figure out what happened and who was involved."

"She *had* to be in the work records," Emma insisted. "She worked all the time. All. The. Time. She was always worn out. I used to play the piano for her, to calm her down." Emma tried to swallow down the growing queasiness in her belly.

"It's probably just a mistake in the records," Jonah said. "Only . . . it's hard to imagine how she could be missing entirely since the work logs were turned in weekly."

"What do you mean by that? What are you trying to say?"

"Nothing. I just don't know why—"

"Are any of the records missing? Or . . . could somebody have messed with them?"

"Why would anyone mess with them?" Jonah said, raising his eyebrow.

Emma began pacing back and forth. Nobody would, she thought. Unless it was someone involved with the poisoning. A person who had something to hide. She looked up to find Jonah watching her like she was a rocket about to go off.

He can read my emotions, Emma reminded herself. Trying not to feel anything just made matters worse.

"Maybe she was there under an assumed name," Jonah said. "That's why she isn't in the records."

Emma was beginning to question everything she thought she knew about Thorn Hill—and that wasn't much to begin with. The mind plays tricks, Emma knew that. But, still, her memories of Thorn Hill were so vivid, like those full-color dreams that you stay in, even after you wake up. Even the air she breathed was so rich and moist and full of life—it was like breathing in the jungle itself. When she closed her eyes, she could see the light of Brazil through her eyelids: the way it filtered through the canopy of trees so that it had a green, growing quality.

Could it all have been just a story her mother told her? Could it have been a lie?

It was like a puzzle where you can't tell what the image is until the last piece falls into place. And then you wonder why you didn't see it before.

Emma's mother had worked for Andrew DeVries, who ran a syndicate of assassins. She'd made poisons for him. Maybe she hadn't come to Thorn Hill to get away from wizards, or to start a new life. Maybe she'd come there on their orders. If Gwen was a sorcerer who made poisons for the Black Rose, she'd be the perfect person to infiltrate what DeVries saw as a hotbed of terrorists. That would also explain why Emma seemed to have escaped the damage that everyone else at the Anchorage had to live with.

That must be why Rowan DeVries and the Black Rose had come to Tyler's looking for information about the poisons used at Thorn Hill. They, more than anyone, would know where to look.

If you were planning a massacre, you wouldn't want to use your own name, would you? That wouldn't be very smart. Tyler had said he'd taken Emma back to the States just before the disaster. Had her mother decided to take advantage of Emma's absence to carry out her plan? The case was growing against Gwyneth Hart. And if she was guilty, then Emma couldn't hate the wizards that had ruined so many lives without hating her mother, too. Maybe wizards had given the orders, but her own mother pulled the trigger.

That probably meant that her mother wasn't really dead. Not even undead. Gwen Hart wasn't on the casualty list after all. She wouldn't poison herself, so she wouldn't be walking the streets as a zombie either. Maybe she was hiding somewhere, like one of those fancy faraway places people move to with blood money. And if Gwyneth was alive, she would have the answers that Jonah so desperately needed.

She should tell them. But that would require confessing all of this to Jonah and Kenzie and Natalie and Rudy. What would they think if they knew that Emma was the daughter of the person who had caused this catastrophe? That she was healthy and well while they paid the price for what her mother did?

"Emma," Jonah said. "What is it? What's wrong?"

Emma looked up to find him watching her closely, eyes narrowed. She pressed her hands into the tabletop to keep them from shaking.

Her stone wasn't damaged like the others, even though people told her it wasn't a mainliner stone. What did that mean? What could that possibly mean? And if her mother were still alive, wouldn't she have come looking for her at Tyler's or Sonny Lee's? Would she really just abandon her?

"That just doesn't make sense," she whispered, almost to herself. Only maybe it did make sense. Maybe it made too much sense. A cold sweat broke on Emma's face as the vomit rose in her throat. "Where's your bathroom?" she croaked.

Jonah pointed, and Emma barely made it in time. When she was finished, she leaned her forehead against the cool porcelain, tears running down her cheeks.

"Here," Jonah said softly (but not soothingly). "Use this."

She looked up, and he was kneeling on the tiles next to her, holding out a wet washcloth. She used it to wipe off her face. Then he handed her a glass of cold water. She rinsed and spat, then sat back on her heels, her forearms on the rim of the toilet.

Why'd you have to tell me that, Tyler? she thought. Why'd you have to tell me that my mother made poisons for Andrew DeVries?

What was it those sidewalk preachers in Memphis used to say? The sins of the fathers . . . or mothers in this case. What it meant was if Kenzie Kinlock died, it would be her fault. And if Jonah Kinlock oozed poison through his skin, it was her fault.

"Would you like me to help you up?" Jonah asked finally. She nodded.

Sliding his hands under her arms, he lifted her to her feet, for once allowing her to lean against him, his arms around her, his heart thudding against her back. "It's been a long day," he said. "It's a lot to take in—all of this very bad news."

"I was better off in Memphis," Emma said, her tears making spots on her green scrubs. "I was better off not knowing."

"I'm sorry," Jonah murmured, massaging her shoulder blades with his thumbs. "Does this help, or do you want me to stop?" He acted like he was walking through a minefield.

"It helps," she croaked through her burning throat. She swiped at her face with the backs of her hands. "I have to go. I've got to get home and get some sleep."

Jonah followed her to the door, and stood in the doorway. She could feel the pressure of his eyes as she strode toward the elevator. "Emma!" he called after her. She didn't turn around. "Promise me you won't go out and look for shades on your own. Some report to Lilith, some don't. And some are just hungry for a warm body."

He was halfway back into his room when Emma called out, "Jonah!"

He swung back toward her, and she swiveled away, so he couldn't see her face.

"If I ask you a question, will you tell me the truth?"

"What's the question?"

"Is Kenzie dying?" Emma stared at the elevator doors, unable to meet his eyes.

"We're all dying," Jonah said simply. "Some of us sooner than others." He cleared his throat. "Kenzie's really sick. His Weirstone is failing. But that new medicine is promising. I haven't given up on him. I will do *anything*—whatever it takes—to save him. And that's the truth." He paused. "It means a lot, I think, that you two are friends."

He might as well have rammed a knife through her heart.

⊗ CHAPTER TWENTY-FIVE ⊗
GOT TO BE SOME CHANGES MADE

With Mercedes Foster on the case, Leesha made a quick recovery from her injuries from the attack in the Flats. Maybe too quick. The old Leesha would have made the most of her convalescence, lolling about while others waited on her hand and foot. Especially since Fitch was one of those at her bedside. Responsible Leesha dragged herself out of bed on the second day so she and Fitch and Emma could meet with the Interguild task force that was investigating the Halloween killings along with the other mainliner murders.

It was like pulling teeth to get Emma to come. Leesha guessed that it was only Emma's growing trust in Leesha and Fitch that brought her to the church for the hearing. Leesha was determined to make sure she didn't regret it. She pre-briefed some of the task force members on the need to be gentle, threatening dire consequences otherwise.

Leesha got that Emma had a whole lot of reasons for

being nervous. She'd admitted that she had a police record,
and that she had no gift for talking in front of people. Being
new to the magical guilds, she wasn't used to having horrible
experiences all the time. Still, Emma seemed unusually nervous. Bordering on guilty. When they filed into the church
parlor, she wouldn't make eye contact with anyone.

The committee members included Mercedes as chair, Jack
Swift, Blaise Highbourne, Seph McCauley, preschool parents
Sylvia Morrison and Hilary Hudson, and Nancy Hackleford,
the parent of a young wizard who'd been murdered back in
the fall with Rowan DeVries's sister. A murder she claimed
was ordered by the council.

Hackleford hadn't been among the original members,
but she'd kicked up a stink about their hand-selected cover-
up committee and insisted that there be representation for
the missing Rowan DeVries. Mercedes had agreed, since
Madison had directed her to include people who were not
actually on the Interguild Council in order to broaden the
perspective of the members.

Leesha didn't think that Hackleford's addition was an
improvement in any way. Diversity has its downside, she
thought. There are too many people on this task force, and
too many of them have their own agendas.

Leesha and Fitch sat on either side of Emma, who'd
dressed in the same somber outfit she'd worn to Grace's
funeral. Seph sat next to Madison, who looked pale and thin,
almost haunted.

"Emma!" Jack said on his way to his seat. "Good to see
you. I hear you're living in town now. I keep thinking I'll run
into you, but I haven't seen you since—for a while."

"I still spend a lot of time at the Anchorage," Emma said. "I'm going to school there." She cleared her throat. "And, you know, the band practices there."

"I've been meaning to text you or Jonah," Jack said. "I've been following the band online, but the page hasn't been updated. I was hoping to catch another show."

"Natalie does that," Emma said. "Maybe she hasn't kept it up since we haven't had any gigs lately."

"Soon, I hope," Jack said. Nodding to Leesha, he found a seat on the other side of the fireplace.

Jack seemed to have taken Leesha's lecture to heart. He was working so hard at not being scary that he reminded Leesha of a friendly Great Dane—a Great Dane who looked like young Hercules in a sweater and blue jeans.

When Hackleford walked in, Emma's eyes widened, and her hands tightened on the arms of her chair. "What's *she* doing here?" she hissed.

"Hackleford?" Leesha leaned in close. "She's not on the council, but her daughter Brooke was murdered, along with Rowan DeVries's sister. She claims that the underguilds are responsible." Leesha paused. "Why, do you know her?"

"N-no," Emma said, but Leesha knew she was lying.

As if cued by the intensity of Emma's stare, Hackleford looked their way. When she saw Emma, she froze for a split second. If Leesha hadn't been looking straight at her, she would have missed it.

How would they know each other? Leesha wondered.

"Don't worry," Leesha whispered, squeezing Emma's hand. "Fitch and I will tell them what happened. You speak up if we get anything wrong. And then we'll all answer questions. Okay?"

Emma nodded, her lips pressed tightly together like she was afraid she might say something by accident.

"Everyone's here, so I suggest we get started," Mercedes said. She looked toward the three witnesses. "This is an informal inquiry to allow the task force to learn more about the incident that occurred two days ago. Just tell us what happened in your own words. Jack will be taking notes, so he might have a question or two for clarity."

"I will, of course, be taking my own notes," Nancy Hackleford said, setting the tone right away.

Mercedes cleared her throat. "Perhaps we should begin by introducing ourselves for our first-timers. I am Mercedes Foster, sorcerer and member of the Interguild Council."

They went around the circle, each member introducing him or herself. Morrison and Hudson introduced themselves as "wizard and concerned parent." Fitch introduced himself as "friend of the guilds."

When they got to Emma, she said, "I'm Emma Lee, a musician. And student."

"What guild are you in, dear?" Morrison asked, squinting at her.

"I'm not really in a guild," Emma said. "I go to school at the Anchorage."

"The Anchorage!" Morrison's expression changed from solicitous to horrified. "But that's—that's—" Sucking in a breath, she plunged on, "That's Gabriel Mandrake's school for magical mutants." She pointed a shaking finger at Emma. "Should she really be here?"

"Sylvia!" Leesha planted her feet and stood. "Shut the hell up. How is it that your daughter Olivia has better manners than you do?"

Vibrating with rage, Morrison opened her mouth to respond.

"People!" Mercedes didn't have a gavel, but somehow she didn't need one. "I will not have any member of this committee badgering, abusing, or slandering these witnesses. They have graciously agreed to come here to help us do our work. I hope you're aware that when it comes to compelling witnesses to testify, we are on shaky legal ground."

Hackleford rolled her eyes. "I remember a time when we didn't have to jump through all these legal hoops in order to get at the truth," she said. Her eyes were fixed on Emma, who seemed to shrink down a little more.

"I remember that time, too," Mercedes said, in a cold, cutting voice. "And we'll go back there over my dead body." She paused to let that sink in. "I've been asked to chair this task force, and I will do my job. The next person who launches a verbal attack will be escorted out of this hearing. I will be the sole judge of what constitutes a verbal attack. Am I clear?" She looked around the room. Emma wasn't the only person avoiding eye contact.

"Now, then," Mercedes said, sweetly. "Leesha? Why don't you begin?"

Leesha told what happened in the least sensationalized way a person could describe a zombie attack. Now and then Fitch broke in to clarify something or add some detail she'd overlooked. Emma said absolutely nothing, just sat there looking miserable.

In that regard, she and Madison Moss were like a matched set of bookends.

Leesha managed to get to the end of the story with no more interruptions. "Are there any questions?" she said.

Concerned parent Hilary Hudson raised her hand. "It seems to me that this entire episode could have been prevented had you taken action after the Montessori incident. It is obvious that the children were telling the truth."

"Is that a question?" Fitch murmured so only Emma and Leesha could hear.

"What kind of weapons did they have?" Jack asked. "Did they seem to be freelancing, or fighting in a coordinated way—like an army?"

"Their weapons seemed to be whatever they could get their hands on," Fitch said. "Iron bars, wooden boards, and axes. Like that. As to whether they were coordinated, I was running for my life, so I couldn't say for sure."

"When you say they were zombie-like, could you explain what you mean?" Mercedes asked. "Did the cadavers appear to be in a state of advanced decay, or—?"

"Some of them were," Leesha said. "Others looked superficially normal. Keep in mind, it was dark and chaotic and—"

"So what makes you think they weren't street thugs, then?" Blaise Highbourne asked. "Members of a local gang. High on meth or something?"

"For one thing, they weren't vulnerable to conjury," Leesha said. "Even if I flamed them, their bodies burned, but they didn't seem to feel it. The only way I could stop them was through some kind of physical obstacle, like if I blew a hole in the pavement and they couldn't get around it."

"If you hacked off a limb, they'd just keep coming," Fitch said, shuddering. "It's like they don't feel pain. Jonah said that the best way to stop them was to take off their legs, so they couldn't chase after you."

"Tell us more about this Jonah Kinlock," Hackleford said. "You claim he just showed up out of nowhere and saved your lives?"

Leesha and Fitch looked at each other. "Pretty much," Leesha said. "I don't know what would have happened otherwise. He's an incredible fighter."

"Isn't it fortunate that he just happened along when he did," Morrison murmured. "That mirrors what the children said. Whenever zombies appear, young Kinlock isn't far behind."

Leesha's face heated. "It *was* fortunate," she said.

"Maybe he's like one of those arsonists who start a fire and then show up to watch the show," Morrison persisted.

"He was not *watching*," Fitch growled. "He was—"

"Participating?" Morrison cocked her head.

Emma leaned forward, speaking up for the first time. "It's not fair, talking behind Jonah's back when he's not here to defend himself," she said.

"Why isn't he here, then?" Morrison asked, looking at Leesha.

"We invited him, but he declined to come," Leesha said reluctantly.

For a long moment, nobody said anything. Then Seph tried to change the subject. "Where exactly were you going when you came under attack?" he asked. "Could they have followed you from somewhere else?"

"We'd only gone to one place—it was called Tonks, I think," Fitch said, looking to Emma for confirmation. She nodded.

"Had you been drinking?" Mercedes asked.

"We'd had a few," Leesha said. "I'd had—what?—three or four Cokes? Fitch was drinking root beer, so he tried to pace himself." Turning to Emma, she asked, "What were you drinking, Emma?"

"Orange soda," Emma said softly.

"So," Fitch said, with a warning look at Leesha. "Emma had heard about this club down in the Flats that showcased indie bands. We—"

"What club was that?" Morrison directed this question at Emma, who blinked up at her.

"I—I can't think of the name of it," Emma said, picking at the fabric in her skirt. "I thought I knew where it was, but then we couldn't find it."

"So *you* were the one who lured them down into the Flats," Morrison said.

"What is that supposed to mean?" Leesha growled. "*We* asked Emma to come along with *us*."

"All I know is that the gifted have ventured into that neighborhood twice, and been attacked by monsters both times," Morrison said. "I've said it before, and I'll say it again—the proximity to Mandrake's school can't be coincidental. I wouldn't set foot down there."

"Really?" Hackleford said, looking amused. "I am not convinced that any of this actually happened."

Everyone turned and stared at the wizard.

"It is simply not credible that you three were attacked by an army of animated cadavers. Cadavers who resist magic and can fight off a wizard. And after this massive battle, a mysterious superhero arrives in the nick of time so that all three of you survive."

"All right, I confess," Leesha said. "I came up with this nefarious plan because I haven't been beaten up in a really long time."

Hackleford dismissed Leesha's injuries with a wave of her hand. "A few cuts and bruises, that's all. Easy enough to fake."

Mercedes was figuratively giving off sparks. "I assure you that Leesha's injuries, while not life-threatening, were—"

"If this is a common occurrence, then why isn't there a city-wide alarm?" Hackleford said.

"I don't know that it's a common occurrence," Morrison said. "We're aware of two instances that—"

"Were only witnessed by children and council insiders," Hackleford said.

"I'm not a council insider," Emma murmured.

"Me neither," Fitch said. Neither spoke loudly enough for anyone but Leesha to hear.

"And we would devise this elaborate scheme because . . . ?" Seph leaned back, templing his fingers and looking out from under his dark brows. In that moment, he looked more like his father, Hastings, than ever.

"It seems to me that this whole episode might be a red herring to distract us from the real targets and the real culprits," Hackleford said.

"Who would be—?" Seph tilted his head.

"Wizards continue to die, and the underguilds don't want the blame, and so they conjure up a story about zombies." Hackleford snorted. "Zombies who resist magic. That, my friends, is preposterous. I surmise that the reason there have been two incidents within thirty miles of us is that it's an easy commute for operatives from Trinity."

By now Morrison was on her feet. Leaning forward, she planted her hands on the table and thrust her head forward into Hackleford's face. "If my Olivia said there were zombies, there were *zombies*," she said through gritted teeth. "What we should do is clean out that nest of vipers downtown and see if these incidents stop."

"I really don't care whether Mandrake's unfortunates are involved in this or not," Hackleford said. "Clearly, they are incapable of organizing this conspiracy themselves, so we know that somebody else was the mastermind. Cut off the head of the snake and the rest will die. Under the old system, at least, there was a mechanism for deciding disputes and eliminating threats to the common good. I've not seen anything of value come out of the so-called Interguild Council. If these killings continue, the Wizard Guild will take unilateral action."

"Really," Seph said, his eyes glinting green. "Being a wizard myself, then, shall I assume that you will keep me apprised of your plans?"

"Hackleford!" It was a new voice. Everyone turned to look, and it was Madison.

"You lost your daughter," Madison said. "I lost my little sister. No one is more interested in solving this than me. If you can get the evidence to prove your allegations, you will see action, and you'll see it quick. But I'm committed to getting it right. If the Wizard Council acts, and you get it wrong, you can expect to pay a huge price. A *huge* price."

Madison turned to Leesha. "It seems to me that the missing piece of the puzzle is Jonah Kinlock. He was at the Halloween party, he was present for this attack, and it sounds very much like he was on-site the night of the Montessori attack. We're not going to clear this up until we talk to him."

"I'm friendly with Gabriel Mandrake," Mercedes said. "It may be that if I approach him directly, he'll make Jonah available for questioning."

Good luck with that, Leesha thought.

When the hearing was over, Leesha, Fitch, and Emma walked into the churchyard. As always, Leesha's eyes were drawn to the small cemetery next to the church. Snow swirled around the gravestones and coated the frail, frozen flower arrangements, now brown and seared with frost.

"Hang on," Leesha said to the others. She entered through the gate and crossed to one particular grave that was as green as it might have been in mid-June, red and white roses blooming everywhere, and vines twining up and over the stone. Their scent perfumed the lean winter air, and the snow melted as soon as it hit.

Unlike some of the others, this gravestone was relatively new. Leesha ran her fingers over the letters cut into the stone.

Draca Heorte

Jason Haley

Gone, But Not Forgotten

And his birth and death dates.

Jason Haley. The boy Leesha loved and betrayed and lost in one thrilling and heart-breaking year. The boy who wanted, more than anything, to make a difference.

Leesha heard the crunch of snow as Emma and Fitch came up behind her. She knelt, and swept away sticks and dry leaves that had collected on the windward side of the stone.

"I'm sorry for your loss," Emma said.

"I like that he's buried here," Leesha said. "So that when I come in and out of these mind-numbing, frustrating meetings I can remember why I'm doing this."

"What does that mean?" Emma asked, hesitantly. "Draca . . ."

"It's Old English," Leesha said. "It means *Dragon Heart*."

⊘ CHAPTER TWENTY-SIX ⊘
HEALER

It was the third time Emma had called Jonah, and the third time it had gone to voice mail. So this time she left a message. "Jonah? It's me, Emma. Call me if you get this. Bye."

Clicking off, she sipped at her coffee, which had gone cold. It didn't really matter, because it was one of those peppermint drinks they have at Christmas, which taste so much like dessert and so little like coffee that even Emma could drink them. Blotting up some doughnut crumbs with her finger, she sucked them into her mouth. The place was crowded with shoppers, and the coffee dude was giving her the evil eye, so she guessed she couldn't stay there too much longer without buying something else.

After school, she'd snuck into the woodshop at the Anchorage and spent several hours working. It was kind of aimless—she had three different projects, and she didn't make a whole lot of progress on any one of them, but to be honest, it was more about the work than anything else. It wasn't like she was going to be selling guitars any time soon. And she could only play one guitar at a time.

Once she got herself sweaty and totally gritty, she shook the wood chips out of her hair and walked over to the fancy grocery around the corner. There was a little café there, and it was the last place anyone would expect to find Emma, which was the whole point.

Leesha had been calling and leaving messages for Jonah for two days, hoping to persuade him to meet with the task force. He never responded. She'd asked Emma to bring it up with him after class, but Jonah wasn't in class, and he wasn't answering his phone. He was like a ghost lately, more absent than present since the attack. It was like he knew, with that spooky sixth sense of his, what she wanted to talk to him about.

There was no hope of persuading him to come, anyway. Why would he? And yet, she couldn't help thinking that sooner or later the whole thing would blow up, and everything and everyone she cared about would be destroyed. Maybe it would've happened already if the magical guilds could agree on anything. They were so busy having at each other that they wouldn't recognize the truth if they stumbled over it.

And now Emma didn't want to return to Trinity, and it didn't feel right to be at the Anchorage, so she was hanging out in no-man's land, waiting for who knows what.

What she should do is try to find her mother. Only she didn't know where to start. She woke her screen, and searched on *Gwyneth Hart*. Nothing. She tried *Gwen Hart*. Nothing. Which was what she'd found the last time she tried it. And that about summed up what she knew about finding a person.

Kenzie. He knew how to find things online. Maybe by now, he'd had a chance to look over Tyler's notebook. And while she was there, she could ask him for wisdom about Jonah.

When Kenzie's phone went to voice mail, she was all out of ideas. "Hi, Kenzie," she said. "I wondered if you had a chance to look over that notebook I gave you. I'm here in town, and thought I could pick it up if you're done with it. And I had a couple things I wanted to ask you about. I'll be here for maybe another hour."

A few minutes later, Emma's phone pinged. A text from Kenzie.

I'll give it to Jonah to give back to you.

But I wanted to see you, too, she texted back.

This time, there was a long delay before he replied.

Not possible. My agoraphobia is flaring up.

Your what?

What don't you understand about no?

No, I understand. Agorawhatever, I don't.

Then, no.

Are you all right?"

No response.

I'm coming up there. I want to see for myself how you are.

A moment later, her phone rang. "I don't need you to check on me," Kenzie spat. "I'm in a damned nursing home, wired up to a dozen monitors. I can't take a dump without somebody weighing and measuring it. If you want to know how I am, just look at the data."

"Please," Emma said. "Let me come up."

"To do what? Change my nappy?"

"I'm just . . . I'm your friend," Emma said, her voice hitching. "I just want to—"

"It's time to start letting go of me."

"I'll call someone," Emma said. "I'll call Gabriel. Or Natalie. They can—"

"No!" Kenzie sounded a little panicked. "Don't. Please don't call anyone. If you want to help, don't call anyone."

"But I want to—"

"You want to hand off the responsibility. You want to make yourself feel better. If you call Nat or Gabriel, they'll move me to Safe Passage. I'm not going to do that to Jonah."

"Wh-what do you mean, Safe Passage? What does Jonah have to do with it?"

Kenzie said nothing for a long moment. Then said, "Harry, hang up the phone." Emma heard the soft *click* as Harry complied.

This time of night, Steel Wool reminded Jonah of a sleeping patient—lights out on the outside, shades closed, dim lights burning on the inside. All of the essential functions continued unseen, under the skin of its walls.

Jonah didn't call first. He didn't intend to give Kenzie the chance to say no. If his brother was sleeping comfortably, he wouldn't wake him.

When he eased open the door to Kenzie's room, it was dark, save for the light from the cinema display on his desk. Kenzie was in bed, lying on his side, covers kicked off, wearing only his pajama pants.

Jonah could hear his brother's labored breathing. He could feel Kenzie's pain clear across the room. He ghosted forward, his heart thudding in his throat, until he was at Kenzie's bed-side, looking down at him. His fine brown hair was plastered to his head, and his face glistened with sweat. His headphones lay next to him on the bed.

Kenzie didn't open his eyes, but he said, "Emma ratted on me, didn't she?"

"She totally did," Jonah said, sitting on the side of the bed. He put his hand on Kenzie's shoulder, and his brother's fear and desperation rocketed through him.

Kenzie twitched. "And here . . . I thought . . . we had an understanding."

"If you want to blame someone, blame me," Jonah said.

"That's my Jonah," Kenzie rasped. "Always takes the blame for everything. Have I ever told you that you have a martyr complex?"

"Incessantly," Jonah said. He stroked Kenzie's hair away from his forehead, realizing that the magic that had always burned over-brightly within Kenzie was nearly out.

"See?" Kenzie said, holding up a trembling hand. "No sparks. I'm much easier to be with when I'm dying."

Jonah bit back a protest, a denial. That would be conde-scending. They'd always been honest with each other, at least.

"How long have you been this way?"

"Couple days." Kenzie licked his cracked lips.

"Was it the blood magic?" Jonah asked. "Is this some kind of a reaction or—?"

"I think I just have a hell of a hangover," Kenzie said.

Why didn't you tell me? Jonah wanted to ask, but he bit back the words, because he knew the answer to that question.

"You don't have your music on?"

Kenzie shook his head. "It just doesn't cut it anymore. I

thought I'd turn it off for a while, and then when I turn it back on, it'll feel like relief."

"Can I get you something else? Do you still have a PRN order for pain meds?"

"I'm maxed out for this building," Kenzie said, leaving unspoken the truth they both knew—that Gabriel didn't want to risk overdosing anyone before Jonah did his thing.

"Where does it hurt?" Jonah asked.

Kenzie held up his hand, extending his middle finger. "That's the only part that doesn't hurt," he said.

"Well, then," Jonah said, shedding his jacket. "We'll just have to use the nuclear option."

"What's the nuclear option?" Kenzie asked suspiciously as Jonah removed his boots, setting them neatly at the side of the bed. Lifting up the covers, he slid in next to Kenzie.

"Wh-what—no!!" Kenzie cried. "What the hell do you think you're doing?"

"This is the nuclear option," Jonah said.

"I told you," Kenzie said, scooting to the far side of the bed. "I'm not doing Safe Passage. I am not going to let you—"

"I'm not going to kill you, bro," Jonah said. "Not unless you keep whining. Turn around, so we're like spoons. I promise not to nibble your ear."

"Get out of my bed, Jonah," Kenzie spluttered. "You know how open-minded I am, but—this is really kinky. People will talk."

Jonah resorted to pleading. "Please, Kenzie. Let me try this. If it doesn't work, we'll never speak of it again."

"Just . . . be careful," Kenzie said. "No kissing, all right? I don't want to have your guilt over my death on my conscience." Still grumbling, he turned onto his side, and Jonah pulled him up against his body. Gingerly, he wrapped his arms around his brother, pretending not to notice that he was skin and bones. Breathing out slowly, trying to relax, Jonah thought, *Let me help somebody for once. Whatever gift I have, let me use it to help my brother.*

It helped that Jonah had seen it work before with Emma and with Mose. It took a little time, but gradually, Kenzie's rigid body relaxed, his hands unclenched as the pain dulled, faded, until it was just a faint ache.

"Better?" Jonah whispered, though he already knew that it was.

"Fishing for praise? That's not like you." Kenzie paused, and the snark drained right out of him. "Yes. It's much better. Thank you. Too bad you can't bottle that. You'd be totally rich." He was silent for so long that Jonah thought he might have drifted off to sleep. "Can you return something to Emma?"

"You have something of hers?"

"She leant me a notebook," he said. "Full of songs. Remember? That night we were jamming and you interrupted us?"

"Oh. Right. And now you want to give it back?"

"Yeah," Kenzie said. "It's over there, lying next to the computer."

"Okay," Jonah said. "Any message for Emma?"

"There's a note in the binder," Kenzie whispered. "I've annotated the pages." After another long pause, he said, "Sing to me?"

"Sing what?"

"One of our songs. Singer's choice."

And so Jonah sang.

❧ CHAPTER TWENTY-SEVEN ❧
ME AND THE DEVIL BLUES

Emma had finished a second peppermint drink and a large cinnamon roll by the time Jonah texted her back.

He's doing better. I'm going to stay with him a while longer. Thank you.

Emma was desperate for more information, but knew there would be none, so she had no excuse to hang around.

There's no point in worrying about something you can't do anything about. That was one of Sonny Lee's favorite sayings. It didn't work for Emma Greenwood anymore.

You are in way over your head, she thought.

Emma pulled on her coat and gathered up her things, then threaded her way to the front of the store and out onto the street. She was so distracted that it took her a moment to collect her thoughts and remember where she'd left her car. Oh. Right. Parking lot on Fourth. Only suppertime, but it was already dark. A light snow was falling, sparkling like glitter in the lights from the restaurants and clubs.

As she walked, the crowds thinned. She turned off the sidewalk, into the parking lot where she'd left her car. There were only a few cars in the lot—all coated in snow, so maybe they'd been there all day. Emma took her usual look-around before she went to unlock the door of the Element. That's when she noticed the black SUV parked, lights out, motor running, on the far side of the lot. The kind of car that crowds other cars off the road.

Every street instinct she had screamed *Bad news!* Fumbling for her keys, she dropped them in the snow. She groped for them as she heard car doors slamming across the parking lot. She tried to jam her key into the lock and missed, scraping metal on metal. She looked up to find four wizards closing in on her from all sides.

Time slowed to a crawl as Emma scanned the deserted street. Even if there had been people there, she wasn't sure how much protection they would be against wizards.

She knew she wouldn't be able to get the door open and slide inside before they were on her. Planting her back against the driver's door, she flipped her key chain case up into her hand. The one with the pepper spray and the built-in siren. As she flipped off the safety, one of the wizards jetted flame at her, engulfing her hand, setting her glove on fire.

Screaming, Emma dropped the charred mess of a key chain and ripped at her glove, sucking at her fingers, which felt like they were still on fire. When her mouth caught fire, too, she realized that her hands were soaked in pepper spray. Turning, she plowed into the nearest wizard, swearing like a roadie, thrusting her pepper-sprayed fingers into his eyes.

Howling, he let go of her, and she almost got away, but

slipped on the snowy pavement and nearly fell, and by the time she got back on her feet there were three sets of hands on her, pinning her arms. She felt power pouring into her like hot metal, heard wizards mumbling all around her, while she kicked and bit and screamed and struggled.

One of them managed to wrestle a hood over her head, then picked her up and shoved her into the backseat of the car. She could smell the leather seats through the hood, so strong she knew it was a new car. Pushing off with her feet, she tried to scramble to the door on the other side, but there was yet another body in the way. She threw out her elbow, aiming blindly, and somebody gripped her arm. Another wizard, judging by the sting.

"Stop it, Emma," he said. "This is a waste of time. Don't you know when to give up?"

It was Rowan DeVries—she recognized his voice. That surprised her enough that she stopped struggling.

"Don't you ever surrender?" he demanded, alive and well and sounding pissed.

"No," Emma said finally, wrenching her arm away. "I don't surrender. So why don't you just leave me alone?"

"I will," he said, "after we talk."

"Can't you get it through your head that I don't want to talk to you? Anyway, everybody says you're dead. Where have you been?"

"I've had some serious health problems," Rowan said. "Maybe you heard? In my line of business, if you can't defend yourself, it's best to go into hiding."

The other wizards climbed in, too, doors slamming all around.

"What's with the posse?" Emma said.

"Associates," Rowan said. "Don't worry, they'll keep their distance unless they believe I'm in danger."

"From me?"

"I don't know," Rowan replied. "You tell me."

"You were right," one of the thugs said. "Conjury doesn't seem to work on her."

"*Hmmm,*" Rowan said. "Use of direct magic does, though. Interesting." He shifted on the seat as he leaned forward. "Let's go," he said. The car clumped over the curb, and down to street level.

"Where are we going?"

"Not far," Rowan said. "Your boyfriend's not the only one who can have a top-secret hideout."

"He's not my boyfriend."

"Coconspirator?"

"He's not that either. Anyway, why should I talk to you?"

"I don't want you to," he said. "Not right now." And then he wouldn't say anything else.

It *wasn't* far. In fact, Emma suspected they took the long way around to make it seem farther. The car rolled to a stop, and she heard a clatter and bang, like steel doors slamming open, then the hum of machinery—maybe a second set of doors. The car eased forward, and the street sounds disappeared, so she knew they were inside a building.

Once the doors were shut she could hear nothing from the outside at all. The car rolled to a stop, the engine cut off, and automatic door locks clicked all around.

"All right, Emma," Rowan said. "You can uncover your eyes."

As she pulled the hood off, the rest of them piled out

of the car. Emma scrambled out after them, blinking in the dim light. They were parked against one wall of an industrial building with a poured concrete floor, like a garage.

"This way." Rowan led them toward the other end of the building, walking with a bit of a limp. A set of doors opened into an office and living area. Here, the wide oak floorboards and battered brick walls said that the building was vintage, probably turn of the last century.

It was warmer in here than in the outer warehouse. Computer equipment was everywhere, video displays and keyboards, like it was some kind of command post. Emma thought of the mini armory in Jonah's room.

Rowan stripped off his jacket and hung it on a hook by the door, then turned to face her. He stuck out his hand. "May I take your coat?"

"I'll keep it on," Emma said. "It's cold in here, and I won't be staying long, anyway." She'd put her street face on, and hoped she looked more confident than she was. He's not going to hurt me, she told herself. He wants something from me.

Rowan shrugged. "Suit yourself." He looked different—thinner than before, almost hollow-cheeked, purple smudges under his eyes. He wore blue jeans and a sweatshirt, which somehow made him look younger despite his worn-out appearance. She noticed a new scar, still pink and puffy, that ran down the side of his neck and under his collar.

"This your hideout?" Emma asked.

"One of them."

"It's not nearly as nice as your old place," she started to say, when she heard the faint clamor of a lift bridge alarm. She looked up, startled, and met Rowan's eyes. She didn't say it—she didn't have to. They were within shouting distance of the Anchorage. Was this really a hideout or the launch point for an ambush?

"In here." Rowan led her through another set of doors, into an inner office. He closed and locked the door behind them, then circled the room, hand extended, murmuring charms. When he pointed in Emma's direction, she flinched—she couldn't help it.

He snorted in disgust. "I'm just making sure we're not overheard," he said. "Anyway, why are you worried, if conjury doesn't work on you?"

She displayed her hand, which was already blistering up between her thumb and forefinger and was throbbing like crazy. "Is there someplace I can run this under cold water?"

He grimaced. "Sorry about that." Showing her into a small bathroom off the office, he stood in the doorway until she said, "Do you mind?" and shut the door in his face. She soaped up her hands and washed off the pepper spray, then held her burned hand under the cold tap until she got some relief. She looked around the room. No windows. No weapons. Pulling out her cell phone, she scanned the screen. No signal.

All out of ideas, she dried her hands, flushed the toilet for show, and returned to the main office, where Rowan was waiting. He gestured toward a grouping of chairs. "Sit."

Emma saw no point in standing, so she sat, board-straight, feet planted.

He sat across from her, so close their knees were nearly touching, his tawny eyes fixed on her. "How's the hand?"

"Terrific," she said. "Whatever you have to say, hurry it up. I need to get home and put some ointment on it."

"You're not giving the orders."

"I'm not giving orders," Emma said. "I'm stating a fact."

He sighed. "I'll stipulate that neither one of us wants to be here. But I'm trying to help you."

" 'I'm a wizard, and I'm here to help'?" Emma snorted. "I don't think so. Let's see—the first time we met, you threatened to torture me."

"That was Burroughs," Rowan said.

"Maybe you felt bad about it, but you were still going to stand by and *let* somebody torture me," Emma amended. "Then the next time I saw you, you tried to kidnap me."

Rowan rubbed the back of his neck, like it hurt. "The first time I saw you, somebody murdered my sister. The last time I saw you, somebody tried to murder me. There's a pattern there, I think. You should've listened to me then. It's even more important that you listen to me now."

"Important to you, maybe?"

He shook his head. "Important to you."

"What do you care about me?"

"I don't," he said. "I just want you to make an informed decision. Jonah Kinlock is going down, and I'd hate to see you go down with him."

That got her back up. "What? You think he's a bad influence on me? Maybe *I'm* a bad influence on *him*." This was nothing to joke about, and yet, Emma couldn't stand the notion that she was some kind of welfare project for this rich wizard.

"I hope for your sake that's not true," Rowan said. "I don't think it is." He pushed back his sweater sleeves, anchoring them above his elbows. His hands were elegant, unmarked, the nails clipped short and buffed to a shine.

Emma always noticed people's hands. You could tell a lot about a person by looking at their hands. What, if anything, they did for a living. How much they cared about appearances. Whether they liked to wear a lot of bling.

Jonah, of course, kept his hands hidden.

As if overhearing her thoughts, Rowan said, "I can't figure out why you're teaming up with the person who murdered your father and tried to murder me." He paused for a beat. "Although now that I know more about you, maybe I shouldn't be surprised." He dangled that out there, waiting for Emma to grab at it.

She didn't. "I'm not teaming up with him—I'm not a team kind of person. And I don't know for a fact that he murdered my father."

Rowan's lips tightened. "Emma, I heard you at McCauley's that night. I heard both of you. So don't tell me you don't know what really happened."

"Look," she said, "I just want to be left alone. If y'all want to kill each other, up to you."

Rowan rubbed the back of his neck like it hurt. "Face facts. Kinlock is making a fool of you. That's what enchanters do, Emma. That's what they're designed for."

Tyler's words came back to her. *Enchanters—stay away from them. They can talk you into almost anything.*

Was she being a fool? Was Jonah Kinlock so charming that she'd lost her head? Was that why she kept making excuses for him?

"I hear you've moved to Trinity," he said, abruptly changing the subject.

"Who told you that?"

He smiled faintly. "If you've spent any time in Trinity,

you know feelings are running high. Yet you're still going to school with the labrats."

"Did you really bring me here to tell me things I already know?" Emma shoved one hand through her hair. "All my life, I've been stepping on toes. To begin with, I'm biracial. Then I'm a girl who thinks she can play the guitar. Now I'm a labrat—or at least I'm hanging with them."

"You'd be better off if you keep your distance from them," Rowan said. "You don't want to be here when the bad goes down."

Emma snorted. "Did you hear that on TV? Maybe you think I was better off at your place, being held prisoner?"

"You were safer there, at least."

"Funny, I didn't feel safe."

"I'm not going to argue that point with you. There are different levels of risk."

"So. Why haven't you talked to the police?" Emma said, hoping Rowan would volunteer something. "I know they're in a hurry to talk to you."

Rowan shook his head. "I have no interest in talking to the police. I'm a wizard. I don't answer to them. But you do." He pulled out his phone, turning it in his long fingers. "I haven't exactly been idle these past weeks," he said. "I know a lot more about you than I did before. It's amazing how much information is available in public records." He paused. "The Memphis police are still looking for you. Did you know that?"

"They got nothing better to do?" Emma said, shrugging. "The crime business must be slow down in Memphis these days."

"I wouldn't say that. You're a 'person of interest' in a murder."

Emma's mouth went cotton-dry, but she tried to pretend that it didn't matter, one way or another. "Really? Whose?"

"Your grandfather's."

"Sonny Lee was murdered?" Her voice came out in a high squeak. "For sure?"

Rowan rolled his eyes. "Please."

"No," Emma whispered. "Sonny Lee—he fell. In his shop." She'd accused Jonah of killing him, but she'd never quite believed it.

"They don't know whether you're an accomplice or a victim."

"Kind of like you?"

"No," Rowan said. "Not at all like me. I'm the heir to a well-to-do family, the innocent victim of a crime."

"Your father was an assassin," Emma said.

Rowan raised an eyebrow. "He was a businessman. Like me. My record is spotless. You, on the other hand—you have a criminal record."

"You call that a record?" Emma snorted.

"It'll do," Rowan said.

"It's all juvie stuff: curfew violations, truancy, underage possession—that doesn't mean I was drinking, mind you; I just go a lot of places where they serve alcohol."

"Breaking and entering?" Rowan raised an eyebrow.

"Girl told me I could spend the night at her place. By the next morning, she'd forgot all about it. Never bunk with a drunk."

"That goes without saying, don't you think?" Rowan said, wrinkling his nose like he smelled something bad. Like finding a place to sleep had never been a problem he'd had to shake hands with. "Receiving stolen property?"

"That was just a mix-up. I bought a guitar from a dude who was down and out, and it turned out it didn't technically belong to him. I should've known by the price it was too good to be true." Emma shut her mouth to keep more words from spilling out. She couldn't seem to stop offering excuses. "Where'd you get that information? That should not be on my record, because those charges were dismissed."

Rowan did the flicker-eye thing. "Maybe your grandfather was too strict, and that kept getting in your way. Maybe you were arguing, and you pushed him. If I were the police, and I looked at your record and the fact you ran off, I'd think maybe you and your grandfather had an argument about curfew, and—"

"Curfew? Sonny Lee?" Emma snorted. "Nobody who knew him would believe that." But somebody who didn't know him? She could see how they might.

"Maybe he decided to keep a tighter rein on you, and you didn't like it. You were arguing, and you pushed him. You didn't mean to hurt him, but—"

"Your making stuff up doesn't make it true," Emma said. "I would never, ever hurt Sonny Lee. Why are you even interested in what happened in Memphis?" The back of her neck prickled. Something wasn't right.

"I need your help," Rowan said. "I want the truth about what happened the night my sister was murdered."

Her ironwood spine hardened. "You mean the night *my* father was murdered? Do you think I'm covering for my father's murderer?"

"Maybe," Rowan said. "There are several possible scenarios. Maybe you were collateral damage, someone who happened to be in the wrong place at the wrong time. Or maybe you were actually involved in his murder. You and your father weren't all that close—you only moved in with him because your grandfather was dead. You just couldn't tolerate a parent telling you what to do. It could have been a setup—a robbery gone wrong. Maybe you're in love with the charming Jonah Kinlock, and you want to protect him."

"You know what?" Emma said. "Every time I start feeling bad for you, you make me regret it."

Rowan ignored this. "Which brings us to the Halloween murders. There are several possible scenarios about what happened then. I just can't decide which is the truth." He looked at Emma, clearly waiting for her to ask the question.

"Several scenarios," Emma repeated. "Like what?"

"Burroughs and Hackleford are pitching the story that Seph McCauley and Madison Moss are behind the murders. They want me to support that view—to identify them or their friends as the killers."

Emma snorted. "Madison Moss killed her own sister?"

"Coldhearted, huh? But perhaps she got caught in the crossfire. Or saw more than she should have. Or maybe she was helping Big Sis and it went wrong—a tragic accident."

"And they did the murders in McCauley's backyard?" Emma shook her head. "Who would believe that?"

"Wizards," Rowan said. "Hackleford and Burroughs aren't that concerned about whether it's true, as long as it serves their purpose: to get other wizards to align with us against the Trinity dictatorship."

"Don't dictatorships usually run better than that?" Emma said, thinking of the hearing.

"The underguilds are dysfunctional by nature," Rowan

said. "But I agree with you that Grace Moss's death makes that scenario implausible. I, for one, don't believe it."

"But you're going to go along with it, anyway?" Emma's voice trembled.

Rowan shook his head. "Hackleford and Burroughs want to start a war with the underguilds, even if they have to lie to do it. They want to use the murders to unite the Wizard Guild. That was never my goal. Now I've lost Rachel, and I have to live with that. I want to stop the murders, and bring the murderers to justice. Then I'm done."

He's telling the truth, Emma thought. About that, anyway.

He leaned forward, looking into her eyes, and went right back to lying. "Here's what I think. A more believable possibility is that you lured me out to the gazebo. Then you and Jonah Kinlock attacked me and tried to kill me."

"Wh-wh-what?" Emma had heard of people spluttering, but had never actually done it herself. "I never—I didn't even know you were at the party until you showed up in the gazebo."

"Do you expect me to believe that?"

"Whatever you believe, it's the truth," Emma said. "If I'd known you were there, you think I'd wander off by myself?"

"Yes, if the goal was to set me up."

"I hoped you'd attack me and try to drag me off?" Emma rolled her eyes. "If I was that stupid, I'd shoot myself. Nobody will ever believe that story."

"You think not? All the evidence points to you, from what I've seen. After all, my blood was all over your shoes and jacket."

"You know damn well why your blood was all over my

clothes," Emma said. "You attacked me, and I broke your nose, and you bled like a stuck pig."

"I'm sorry," Rowan said. "I don't remember it that way. And if it comes to a judge deciding between the two of us, who do you think he'll believe? A teenage runaway who's a suspect in her grandfather's murder? People might question whether one teenage girl could be the perpetrator of so many killings, but Jonah's involvement gives the theory a bit more . . . credibility." He looked at her dead-on. "That's why I wanted to talk to you, Emma. Just me. No Burroughs, no Hackleford. I hoped if I could get you away from Kinlock, you might be able to think clearly enough to see that he's been using you."

Emma planted her feet and stood, hands on hips. "You listen to me, DeVries. I am not the kind of girl who gets used. I learned that lesson a long time ago. This is business. We're in a band together, that's all."

"Is it?" Rowan raised an eyebrow. "I watched you and Kinlock onstage. It's like, get a room. And later, when you were dancing, you heated up the place. I've seen the way you look at him." He steepled his hands. "I've heard about enchanters, which is what he apparently was before the accident. I'm sure the sex is amazing, but you can't let that—"

"Now I'm done," Emma said, her cheeks heating up as the blood rushed in. "Just keep right on with your nasty fantasies, but I'm not gonna play." She strode to the door and pounded on it until the heel of her hand stung.

"I'm sorry," Rowan said, still in his chair. "Forgive me. That was out of line."

Emma kept pounding.

"Please," Rowan said. "Come sit down. There's not much

more, and you're not going anywhere until I get it said. Then you can go."

Emma turned, put her back to the door, and folded her arms. "I'm listening."

Rowan blew out a long, disgusted breath. "The point is, when Jonah showed up, I realized it was just a bit too convenient. And then, when I found out about the other dead, it just confirmed it."

"Confirmed *what?*"

"The identify of the person responsible for the Weir murders."

"Jonah?" Emma nearly choked on his name. "You think Jonah's been running around the world killing mainliners?" She tried to tamp down the flame of suspicion that had been smoldering since Halloween. That now once again flared brighter.

"It's unlikely that he is responsible for all the killings," Rowan said. "From a logistical point of view, that's simply impossible. I suspect that the conspiracy centers on the Anchorage, and Gabriel Mandrake is the ringleader."

"What possible reason would Gabriel Mandrake have to be killing mainliners?"

"You'll have to ask him," Rowan said. "But maybe it's not so surprising. Mandrake was one of the founders of Thorn Hill. The purpose of Thorn Hill was to destroy wizards."

"Says you. Jonah was right when he told me not to believe anything a wizard says." Frustration boiled up inside her. "I just can't figure out why you're doing this. What did I ever do to you?"

"What did you ever do to me?" Rowan extended his hand, ticking off on his fingers. "You were there when my sister was murdered, and yet you claim that you don't remember a thing. The next thing I know, you're living at the Anchorage with the murderer. In fact, you're in a band with him. A band that played at the scene of another set of murders. You tell me you're not stupid. Well, I'm not either."

"You always leave out the part where you threatened to torture me unless I told the right story," Emma growled.

"Not my idea," Rowan said. He leaned back, lacing his fingers across his chest. "There is another option," he said. "Don't you want to hear the third scenario?"

Emma's head was spinning, so it took her a minute for that to sink in. "What do you mean? What other scenario?"

"Jonah acted alone. You and I were talking in the gazebo, and Jonah attacked us. You ran—"

"I *ran*, and I didn't say anything to anyone? I just left you for dead?" Emma shook her head. "No. I wouldn't do that."

"You're frightened of Jonah Kinlock, Gabriel Mandrake, and the others. You've realized just how deadly he is, and you were afraid of what they'd do if you gave him away."

"You act like there's all these different stories, and it's just a matter of picking the one that we agree on," Emma said. "But only one of them is the truth. Which one is it? Who attacked you? What did you see that night?"

"I don't really know the truth about *your* involvement— whether you were an innocent bystander or a coconspirator. But I can tell you what I remember." He kept looking at her, as if she might decide she didn't care to know after all.

"I'm waiting."

"As you know, I left the gazebo ahead of you both, but I hung around outside, because I was worried about you.

When I saw you leave, I gave you a few minutes, then began walking back up the hill toward the house. I heard running feet, and then someone grabbed hold of my jacket collar and slashed my throat." He fingered the fresh scar. "I twisted away, but I stumbled, and he came after me. I tried using an immobilization charm, and then a killing charm, but it had no effect that I could see. I scrambled away on all fours, but when he caught up with me, I rolled onto my back, and saw that it was Kinlock."

Emma's heart quivered. "You're positive it was him?"

"Yes." He said it without hesitating. Maybe Emma wasn't a good judge, but she'd have said he was telling the truth.

"Really? What was he wearing?"

Rowan sighed. "His usual. A black leather jacket, jeans."

Emma tried to recall what Jonah was wearing that night. "I don't remember him wearing a jacket in the gazebo. Did you see his face?"

"He wore a ski mask."

"So you didn't see his face," she said, trying to ignore the voice that said, *Jonah wore a ski mask the night your father died.*

Rowan rolled his eyes and ticked his arguments off on his fingers. "Use your head, Emma. It was Jonah. He was resistant to conjury, extremely strong and quick, and had leather gloves on his hands. Can you think of anyone else who fits that description?"

"He was wearing gloves?"

Rowan nodded.

"Did he say anything?"

Rowan shook his head. "I guess he did all his talking back at the gazebo. If you'll recall, he said he was going to kill me, and so that's what he tried to do. Simple as that. He would have succeeded, but we got interrupted. I heard somebody crashing through the brush, calling Jonah's name."

"Calling Jonah's name?"

Rowan nodded. "I think it might have been Madison Moss's little sister. Kinlock stabbed me again, through my rib cage, then took off running. I don't remember much more. I was pretty weak from loss of blood by then, and I must have fainted. That's the last I remember until I woke up in the hospital." He paused, then added, as if exasperated, "Don't you want your father's killer brought to justice?"

"You were the one who burned up the bodies and destroyed all the evidence at the house."

"Look, neither of us wanted to bring in the police. That's not the way it works in our world. Why would we want to answer to Anaweir authorities? This way, justice is served, and we're not implicated."

"Unless Jonah is innocent."

"I was there, remember? Remember what you said? *You're going to kill him, just like you killed my father.*"

"I shouldn't have said that," Emma mumbled.

"He confessed to you, didn't he?"

"Not exactly," Emma said. "He doesn't remember."

"Oh, right. It's an epidemic of amnesia." Rowan gave her a pitying look. "Think about it, Emma. You've left a trail of death behind you. Your grandfather was murdered, your father was murdered, and now, once again, you're on hand for another series of killings, and this time you're covered in blood. Who has the criminal record? Who's the most obvious suspect? Not Jonah Kinlock. You. Do you really want to—what's the word—take the fall for him? *Do* you?"

Emma thought of Ross Childers, how kind he had been. And wondered how he would react once he knew her history and heard what Rowan had to say.

"I want to be left alone," Emma said, through gritted teeth. "I want to build guitars and forget about all this. I don't know how I ended up stuck in the middle." But a voice inside her head whispered, *Your mother was the cause of the Thorn Hill Massacre. Maybe you are right where you deserve to be.*

"I wanted to be left alone, too," Rowan said. "I never intended to go into the family business. And then someone murdered my father, and now someone's murdered my sister, and it seems clear to me that someone is going to keep on murdering until I put a stop to it. And I intend to—with or without you. You need to decide which it's going to be."

"I don't get it," Emma said. "Do you or don't you think I'm guilty? And if you do think I'm guilty, why would you let me off the hook?"

Rowan thought about this for longer than Emma expected, a muscle working in his jaw. Finally, he said, "Have you ever heard the saying about people in glass houses?" He turned his phone in his hands, over and over, avoiding her eyes. "Maybe it's a little of that. Maybe I think you've gotten a raw deal, and I owe you one."

"What's going to keep the police from blaming me anyway?" Emma said. "It's like you said: I'm the one with the criminal record. It would be my word against Jonah's."

"No," Rowan said, "it would be *our* word against his. That's why I need your support. Like I said, I don't intend to take this to the Anaweir authorities. I have no interest in seeing Kinlock twist a jury around his finger. This is better handled by the Interguild Council. They know the history.

They're better able to analyze the risk and determine how the situation should be handled. That's who I have to convince."

Whatever happens, it's a disaster, Emma thought. It doesn't matter whether it's the real police or a group of magical vigilantes. When they find out about Jonah's "gift" he'll get the blame for every suspicious death in the whole state.

"Well?" Rowan asked, as if he didn't want her to think on it too long.

"I just can't believe that Jonah Kinlock would kill a twelve-year-old girl," Emma said. "He—he has a younger brother that he's crazy about, just a little older than Grace was. He had a little sister who died at Thorn Hill."

"Don't be naive," Rowan snapped. "What better reason for Kinlock to target the guilds? Many of the labrats still believe that wizards somehow caused the disaster. Revenge is a powerful motivation, especially for someone with nothing to lose." He leaned forward. "This is a pivotal time. Somehow we have to have a reconciliation process if we're to put all this history behind us and go forward. We have to stop the killing. Otherwise, there will never be peace among the Weirguilds. It's time the Interguild Council decides how it's going to handle disputes and criminal cases now that the Rules of Engagement no longer apply. Now that wizards are no longer settling disputes. We'll see how they do."

"Why talk to me?" she said finally. "Why didn't you just go straight to the council with this?"

He took a quick breath. "If you help me, I think I can make sure that you're not implicated."

A ping of warning sounded in Emma's head. "What do you mean? Help you how? What would I have to do?"

"You'll have to testify before the council in support of my account."

"You want me to lie."

"No. I'm asking you to use your common sense and see justice done. Tell them what happened in the gazebo, what Kinlock said and did. Tell them what happened the night your father was killed. That's all." He rubbed his eyes with his thumb and forefinger.

"What about the part where you tried to drag me off and Jonah stopped you?"

"What is *wrong* with you?" Rowan growled. "I'm trying to help you. Your cooperation sends a strong signal that you were not involved in all this, and it makes it less likely you'll change your story later. I need to make a good case in order to convince Burroughs and Hackleford to align with me. They are still scheming to hang it on Madison Moss and her friends."

"While you're scheming to hang it on Jonah and the other Thorn Hill survivors."

"That's not a problem if they're guilty," Rowan said.

No matter how much hand waving you do, Emma thought, you're still asking me to lie. She thought of what he'd said at the beginning—that he wanted her to make an informed decision. What else did she need to know?

"What will they do to him? If they decide he's guilty?"

Rowan's tawny eyes met hers, flat and hard as agates. "I know how it would have been handled in the past," he said.

"You're going to kill him," Emma said flatly. "Do you have a plan for that?"

"If the council elects to proceed against him, you'll

persuade Jonah to come to Trinity so he can be . . ." Here he stumbled a bit. "So he can be taken into custody."

"You want me to lead him into a trap?"

"Kinlock has shown how dangerous he can be. Remember, he took down seven wizards at once at your father's house. I'd like to handle this with as little bloodshed as possible."

Good luck with that, Emma thought. "What about the others? At the Anchorage, I mean?"

"That remains to be seen," Rowan said, "depending on what the evidence shows about their involvement. As I said, it stands to reason that Mandrake is involved in some way."

"What about after? Do I just disappear?"

"I know you're worried about where you'll end up when this is all over. That won't be a problem. I have considerable resources—I can offer you protection and a place to settle. I can hire tutors, send you to a private school, or set you up in business if that's what you want."

"Why would you *do* that?" Emma blurted.

"You'll be taking a risk," Rowan said. "If Kinlock and the others find out what you're doing, you'll be a target. Anyway, I don't have a family. Not anymore. I don't have anyone else to spend it on."

"What—you're going to *adopt* me?" Emma rolled her eyes. "Anyone who looked at us could tell we don't belong together."

"You're welcome to decline my help if you don't want it," he said stiffly. "I just wanted you to know what's on the table." He pulled out his phone, scanning the screen as if the conversation was almost over.

Rowan DeVries was smart—smart enough to figure out

what Emma really wanted. More than anything, she wished none of this had ever happened. If not that, then she wished that she could forget about all this and build guitars.

What was the argument Jonah had used to persuade her to stay on at the Anchorage? Self-interest. Act in your self-interest. If she had any sense, there was no question which way to go. She could share the blame for murders she didn't commit. Or she could leave all this behind and start a new life, doing what she was meant to do. And put all this trouble in the place where the bad dreams go.

But bad dreams have a habit of coming back to haunt you. And maybe Rowan DeVries wasn't as smart as he thought he was.

She needed to warn Jonah. And that meant she had to persuade DeVries to let her go.

"All right," she said, avoiding his eyes. "I'll speak to the council. I'll testify."

"Good," Rowan said, gripping her hands, sending a bit of a buzz through her. "You're doing the right thing." Letting go of her hands, Rowan continued, his voice brisk and businesslike. "I've scheduled a closed hearing in Trinity for Saturday. It's best if you stay here until then—that's the safest option." It was like he was trying to rush through that part, so maybe she wouldn't notice.

"No, thanks," Emma said. She stood. "Can I go now?"

Rowan growled in frustration. "Not a good idea. If Kinlock gets wind of what you're planning, you'll be in real danger."

"I'm not stupid," Emma said. "I know how to take care of myself. And if you have any plans to hold me prisoner until the hearing, the deal's off. If you keep me here against my will, there's no telling what I'll say when I get in front of the council."

"Please, Emma," Rowan said. "If you see him—if you even talk to him, it could ruin everything. This is someone who can charm the skin right off your bones."

"Are y'all finished?" Emma said, trying to project more confidence than she was feeling. "I've got places to be."

"Fine!" Rowan stood himself. "Just remember—it goes forward with or without you. And if you're thinking of running, I suggest you think again. Like I said, you're not very good at covering your tracks."

Maybe, Emma thought, I just need a little more practice.

⊗ CHAPTER TWENTY-EIGHT ⊗
TRIPLE CROSS

"**A**re you sure it's even safe to go in there?" Alison asked, as she geared up for the planned ambush of Lilith Greaves. "From the outside, it looks like a dump. It might collapse while you're in there."

That's the least of my worries, Jonah thought.

"Couldn't you have planned this meeting for, say, a coffee shop?" Mike said. "There's a great one down on West—"

"It has to be on neutral ground," Jonah said. He knew they were trying to relieve the tension of the moment, but he was not at all in the mood for jokes. Especially since he had a whole different set of reasons to be tense. "I don't know about you, but I don't really want people gawking at us when the knives come out. I don't want to have to explain to Cleveland's finest that the person I'm murdering is already dead. Last time I saw Lilith, she was hosted, and she looked pretty much like anybody else."

"Really? When did you two get together?" Alison asked,

strapping a quiver of shivs over her chest. "When we saw her at the bridge, she wasn't hosted."

The question caught Jonah by surprise, as it was intended to. It took him a minute to find his footing. "It must've been that time the two of us met for breakfast at the Pancake Palace," he said. "Or was it the weekend in Chicago?" He paused, and when Alison opened her mouth to press him, he hurried on. "The point is, I don't know if she'll come hosted or not. If she's wearing a body, people might start asking questions when I hack her to pieces."

Gabriel didn't seem to notice the slip. He studied him critically. "What are you bringing in the way of weapons?" He looked over Jonah's shoulder, at the place usually occupied by Fragarach's massive hilt.

"I can't very well bring a sword to a peace parley," Jonah said. "That would send the wrong message." Accessing multiple hidden sheaths in his coat and jeans, he displayed an array of cutting blades, hatchets, and shivs, all of them perfectly hidden when he stowed them back away. "Two of these are giveaways. They'll find them when they search me. The others, hopefully not."

Gabriel nodded, his eyes still searching Jonah's face. Jonah's mentor wore jeans and a heavy sweater, with a fleece-lined leather bomber jacket over top. He looked more haggard than usual, his eyes muddy with fatigue. Or maybe cluttered with secrets.

"I appreciate your volunteering for this, Jonah," he said. "I know it's difficult for you. I hope you realize now that we have no other choice."

Jonah nodded, not meeting Gabriel's eyes.

"I'd like this better if we could be hiding inside," Alison

said. "Too many things can go wrong with this plan, and we'll be too far away to get there in time."

"If you wanted to do that, you should've moved in three days ago," Jonah said. "If we're already watching the building, we can assume that they are, too."

"You're giving them an awful lot of credit," Alison said.

"It's better to overestimate your opponents than to underestimate them."

"We'd better get moving," Charlie said. "We're supposed to be in place in half an hour."

They took the familiar path down into the Flats. Thérèse waited at the foot of the hill, her cheeks pinked up with excitement and cold. Mike, Charlie, Silkie—there were a dozen of them in all, not counting Gabriel.

It was peculiar, having Gabriel along. Though Gabriel had been intimately involved in the establishment and training of Nightshade operatives, Jonah couldn't remember that he'd ever come along on a riff.

Let's see how you like it, Jonah thought.

When they reached their preplanned staging area, Jonah said, "Everybody know where they're going?" They all nodded. Just to make sure, Jonah said, "Lilith's shades will be lined up along the same perimeter to keep us honest. They'll be watching to see who goes into the building. They're not to be harmed—that's the agreement. Nobody uses this as an opportunity to build their kill count. Everybody get that?"

Heads nodded all around.

"Once the others are in place, Thérèse and Charlie will search the area around the terminal, and make sure there's no hidden ambush, it's not wired up with explosives, etc. Once the area is cleared, you'll keep watch to make sure it stays that way. Any activity we should know about, anybody tries to approach the building, you'll hit the alarm."

"What if there's a full-scale assault?" Thérèse asked.

"That building is built of stone, and the walls are a foot thick. I think it will hold up long enough to prevent a surprise attack." Jonah turned to Gabriel. "When we get to the door, I'll go inside to clear the building. Then we'll wait inside for Lilith."

"What about snipers?" Charlie asked. "Is there any chance of that?"

"I've been over this area four different times. If you all are in your places, I don't think there's anyplace somebody can get a clear shot without your seeing them."

"Besides, their armament is pretty limited," Alison said contemptuously. "You can only throw a hatchet so far."

"Charlie has a good point, though," Jonah said. "We're a lot easier to kill than hosted shades. One good shot, and Gabriel or I go down. Fill a hosted shade full of holes, and the shade goes hunting for a new host." He looked around the circle, meeting everyone's eyes. "That's why it's so important that nobody gets trigger-happy and tries to claim the riff early. It's unlikely to kill Lilith. All it will do is spook her, and this chance will be gone forever."

"I don't like it," Thérèse said. "It seems like we're taking all the risks."

"That's why we get paid the big bucks," Jonah said. "Anyway, the status quo is unacceptable, at least for me. The trickiest part is after. When Gabriel and I come out of the building without Lilith, things could get ugly real fast. Give us some cover, and let's all of us get out. Don't hang around, hoping to put a few more notches in your belt. The numbers don't work in our favor. We also need to anticipate the possibility of retaliatory attacks on the Anchorage. They've had access to inside information, since some of our alumni have crossed over. They know what our vulnerabilities are."

Jonah could feel the pressure of Gabriel's gaze on him.

"Any questions?" There were none, so Jonah said, "Let's do it."

The others scattered to go to their assigned stations, leaving Gabriel and Jonah alone.

"The adrenaline really kicks in, doesn't it," Gabriel said, looking around. "I don't know why I haven't gone out with you before."

"The excitement wears off after a while," Jonah said. "Are you armed?"

Gabriel's eyes narrowed. "Why do you ask?"

"If it goes wrong, I just wondered whether you'd be able to protect yourself."

"It won't go wrong," Gabriel said. "I have faith in you." That comment had all kinds of sharp edges, or maybe it was Jonah's imagination. It also wasn't an answer to his question.

Jonah said nothing. Gabriel, however, seemed to feel the need to fill the silence between them. "Jonah, I'm still not convinced that this person we're meeting is Lilith Greaves. But on the off chance that it is, there's something you should know: something I haven't told anyone else."

Jonah waited.

"I have reason to believe that the woman I knew as Lilith was at least partially responsible for the Thorn Hill Massacre," Gabriel said. "If there's anyone who deserves to die, it's her."

That echoed what Lilith had said. *He thinks I'm the one responsible for Thorn Hill.*

"Really?" Jonah said, thinking, Shouldn't we be keeping her alive, then? So we could maybe find a way to help the few survivors? But by now he knew that speaking it aloud would do no good. And it might give away the game.

Gabriel gripped Jonah's shoulder. "I hope that, once this is behind us, we can go back to the way things were. We've always been a great team."

"There's Charlie," Jonah said, seeing the slayer wave from atop the lift bridge. "He says it's clear. Let's go."

The old railroad terminal squatted amid parking lots and industrial buildings next to the river. Grass and weeds had broken through the pavement in several places. The terminal was brick and stone, stained by more than a century of industrial smoke and city grit. The windows were boarded over, graffiti-covered, barred. *That* seemed pointless, since it was hard to imagine anyone wanting to get in there that badly. Still, it suited Jonah's purposes.

Slayers and shades ringed the building, keeping an uneasy distance between them. All of the shades were hosted, and all of them looked relatively fresh.

Putting our best foot forward, are we? Jonah thought.

One of them stepped into their path. Mid-fifties, maybe, stubble-faced, buzzed hair, his muscled arms covered in tattoos.

Hello, Jonah, he said mind-to-mind.

"Brendan!" Jonah looked him up and down again. "What happened to your old host?"

Turned out that body had too many enemies, Brendan said, all brisk and businesslike. *I was tired of getting into fights. Now. I'm going to search both of you.*

Jonah turned to Gabriel, who was looking on in confusion

and alarm. "This is Brendan Wu," Jonah said. "He's going to search us for weapons." When Gabriel opened his mouth to protest, Jonah met his eyes and mouthed a no.

During Jonah's pat down, Gabriel stared at Brendan as if transfixed. And a little horrified. Shifting his gaze to Jonah, he muttered, "Are you sure it's Brendan?"

"I'm sure," Jonah said.

Brendan surfaced Jonah's giveaway blades, but nothing else, then turned to Gabriel, who stood, rigid, fists clenched, visibly sweating, during the search.

Finally, Brendan stepped back, satisfied. *Could you tell him I don't bite?* he said to Jonah. He jabbed a thumb into his chest. *I'm a shade. Not a vampire.*

"This does take a little getting used to," Jonah said with a tight smile. "All set? Are we good?"

Brendan nodded.

"Now let's go clear the building."

The three of them crossed the parking lot, Jonah in front, Gabriel in the middle, and Brendan coming behind. Pulling keys from his jacket pocket, Jonah unlocked the metal gate protecting the door.

"You have a key?" Gabriel whispered.

"I had it made," Jonah said. He didn't find it necessary to add that he'd installed the gate as well. And bars on the insides of the windows. Jonah Kinlock had created a small fortress, here on neutral ground. He'd already changed the lock on the inside door so he could open it with the same key.

"Wait here," he said to Gabriel. "We'll clear the inside." They were coming up on another risk point. It was possible that Lilith had set a trap, that she was just as clever as Jonah Kinlock, just as clever and twice as desperate. Gabriel's solution to Lilith's army was to kill Lilith. Maybe Lilith's solution to Nightshade was to kill its leader.

But Jonah didn't think so. He hadn't read her that way. He was betting a lot on that reading.

The inside was just as he'd left it—nobody lurking in ambush. He'd removed the junk and rats' nests from one end of the building, piling it all to the right of the door. He'd even set up three chairs in a little triangle. He wondered if anyone would actually sit in them. He wondered if they would actually survive this.

Looks okay to me, Brendan said. He paused. *How'd you find this place?*

"I walk by here all the time," Jonah said.

Brendan still hesitated. *You're being straight with us, right, Jonah? No double cross?*

"No double cross," Jonah said, thinking, *Double cross* is too honest a word to describe this plan.

I'll go get Lilith, Brendan said.

When they emerged into the sallow light of the mercury vapor lamp. Gabriel was waiting, pressed back into the brick and stone of the building as if he could disappear into it, his upper lip beaded with sweat.

I don't think I've ever seen Gabriel Mandrake sweat before today, Jonah thought.

Brendan walked away, back across the parking lot toward the road.

We're good. Let's go in. He stood aside, letting Gabriel precede him through the door.

Inside, Gabriel said, "You didn't seem worried he'd find your weapons."

"Their hands don't have much sensitivity," Jonah said. "Brendan told me once that their skin is basically numb. So I counted on that, plus my near-legendary skills of concealment." He gestured toward the chairs. "Sit," he said. "I'll wait for Lilith by the door."

"Jonah," Gabriel said. "I don't really need to—to talk with her. Or see her. Just . . . finish her, so we can go."

Oh, no, Jonah thought. It's important that you participate in the full slayer experience. You're like the politicians who're so quick to send other people's sons and daughters to war.

What he said was, "No worries. You know how efficient I am."

Gabriel frowned, as if reading something worrisome in Jonah's attitude.

Jonah crossed to the door, standing a little to one side so that Lilith would step past him before she knew he was there. So that if she'd planned an ambush, he'd have the element of surprise.

He stood, a shadow among shadows, waiting, heart throbbing, his breath coming fast, senses tuned to the world outside the building.

Then he felt it—a stir of emotion, all around them. A break in the attention focused on the building. Quick footsteps on the street outside. Someone was coming. If it was Lilith, she was hosted. Jonah had expected she would be; it was safer for her that way.

Jonah glanced back at Gabriel, who showed no eagerness for this reunion.

Someone fumbled at the door, eased it open. Hesitated a moment, then came forward into Jonah's view. He released a long breath, his first in a while. Lilith Greaves had come alone, as agreed, wearing the same cadaver as she had the last time Jonah had seen her. The same clothes, too, of course.

Jonah moved to the door and locked it behind her.

She whirled to face him, bringing both hands up in defense. She dropped them a little when she saw no weapon. *You're locking us in?* she said, her gaze sweeping the dark interior.

"So we aren't interrupted," Jonah said. He felt much better now that the three of them were enclosed within the brick and stone of the old terminal. He jerked his head toward the back of the room. "We'll talk over there."

Lilith followed him back to where Gabriel waited.

The sorcerer stared at her as she approached, his eyes wide, hands clenched. He seemed absolutely riveted, even though she couldn't possibly look anything like the woman he remembered. His former lover, if what Lilith had said was true.

Lilith stared back. It had been ten years, and a lot had happened in the interim to age Gabriel, but he must at least somewhat resemble the man she knew. The man she'd fallen in love with.

Shifting his gaze to Jonah, Gabriel nodded, signaling him to go ahead and make the kill.

Jonah pretended not to see it.

Gabriel! Lilith said, in what sounded to Jonah like mind-to-mind shouting. *I'm so glad you've come. It's been a long time.*

Gabriel flinched back. "I can hear you," he said, going paler than before. "It's faint, but—" He licked his lips, swallowed hard, looked at Jonah. "Why is it I can hear her?"

That's the power of blood magic, Lilith said. *I've loaded up for this meeting. With enough power on board, even the living can hear us. That's just the beginning.*

Gabriel said nothing, his eyes smoldering like scorched slate against chalk, burning into Jonah.

Instead of sitting, Jonah stood behind his chair, his hands resting on the back, knowing he might have to move quickly. "I told the other slayers to give us about an hour before they begin to worry," he said. "That should give us plenty of time to talk."

I did the same with my shades, Lilith said.

"Jonah." Gabriel raised his eyebrows, tucked his chin, and lifted both hands, palms up, the universal gesture for *What the hell?*

Jonah turned away, toward Lilith. "How is your hearing? Do I need to repeat what Gabriel says, or are you able to make it out? He isn't used to speaking mind-to-mind."

My hearing isn't great, but I should be able to make out what Gabriel says in a quiet room.

Jonah turned back toward Gabriel. "I may repeat some of what you say, if it's unclear, but you should be able to speak directly to Lilith."

"Jonah," Gabriel repeated. His face was bloodless, his lips white with anger. "We made a deal."

"We did," Jonah said. "But I made a deal with Lilith, too. Her price for talking to me was the opportunity to talk to you."

"And so you lied to me. After everything I've done for you."

"If you'll remember, I asked you to talk to Lilith. I begged you. Several times. And you refused."

"And that should have been the end of it," Gabriel said. "I know Lilith Greaves a lot better than you do—"

"So I hear," Jonah said, tipping up his chin and looking him in the eye.

Even though Jonah was expecting it, Gabriel moved faster than he'd have thought possible. In one quick motion, he lunged forward, gripped Lilith's hair with one hand, and cut her throat with the other.

❦ CHAPTER TWENTY-NINE ❧
THE THINGS I USED TO DO

In a split second, Jonah had Gabriel imprisoned in an iron grip. He increased the pressure on Gabriel's wrist until he dropped the knife. Jonah kicked it away. His pounding heart was beginning to slow a little. He turned to look at Lilith.

There was no blood whatsoever, just a slice into the flesh that went halfway to the windpipe. She sat upright, supporting her head with a hand on either side. *Oh, Gabriel,* she said. *I was comfortable in this body. I thought I'd be able to use it another month or more.*

Gabriel struggled briefly, then settled again.

Jonah turned back to Lilith, who was exploring the wound with her fingers. "Are you sure you're all right to continue with this? Do you need—?"

No problem. I've waited for this too long to let anything stand in my way.

"Jonah, I'm warning you," Gabriel said. "I've tried to

provide you with a path forward, to honor your growing independence, but—"

"But you didn't expect me to actually think for myself. That's what you get for turning us into grown-ups so quickly. Oh, right, all the grown-ups died, so you didn't have anybody else to work with." Jonah patted Gabriel down methodically, retrieving two more knives and two shivs. He was much better at it than Brendan. Pushing him down into one of the chairs, he handcuffed him to the arms. "By the way, for future reference, it takes a much heavier blade to decapitate someone. See, you use the momentum of the—"

"Jonah," Gabriel hissed, pulling at his bonds. "What's happened to you?"

"Those are the rules. The first one who tries to kill the other person gets shackled."

He's just being what he was meant to be, Gabriel, Lilith said. *Brilliant, strong, beautiful, deadly. You know that. He's a spectacular success, if you look at it that way.*

"What are you talking about?" Jonah looked from Gabriel to Lilith.

Lilith settled into another of the chairs. *Gabriel, it's time you were honest with Jonah and all of the other children of Thorn Hill,* she said.

Gabriel said nothing, only glared daggers at Jonah.

I know you think I'm to blame for what happened, Lilith said, *but it's not true.* She paused, waited for a response, got none.

She's here to win Gabriel over, Jonah thought, with a prickle of unease. What will happen if she does?

Gabriel seemed to be trying to ignore the fact that Lilith was in the room. He remained hyper-focused on Jonah, as if still hoping he might follow through on the riff. It was like an odd love triangle: Lilith focused on Gabriel; Gabriel fixed on Jonah; Jonah intent on Lilith now that Gabriel was fixed in place.

"Jonah. I warned you about her. I told you not to listen to her—that she would mislead you. And, apparently, she has."

If you won't tell the truth, I will, Lilith said. *Trust me, you're better off telling it from your point of view—you're a lot more likely to come off as the hero.* She paused, then said, *Please. I want to work with you to make this right, or at least to see justice done.*

Gabriel leaned forward in his chair as far as his manacles would allow, his eyes fixed on Jonah. "Listen to me. I've spent my entire life trying to undo what *she* did. What I'm saying is, this is not my fault. I trusted her. But if word gets out that—that— Kill her, please. Kill her now. Don't let her destroy everything we've built together."

Jonah tried to sort through these conflicting fragments and put them together into a picture. "Are you saying that Lilith was the one who poisoned us? Or that she was the one who betrayed us to the Wizard Guild?"

"Maybe she never meant to poison us," Gabriel said. "Maybe it was unintentional, but the end result was the same."

I was working for you, Lilith said. *I never dosed anyone except on your orders.*

"Well, you must have gotten it wrong," Gabriel said.

Jonah looked back and forth between the two of them, a sick suspicion boiling up in him. "So," he said slowly. "You're saying that the two of you cooked up the poison that killed thousands of people at Thorn Hill? That is still killing us."

No! they said in unison. But it appeared that they even disagreed on no, because they immediately began issuing discordant disclaimers.

"I didn't poison anyone," Gabriel said. "She did."

I didn't poison anyone either, Lilith said. *That's what I'm trying to tell you.*

Jonah came and stood over Gabriel. "Gabriel, here's your chance. Start at the beginning, and don't leave anything out."

"What does it matter now?" Gabriel said. "Don't you see? If word gets out that—"

"Thousands of people died, and you're worried about your *reputation?*" Jonah methodically removed his gloves and tossed them aside. "Perhaps you misunderstood. That wasn't a request. It was an order. I'm not going to charm you into doing the right thing."

Gabriel made one last desperate effort. "Why don't we go back to the Anchorage, so that we can discuss this in more comfortable surroundings? There's no need to hide out in a bunker in order to—"

"I've waited ten years to find out what really happened at Thorn Hill, when all along the answers were within reach. If you don't tell me the truth right now, I will kill you. You can't really complain, because, after all, you're the one who turned me into an assassin." Jonah was bluffing, of course. There was no way he'd kill Gabriel until he'd pried free the secrets he'd been holding close for so long.

Maybe Gabriel believed him. Or maybe he was just worn out with lying. "All right," he said. "I'll start at the beginning. I'll tell the truth as I know it." He closed his eyes, as if to avoid Jonah's. Plus it was easier to speak of dark things in the dark.

"For years," Gabriel said, "wizards have claimed that Thorn Hill was a training camp for rebellious underguild operatives."

"I believe the term they used was *terrorists*," Jonah said.

"That is an inflammatory word," Gabriel said, "but there is an element of truth in it. The commune *was* the site of a . . . an experiment in self-defense." He looked to Jonah for a reaction, but Jonah said nothing, so Gabriel continued. "Keep in mind, this was before the last tournament at Raven's Ghyll, the establishment of the Sanctuary at Trinity, the emergence of the Dragon—none of that had happened. The underguilds were little more than slaves to their wizard masters. There were many of us who were quite wealthy—myself included—but we were as much at risk as those with few resources. In fact, we were even more at risk of discovery, because we were visible. We sorcerers are the makers, so to speak, and so we were especially valuable. Wizards were the takers, who profited from the fruits of our labor."

Gabriel paused, and Jonah looked at Lilith. She shrugged slightly. *I was born into a so-called "servant" family—sorcerers who had worked for wizards for generations.* She turned to Gabriel. *Tell him about your family.*

For the first time, Gabriel responded directly to something she'd said. "The wizard houses have always been ruthless in putting down guild rebellions. That's one thing the Red Rose and the White Rose agreed on. My sister and brother were killed in the last serious sorcerers' rebellion."

"And yet," Jonah said, "when I asked why we weren't targeting the wizards who caused so much misery, you preferred to finish the job they began at Thorn Hill."

"Hear me out, then maybe you'll understand," Gabriel said. He took a deep breath, then continued. "Given the nature of our gifts, some of us—mostly sorcerers—had begun to realize that there was no way we would ever prevail. The fight was too one-sided. We wanted to change that. We wondered whether it might be possible to strengthen ourselves in ways that wizards could not counter. The biggest wizard advantage was conjury. It was so flexible, so nuanced, so versatile, that we had no defense against it. We thought, what if we could develop Anawizard Weir who resisted conjury? Wouldn't that be a huge advantage?"

Gabriel leaned forward in his seat, eyes alight with enthusiasm. In him, Jonah saw the vestiges of the young sorcerer who believed that sorcery could solve every problem. "So we brainstormed, assuming that anything was possible. For instance, another advantage that wizards have is that they are so long-lived. What if we could make ourselves immortal? If it came to a fight, what if our healers could heal wounds in new ways? What if they could look right into a client and identify the disorder without scans or surgeries?"

What if we had warriors who were savvy, amazingly strong, agile, and quick to heal? Lilith put in. *What if we had assassins who could kill painlessly, kindly, even pleasurably? If you're planning on going to war, wouldn't that be an advantage?*

For a long moment, Jonah's throat locked up, and he couldn't force any words out. "Did you ever think of the person who had to do the killing?"

The two sorcerers looked at each other, as if each hoped the other one would speak up. Neither volunteered.

"Tell me about Thorn Hill," Jonah said, once it was clear that no answer was forthcoming. "How did that get started?" He didn't want to listen to a pitch for genetic engineering, especially since he had to live with the results.

"We knew we were taking a risk," Gabriel said. "We knew what happened to members of the Weirguilds—even wizards—who conspired against the regimes in power. Leander Hastings, for instance. Because Hastings was a well-known subversive element, he was constantly on the run. As was Linda Downey, who, of course, had to hide her identity in order to protect her family. But we couldn't do the hit-and-run-type thing. We needed time to do our research in a protected environment, to trial therapies and evaluate results. But the Roses had spies everywhere. And we needed resources to fund our research.

"So I bought the property in Brazil. The mines were already operating. I had a diverse portfolio, so nobody questioned it. The mines provided income to support the commune, to build the labs we needed, to develop agriculture so that we could be self-sustaining."

"Where did Lilith come in?" Jonah asked.

"I recruited her," Gabriel said. "She came highly recommended. I was told that she was the most talented sorcerer of this generation. I believed it."

Because it was true, Lilith said.

"I knew she had a rather shady background—"

If you wanted somebody with my experience, Lilith said, *it wouldn't be someone unsullied by contact with wizards.*

"What kind of expertise were you looking for?" Jonah asked, wary of the answer.

"Lilith had been working for wizards to research methods of modifying Weirstones," Gabriel said.

"Why would wizards be interested in that?" Jonah opened his stance a bit, resting his hands on the back of a chair, preparing for a lie or a long story. "It seems like they already have every advantage."

Oh, they had no intention of experimenting on themselves, Lilith said. Then looked at Gabriel, as if to encourage him to carry on.

"You're aware that the wizard houses have a long history of holding tournaments between warriors and gambling on the result," Gabriel said. "They mimicked racehorse owners, always looking to breed a stronger, more bloodthirsty warrior. But selective breeding in humans takes a long time to achieve, especially given the fact that there was and is a real shortage of warriors, because most of them have been killed off. So it occurred to some wizards that it might be possible to genetically engineer warriors who would be impossible to defeat. Or modify the Weirstones of members of the other guilds to turn them into warriors."

A memory came back to Jonah, of the swordplay demonstration in Trinity, when Ellen had called Jack Swift a "mongrel." "Is that what happened to Jack Swift?"

Lilith shook her head. *As I understand it, that was a surgical procedure. Really risky, and it still requires finding a warrior stone. My employers thought it might be possible to use treatments to gradually change, say, a sorcerer Weirstone into a warrior stone, or at least one that was close enough to fool a stone reader. If, at the same time, it was possible to enhance the warrior's fighting capability, even better.*

"So you have a long history of experimenting on unwilling subjects," Jonah said, allowing his bitterness to show through.

Unwilling sorcerer, unwilling subjects, Lilith said. *I hated it. So when Gabriel contacted me with a proposal, I was immediately intrigued. Not only would it provide a means of escaping the situation I was in, it might mean freedom for all of the Weirguilds.*

"At least you meant well," Jonah said. "Everybody makes mistakes."

That's the point—I did not make a mistake, Lilith said.

"But you were still experimenting on unwilling subjects," Jonah said, looking from one to the other.

"Don't make assumptions until you know the facts," Gabriel snapped.

"What a shame, then, that nobody has told me the facts up to now," Jonah said.

"Our subjects were volunteers," Gabriel said.

"I don't remember volunteering."

We began with adults, Lilith said. *We actually had to turn people away.*

"You had to turn people away," Jonah repeated. "So—everyone wanted to be Spider-Man?"

"Imagine that you are enslaved by a self-styled superior race," Gabriel said. "Consider that the disparity in power was so great that you had no hope of throwing off the yoke on your own."

"And yet it happened," Jonah said.

"The end of that story isn't written yet," Gabriel said. "Don't count wizards out too soon. They always find a way to win. Anyway, hindsight is twenty-twenty. As I was saying—wouldn't it be tempting to take a chance on a treatment that might set you free? That might allow you to take revenge on your oppressor?"

And so we set up our lab, recruited our volunteers, and the research began, Lilith said. *But we soon found that our treatments didn't work well on adults. That was consistent with my previous research as well. Apparently, the therapies work best on stones that are biologically active, growing and developing, so that a new matrix can be laid down that reflects the desired profile.*

"So . . . you recruited kids?"

"Parents volunteered their children," Gabriel said. "Again, imagine if you could offer your children a better life."

"My parents volunteered me and Kenzie and Marcy?" Jonah's stomach twisted. "They said, 'Go ahead, experiment on our children'?"

"Those weren't the words they used, but yes. They were involved in the planning and decision-making process. They were members of the governing council of the collaborative."

Jonah felt cut loose, set adrift by these revelations. Like most orphans, he'd put his dead parents on a pedestal. Had created in his imagination the kind of life he would have had if they'd survived. Another daydream exploded, reduced to ash. He could almost taste it on his tongue.

"What did you do to us?" Jonah asked. "Gamma rays? Radioactive spiders? Gene splitting? Alien sex?"

Lilith flinched a little. *I compounded potions designed to enhance and expand native capabilities in the gifted by modifying their Weirstones.*

"That sounds so much better than 'We did random experiments on helpless children,'" Jonah said.

It was all science based, Lilith said. *I'd been working in that field for years. I was the foremost expert in the world.*

"That's what she told me," Gabriel said, with a sidelong look at Jonah.

"Did everybody get the same stuff?"

She shook her head. *It was formulated individually based on what guild the subject belonged to and an individual assessment and treatment goals.*

"When you say 'treatment goals,' did you try to remake people to fit into a slot, or did you go with—"

Jonah, Lilith said. *We never meant to do you harm. I don't know if there's any way to convince you of that, but—*

"It sounds to me like thousands of people knew exactly what you were up to at Thorn Hill," Jonah said. "How did you hope to keep it a secret?"

"Volunteers were required to agree to memory modification," Gabriel said. Seeing Jonah's expression, he said, "We had no choice."

"So people volunteered, and volunteered their children, and then you erased the memory of that, so they had no idea what was being done to them as it progressed? Must've been tempting to just skip the volunteer part."

"There was no need for that, since we had so many volunteers." Gabriel sighed in exasperation. "They signed informed consent forms. Would it have been more acceptable to you if we'd imprisoned people at Thorn Hill after the project began to prevent word from leaking out?" Gabriel seemed to be regaining his usual confidence. He was the kind of person who always landed on his feet. "We wanted people to have the freedom to come and go without compromising the project."

"Just not the freedom to make informed decisions," Jonah said. "And all of this was strictly for self-defense? Since when is assassination a defensive weapon?"

"It can be, used judiciously," Gabriel said.

"You're saying there were no plans for a frontal assault on the Wizard Guild some time down the road?" Jonah persisted.

Gabriel looked away. "In any large group of people, there will be differing philosophies and agendas," he said. "There were some among us who believed that the only way to convince wizards to leave us alone was to make them pay a blood price. Who favored creating an army of savants and assassins, to be called *Nightshade.*"

"Catchy name," Jonah said. "What about you, Gabriel? Where did you fit on that continuum?"

"That's not important," Gabriel said.

"It's important to me," Jonah said. "You were the one who bought the property, who established the commune, who hired Lilith to brew up her potions. What did *you* intend?"

Gabriel stared straight ahead for a long moment, clenching and unclenching his jaw. Then he looked up at Jonah without a trace of apology. "I intended to go to war," he said.

Jonah cocked his head. "You . . . you meant to hurt them enough to convince them to leave us alone? To demonstrate that we could defend ourselves?"

Gabriel smiled, a hard-edged bitter smile without a trace of amusement in it. "I intended to hunt down and destroy every last member of the Wizard Guild. I intended to extinguish that genetic line."

Jonah staggered back a step, wrapping his arms around himself, feeling as if he'd taken a serious punch to the gut. "Wh-what?" he choked out.

"Consider this, Jonah," Gabriel said, briskly, as if referencing an argument he'd made many times. "From the very beginning, from the founding of the guilds in Dragon's Ghyll, from that original betrayal, wizards have never swerved from their purpose: to gain power by oppressing others. It's gone on for centuries. I believe the desire for power is built into the matrix of their stones. They cannot change, and we can't live with that any longer."

Jonah's skin pebbled as he broke into a cold sweat. "DeVries was right," he whispered. "DeVries was right all along."

✂ CHAPTER THIRTY ✄
THE THRILL IS GONE

"**W**hat did you say?" Gabriel asked, though Jonah was sure he'd heard.

"Rowan DeVries. He claimed that Thorn Hill was conspiring against the Wizard Guild, that it was a nest of terrorists, and they died of a self-inflicted wound. I told him he was wrong."

He is *wrong,* Lilith cut in. *About that last part, anyway.*

You wanted the truth, Jonah thought. Be careful what you wish for.

"So." Jonah extended his hands, palms up. "Lilith says I'm a spectacular success. A success at what? What was my role supposed to be?"

"Whatever I intended, it didn't work out," Gabriel said, shrugging as if to dismiss the question.

Jonah slammed the chair aside so that it hit the floor with a clatter. "No," he growled, gripping the front of Gabriel's leather jacket and lifting him, chair and all, off the floor.

"Don't think you can put me off with a pat on the head this time."

"Jonah!" Gabriel cried, staring down at Jonah's ungloved hands, his face shiny with sweat. He struggled once again to free his arms.

Jonah! Lilith cried. *Put him down. We need him. Enough knowledge died at Thorn Hill.*

Jonah took a deep breath. Let it out. Set Gabriel down.

I knew this would happen, Lilith murmured.

Jonah whirled on her. "Why? Because the two of you created a monster?"

You were meant to be a weapon, not a monster, Lilith said. *The keystone of our defense. A physically gifted predator who could adapt to multiple situations. Who could go unarmed into secure facilities and come away with a kill. Someone with acute hearing, vision, and sense of smell. Someone so physically strong that you would prevail in any physical fight, and so beautiful and charming that no one would ever question your intentions.*

"Someone who could kill his little sister with a kiss," Jonah said, feeling oddly hollow, as if even his most painful wounds had lost their ability to torment him.

No. Lilith took a step toward Jonah. *That was not part of it. That was not our doing. Why would we create someone who kills accidentally?*

"So you're saying that you had nothing to do with the fact that your assassin has a killing touch?"

Gabriel and Lilith looked at each other, radiating mingled guilt and deception.

"If you wanted to get away with lying to me," Jonah said, "you shouldn't have created an empath."

"All *right*," Gabriel said. "That *was* part of the build. But it was meant to be a weapon, not a curse. You were supposed to be able to turn it on and off at will."

"Whose will?"

"Yours," Gabriel said.

"Oops," Jonah said. "You want credit for my uncanny good looks and my remarkable grace and skill with weaponry, but not for—for this." Jonah held up his bare hands.

Lilith and Gabriel said nothing, like parents who don't know what to do with their tantrumming child.

Jonah wished he could bring the other shadeslayers in, and let them listen to these revelations directly. But he was afraid that it would turn into a melee.

"There's something I don't get, though," Jonah said. "Why just one of me? While you were at it, why not create an army?"

You must understand, we were in the beginning stages of our research, Lilith said. *We did not know what the possibilities and limitations were. Some therapies didn't turn out the way we expected, and it often took years to find that out. If we'd had a tested protocol from the beginning, we might have been able to create an army of Jonahs. As it was, you were the best candidate and the best outcome in the military trials.*

"So what with all this trial and error, you don't think you could have messed up and poisoned us? Assuming that you didn't intend to kill thousands of people."

"You'll have to ask Lilith," Gabriel said. "I wasn't there."

How many times do I have to say this—I did not *make a mistake.* Even without the benefit of facial cues, even mind-to-mind, Jonah could tell that Lilith was furious. *Believe me, I've had a lot of time to think about it. There was* nothing in my *therapies that could have caused these results. Besides, I just told you that each person received personalized therapy. So how could it be that on one particular night, everyone was poisoned?*

"There wasn't some common element in all the treatments?" Jonah persisted, "Something that could have been contaminated or used at too high a concentration or—"

No, Lilith said. Then paused. *That's not entirely true. Everyone received life-extension therapy, no matter what their ages or home guild.* She paused. *I'm guessing that's why we've persisted as shades. Our bodies were damaged beyond repair, but our minds and memories survive.*

"Where is your evidence, Lilith?" Gabriel exploded. "It may be appealing to blame this on some mysterious poisoner, but in science we go with the least-complex explanation. I know you never meant for it to happen, but it did. The only justice in all of this was that you were a victim yourself."

Jonah had an epiphany. "Gabriel. *That's* why you refused to target wizards, even though you told us they were to blame for the massacre," he said. "You were ready to slaughter them to begin with, but now you couldn't, because of your own guilt."

Gabriel resisted the admission for a long moment, then nodded. "How could I favor bringing wizards to justice when I was responsible—at least in part—for the largest slaughter of Anawizard Weir in history?"

"Especially when you're still walking around free," Jonah said. "Awkward."

Gabriel bowed his head. "Even if I didn't intend it, it happened. For months after the disaster, I couldn't bear to return to Thorn Hill. I even considered suicide. When I did go back, and I saw what was going on there, I realized that the survivors needed an advocate to protect their interests."

"So you decided not to kill yourself," Jonah murmured. "Damn noble of you."

Gabriel bit back his first response. "I couldn't undo what had happened, but knew that I could be of more help to the survivors by establishing the Anchorage and developing treatments that might help them. I kept the mines going in Brazil, and did a lot of my ongoing research there until the Anchorage was built. At first, I hoped for a cure. But, despite Lilith's meticulous lab reports, nothing seemed to help. All I've been able to do is treat symptoms."

That's because you're not treating the real problem, Lilith said. *The problem is not the therapies I compounded. We were poisoned, plain and simple. The poison interacted with our treatments, producing this result. Who would want to do that? It had to have been the Wizard Guild.*

Gabriel was still shaking his head.

Don't forget that my daughter died, too. And that proves it was the water supply or an aerosol or some other method of poisoning, because she was not receiving any therapy at the time. In fact, there were a number of people who were in the middle of a treatment window. They still died.

That argument seemed to make an impression. Gabriel thought about this for a while, then said, "You're sure it wasn't a cumulative effect?"

All at once? On the same night? Lilith snapped. *On thousands of people receiving starkly different therapies? No, I don't have any proof. Being dead, I haven't been able to do a thorough investigation. That, it seems to me, was your job. But you were too busy blaming me and trying to hide your involvement. You cared more about your reputation than finding real help for these victims.*

"That's not true," Gabriel fired back. "I have dedicated

my life to the survivors. The profits from the club, every-thing from the mines, relentless fund-raising—it all goes to provide for them. I relocated here, because it's much easier to access staff and supplies, and it's a good place to raise funds for support of the foundation."

"Couldn't there have been accidental contamination of the water supply, as the Wizard Guild claims?" Jonah said, eager to get back to possible causes of Thorn Hill. "Something that came from the labs?"

Lilith shook her head. *I just don't see how it's possible,* she said. *A totally separate water supply served the labs, and we were acutely conscious of protecting the environment against spills and contamination. I'm a scientist, and I was extremely selective in choosing the staff who worked with me.*

"Were you working on poisons as well as genetic modification?"

Lilith glared at Gabriel. Finally, reluctantly, Gabriel nodded.

He did, I didn't, Lilith said. *Poison is—poison is—* She shuddered.

"So," Jonah said, "you created your own chemical dump in the Brazilian jungle, and yet you think it's more likely some unknown person crept in and put poison in the water?"

We used very careful techniques and controls, Lilith said. *I've worked around dangerous compounds for years. My little girl was living there, for God's sake. Even if I were careless with my own life or that of my friends—which I'm not—I'd never risk her. I was doing it for her, after all.*

"That's what motivated most of the parents at Thorn Hill," Gabriel said. "They didn't want their children enslaved in the same way that they had been, to have to look over their shoulders all of their lives. To risk death if they ran away." His voice trembled.

"What about you two?" Jonah asked. "Were you receiving treatment as well?"

Gabriel nodded. "At first. But, as I said, the treatments seemed to have little effect on grown people."

You are not responsible for what happened, Lilith said. *Don't you see? The difference between us is that I was there the night of the massacre, and you were not.*

Hope flickered across Gabriel's face. More and more, his attention was shifting away from Jonah and toward Lilith. She's winning him over, Jonah thought. She's telling him what he wants to hear. He wants desperately to believe it after a decade of blaming himself.

"How did you find out about shades?" Jonah asked Gabriel, trying to nip the lovefest in the bud. "How did you know they existed? What made you decide to make them a target?"

Gabriel looked from Lilith to Jonah, licked his lips, and said, "I stayed in Brazil for two years after the accident, treating the survivors, burying the dead, and optimizing the mines. Most of the shades remained near the site of the massacre—at first, anyway."

"Like ghosts of the murdered, haunting the scene of the crime," Jonah murmured. "Maybe hoping to get their bodies back."

"Maybe," Gabriel said. "We began hearing wild reports about zombies, some from our own employees. Turnover increased—it became difficult to keep fully staffed for any length of time. In those days, of course, shades were merely possessing those who were already dead. We had no idea what was going on. We began hunting the undead, but when we chopped them to bits, the shades slipped away invisibly. We didn't realize what was going on until we discovered that the Nightshade amulets made them visible."

Jonah recalled wondering how Emma had acquired a pendant. "You know, Gabriel, I thought you had those pieces made for us, to help in the hunt for shades."

Lilith shook her head. *Those were made before the massacre, to help members of our community to find the gifted at a distance—to pinpoint the gifted over a large area.*

"So you could hunt them down?"

"So we could locate our enemies—or our friends," Gabriel said. "Shades must have a magical component, or aura, because the amulets make them visible."

This is what I don't understand, Lilith said. *How did that hurt you, that we sought out cadavers to live in?*

"Because we couldn't communicate with you, we didn't know what your intentions were," Gabriel said. "And once you discovered the advantages of claiming a fresh corpse, we knew we had to take action. I knew that I had an obligation to help them, too—to put them to rest."

Willingly or unwillingly, Lilith said wryly. *You might have asked whether we wanted your help.*

"How could we do that?" Gabriel snorted. "It wasn't until Jonah joined Nightshade that we realized that he could communicate with you."

"How disappointing this must have been," Jonah said. "We were supposed to be holy warriors, fighting the oppressors, our signia emblazoned on our arms." Jonah ran his fingers over his sleeve where the tattoo was. "And now we're fighting with one another. The Wizard Guild should be laughing at us. Maybe they are."

It doesn't have to be this way, Gabriel, Lilith said urgently. *We still have an army. If we join forces, we can restore the dead warriors of Nightshade. And then nobody can stand against us.*

⟡ CHAPTER THIRTY-ONE ⟐
NOT FEELING THE LOVE

Jonah paced back and forth. "You enjoy being a saint, don't you, Gabriel? Hosting your big benefit concerts, having everyone marvel at how much you've sacrificed for 'Gabriel's Kids.' It was perfect. The grown-ups all died, and the kids didn't know. Once we all die off, you can forget about all this and get on with your life."

"No," Gabriel said. "You're wrong."

"What a shock it must have been to discover that the dead were still around to haunt you. Even worse, I could communicate with them, and I kept pestering you about meeting with them." He spun and faced Gabriel. "The question is, why am I still alive? It would have been so easy. Slip a little something into my meds, and I'd be just another shade, voiceless and invisible except to those hunting us."

"No," Gabriel said. "No. I would never hurt you. How can you say that?"

"You mean, after all you've done for me?"

Jonah, Lilith said. *You're wrong about Gabriel. He loves you. He always has.*

"Not feeling the love right now," Jonah said. "How do you think the remaining Thorn Hill survivors will feel when they find out you've been lying to them for a decade? That you were experimenting on them? And you've been using them to clean up the mess you made?"

For once, Gabriel had no answer. So Lilith spoke up. She faced Gabriel directly. *Gabe. I want to help you fix this, as much as it can be fixed. Even though I don't know what caused the catastrophe at Thorn Hill, I'm the one most likely to figure it out. I've already discovered some treatments that help.*

"Like blood magic?" Gabriel said. "I never thought you would resort to tactics like that."

How many sides of an issue can he be on? Jonah thought.

Here's the difference between us, Lilith said. *You haven't been willing to bring those responsible for Thorn Hill to justice, because you couldn't wash the guilt from your own hands. Some might question our tactics, but I know for a fact that I am not responsible for the massacre. The children of Thorn Hill were healthy, and happy, and blooming like roses until the night they were poisoned. It was wizards who poisoned us; it had to be. Who else stood to gain from that catastrophe?*

Gabriel stared at her, hope flickering in his eyes.

Yes, Lilith said. *If I'm not guilty, you're not guilty either. Not of this, anyway.*

Clearly, Lilith was wooing Gabriel. So she needed him for something. But what?

I know you've had grievous losses, Lilith went on, *but you lost no family at Thorn Hill. I lost my daughter, who was all the family I had left. She meant the world to me. I will do anything possible* to help the innocent survivors of Thorn Hill. *And I will not leave Claire's death unavenged. I will see that mainliners pay the price for what they did.*

"Isn't that mission creep?" Jonah said. "First it was wizards, and now it's all of the magical guilds?"

Lilith turned on him. *It's been open season on savants ever since Thorn Hill, and the underguilds are some of the worst offenders. So many have died who should have lived. I should know—the victims come to me at the end of it. Any mainliners who are not part of the solution are part of the problem.*

Turning away from Jonah, Lilith crossed to Gabriel, put her hand on his shoulder. *The thing is, I can't work. Not like this. I don't know how much longer this body will last. Even at my best, I have no fine motor skills. I can't communicate with anyone but Jonah without a heavy dose of blood magic. I have no lab. We need to work together, like we did before. And that means you're going to have to stop trying to kill me.*

Gabriel's eyes flicked to Jonah, then back to Lilith. "I don't know what Jonah's told you, but—"

Let's not begin this thing by lying to each other, Lilith said. *The number of people who know the truth about Thorn Hill is growing, so don't think you can keep this quiet by silencing me. Or Jonah.*

Gabriel shifted in his chair. Once again, he pulled at his shackles. "All right," he said. "I'll call a cease-fire for now, and we'll continue to talk."

"Does the cease-fire extend to mainliners?" Jonah demanded. "Or is it open season now?"

Open season? Lilith seemed puzzled. *What do you—?*

"I mean, will you continue to kill the gifted, and we'll continue to get the blame?"

"Jonah," Gabriel said. "I don't think we—"

He deserves to know, Lilith said. She turned her full attention to Jonah, for almost the first time since Gabriel had arrived. *While we negotiate, we'll continue to need blood magic in order to function. We'll do our best not to embarrass you or make you a target. Perhaps blood magic can be collected elsewhere, so that you don't come under scrutiny.*

"You think I'm worried about being *embarrassed?*" The turmoil in Jonah's gut had turned into what felt like a lead weight. In less than an hour, it seemed that Gabriel and Lilith were forming a team again. Who knew where that would lead? As for Jonah, he knew a lot more than he did before, but none of this would help Kenzie or anyone else. "It seems like we're back where we started," he said. "Somebody poisoned the water supply. We don't know what was used, and we don't know how to treat it. And before long, we'll all be dead."

Have a little faith, Lilith said. *I haven't given up. I will find a way to fix this. Your participation will be critical as we move forward.*

"If you're expecting me to go out and kill mainliners, that's a nonstarter. I'm done with being the assassin on call, for Gabriel or anyone else." Jonah reached for the chain binding Gabriel to his chair, and Gabriel flinched back. "Don't worry," Jonah said. "I'm not going to *touch* you. People don't always get what they deserve." He gripped the chain, hard, until the links crumbled and the chain broke into pieces.

Lilith leaned close to Gabriel. *He'll come around,* she whispered. It sounded like betrayal in Jonah's ears.

"I don't want to play a role in any of your schemes," Jonah said. "In fact, I'm having a hard time being in the same room with you."

He turned and walked out.

When you storm out of a place, it really helps if you have

someplace to storm to. And a plan for what to do after you get there. And an awareness of who might be waiting outside.

When Jonah walked out of the terminal alone, he hadn't gone more than a dozen paces before Alison and Charlie were incoming. "Where's Gabriel?" Charlie demanded, looking over Jonah's shoulder.

"In there," Jonah said, pointing. "He and Lilith are still talking, making plans, catching up on old times. I really felt like a third wheel."

Alison scowled at Jonah. "What do you mean, 'old times'?"

"Did you know they were, shall we say, *going out*, back in the day? I sure didn't."

"Going out?" Alison grabbed Jonah by the front of his jacket and jerked him close. "What are you talking about?"

"Alison," Charlie said quietly, as if to avoid startling either of them. "Gloves are off."

Alison immediately let go of Jonah and leaped back. Then tried to act like it was some kind of deft strategic move.

"How could they be in there talking?" Charlie said, keeping his distance. "I thought the only way to talk to shades was through you."

"I thought so, too," Jonah said. "Lilith is using blood magic to amplify her voice. Who knew that was possible?"

"Cut to the chase," Alison said, cradling her shiv-launcher. "Did you kill Lilith or not?"

"Not," Jonah said. "I think Gabriel's changed his mind about killing her."

"Is that what he said?" Alison persisted.

"Not in so many words," Jonah said.

"Did you make some kind of deal with Lilith?" Alison's voice rose. "Did you agree to give her Gabriel?" She leveled her weapon at Jonah. "Is that why he didn't come out with you?"

"Don't point that thing at me," Jonah said. "Gabriel's fine. He's feeling better than he has in years. He just dumped a crapload of guilt."

They both squinted at him, channeling suspicion.

By now, Thérèse and Mike had emerged from hiding, and Jonah waved them over. "Want to know what Thorn Hill was all about? Here's the news. Lilith and Gabriel were in the business of turning children into their personal army of customized mutant Weir."

After a long moment of silent gaping, Alison was the first to speak.

"You're lying," she said flatly. "You used to be loyal to Gabriel, but now you never miss a chance to stab him in the back."

"I'm telling the truth," Jonah said. "Gabriel is the one who's been lying to us. We were part of a massive experiment in genetic engineering. According to them, our parents *volunteered* us."

"They told you that?" Thérèse said.

Jonah nodded.

"So—we're savants because of something they did?" Thérèse said, still dissecting what Jonah had just said.

"Lilith claims that our condition is multifactorial. Her theory is, after they modified our Weirstones, we were poisoned."

A half dozen shades had appeared from among the surrounding buildings, Brendan in the lead.

What's going on in there? Brendan asked Jonah. *Where are Lilith and Gabriel?*

"They are talking," Jonah said. "Isn't that what you wanted?" He tipped his head toward the terminal. "Don't take my word for it. Have a look for yourself."

"Fine, I will," Charlie said, turning away, toward the terminal.

No! Brendan said, stepping into Charlie's path.

Though Charlie couldn't hear him, his intention was clear. "Get out of my way," Charlie hissed.

The rule was we all stay outside, Brendan said. He pointed at Alison. *Jonah, you promised. No weapons. No double cross.*

Some of the hosted shades were gripping metal bars and broken bottles, creeping closer. The other slayers clustered around Charlie, protecting his back. It was like two angry mobs, with Jonah trying to play peacemaker.

"Better stand down," Jonah messaged them. "Lilith's called a cease-fire. She'll be upset if you mess it up. Besides, if anyone's been double-crossed, it's us. The children of Thorn Hill."

Jonah found it hard to play the role of peacemaker while channeling rage. It was like he'd forgotten how to be charming.

"Sorry," Jonah said. "I can't do this anymore. I'm going back to Oxbow. I promised to tell Natalie and Rudy what's gone down. You can come with me if you want, or stay here, but I suggest that you talk to Gabriel and Lilith before you start fighting."

"I'll go with Jonah," Alison said abruptly. "The rest of you, check out the terminal and see what's what. Let me know what you find out."

"Come on, then," Jonah said, turning away.

❦ CHAPTER THIRTY-TWO ❧
PAYDAY

All the way to Oxbow, Alison walked a few paces behind Jonah, her shiv-launcher slung over her shoulder, radiating resentment. Jonah tried to ignore the prickling between his shoulder blades.

Alison seems angrier with me than she is with Gabriel, Jonah thought. Is it that she doesn't believe me, or is it that she just doesn't care?

When Jonah walked into the practice room, he'd expected to find Natalie and Rudy waiting for him. He hadn't expected to find Emma there, too. She was seated on the floor, elbows on her knees, the three of them a triangle of tension.

Emma looked up at Jonah, and her emotions washed over him, a tangle of guilt and regret. His first thought was that it had to do with what had gone down in the Flats. But, no. How could it?

Alison stopped dead when she saw Emma. "What are *you* doing here? You're not in this."

"She can stay," Jonah said, adding quickly, "if she wants to."

"But—"

"She deserves to know what's going on," Jonah said. "She's one of us."

"She's *not* one of us!" Alison hissed. "At least not—not in that way."

"She's a Thorn Hill survivor," Jonah said. "She knows about Nightshade, Lilith, all of that. Her mother died at Thorn Hill. Her father—her father's dead, too. She's in."

Alison scowled. "Does Gabriel know that she—?"

"I don't give a flying—" Jonah paused, took a deep breath, let it out, then said, "Why, no, Gabriel doesn't know. When he stops keeping secrets from us, we'll stop keeping secrets from him."

"Look," Emma said, "I came over because I need to talk to Jonah. But, listen, if you all want me to wait outside while you talk, I'll—"

"No," Jonah said. "Stay and hear this." His gaze met Alison's, and she looked away first. She slumped into a chair and sat, staring down at her hands.

After an awkward silence, Natalie said, "So. What happened at the meeting with Lilith?"

And so Jonah told them. Rudy and Natalie listened with expressions of growing disbelief. At first, they interrupted with questions, but those dwindled as the full import began to sink in.

Emma just sat frozen, saying nothing, her expression peculiar, almost a plea for forgiveness.

When Jonah came to a stopping point, Natalie and Rudy looked at each other, then back at him.

"They were . . . experimenting on us?" Natalie's voice was pitched higher than usual.

"Gabriel keeps trying to call it something else, like we were coconspirators or something," Jonah said. "But, yeah. Basically."

"And so—you're saying it was *Gabriel* who poisoned us?" Rudy said.

"You be the judge," Jonah said. "I've pretty much told you exactly what they said to me. He says it wasn't him, it was Lilith, and Lilith says wasn't her, it was wizards. So maybe we weren't poisoned at all, it's all been a misunderstanding."

"If we have to choose who to believe, wouldn't we have to choose Gabriel?" Natalie said. "I mean, I know you and Gabriel have had your differences, but he's the one who's been here for us."

"Lilith has lied about other things," Rudy said. "I mean, she claims she had nothing to do with the killings at Seph McCauley's."

Alison's head came up. "It was her," she muttered. "It had to be."

Jonah shrugged. "I guess McCauley has plenty of enemies. My point is, Gabriel's been lying to us, keeping secrets for years about the true purpose of Thorn Hill. They've both admitted that they experimented on us. I think we have to ask whether his obsession with riffing shades has more to do with keeping his secret than putting restless souls to rest."

"What secret?" Rudy asked.

"All this time, he's been worried that if it came out that he and Lilith were feeding us potions to turn us into an army of mutants—"

"Savants," Natalie said.

"Army of *mutants*," Jonah repeated. "He'd be blamed for the massacre."

"And are you?" Rudy asked. "Blaming him for the massacre, I mean?"

Irritably, Jonah raked his fingers through his hair. "I don't know what to think."

"Well," Natalie said, "you could argue that if mainliners knew what was *really* going on at Thorn Hill, they'd exterminate all of us. Gabriel *may* have been trying to protect us."

Jonah bit his lower lip. "The ironic thing is, Gabriel kept warning me not to talk to Lilith, that she would charm me into believing her lies. Now I think *he* really wants to believe it. He wants to be a hero in the worst way. And she's giving him that chance. In one conversation Lilith has persuaded Gabriel that the story he's been telling us is true—that we were poisoned on orders from the Wizard Guild. We don't know who did it, and we don't know what poisons were used."

"What if it's the truth?" Emma blurted out.

For a long moment, nobody said anything. Until Natalie said, "Why do you say that, Emma?"

Emma shook her head. "Never mind. You're right. I don't know why I'm even butting in, talking about things I know nothing about."

She feels guilty, Jonah thought, confused. Why would that be? Because she's healthier than the rest of us?

"Do we even know that this Lilith is who she says she is?" Rudy asked. "I mean—she's not in her original body, right? She could be anybody, pretending to be Lilith."

"Gabriel seemed convinced, and he should know," Jonah said. "They weren't just business partners; they were lovers."

"What?" Natalie leaned forward, hands on her blue-jeaned knees. "That's—no. No way."

"Surprise," Jonah said. "For weeks, we've been hunting Lilith down on Gabriel's orders, and it turns out we were assigned to riff Gabriel's old girlfriend, who is one of the few people who knew the truth about Thorn Hill. She's a sorcerer, and apparently an expert in developing potions that modify Weirstones. Gabriel hired her to do that at Thorn Hill. She has her own reasons for wanting to dodge responsibility. She lost a child there."

"You think she poisoned her own child?" Natalie said, frowning.

Jonah snorted. "Right now, we don't have enough information to sort the truth from lies. All I know is that we went through this whole farce of a meeting with Lilith, and we're no closer than we were before to finding out how to . . . how to fix this. Fix us."

"But . . ." Natalie's face was lit up with hope. "If Lilith was the one who compounded the potions, shouldn't she be able to tell us what she used?"

"This is not new information to Gabriel, remember," Jonah said. "He's been using Lilith's notes for the past ten years, trying to come up with a therapy that works. Lilith says that's because she did not make a mistake. None of this is her fault, so Gabriel's been wasting his time. If there's any good news coming out of this, it's that Lilith and Gabriel have called a truce. Gabriel agreed to leave off riffing shades for now. Lilith, however, has no plans to stop killing mainliners. I just don't see how this ends well."

"What are we going to do?" Rudy said.

"Don't look to me for answers," Jonah said. "I'm all out of

wisdom." All out of hope, too. Discouragement weighed on him like a lead cloak. I'm going to lose Kenzie, he thought. He hadn't realized how much he'd banked on this meeting with Lilith to provide a way out.

"Jonah," Natalie said. "Don't you think we should wait until we figure out who's telling the truth before we do anything rash?"

"What makes you think that will ever happen?" Jonah snarled. "Nobody's told us the truth up to now. I see no reason to think that'll change before we're dead." He pressed the heel of his hand against his forehead.

"Jonah?"

He looked up to see that Emma had pulled on her flannel shirt and the winter coat she'd bought at Goodwill. She was shifting her weight from foot to foot like she was eager to be on her way.

Who could blame her?

"I need to go, but I wanted to talk to you in private if I could."

Jonah's weary synapses finally fired. "Right," he said, unfolding to his feet. "Anyway, I have something for you. From Kenzie."

"Something from Kenzie?" Emma looked mystified.

"A music notebook? He said you gave it to him and asked him to look it over. It's at my place. If you can wait a minute, I'll—"

"I'll come with you," Emma said. "And leave from there."

꧁ CHAPTER THIRTY-THREE ꧂
AIN'T NOTHING LIKE THE REAL THING

They rode the elevator up in silence, past the eighth floor, where Emma's room still waited for her, to the twelfth, where Jonah's room was, one floor below Gabriel's.

She waited while Jonah went through the security routine, opened the door, and stood aside so she could enter.

Following her in, he shut the door and disappeared into the studio.

Emma planted her feet, waiting until he returned, carrying Tyler's notebook in his two hands. He'd replaced the leather gloves, she noticed, as if he felt naked without them.

"How is Kenzie doing?" Emma asked, as he handed it over. "Is he any better?"

Jonah's eyes tightened in pain, and he shook his head. "He just keeps losing ground."

"What about that new medicine?" Emma clutched the notebook like it was some kind of life raft. "That seemed to help."

Jonah spun away from her, staring out the window into gray smears of snowflakes. "That's not an option."

"But if it—" Emma stopped talking when she saw the granite windowsills crumble under Jonah's hands. She cleared her throat. "What are you going to do?"

"About—?"

"Gabriel. And Lilith. All that. Where do you go from here?"

"I haven't a clue," Jonah said. "Like I said, I'm all out of wisdom."

Emma took a quick breath. "What you need to do is leave here. Now."

"You think I *want* to stay here?" Jonah said, his voice edged with desperation. "I'd love to go someplace else—but I can't."

"Because of Kenzie?"

Jonah just looked at her, lips pressed together, because, frankly, it was a really dumb question.

The conviction came back to her, stronger than ever. *This is not a person who could kill a twelve-year-old girl. An innocent.*

"Look here," Emma said. "The committee that was looking into the Montessori thing is now checking into the Halloween murders. They're going to want to talk to you about it."

"I've already spoken to the police," Jonah said.

"I know. This—this is a separate investigation. By the council." Emma licked her lips. "Rowan DeVries is going to accuse you of murder."

"DeVries?" Jonah's eyes narrowed. "I thought he disappeared."

"He's been in hiding. Now he's recovered enough that

he's ready to testify that you attacked him and tried to kill him at McCauley's. There's a hearing scheduled for next week. Saturday."

"How do you know?"

Emma knew that she was on a slippery slope, beginning that long slide, with no way to grab a handhold. "He told me."

"Why would he tell you that?"

Emma ran out of words. She just froze like a small animal caught in the headlights.

"Why would he tell you that?" Jonah repeated, his voice piercing her soul like splinters of ice.

"He wants me to testify," Emma said. "He wants me to support his story."

"And will you?"

"I told him I would, but I won't."

"But you won't. So who did you lie to, Emma?" Jonah asked. "Him or me?"

"Him," Emma said, realizing it was a lot harder to go through life telling the truth than she'd ever thought.

"That's reassuring, because I didn't do it." He showed his teeth in a bitter smile. "If it had been me, he would have stayed dead."

He closed the distance between them, and all at once Emma was acutely aware of being in the presence of a predator. Some part of her mind heard the thud as the notebook hit the floor.

Jonah rested his gloved hands on her shoulders, gently encircled her neck with his leather-clad fingers. Her skin pebbled and burned under his touch, sending *do something* signals to her brain, a mangled mix of terror, guilt, and desire.

Should she tell him that DeVries had grabbed her off the street and threatened to turn her into the police? That he had threatened to implicate her in the Halloween murders if she didn't play nice?

No. Jonah would go after DeVries for sure. Emma could see the tragic ending of that story, and she didn't want to go there.

"Why are you here, Emma? Are you spying on us? Gathering a little more evidence before the hearing?"

"No," Emma said. "I came here to see you—to see everyone. And tell you what was going on."

"Maybe," Jonah said, "or maybe DeVries sent you here to lead me into a trap."

"That's what he wanted," Emma said. "But—"

"But now that you're here with me, you're having second thoughts, aren't you?" His voice was a caress, like a melody that went straight to the soul.

"Don't," Emma said, cheeks burning, trying to keep her head above water. "Don't you get it? I'm on whatever side you're on."

"Of course you are," Jonah murmured. "I'm irresistible. When you're with me, you're on my side. All I have to do is turn on the charm. Once you leave, no doubt you'll regain your senses."

"That's not it," Emma said, planting her hands in the middle of his chest and pushing. She might have been pushing against a brick wall.

"It's so much easier to kill the living than the dead, Emma." Jonah's lips were so very close to her skin, his eyes all blue ice and shadow, like the kind of death that comes in the wintertime, when the cold creeps into your bones. "So many ways to do it, and I'm good at all of them. I'm a monster by design."

Emma wished she could say something that would convince him that he was wrong, but she had no skill for that. So what she said was, "Just shut the hell up."

Jonah stared at her, the blank, hard expression on his face nudged aside by surprise.

"I'm so sick and tired of you talking crazy shit like that."

"Maybe I *am* crazy," he said.

"These are hard times," Emma said. "It's hard to know who or what to believe in. But I believe in you, and it has nothing to do with your damn pretty face and your big, blue eyes. Do you take me for that kind of a fool?"

For once, smooth-talking Jonah Kinlock seemed to be at a loss for words. "N-no," he said. "It's just that I—"

"Now, I'll admit, it took me a while to figure it out—what I saw in you. You had me convinced that it was all about your good looks and your whiskey voice. That I was being enchanted or charmed or something. I'm not good with people, and so I doubted my own common sense.

"Now I know. It's not about what you look like. It's who you are. Don't forget—I've seen you in action. I've seen you with Kenzie. I've seen you risk yourself to save other people. And I have heard you. I have heard your music. I've listened to those words that come straight from your soul, and I am here to tell you that they come from a *good* place." She took a quick breath. "A good place."

She slid her arms around him and pulled his body close, pressing her face into his shirt so that she could feel his wildly beating heart just inches away. His body rigid, as usual. Her frustrated tears soaked into the fabric.

"You are not a monster. This is real. If there's anything in this world that's real, this is it. This is not about the magic. It's about you."

His hands fell away from her neck and he wrapped his arms around her, crushing her to him. "Don't you see?" he whispered, each quick breath warming her ear. "This just makes it worse."

"We could leave together," she said. "We'll take Kenzie—we'll work out something. Find a cabin in the mountains somewhere. I—I have a little money."

Jonah shook his head. "You can pass as a mainliner. Kenzie can't. I can't take Kenzie out of the only place he's ever been safe. And if they ever find out about—about me, the mainliners will hunt me down. You know they will."

"That's why you have to leave," Emma persisted. "They *are* coming after you."

Jonah shrugged. "Let them come. I'm not going to run from them. I'll stay and fight. But I won't get you tangled up in it."

"It's already happened," she said, her voice thick with emotion. "Too late."

"No," he said. "It's not too late. Not this time." He gently peeled her away from him. "If you play it smart, you can survive this. Leaving is a really good idea—for you. Something bad is about to happen, and my advice is to be as far away as possible when it does. Keep your head down, blend in, and survive."

Scooping the notebook off the floor, he shoved it toward Emma. "Now, go."

CHAPTER THIRTY-FOUR
HOME

Emma turned her back to the rising sun and headed toward Trinity, so tired and distracted by worry she nearly went the wrong way on the freeway.

One thing she knew, and had known from the start: she was not going to go into a hearing and help Rowan DeVries make a case against Jonah Kinlock. Even if she did it by telling the truth, there are ways to tell the truth that end in a lie.

If she'd made a mistake, it was listening to Rowan when he'd told her that it was Jonah's gift of persuasion that had turned her head. It wasn't about his blue eyes—it was what lay behind them. She did not believe that Jonah would murder a twelve-year-old girl. And if it was somebody else, there was a whole piece of the story she didn't know. And another murderer out there.

She didn't want to walk out on these people who had come to mean so much to her. Jonah. Kenzie. Natalie. Rudy. Leesha. Even Alison. If she ran away, they'd think she was guilty for sure. And a girl on her own can get backed into the wrong kind of corner. Besides, she had nowhere to go, other than Memphis, where the police were still looking for her.

But what was the alternative?

She thought about Chief Childers, how kind he had been. But that would change once he knew who she really was, that she had a police record, that she'd left Memphis after her grandfather was murdered.

By the time she exited the highway downtown, she'd decided. She would leave. DeVries couldn't make her testify if he couldn't find her. The police couldn't arrest her either. She could take her few thousand dollars and find a hole to hide in.

Nobody was home at Aunt Millie's. Emma changed clothes, washed her face, and scraped her hair back into a rubber band. Then carefully sorted through her clothes, picking out socks, underwear, a few shirts and pairs of jeans, and stuffing them into a duffel bag. She slid her money stash into a side pocket. It was the cash she'd been saving to set up her own woodshop. If she lived cheap, she could make it last a while.

That's what happens to dreams, she thought. They get sanded away by real life.

When she'd finished packing, she looked around to make sure she'd left enough behind that her room still looked lived-in. That should give her a little time. It helped that the council didn't mean to involve the police, so there wouldn't be some kind of bulletin put out on her.

She loaded the little she was taking into the Element, then did a quick look-around. That's when she spotted Tyler's notebook. It still lay where she'd dropped it on a table by the door. Running her fingertips over the plastic cover, she debated. She didn't really need a big old binder to carry around. But it was, after all, the only remnant of her father left to her. Lifting it from the table, she saw that one section bristled with those tiny sticky notes. The section dedicated to Emma. Pinned to the divider was a note from Kenzie.

The note was typed—she imagined Kenzie dictating it to Harry, his face illuminated by the light from the screen.

Emma—

> *Harry and I analyzed it every which way. Also took a whack with Sibelius. The one pattern I identified was that the time signature is not consistent. In other words, some measures are longer than others—some are 4:4 time, some are 4:5 or even 4:8, because some of the notes are the wrong duration and pitch. There didn't seem to be any repeating pattern. Here's a list of all the messed-up songs. You'll see that I went through and highlighted all of the inconsistent measures. I tried a mathematical analysis on the music. Still nothing. I think it's code that you might know the key for. Hope it means something to you.*

> *—K*

This was followed by a winnowed-down list of songs. Emma scanned them, looking for a clue. Kenzie had transcribed the titles in order as he went through the notebook. They weren't alphabetical—the arrangement didn't make any sense that she could see. Sometimes three or four songs were clean, followed by two annotated ones.

Emma flipped through the tagged songs, one by one, studying the marked measures. Finally, she grabbed a tablature notebook and an ink pen. She went through and wrote down all the mistimed notes. When she had a list, she looked it over. Nothing came to mind. Scooping up her guitar, she plunked them out. The sound was random, off-key, not any tune she'd heard before.

She went through the songs again, this time recording the lyrics opposite the extra notes in each marked measure. When she'd finished, she scanned the results, her pulse quickening.

Emma: 324 Venable Chapel Rd, Beasley, TN. Mickey has the key. I'm sorry.

Beasley? Where the hell was Beasley? She was firing up the computer to look when she stopped cold. Couldn't that kind of thing be traced, what you search for on a computer?

It was someplace in Tennessee, anyway. Now Emma knew, without a scrap of doubt, that she had to head south, though that was exactly what everyone would expect her to do.

She weighed her phone in her hand. Cell phones could be traced, too. But she didn't want to leave it here, because when she didn't show up, they'd be calling it and realize she hadn't taken it with her. So she packaged it up and addressed it to herself at the Anchorage so it would be waiting for her if she ever came back. She pasted all of Aunt Millie's stamps on it, and left a twenty to square things.

She knew she should slip away while she had the chance, without answering any questions or risking getting into a tangle. But she couldn't leave without saying good-bye to Leesha, who'd been kinder to her than just about anybody.

So she wrote a note and left it on the dining room table.

Leesha, I'm staying over in Cleveland for a few days, but I'll be back on the weekend. I just want to say thanks again for being such a friend to me. Your friend, Emma Lee.

On her way out of town, she dropped her packaged up cell phone into a mailbox.

⊙ CHAPTER THIRTY-FIVE ⊙
SAFE PASSAGE

The day after the meeting between Gabriel and Lilith, Gabriel called an all-hands meeting of Nightshade. Jonah slept in and went to the gym instead. Two hours later, he'd worked himself into a lather of sweat and his muscles had that familiar, wrung-out ache.

That's when he noticed that Natalie was waiting for him down on the floor.

He dropped lightly onto the hardwood beside her. "Hey, Nat," he said.

She radiated guilt, not meeting his eyes. "We missed you at the meeting," she said.

Jonah slapped his forehead. "Damn! Was that this morning?" He paused, and then asked, "How'd it go?" because Natalie seemed to be expecting it.

"It was . . . interesting," Natalie said. "Maybe even a little encouraging. Lilith was there."

"Was she?" Jonah said, pretending disinterest.

"Both she and Gabriel seemed disappointed that you weren't there."

"Really? Did she say that, or just, you know, use hand gestures?"

"She was hard to understand, but she was audible," Natalie said.

"You understand the cost of that, right?" Jonah said.

Natalie shifted her weight from foot to foot. "She let Gabriel do most of the talking."

"Gabriel does like to talk." Jonah toweled off. "What did he say?"

"He issued new ground rules for Nightshade. The field operatives are not to harm any shades, hosted or not. In return, shades are not to kill any more gifted here in Ohio."

"Terrific," Jonah said. "How was that received?"

"There were a lot of questions. I think most of us would like to give it a chance."

"What did Alison say?"

That was a direct hit, Jonah could tell.

"She . . . um . . . had reservations."

"The shades were on board, too?" Jonah cocked his head.

Natalie flushed. "There weren't any shades there."

"Ah. I see." Jonah slung his towel around his neck. "A cease-fire only works if both sides agree."

"Lilith is going to meet with them separately."

"Lilith controls only a handful of shades," Jonah said. "Otherwise, it's the Wild West out there." He paused. "What happens when she runs out of blood magic?"

"Lilith has a limited supply on hand. And there are some other therapies she'd like to try, based on her research."

"That's going to take a while," Jonah said, "and I don't think we have a while."

"We have to *try*, Jonah," Natalie said, tears pooling in her eyes. "I mean, what's the alternative?"

Jonah felt a twinge of guilt. It wasn't like he had one to offer. "So what's the plan?"

"We're going to begin a process of reconciliation," Natalie said.

"That's hard to do when you can't communicate."

"Gabriel is hoping that you will help with that."

Jonah just looked at her, his lips pressed tightly together.

"Well. Anyway. I thought you might want to know what went down," Natalie said, turning away.

"Thanks, Nat," Jonah called after her. "Thanks for filling me in. I hope this all works out."

After his shower, Jonah found himself walking to the Steel Wool Building for the second day in a row. He'd stopped in the night before and briefed Kenzie on what had gone down at the meeting between Gabriel and Lilith. Kenzie seemed to follow what Jonah was saying—he asked a couple of questions, but otherwise it seemed that staying alive consumed all of his strength and attention.

Stay with me, Kenzie, Jonah thought. I could really use your advice right now. Kenzie had a way of cutting through the bullshit. Maybe continually dancing on the knife's-edge of death did that to a person.

Jonah beat down the thought that if he could get his hands on more blood magic, he could restore Kenzie's health enough that they could leave the Anchorage together.

The streets seemed oddly deserted. He'd thought he might run into some Nightshade operatives who could tell him what had gone down at the meeting. He saw a few of the civilian students amid the usual pedestrians. Nobody from Nightshade.

But when Jonah reached Kenzie's room, the door was locked. Jonah pounded on the door. No answer. He called Kenzie's phone. It went to voice mail. He checked the time again. It was only six P.M. He might be asleep, but . . .

He keyed in the access code to the tablet outside Kenzie's room. It came up VACANT. A cold finger of fear ran down Jonah's spine. A voice shouted inside his head. *Too late!*

He turned, and charged down the hallway to the nurse's station. Todd Doherty, the evening shift nurse, had his head down, keying notes into a chart. He looked up at Jonah, and his face turned the color of library paste. "Jonah! It's good to—"

"Where is Kenzie? Why didn't anyone tell me he's been moved?"

"He's safe and comfortable, don't worry." Todd stared at Jonah's gloved hands.

"I'm so glad he's safe and comfortable; now tell me where he is," Jonah said, forcing the words between stiff lips.

"I can't," Todd said.

Jonah knew Todd, he liked Todd, but just now it was all he could do not to lunge across the desk between them and close his hands around Todd's throat. Instead, he said, "You can't? Because . . ."

"I can't because I don't know where he is."

"Really? How is it possible that you don't know?" Jonah said, his voice low and deadly.

Todd swallowed hard. "Mr. Mandrake said that if you had any questions you should come see him."

"Did he now?" Jonah leaned closer.

Todd scooted his chair back until it hit the wall, raising both hands to fend Jonah off. "Mr. Mandrake is in his office."

"Thank you," Jonah said on his way out the door.

"I'm so sorry, Jonah," Todd called after him.

Before heading to the Keep, Jonah made a quick detour around the back of Steel Wool to the back entrance—the entrance to Safe Passage. Jadine, the duty nurse, jumped when Jonah burst through the door.

"Jonah!" she said, coming quickly to her feet. "What brings you here? We don't have any residents right now. . . ."

Jonah didn't answer, but quickly circled the nurse's station, looking into every room, opening every closed door. All were empty of patients.

"Is there something I should know about?" Jadine asked.

"Have you seen Kenzie?" Jonah demanded.

Jadine shook her head. "Kenzie? No, I haven't seen him." Her face clouded with worry. "Why—were you thinking he'd been transferred here?" she asked gently.

"Thanks, Jadine," Jonah said, and slammed out of the door.

Jonah knew that Gabriel would have had plenty of advance warning that he was on his way over. Briefly, he debated whether it was wise to come in the front door. His instincts told him to be wary of a trap. And yet he tried to tell himself that this was Gabriel. He'd been looking out for Kenzie for years. He'd probably made the decision to move Kenzie to Safe Passage in an undisclosed location. Jonah would just have to find a way to make him understand that it was the wrong thing to do. That Kenzie wasn't ready to go there.

He was good at persuasion, right? Only just now he was not in a persuasive mood.

The alley door yielded to his entry code, and Jonah loped up the stairs and through the second security gauntlet. The outer office, where Patrick Murphy generally stood guard, was empty. Jonah gingerly tried the door to Gabriel's office. It was unlocked. Jonah listened. This office was occupied—at least two people were inside.

Turning the handle, Jonah nudged the door open with his foot, ready to leap aside in the event of attack. None came. Jonah edged around the door frame and into the office.

Gabriel stood behind his desk, clearly waiting for him. Lilith perched on the edge of his desk. Jonah was surprised to find her occupying the same body, the one Gabriel had nearly decapitated at the old B&O Terminal. It appeared to be all healed up—Lilith practically glowed with health.

Clearly, she'd been dosed up with blood magic. Jonah couldn't help wondering who had died to put those roses in her cheeks.

"Hello, Jonah," Gabriel said.

"Gabriel." Jonah looked from Gabriel to Lilith.

"We missed you at the meeting this morning," Gabriel said, running a hand over his close-cropped hair.

"I couldn't be there," Jonah said, forcing a neutral tone.

"I hope we're not going to be at odds from here on in," Gabriel said.

"Actually, I was busy looking for my brother. He seems to have disappeared. Any idea where he might be?"

Gabriel and Lilith looked at each other. Gabriel gave a little headshake.

"Is he dead?" Jonah's voice rose. "Is that what you don't want me to know?"

Kenzie's fine, Jonah, Lilith said in a reasonably clear voice. *He's responding to therapy really well, in fact.*

"What do you mean by that?" Jonah asked, though he thought he knew.

It's amazing what a little blood magic will do, Lilith said. *But then, you know that already, don't you?*

Jonah leveled his gaze at her. "I'm glad to hear that he's doing well," he said carefully. "I'd like to see for myself."

"I'm afraid that won't be possible," Gabriel said.

"Because . . . ?"

"Because you've made your position clear—that you disapprove of our collaboration with the undead survivors of Thorn Hill."

Jonah saw where this was going, but he wanted to hear it plainly. "What's that got to do with Kenzie?"

"We need to make sure that you don't do anything to sabotage our plans," Gabriel said.

"What plans?"

A plan to save all of the Thorn Hill survivors, living and dead, Lilith said.

"Except, I assume, for the shades we've riffed on Gabriel's orders," Jonah said.

Except for them, Lilith said. *Unfortunately.*

"But in order to make that happen, we're going to have to work together," Gabriel said. "All of us. Including you."

"Sounds fantastic," Jonah said. "Why would I sabotage a plan like that?"

"Why indeed?" Gabriel said.

"Then why are you holding Kenzie hostage?"

"*Hostage* is such a loaded word," Gabriel said. "We have his best interests at heart. We want to assure his survival until we're in a position to offer curative therapy."

"You think I don't want that?" Jonah said through gritted teeth. "Now, are you going to tell me where he is, or do I have to take this place apart brick by brick?"

"I am *not* going to tell you where he is, and you are *not* going to get your way by threatening me or the institution that has taken care of you and your brother for ten years," Gabriel said. "That continues to care for all of the survivors of the Thorn Hill disaster."

"Says the man who poisoned us in the first place."

Gabriel did not poison you, Lilith said. *Nor did I.*

"What are you planning to do?"

"We'll go over the plan in detail when the time comes," Gabriel said. "When you need to know it."

"I thought we were all working together," Jonah said, his voice dripping with derision. "Guess not."

Gabriel leaned forward, planting his hands on his desk, his voice steely. "I am doing what I believe to be in the best interests of the survivors of Thorn Hill. As I always have done. There was a time that you believed that, and I hope we can get back there again."

"How do I know that Kenzie is still alive?" Jonah said.

What are you so worried about? Lilith said. *Kenzie is immortal, just like the rest of us.*

Gabriel shot Lilith a warning look, then turned back to Jonah. "Jonah, if you can demonstrate that you've regained your senses, perhaps we'll allow you to see your brother. I think you'll be pleased with his progress."

Jonah took a deep breath, released it. Let go of his rage,

replacing it with cold calculation. He had to play it smart. And he would. If they were telling the truth, and Kenzie was alive and improving, his brother would find a way to get in touch. If they weren't telling the truth, well, he'd deal with that, too. Storming out and slamming doors might be satisfying in the short run, but in the long run it wouldn't get him where he needed to go. Best not to burn bridges until he managed to drag his brother to the other side.

How far would he go to save his brother? As far as he needed to go.

"All right," Jonah said, with a stiff nod. "Let me know what you need me to do."

❦ CHAPTER THIRTY-SIX ❧
THAT'S HOW I GOT TO MEMPHIS

Maybe the weather gods had decided that Emma shouldn't ever get to Memphis. They'd stuck a big winter storm in her way, one of those that come up out of the south and ambush you. It was snow all the way to Cincinnati, and then ice through Kentucky. Though the Element was all-wheel drive, Emma guessed that the tires were almost as old as she was. She passed this big billboard along the highway that said, in black letters on stark white, ARE YOU READY TO MEET GOD?

Not quite yet, Emma thought. Not until I figure out a few things.

So she waited out the storm at a truck stop off I-65 that must have been near Mammoth Cave because there were brochures and posters all around, trying to get her to go there. Right now, a cave sounded sort of appealing. After she crossed into Tennessee, it turned to all rain, which she was at least used to. After that, she made good time.

Hopefully, they'd think she was too smart to go to Memphis. With any luck, she could check out the clue her father had left for her and get out of town before anybody caught up to her.

Emma parked in the central library parking lot. It was a hike from Beale Street, but between the library, the McDonald's, and the shopping center, she figured there was enough parking that she could sleep in the SUV if she had to without being noticed. Plus clean up in the library and use the computers there.

When she searched on the computers in the library, she found that Beasley was in middle-of-nowhere Tennessee. Almost in Mississippi. Was this a wild goose chase or what?

She took the bus down Poplar to Mickey's so nobody would spot the truck on her old stomping ground. It was peculiar to be walking in a place that was so familiar and now so different through her eyes. So much had changed since that night she found her grandfather dying on the shop floor.

People were bundled up like it was freezing, but after a half year in Cleveland it didn't feel so bad. Up north, the cold wrung all the life from the air, so it was harsh and tasteless. Here, the air was a thick brew, warm and rich with the scents that meant home.

It was mid-morning, before the lunchtime rush, but Emma knew that people were in and out of Mickey's all day long. Chances were high she might run into somebody she knew.

So she walked around the back and into the alley that ran behind the bar. Upending an old pickle bucket, she sat. She knew it wouldn't be long before Mickey came out here for a smoke. He always liked to get one in before he had to work lunch.

Maybe ten minutes later, the back door slammed open and Mickey shuffled out, already thumbing his lighter.

"Hey, Mickey," Emma said.

Mickey jumped and spun around. The lighter clattered onto the bricks. "Emma!" He stared at her as if he'd seen a ghost. "My God, girl, where'd you come from?"

"I just got back to town," Emma said.

"Why'd you disappear like that, and not tell anyone where you were going? I've been worried sick about you."

"I went to stay with my father," Emma said.

Mickey's face went ashy. "Tyler? You were with *Tyler*?"

Emma didn't know what to make of that look he was giving her. "I was. Why?"

"But . . . you shoulda said something, honey," Mickey said. He looked up and down the alley. "Tell me. Does your daddy know you're here?"

"Tyler's dead," Emma said, thinking, Mickey knew about Tyler. He knew about Tyler all along. Was that going to be her whole life—one secret, one betrayal after another?

Mickey wet his lips, his face sagging with sorry. "Oh, honey," he said. "Let's get you inside out of the cold." Turning, he pawed at the door handle.

"Are you by yourself?" Emma asked quickly. "I don't want anybody to see me."

"Nobody's in there but Riley, cleaning up before—" Mickey stiffened, turned. "Is somebody after you?"

"Well . . ." Emma didn't know how to answer that question. "I know that the police suspect me in Sonny Lee's murder."

Mickey's eyebrows shot up. "Murder? Who said he was murdered?"

"Well . . . I mean . . . he fell and hit his head. And I thought that maybe . . . maybe somebody knocked him down." Emma felt like she'd fallen into a sinkhole, and now she was flailing around, getting herself in deeper.

"I guess he could've been . . ." Mickey said, slowly. "But I ain't heard nothing about that. Old men fall down sometimes. I think the police couldn't tell one way or the other. Unless you know something I don't."

Emma's mind was racing, trying to keep up with what Mickey was saying. "So the police aren't looking for me?"

"No, honey." He scrunched his face, looking guilty. "I did report you missing when you disappeared. I think the police figured you'd run away, so I don't know that they tried that hard to find you."

Well, Emma thought, I've been stupid. Again. "Let's go inside," she said, straightening. "It's cold out here."

Mickey hauled open the door, ushering her inside. "We can stay back in the boardroom," he said. The boardroom was a spare room Mickey had hoped to expand into one day. It was mostly used for storage and late-night poker games. "You want some breakfast? There might still be some bacon set aside for the—"

"Just coffee," Emma said, helping herself to the backroom pot and loading it up with sugar and cream. Hanging her coat on the back of a chair, she sat down at the battered poker table, and Mickey sat down opposite her. She studied his hands, amazed at how old they looked to her now, the knuckles all gnarly with arthritis, the skin speckled with scars and sunspots.

"How'd you and Tyler find each other?" Mickey asked. "I didn't—" He cleared his throat. "Did he get in touch with you?"

"Sonny Lee left me a note with Tyler's phone number on it."

Mickey's shoulders slumped. "That Sonny Lee. He could never quite let go of the notion that Tyler had some good in him. That he'd turn himself around. Didn't matter what he did." He snorted in disgust. "Who was it killed him?"

Emma took a drawn-out sip of coffee to give herself time to think. "How do you know he didn't die on his own?"

"Tyler Greenwood was not the kind of person who dies in bed," Mickey said.

"Then you know something about him I don't," Emma said. She waited, that next question hanging in the air between them like the smoke in some after-hours club.

"What brings you back down here?" Mickey asked.

"Tyler left a message for me to read after he died. It just took a while for me to find it. He told me to come to Memphis. He told me to talk to you. That you   that you had the key."

"He did?" Mickey's eyes widened in surprise, which switched into horror. "He told you to come see me?" Now he fumbled in his pocket, pulled out his cigarettes and lighter, and tried to light one, but his hands were shaking so badly he couldn't connect. "He knew," he whispered. "He knew all along."

"Knew what?"

"He knew that I was Sonny Lee's backup."

"Mickey, I don't understand a word you're saying." Which made sense, because he seemed to be talking to himself.

Mickey's eyes flicked away. He twisted a paper napkin between his fingers. "Look here, Memphis. It sounds to me like everybody's dead that was involved in this thing. Nobody left to get hurt but you, and I don't want that to happen. Maybe it's better to let sleeping dogs lie and move on."

"That's just the thing," Emma said. "Not everybody is dead, and people are still dying, and I think it's going to keep right on unless I find out the truth."

Mickey sighed, and it turned into an old man's cough. "I knew you'd say that. Sonny Lee always said that you'd chew on something until you stripped it to the bone." He looked into Emma's eyes, which he almost never did, so she'd know he meant it. "He loved you more than anything, Emma Claire—that's one truth you can believe in. But if there was somebody in second place, that would be Tyler."

"Really?" Emma rubbed her tailbone, which was sore from sitting in the truck all night. "Tyler seemed to think Sonny Lee was mad at him."

"He was, and he had good reasons," Mickey said. "But sometimes we get the maddest at the people we love the most."

Emma kept quiet, knowing that people will keep talking on just to fill a silence.

And Mickey did. "Sonny Lee couldn't forgive some of the things Tyler'd done, but I guess at the end of the day, he decided you were better off with your daddy than with the county. He never did trust them much."

"Sonny Lee never had a good word to say about my mother either," Emma said, hoping this shot in the dark might hit something.

Mickey snorted. "There was no love lost between

Sonny Lee and Gwen, but she didn't deserve having Tyler Greenwood for a husband."

"Why? Because he was a musician?" Emma guessed.

"Sonny Lee always told me not to fall in love with a musician— that it just led to cheating, hard times, and heartbreak."

I didn't take your advice, she thought.

Mickey just looked at her, like he wished he could get out of this corner and go anyplace else where Emma wasn't looking back at him. "Listen here," he said, finally, planting both hands on the table. "I should have done better by you after Sonny Lee died. I was scared, and I'm not used to being responsible for somebody else. Your granddaddy and I have been friends forever, and I owe him." He waved a hand, taking in their surroundings. "This ain't much, but I own this building, and I make a living. You can stay here as long as you want, and work part-time for me if you need spending money."

"I've got money," Emma said automatically.

"Well, you may want to spend it for college or trade school or something," Mickey said. "If you're at all interested in this place, we could make a deal. It could be a lot more than it is, but I just don't have the energy to put into it." He looked up at her, all hopeful. "What do you say?"

"That's a real kind offer, Mickey," Emma said. "I'll think hard about it. Now—what do you know about Tyler that I don't? What was the secret you and Sonny Lee were keeping from me?"

Now Mickey slammed his hands down on the table, rattling Emma's cup and saucer. "Damn it all, Memphis, can't you let go of that? You won't be happier after you hear it, I guarantee that."

"I'm not happy now, so what's the difference?" Emma said. She reached into her backpack and pulled out Tyler's notebook, flipped it open to the annotated section, turned it so it faced Mickey. "Tell me what this is all about. Why did he pick these songs in particular?"

Mickey's eyes shifted back and forth, and his lips moved a little as he read. When he'd got through the first page, he swore softly, then flipped around, sampling different ones.

"Typical Tyler," he muttered. "Wants to hand this thing off to you and get it off his own chest."

"Well," Emma said, "he *is* dead. I don't guess he's worrying about it much."

Mickey put his chin down on his chest, shoulders shaking, and it took Emma a while to realize that he was laughing. "You're right," he said, wiping at his eyes.

"*You* were right, by the way," Emma said. "Tyler *was* murdered, and I was the one to give him away to his enemies. Ten years he's been in hiding, and then I come to live with him, and then suddenly he's dead."

"That's exactly why you don't want to mess with this," Mickey growled. "Safest thing would be to forget all about it."

"You think they won't find me here?" Emma shook her head. "I got myself into a tangle up north. It won't take them long to find me. The safest thing is for me to know who my enemies are and why."

Mickey sat quiet. He was grinding his teeth—Emma could tell by the way his jaw worked. "I just don't get why Tyler would send you to me, after all this time," he said.

"I think maybe he got to know me well enough to realize that I'd want to know the truth, no matter how much it hurt," Emma said. "Maybe he thought I deserved to know, but he just wasn't man enough to tell me when he was alive. Or he thought I was safer not knowing." She paused, recalling what he'd said in his note.

I used to think that I was tough, but now I know I'm the biggest coward that ever lived.

"I might be a fool, Mickey, but I do think he cared about me." She pulled out the sheet of paper on which she'd written the words she'd ferreted out of Tyler's notebook. "He gave me this address." She handed it over. "I'm going, with or without you. Do you know how to get there?"

Mickey barely glanced at the paper, then nodded. "You're sure?"

"I'm sure."

Mickey stood. "Get your coat back on. I'll drive."

❧ CHAPTER THIRTY-SEVEN ❧
FIND YOURSELF ANOTHER FOOL

Leesha Middleton pulled on her red Gucci python boots—the ones that always gave her confidence. Not to mention five extra inches of height.

Aunt Millie eyed her critically. "I worry about you, Alicia, in those boots. They are lovely, to be sure, but not exactly practical on icy sidewalks."

Leesha lifted her foot, showing off the heels. "These are actually great on the ice. Like spikes."

"You're sure you don't want me to have Martin pull the car around?"

"Martin's not here, Aunt Millie."

"*Another* day off?" Millie frowned. "That man is never here."

"That's because he died three years ago."

"Ah. That would explain it," Aunt Millie said with a sigh. "I am getting terribly forgetful, aren't I?"

"You are," Leesha said. "The thing is, the older you get,

the more you have to remember." She kissed her aunt on her forehead, breathing in the scent of patchouli and sage.

"Where are you off to, dear?"

"Another meeting." Leesha tried not to roll her eyes. Aunt Millie didn't approve of eye rolling.

"You've been all wound up ever since Emma left," Aunt Millie said. "She's not coming back, is she?"

The thing about Aunt Millie was, she missed a lot, but you couldn't count on her *not* noticing stuff.

Leesha shook her head. "I don't know what you're talking about." She edged toward the door, hoping to make her escape without having to elaborate.

"It's because of me, isn't it, dear?" Aunt Millie said sadly. "I know I am hard to live with sometimes—this problem I'm having. I seem to have lost my knack for magic, but it's very hard to give it up."

"I wouldn't want to give it up either, if I were you," Leesha said. "You've always been so good at it. But Emma didn't leave because of you. She's very fond of you, Aunt Mill."

There came a knock at the front door. "That'll be Fitch," Leesha said.

"I do like that young man," Aunt Millie said. "He looks to be a bit of a ruffian, and *Fitch* is an odd sort of name, but he has a very warm smile. And he comes to the door. None of this horn-honking."

"He does have a very warm smile," Leesha said.

Aunt Millie cocked her head, studying her through narrowed eyes. "Are you *blushing*, Alicia?"

Exactly. That thing about Aunt Millie.

"Bye now. I might be a while."

She pulled open the door to find Fitch smiling his warm smile, a navy watch cap pulled down over his ears. "You ready for this?"

"Sure, why not?" Leesha said. "Maybe I'll be hit by a car on the way over."

The church was already half full, with people gathered into the usual factions. Seph and Maddie and Jack and Ellen huddled together, talking.

Leesha spotted Rowan DeVries right away. He stood alone, or as alone as a person can be when he's surrounded by bodyguards. He looked thinner than before, his bones more sharply defined.

He looked like a person on a mission.

As Leesha watched, Hackleford and Burroughs joined him. They nodded curtly to each other, like they were frenemies, forced together by circumstance. Hackleford, in particular, resembled a crow waiting to get at a fresh kill.

As soon as DeVries saw Leesha, he headed right for her, his bodyguard posse swarming after him. Gripping her elbow, he tried to pull her aside, but Fitch came right along.

"Who are you?" DeVries demanded, looking Fitch up and down.

"He's *my* bodyguard," Leesha said. "Now, take your hands off me."

"Who is guarding whom?" DeVries said, rolling his eyes. But he did let go of her.

"I'm glad to see that you are recovering," Leesha said, trying to be gracious.

DeVries brushed that aside. "Have you seen Emma?"

"Emma?" Leesha shook her head. "Not lately. Why?"

"She was supposed to be here," DeVries said. "She's not answering her cell phone either. Isn't she staying with you?"

"She is, but I haven't seen her in several days. She said she was going to stay over in Cleveland." She's not answering *my* phone calls either, Leesha thought.

"Downtown!" DeVries seemed stunned. "At that—at the Anchorage?"

Leesha nodded. "She still has an apartment there, I guess."

"Why would she *do* that?" He looked almost . . . distraught. Betrayed?

"Maybe she was afraid the roads would be bad and it would be too hard to drive back and forth," Leesha said. She paused. "Not to be nosy, but why are you so concerned about Emma's whereabouts? I didn't realize that you two even knew each other."

DeVries pressed his lips together, straightening his body. "Either I misjudged her," he said, his voice clipped and cold, "or someone has made certain that she wouldn't be here."

"What are you talking about?" Leesha said. But just then the side door banged open, and Mercedes entered. "Let's get this thing started, shall we?" she said, letting the door slam behind her.

The buzz of conversation ended, and people found their seats with amazing efficiency.

"Now, then," Mercedes said, "I have called this meeting of the task force because Mr. DeVries tells me that he has new evidence to offer relating to the Weir murders, including those on Halloween. As usual, we will proceed in an informal manner unless we are compelled to impose more stringent rules." She paused, her gaze flicking to each person in the room, allowing time for the threat to register. "Mr. DeVries, I'm sure I speak for many when I say that I am glad to see that rumors of your death were, at the very least, exaggerated."

DeVries smiled thinly. "Perhaps, but I suspect my recovery is disappointing to so many more," he said. "I appreciate your calling this meeting on such short notice. Now that I am improving, this matter needs to be dealt with before any more lives are lost. I'll remind you that these have been wizard murders, primarily, and so we have a special interest in seeing this handled. My colleagues and I"—he gestured toward Burroughs and Hackleford—"we believe that we have identified those responsible."

"By all means, enlighten us," Mercedes said. "We can scarcely stand the suspense."

DeVries seemed unruffled. "If you'll recall, we came before the full council back in the fall, to report that eight wizards had been murdered not far from here, in Cleveland Heights." The wizard paused. "A massacre, if you will."

The usual wizard blah blah blah, Leesha thought, reading a similar response on the faces of the rest of the task-force members. A flicker of movement caught her eye, up on the stairs to the gallery. Was somebody eavesdropping? Leaning forward, she focused in. Nothing. She finally decided it must have been shifting shadows from the bare-limbed trees outside.

Her attention was drawn back to what DeVries was saying. "Since the last time I was here, there has been an attack on gifted preschoolers in downtown Cleveland, which, fortunately, did not result in loss of life; and, of course the attack right here in Trinity on Halloween in which I was gravely injured and three lives were lost." He paused. "I want to apologize to all of you for some of the things I said the last time I came before council," DeVries said.

That got everyone's attention. A wizard apologizing? You could have heard a pin drop in the room.

"At the time, I believed that members of the underguilds must be complicit in the ongoing murders. In particular, I suspected that members of the full council might be involved in protecting these responsible. Now, I realize that this probably isn't true."

"Whoa," Jack murmured, nudging Ellen. "I feel so— I don't know—redeemed."

"Once we opened our eyes to new possibilities, we quickly realized that the most likely culprits are those with a long history of terrorist activity, who still carry a grudge against the wizard guild."

"And so, your theory is . . . ?" Seph said impatiently.

"We believe Gabriel Mandrake and the survivors of Thorn Hill are at the center of a conspiracy to murder the gifted," DeVries said. "Wizards in particular."

"The labrats," Sylvia Morrison said. "I knew it."

Mercedes gave Morrison a look, and then turned back to DeVries. "That is a serious accusation," she said. "Is it only a theory, or do you have some proof?"

Morrison seemingly couldn't restrain herself. "How much proof do you *need*?"

"Some, as opposed to none," Mercedes said dryly.

DeVries ticked his arguments off on his fingers. "It's widely believed that the facility at Thorn Hill was being used to develop powerful magical weapons until something went wrong. Many of the survivors have accused wizards of some how engineering the accident. The Weir murders began ten years ago—not long after the disaster, and have continued since sporadically. The killings have disproportionately targeted wizards."

That doesn't prove anything, Leesha thought. I got my braces off ten years ago, too, and it had nothing to do with Thorn Hill. Or the Weir killings.

"Maybe so," Seph said. "But if these killings are being carried out in revenge for Thorn Hill, then why have some of the slain been Anawizard Weir? The killers seem to be very good at what they do. I can't imagine that they would make that sort of mistake."

Mercedes cleared her throat, fingering the bracelet on one bony wrist. "After the catastrophe in Brazil, there were some who believed that dispatching the survivors was the best solution. There were members of several guilds involved in so-called 'mercy killings.'"

"Can labrats even read Weirstones?" Hackleford asked. "Does anyone really know?"

"That doesn't really matter," Leesha said. "We can't go accusing *anyone* of a crime without witnesses."

"That's been difficult," DeVries said, "since until recently, the killer or killers have left no witnesses alive. Indeed, that's what we believed the last time we came before council. But now we know that's not quite true."

"If you're talking about the preschoolers, we did interview them," Leesha said. "So did the police. Many of their stories were so wildly different that we didn't know what direction to take the investigation."

"My Olivia was a witness," Morrison said. "She has a very good memory. And when you and your friends were attacked, what you saw was consistent with her testimony.

Down to that one particular labrat. Kinlock. It seems that whenever he shows up, the zombies are close behind."

Unless it's the other way around, Leesha thought.

DeVries looked as if he'd prefer to have a little less support from Morrison. "More important, it turns out that there *was* a witness to the slaughter in Cleveland Heights who survived," he said. "Emma Greenwood."

"Emma Greenwood?" Jack cocked his head. "Who's that?"

"You know her as Emma Lee, but her name is actually Greenwood," DeVries said. "She's been living under an assumed name. She came here from Memphis, where she's being sought for questioning in a murder."

Murder! The word blew through the sanctuary like gossip through a small town.

Leesha came to her feet then. "I don't believe that," she said, clenching her fists so the nails dug into her palms. "No way."

DeVries ignored her. "The Cleveland Heights murders took place in her father's house, and her father was one of those killed. Emma, however, survived, and again disappeared before the police arrived."

"Something's not right," Fitch murmured, at Leesha's elbow.

"Her father was one of the dead wizards?" Madison asked.

DeVries shook his head. "No," he said shortly. "Sorcerer. Emma may or may not have been involved in the killings. But she was there, and so was Jonah Kinlock."

"And you know this how?" Jack said, wearing that familiar skeptical expression.

"Emma told me," DeVries said.

Leesha snorted. "Why would she confide in you?" she asked.

"If you'll give me the chance to explain, I'll—"

"Jonah went up against eight wizards all by himself?" Ellen's voice was laced with a hint of admiration. Maybe envy.

"He may have had help," DeVries said. "We just don't know. But the more we are learning about these magical aberrations, the more we're understanding how it is that they've been so successful at slaughtering us."

"Is that where the zombies come in?" Morrison asked breathlessly.

Maybe it was the mention of zombies, but Leesha thought she heard something—what sounded like a stealthy footstep overhead. Once again, she peered at the church balcony, festooned with greenery and red satin bows. Saw nothing.

She leaned toward Fitch. "Did you hear somebody moving around upstairs?"

He shook his head. "This place makes a racket in the wind, though. All this talk about zombies doesn't help." He squeezed her hand. "You okay?"

Leesha nodded.

"Let's back up," Mercedes said. "I'm still hearing accusations, but I have yet to hear any evidence." She shot a warning look at Morrison to prevent another outburst.

"It's difficult to know where to start," Hackleford said.

"Start with Halloween," Madison said.

DeVries nodded. "That's actually a good place. The night of the party, I went outside to get some air."

As, apparently, did half the people at the party, Leesha thought.

"I walked down toward the lake. When I got down to the water's edge, I heard somebody crying. It seemed to be coming from the gazebo. I went in to see if whoever it was needed help, and saw that it was the girl you know as Emma Lee. A member of the band from the Anchorage. A labrat. When she heard me come in, she looked terrified. Then she saw it was me, and seemed—well, she seemed relieved."

Not a common reaction to wizards, Leesha thought.

"I asked her what was wrong, if I could help, and she said nobody could help her and to leave before I got hurt. She was literally shaking. I asked if somebody was hurting her, and she wouldn't answer, just kept after me to leave. That's when Kinlock showed up. When he saw us together, he attacked me."

"Attacked you how?" Mercedes asked.

"He slammed into me, knocking me down. I tried to immobilize him, but it didn't even slow him down. It was like it didn't work on him. Emma tried to help me up, but Kinlock ordered her up to the house and told her to wait there for him. She asked what he was going to do, and he said it was something he should have done in the first place. And, she said"—he swallowed hard—"she said, 'You're going to kill him, aren't you? You're going to murder him, just like you murdered my father, just like you murdered his sister, just like you tried to murder me.'"

At this, the brushfire of conversation in the room was extinguished. This had the ring of truth. The wizard's expression, his voice, the specificity of his language suggested that those words had been engraved on his heart.

"Emma was obviously afraid of him," DeVries continued. "She was all covered in my blood. But she—"

"Whoa," Leesha interrupted. "Where did all the blood come from?"

DeVries looked momentarily stumped. "I don't know. I guess my nose was broken, and I hit my head. Anyway, she still stood up to him. She told him not to kill me, and told me to leave. And I did."

"He let you go on Emma's say-so?" Mercedes looked up from her note taking.

DeVries nodded. "I didn't know what to do. I didn't want to leave Emma there, but I—I did." His voice faltered. "He came after me, though, and caught up with me in the woods. My first clue was when he stabbed me in the back. I tried to run, but I fell, and he came after me and cut my throat, and then stabbed me through the chest. He would have made sure he finished the job, I think, but he heard somebody coming toward us, calling his name, and ran away." He looked up at Madison. "I think it was your sister. I tried to call out to her, to warn her, but I guess I passed out."

Madison folded, like she'd taken a hard punch to the gut.

"Why would he try to kill you in a place where he was so likely to be seen?" Leesha asked.

DeVries stared down at the table. "He was angry. I'm not sure he was thinking clearly."

Leesha looked around. None of the other members of the task force seemed inclined to ask more questions, so she forged on. "I have a few more questions," she said. "Was Kinlock carrying a weapon when you saw him in the gazebo?"

DeVries frowned. "I don't remember seeing any sort of weapons—not while we were inside."

"What was he wearing?"

He shrugged. "I don't know—his usual. What he was wearing onstage. You saw him."

"Which was—?"

"Jeans, T-shirt, leather jacket, I guess. And those leather gloves he always wears."

"Is there a point to all this?" Hackleford demanded. "This isn't a formal court. Why are you cross-examining him?"

"I just want to get a few things on record while they're still fresh in his mind," Leesha said. She looked at Jack, who was taking the official notes. "Did you get all that down, Jack?" She turned back to DeVries. "How much time had passed after you left the gazebo before you were attacked again?"

"I don't know. I was kind of stumbling around. Not long."

"Okay," Leesha said, "so moving along to the attack: what was your attacker wearing?"

"I think he's already answered that question," Burroughs interjected.

"No, I already asked what Kinlock was wearing," Leesha said. "Now I'm asking about the person who stabbed him in the woods."

DeVries seemed to be struggling to keep his temper. "Like I said. Jeans, T-shirt, leather jacket, gloves."

"What Kinlock was wearing in the gazebo."

"Yes. It would have been," Rowan said through gritted teeth, "since it was the same person."

"And what Kinlock was wearing onstage, before the break."

"Probably. I did not pay a lot of attention to the band."

"So anyone who saw the band would know what Kinlock was wearing."

"I suppose so," DeVries said, his voice low and tight.

"Now we're out in the woods. What did your attacker stab you with?"

DeVries thought a moment. "It happened really fast. It seemed like it was some kind of—of sword, or dagger. When he stabbed me in the back, the blade went clear through my body."

The members of the task force murmured to one another. There was plenty of blood in the woods, but no weapons had been found.

"And Kinlock was alone, right? Out there in the woods?"

"He was alone," DeVries said. "At least, I didn't see anyone else."

"So he must have been carrying that big blade in the gazebo."

"I suppose so, yes. The point is—"

"But you didn't notice him carrying a sword or a dagger or any kind of weapon in there?"

"No," DeVries said. "I did not. Maybe he had it hidden out in the woods somewhere. Maybe he had a magical sword that shrinks and grows. All I can say is that it was extremely sharp, and he knew how to use it." He fingered the puffy scar on his neck.

"Why are you giving this witness such a hard time?" Morrison said. "He's just trying to tell you what happened."

"I'm uncomfortable with this rush to judgment," Leesha said. "Isn't it possible that he was set up? Jonah Kinlock saved my life a few weeks ago—and Emma's and Fitch's. He probably rescued the Montessori children, too, if we can believe your own daughter's testimony. I think that should count for something."

"It seems to me that we need to question this Emma Greenwood or Lee or whatever she's going by today," Burroughs said. "It seems to me, with the proper persuasion, she would—"

"She was supposed to be here," DeVries said. "She promised to come and testify. The problem is *not* a lack of persuasion."

What's going on between those two? Leesha wondered, looking from one to the other. Some private dispute?

"Why would she speak up now, after all this time?" Seph asked. "Why didn't she tell all this to the police?"

"I can't say for sure," DeVries said. "With her history, you can imagine why she didn't want anything to do with the police. I think when she discovered I'd survived the attack and intended to testify, that encouraged her to speak up herself. But now she seems to have disappeared." He shot a look at Leesha. "Apparently, Ms. Middleton hasn't seen her lately either."

"I don't know that we can say she's *disappeared*," Leesha said. "Last week, she packed up a few things and left me a note saying that she was going to be staying at school for a few days. I haven't been able to reach her since then."

"Did she say anything to you about—about all this?" Mercedes asked. "Did you know she intended to testify?"

Leesha shook her head. "She never said anything. She was a very private person. She kept things to herself." Leesha stopped, realizing that she sounded like the kind of person who gets quoted in the newspaper about a killer or a victim. "I just can't believe that Emma would be involved in murder. She—she's the most honest person I've ever met."

"Clearly." Burroughs snorted. "She's a runaway with a rap sheet who has been lying ever since she got here. How much credence can we give to your opinion when you don't even know her real name?"

Leesha eyed Burroughs. She couldn't help wondering if there was some history between this bully of a wizard and Emma. "Everybody has secrets. I know her well enough to trust that if she's using an assumed name, she has a good reason for it. As for Jonah, I don't know him that well, but why would he have rescued us if he's in on this scheme? I never had any indication before now that Emma was afraid of him."

"Could that have been why she decided to move into Trinity?" Mercedes asked thoughtfully. "Could it have been because she was afraid of Kinlock?"

"She said she wanted to learn more about mainliners," Leesha said.

"Mainliners?" Seph cocked his head.

"That's what savants call members of the guilds," Leesha said.

"Maybe she wanted to find out our strengths and weaknesses," Hackleford suggested.

"Where do *you* think she is, Leesha?" Seph asked. "I mean, assuming she's not being held captive at the Anchorage. Any theories?"

"If I had to guess," Leesha said, "I'd guess she went back to Memphis. Remember when she came with me and Fitch to that hearing? She'd do almost anything to avoid getting up in front of people and testifying."

"It would help to have someone here from the Anchorage to answer these allegations," Seph said. "We can speculate and guess all we want, but none of us knows the truth of this. And it seems unfair to accuse them behind their backs."

"I don't think we can afford to wait," DeVries said. "I'm worried that if Emma isn't already dead, she may soon be. The best case scenario is that she's being held prisoner, probably somewhere in the Anchorage complex."

"What do we care about her? It sounds to me like she's getting what she deserves," Morrison snapped.

"That's not true," DeVries snapped back. "She doesn't deserve this."

It's odd, Leesha thought, that DeVries is so quick to defend Emma, after suggesting she might have been in on the Halloween murders.

DeVries collected himself, and continued smoothly, "Besides, she's the only witness we have, aside from the preschoolers. This is guild business. If we're going forward with a trial, we'll need testimony from her. Which is why time is of the essence."

"Do you think they'll just let us walk in there and take a look around?" Burroughs snorted. "We need to go in numbers, and we need to be ready to use lethal force if necessary. Remember, these people are mutants—monsters, many of them, who've been implicated in God knows how many murders. Who knows what they are capable of?"

Speaking of a rush to judgment, Leesha thought. "We need to give them a chance to respond to this testimony. We should contact Mandrake and ask him to make Jonah available to talk to us. And ask him about Emma's whereabouts."

"No," Hackleford said. "We need to take them by surprise. If we alert them to our suspicions, they'll destroy all the evidence."

Leesha wasn't buying the born-again Hackleford and Burroughs, ready to join hands with the "underguilds," even to fight a common threat. It was so . . . unwizardly of them.

"I'm worried about Emma, too," Leesha said. "In fact, of everyone here, I'm the only one who might call her a friend. But I don't think it will help her to go charging in without a strategy in mind. If she is there, and they mean to kill her, she's already dead. If not, then we probably have the time to plan more carefully."

Burroughs snorted. "What we need is the kind of all-out magical assault that will convince them that resistance is futile. How much planning does that take?"

"They are resistant to conjury," DeVries said. "Or at least Kinlock and Greenwood are."

"I still find it difficult to believe that conjury doesn't affect them," Burroughs said. "Is it at all possible, DeVries, that you simply missed?"

"I'll concede that, Burroughs," DeVries said, "if you explain to me how hundreds of now-dead wizards all over the world missed as well. Or perhaps you think they were shooting blanks?"

"I agree with DeVries," Leesha said, astonished to hear herself saying that. "We don't really know what we're walking into. We can't rely on magic to win the day."

"What are you proposing?" Hackleford said, grimacing. "Are you suggesting that we carry *guns*?" From her expression, it was as if she'd suggested they use slingshots and catapults.

"Do guns even work on zombies?" Morrison asked.

"Why not just drop a bomb on them?" Jack murmured. "Think of the lives we'll save."

"Shut up!" Leesha said in her outside voice.

To her amazement, everyone shut up.

"I'm not suggesting guns or bombs or an all-out magical assault. All I'm saying is we treat them like human beings who have the right to confront their accusers."

"Leesha's right," Madison Moss said into the silence that followed.

Everyone turned to look at her.

"I know all about witch hunts, and I don't much like them. I have more reason than most of you to want to get to the truth of the matter. Some would say that I have more reason than most of you to seek revenge on the—on those responsible for Grace's death. That's sure the way I felt right after the murders." She twisted a tissue between her fingers. "But I would have to include myself in that number. If I hadn't shirked my responsibility, maybe this would have been resolved sooner—in time to prevent all of these deaths. Life handed me a destiny I didn't want, so I did as I pleased and left other people try to clean up this mess. Peace takes work, and I didn't do it. I've paid a really high price."

"Maddie," Seph murmured. "It's not like you asked for—"

"Don't you make excuses for me, Seph McCauley," Madison said. "You've been making excuses for me for way too long. Doesn't matter if I asked for this thing; it landed in my lap, and it was up to me to use it to make things better. There are too many wounds still festering from the past. I'm finding out that you can't just ignore them. So. If we vote to go to the Anchorage, I'm coming along—to *talk* to people, not to attack them. If I see this thing turning into a slaughter, I will act."

"What if *we're* the ones being slaughtered?" Hackleford said, looking around the table for support. "What will you do, then?"

"The thing is," Mercedes said, a little hesitantly, "we know that you exert power over all guild members. But it's not clear that you have the same control over the savants."

"Savants?" Morrison looked blank. "Are you talking about the zombies?"

"I'm talking about the magically altered Thorn Hill survivors," Mercedes said, acid dripping from her voice. "It may be that our links with them are broken. If it's true that conjury doesn't affect them, it raises questions."

"It doesn't matter," Madison said. "I may not be linked to them, but I am linked to you."

"I, for one, do not believe in zombies," Burroughs said flatly. "That doesn't change the fact that it's a preposterous plan."

"Because . . . ?" Madison said, her voice getting that growly tone Leesha knew well.

"*You* need to remain in a place of safety. If you're injured or killed, what happens to all of us? The mutants might be the only ones left with power."

"I agree," Hackleford said. "If you use your common sense, young lady, you'll realize that involving yourself in this battle is an incredibly selfish act."

Well, Leesha thought, *that's* a mistake.

Madison stood, flames coming up under her skin, so bright they hurt the eyes. Ever since Grace's death, the magic inside Madison had seemed to dim, barely smoldering, like a fire made with damp wood.

Before their eyes, she seemed to grow, until she stretched nearly to the ceiling of the sanctuary. Her clothes and hair thrashed around her as if driven by a wind that no one else could see. She resembled a pillar of flame, with glittering scales, reptilian eyes, and wings of fire trailing her arms, sparks falling all around her.

Most of those around the table had seen Madison like this—everyone except Burroughs and Hackleford. They drew back, hands raised in defense, mouths gaping in surprise, their skin reflecting back the many colors that flame can take. Then they both dove behind the table.

"Let me tell y'all something," she drawled, her Appalachian accent clanging against expectations, coming from a creature like this. "First of all, I am in no way a lady. Second of all, I may be young, but I'm getting older by the minute. And the older I get, the less patience I have for people like you."

Burroughs and Hackleford peeked out, ducking out of sight when they saw Madison glaring at them.

"Well? Do you have anything else to say?"

Madison waited, but no response came from under the table. Gradually, she shrank back to her usual self—tall, thin, and weary-looking. The scales on her cheeks flashed once in the light from the windows, then faded away. "You can come out now," she said, sitting again.

The two wizards poked their heads up again, finally gaining enough courage to return to their seats. Hackleford seemed visibly shaken. Burroughs's expression was more thoughtful. Calculating, even.

"Now," Madison said. "How can we go about setting up a meeting?"

Burroughs frowned. "Is Mandrake really going to agree to a meeting if he knows the jig is up? That we know what he's been up to. I mean, why would he?"

"With all due respect," Jack said, "we don't know if he's guilty. If he's innocent, he has no reason to be alarmed. Even if he's guilty, he may think he can give us Jonah, and that will be the end of it. Or that Jonah will be able to charm his way out of it."

"Me, I expect a really short meeting," DeVries said. "We talk to Mandrake, he says he doesn't know anything. Or, let's say we get access to Kinlock, he says I'm lying and he doesn't know anything and Emma's not there. This is a waste of time unless we search the premises, too. If Mandrake is behind the Weir murders, it should be easy enough to find evidence of it."

"All right," Madison said. "We request a meeting, and permission to search the campus. We bring enough people to do that."

When they took a vote, it was all yeas.

"Motion carries," Seph said. "We go."

"And if they say no?" Burroughs said.

"We'll cross that bridge when we come to it," Madison said.

"I'll give Mandrake the chance to cooperate," DeVries said. "But if he says no, and you don't force the issue, I will bring my own team to the Anchorage, and I will turn over every rock, and I won't leave until I get answers. I think we have to consider the very real possibility that Kinlock has already murdered Emma."

Leesha didn't like it. She didn't like it at all. There were just so many ways it could go wrong. And yet—Madison was right. You can't give evil free rein because you're afraid to confront it.

"All right," Ellen said, as if glad the debate was over and they finally had an actionable plan. "Let's assume they say yes. If we're going to do a thorough search, we need information—detailed maps of the area around the Anchorage, and blueprints of the buildings."

Jack leaned forward. "I think I know where to access some of that on the city of Cleveland Web site," he said. "Because the school's a nonprofit, they may have information online, annual reports, photos, and like that. The library at the college has access to—"

The conversation faded as the voices in Leesha's head grew louder. I'm sorry, Jason, she thought. Here we are again, planning for yet another confrontation that I have to hope doesn't turn into a battle.

Unable to sit still any longer, Leesha slid out of her seat and headed for the back of the church. As she turned toward the restrooms, she nearly collided with a tall, muscled boy in a down jacket, totally bald. He looked familiar, somehow

"Hey!" Leesha said. "The church is closed for a meeting. What are you doing here?"

"I was just leaving," the boy said, brushed past her, and was gone.

✥ Chapter Thirty-eight ✥
Hide Away

Beasley, Tennessee, was one of those places so far out in the middle of nowhere, it made you wonder how anyone ever decided they wanted to live there. Maybe somebody was driving cross-country and ran out of gas and there was no gas station for miles around, so they stayed put.

But maybe there had been a reason to stay there, once. Back in the day, you needed a little town like this every so often to serve the farms all around. A place to do your banking and grocery shopping and whatnot. A place you might meet a boy to flirt with, and buy ice cream on a Saturday night.

Now it was just closed storefronts and a few scattered houses around a crossroads. Not even a speed trap. Emma guessed that anybody who lived there wouldn't blame a person for wanting to get out of town quick. And that was before they turned off the paved highway.

I'm an orphan now, Emma thought, but I might as well

have been my whole life, for all I know about my family. Even as a child, she'd understood that questions about her father, her mother—any other part of her family—were forbidden. If asked, Sonny Lee would put up the shutters and start drinking until he passed right out. So she quit asking.

The address Tyler had left her wasn't even close to town; it was twenty miles away, at the end of a dirt road. All the way there, Emma kept wondering if she hadn't made some kind of a mistake in figuring out Tyler's code. But then, Mickey seemed to know about this place. He didn't bat an eye or ask a question when she gave him the address.

Maybe, in a way, she hoped it would be a mistake, because, more and more, she didn't think she would like what they'd find at the end of that dirt road. In scary movies, that was always the scene of the crime.

"How did you know Tyler?" Emma said, picking at the cracked vinyl on the front seat of Mickey's truck, trying to take her mind off all the bad possibilities.

Mickey stole a quick look at her. "His mama used to send him down here to stay with his grandmother—in the summers, mostly. Your great-grandmother, I guess. Even then, Tyler was a handful, and I guess she was the only one could make him mind. Sonny Lee would pick him up on the weekends to come stay with him."

Emma eyed Mickey, wondering if he knew anything about the magical thread that ran down through the family. "Did you know my grandmother?"

Mickey grimaced. "Not well. She's the one owned the Beasley property, and it's a long way away when you got no reason to go there."

"What was her name?"

"Sarah Vann. I know she was part Cherokee—her family's lived in this county since before the Revolutionary War. Somehow they managed to avoid getting shipped off west."

"Is she still alive?" Emma asked, with a spark of hope.

"No, honey," Mickey said. "The farmhouse burned down when Tyler was just a little older than you. She died in the fire, and he inherited the place from her. It used to be a farm, but it's gone back to woods. Tyler built a workshop on the property. Even after he was grown, he'd come down here several times a year."

That made no sense. There'd been no workshop at Tyler's place up north until Emma moved in. "A workshop? You mean—for woodworking?"

Mickey shook his head. "Different kind of workshop."

"Is that what we're going to see?"

"Yup." Mickey stared back forward, through the bug-spotted windshield. He was still grinding his teeth.

"You gotta stop that," she said.

"Stop what?"

"Grinding your teeth. You'll wear them down to nubs."

Mickey growled something. And then, unexpectedly, began to talk. "Sonny Lee kept a lot of secrets, so there's a lot I don't know. What I do know is that he was in a world of pain, and I can't believe he deserved it. He made some mistakes. Never should have married Lucinda—there was always something peculiar about the Vanns. Kept to themselves. Some said they were granny women."

"Granny women?"

"Healers, witches, like that. People around here say the reason they stayed when the other Cherokee were forced out was because people were afraid to mess with them."

"Well, good," Emma said. "From what I hear, they were robbed."

Mickey laughed. "Sonny Lee was in over his head, that was for sure. Lucinda didn't stick around long. Foolishness about women seemed to run in the family, though, because then Tyler married your mother."

"And that was foolish?"

"Your grandpa seemed to think so."

Maybe it's just foolishness, period, Emma thought. That's what we Greenwoods do—we fall headfirst in love with the wrong people. If there were a picture of a person she shouldn't fall in love with, it would be Jonah Kinlock.

Then, without warning, they were there—at the end of the road. They faced a gate in a falling-down, split-rail farm fence, plastered with about a half dozen KEEP OUT and NO TRESPASSING signs.

"Open up the gate, will you, honey?" Mickey said.

Emma jumped down, set her heels, and dragged open the gate. It wasn't used to being opened, and she guessed it would be next to impossible in the summer, when the weeds were grown up all around.

She climbed back up into the truck. "Is that supposed to keep anybody out? All those signs just make a person want to go in and see what's there."

"Just hang on," Mickey said. They drove down a narrow lane through a tangle of thin saplings and briars for what seemed like a long time, until they came to another fence. This one was ten feet high and topped with barbed wire. These signs said: DANGER! KEEP OUT! SEVERE ELECTRICAL SHOCK!

Mickey held out a tiny gadget, pressed a button, and the gate swung open silently.

Emma's stomach boiled up with worry again. That was the kind of fence you put up when you really had something to hide.

They rattled along the rutted road a way farther, and came up on a large red barn, surrounded by yet another fence. The barn looked weather-beaten, the paint fading, like it had been there forever, but when Emma looked closer she could tell that it wasn't as old as she'd thought, and that a lot of money had gone into it.

They pulled through another electric gate and rolled to a stop in front of the large double-entry doors.

"This is it," Mickey said. "Tyler's workshop."

"Is—is there a house, or—"

"Nope. Just this."

"You've been here before?" Emma asked.

Mickey nodded. "I came here a couple times with Sonny Lee, so I'd know the way."

"Did Tyler still come here, up until—up until he was killed?"

Mickey shook his head. "I don't think so. I don't think he's been here since you come to live with Sonny Lee. That was part of the deal. He wasn't supposed to contact you, or contact Sonny Lee, or come back to Tennessee."

"Have you been inside?" Emma jerked her thumb at the building.

"No." Mickey looked down at his hands. "I'd rather you didn't go in there neither. We could just drive away, honey, and never speak of it again."

"You know I can't do that," Emma said. "You know I need to know the truth. I'm hoping that somehow it will help me keep the people I care about alive." She paused. "Why didn't you say anything about this before?"

"I was following Sonny Lee's orders. He figured the best way to protect you from the past was to hide it from you. I wasn't supposed to tell you about the place in Beasley unless something happened to him."

"Which it did," Emma reminded him.

"Yeah, but nobody said anything about murder until you did. I thought it was best to leave well enough alone." He swallowed hard. "To be honest, I was scared."

"Scared of what?"

"Scared of your daddy."

"Why?"

"Because he was a bad man, Memphis," Mickey said. "Because he was a killer." He hit the button to open the doors.

◌ CHAPTER THIRTY-NINE ◌
EVIL

It felt like when Emma rode a roller coaster for the first time. She got up to the top of the first hill, looked down, and realized the only way to get off that thing was to plunge down that hill and every hill after until she got to the end of the line. There are some things you just have to hang on and get through.

Mickey pulled the truck inside the building and shut the doors behind them. It was obvious that nobody was supposed to see the inside, because the inside didn't look anything like a barn. They were on a concrete pad, in an area clearly used as garage space. There were still some KEEP OUT signs, but it was kind of halfhearted, since anybody who'd gotten that far wasn't going to pay attention to any signs.

Mickey rolled to a stop, but neither one of them made a move to get out.

"What do you mean, he was a killer?" Emma said, her fingers making sweat marks on the vinyl seats.

"That's what he did for a living," Mickey said.

"He was a musician," Emma said, through gritted teeth. "He played the bass guitar." She looked up. "He was good, Mickey. He was damn good."

"I don't disbelieve you," Mickey said. "People ain't just one thing—they're a lot of different things. And Tyler Greenwood was a killer—a killer for hire."

"Who hired him?"

Mickey shook his head. "I don't know. Sonny Lee shouldn't of told me as much as he did, but he needed me to know how dangerous this was before I agreed to help him." He swallowed hard. "See—he knew that Tyler hated giving you up on Sonny Lee's terms. Sonny Lee told him that if he came to see you, if he tried to contact you, he would tell you all about your daddy, about some terrible things he did. And if anything happened to Sonny Lee, he'd set it up so you'd find out anyway. That was my job. I was supposed to bring you here."

"And Tyler wasn't supposed to know that?"

"No," Mickey said, running a hand over his bristly chin. "He wasn't supposed to know. Because then he'd just kill the both of us, you see." From the matter-of-fact way he said it, Emma knew that he believed it to be true. "Keep in mind, Sonny Lee set this up almost ten years ago, when you came to stay with him."

"Do you think Sonny Lee was the one that told him?" Emma said. "About you, I mean?"

"I just can't picture that," Mickey said. "He wouldn't put me at risk that way. I'm thinking Tyler must've known all along. Which gives me the shivers, to tell you the truth. Funny how life gets more precious when you don't have much of it left."

Mickey climbed down from the truck, peering around as though he thought danger might come at him from every side.

"He's dead, Mickey," Emma said, jumping down herself and striding toward a set of doors on the far side of the garage.

"Hang on a minute," Mickey said, hurrying after her. "Don't go rushing into things."

The door was fastened with a keypad lock on it. Mickey pulled out a slip of paper and tried three times to key something in, but had no luck with his trembling fingers.

"Let me," Emma said. Mickey handed her the paper, which had a string of numbers on it. Emma punched in the code and heard the sound of metal against metal as the locks shifted. Bracing her feet, she pulled open the door.

The area beyond looked like the kind of office you'd find in a factory, maybe—not fancy at all. The equipment, the desks—everything was covered with a thick layer of dust. At one end of the office, she saw another set of doors and another keypad.

"You're right," Emma murmured. "Nobody's been in here. Not for a long time, anyway."

Mickey walked around the room, unlocking one cabinet after another, swinging the doors wide. They were full of weapons of various kinds—knives, daggers, handguns, rifles. Some she wouldn't have recognized as weapons, but she guessed they must be.

Emma used the same code on the second set of doors, which swung open to reveal another room lined with white tiles on the floor and walls. It looked kind of like one of the chemical laboratories in high school, with stainless worktables and sinks with high faucets, and metal exhaust hoods to get rid of nasty fumes.

"Just . . . be careful, honey," Mickey said just behind her. "There's no telling what's in there."

"I'll be careful," Emma said. She made a slow circle around the room, taking in the equipment, the gas burners, the shelves lined with jars and bottles full of different colored powders and liquids. Some held what looked like dried plants. They were labeled—some with names, and some with letters and numbers—all handwritten.

Cicutoxin. *Eupatorium rugosum. Aconitum napellus. Scopolamine. Nerium oleander. Atropa belladonna. Cerbera odollam. Solanum carolinense. Datura stramonium. Dieffenbachia. Amanita phalloides. Ricinus communis.*

Who knew that Tyler spoke Latin? Emma didn't know what they all meant, but she had a bad feeling.

Others were labeled with numbers and letters, like PSD320.

She was very careful not to touch anything. She even tried not to breathe, though they were all locked inside glass-fronted cabinets.

In another cabinet were books about nasty plants, poisons, folk medicines, and an entire row of neatly labeled binders. This cabinet was not locked. Emma pulled out one of the binders and flipped through it. It seemed to be a kind of recipe book—recipes for murder.

Emma shoved the binder back into the cabinet and backed away slow. Then turned and rushed past Mickey and out of the lab and into the outer room. There she stood, head down, breathing hard as if making up for all the breathing she hadn't done inside. She heard the doors slide open and closed as Mickey followed her out.

"Come on, Memphis, sit down here before you fall down." He pulled out the desk chair and she collapsed into it. "Need anything? Can I get you some water or—"

Emma shook her head. Then rested it on her arms on the desk and wept, shoulders shaking. She could hear Mickey shuffling around the room, opening a cabinet. He plunked something down on the desk in front of her. "You're supposed to read this. Sonny Lee made Tyler write everything out for you. I don't know if this will help or not." He hesitated. "No rush. I got all the time in the world. I'll be outside, having another smoke." The outside door hissed open and then closed again.

It wasn't long before Emma blotted her eyes on the sleeves of her shirt and sat up. Maybe Mickey had all the time in the world, but she did not.

There was a folder on the desk in front of her, the kind she used to put reports in for school. She flipped it open, revealing notebook paper covered in Tyler's familiar writing.

Emma—

Your grandfather made me write this. He means to use it to keep me away from you. If you're reading this now, I guess it didn't work or I messed up or I'm dead. Anyway.

There were some scratched-out words and then it continued.

I may be telling you some things you know already, but here goes. The truth is, for years, I worked for a man named

Andrew DeVries. I know that you're gifted, you have that shine, but I don't know how much you know about magic. So it may or may not be important for you to know that I am a sorcerer, and DeVries was a wizard, and a lot of sorcerers work for wizards, doing things they'd rather not do. I'm not making excuses. Well, maybe I am.

My job was killing people. I traveled all over the world doing it. Being a musician was a good cover for me. I killed people all different ways, but, being a sorcerer, I mostly used poisons, because I have a real talent for potions and plants and like that. Some of that I learned from my grandmother, your great-grandmother. Most of the people I killed were wizards that some other wizard wanted dead. So I told myself that wasn't so bad. And poisons are a good way to kill wizards, because they ain't looking for it, and because it takes them down as quick as it does anybody else. But sometimes I killed people in the other guilds, too. Mr. DeVries was the one who handled the contracts, and he didn't discriminate, so I didn't either.

Your mother worked for Mr. DeVries, too, but she was working on a project that was kind of a sideline for him. Her specialty was using potions and treatments to change Weirstones—that's the magical source inside of a gifted person. DeVries hoped to make improvements in the basic model, or even create new magical guilds to meet a need, or turn a sorcerer into a warrior, say.

Gwen absolutely hated that work, but, like I said, a lot of people do things they'd rather not do. That's just the way the world is.

So that's how we met, and one thing led to another, and we got married. If that wasn't bad enough, we hadn't been married a year when we found out Gwen was pregnant. I wanted no part of being a father until you were born. And then I was totally head over heels in love with you. I hated traveling because every time I came home, you'd done some new thing and I'd missed it. But Gwen was more and more unhappy with her job. She kept saying we should both leave, we should run away, but I knew how dangerous that would be. We fought about it a lot until I came back from a business trip and found the two of you gone.

It didn't take me long to find out where you'd gone—your mama had been talking about this commune in Brazil before you left. I knew DeVries would be keeping a close watch on me. I hoped that if I stayed, he would decide it wasn't worth going after you. I was scared to death he'd find you and kill you both. He wasn't the kind to give second chances.

You'd been gone eighteen months when I decided it was safe to come find you. I didn't call ahead—I wasn't sure how Gwen would take it if I showed up, and I didn't want to give her a chance to run off and then who knew if I would find you again.

There was some more scratching out, and he drew a line out to the margin and added:

She was scared of me. There was times that I hurt her—I didn't mean to, but I did. I never laid hands on you, though.

So I went to Brazil, and slipped into camp, meaning to surprise you. But when I got there, I was the one who got the surprise. I found out that your mother was experimenting on you. On her own daughter. On my daughter. Not only that, she had taken up with somebody else—a man named Gabriel Mandrake, who was the mastermind behind the Thorn Hill project, as they called it. The three of you were a family . . .

and your mother looked happier than I'd ever seen her. Here I'd been doing everything I could to protect the two of you, while she was cheating on me.

I'd like to say I went a little crazy, but I knew exactly what I wanted—I wanted to hurt your mother and destroy Mandrake and everything he'd built there. I didn't want him dead. I wanted him to have to live with it. So I bided my time, kept out of sight, and waited until Mandrake was away. Then I poisoned the wells at the camp and took you back to the States with me.

It wasn't like Emma didn't know it was coming, but it was still like a body blow. She sat back in her chair, and closed her eyes, and let the tears fall. It was some time before she could go back to reading.

I knew that as long as DeVries was alive, you'd be in danger. So the first thing I did when I got back was kill him. But you were still in danger, if you were living with me, and so I went to Sonny Lee and told him I wanted to fake my death and I asked him to take charge of you.

Your grandpa was furious with me. Furious. It took a lot to talk him into having any part of it. And then he set some conditions. I was done with you. I was not to come back to Memphis or contact you or try and check up on you. I could keep him up to date with how to contact me—that was all.

So this is part of the deal. I had to write a true confession, and he'd keep it in a safe place. And if I broke that promise, he'd let you know what kind of a man your father was.

So, there it is. I'm sorry, Emma. I am so sorry. I've hurt a lot of people—in fact, I've destroyed everybody and everything

I've ever loved. I'm hoping that by staying away from you I can keep bad things and bad people away from you. The best thing that can happen is that you live your whole life without having to read this. Without knowing what kind of evil there is in the world. Without knowing your father. Because you're the one good thing I've done. You're the thing I love most in the world.

—*Your father,*

Tyler Greenwood

ᚙ Chapter Forty ᚙ
Nobody Knows You
(When You're Down and Out)

On his way to the Keep, Jonah checked his incoming messages one last time. Still nothing from Kenzie. He swore softly. He'd been conducting a methodical search of all of the campus buildings, using all his skills to get into places he wasn't supposed to be. So far he'd come up empty. He'd asked Rudy to look for Harry's IP on the network, but it wasn't there. He shouldn't be surprised. By now, Gabriel knew better than to allow Kenzie to get online.

He could be off-campus somewhere, but that seemed unlikely. It would be a hassle and a risk, especially since Kenzie was so medically fragile. It took considerable effort to keep from adding "if he's still alive" to every speculation. But that way lay madness.

As usual, a handful of hosted shades loitered around the front entrance to the club. Most people would assume they were panhandlers or the homeless. When Jonah arrived, they scattered. Understandably, they were still leery of him.

Jonah entered through the front doors, past the placards that read CLOSED FOR RENOVATIONS. SEE YOU NEXT YEAR.

He ran into a tense standoff in the foyer.

To be specific, it was Alison confronting eight hosted shades, most brandishing makeshift weapons. Alison had a shiv in each hand, and a gash over one eye.

Didn't anybody tell you? Jonah thought. It's supposed to be all kumbaya now. It seemed these survivors had not got the memo.

Jonah stepped between Alison and the shades, standing sideways so he could keep an eye on both. "What's going on?" he demanded.

"How the hell should I know?" Alison swiped away blood with her sleeve. "They just showed up here, and when I wouldn't let them in, they attacked me. Am I supposed to just *let* them? Is that the new rule?" Her voice was shaking.

Jonah turned and faced the shades, who shuffled and seethed, but stood their ground.

"What's up?" he asked.

One of the shades stepped forward, a haggard-looking man in ragged clothes, wielding a broken bottle. *We want to see Lilith!* he messaged Jonah.

"Lilith and Gabriel will be meeting with you in small groups once they come up with a plan. They don't have one, yet." At least, not one they've shared with us, he added to himself.

You're keeping the blood magic all to yourselves! one of the shades shouted. Well, it sounded like shouting, mind-to-mind.

"It's not like they're hoarding it," Jonah said. "There's a limited supply. It's not that easy to come by." And it's going to a select few. You lose.

Lilith promised that if we did as she said, and stopped killing mainliners around here, she'd supply us with blood magic, the shade persisted. *Where is it? We want to meet with her.*

"She *will* meet with you," Jonah said. "But you have to give them some time."

How do we know you aren't holding her prisoner? How do we know she's still alive?

"You'll just have to take my word for it," Jonah said, beginning to lose patience. "I can't make her come down and meet with you."

I like this body, the shade said. *And I want to keep it. But it's already disintegrating. Unlike yours.*

Well, what do you expect? Jonah thought. I'm not dead. Yet.

But, no. That was not politically correct. We're all equal now, all Thorn Hill survivors. All in this together. Until we're not.

The shade waved the bottle menacingly. *If they're going to meet with us, I want to know when.*

"Where are they, anyway?" Jonah muttered to Alison out of the corner of his mouth.

"Upstairs," Alison said. "Having a meeting. Again. Still. Gabriel isn't answering his phone."

Jonah was in no mood to run interference for Lilith and Gabriel while they planned and plotted. But he had to try.

"I'm sorry," Jonah said to the shades. "I can't say when they'll be meeting with you. As soon as I know, I'll tell you. Right now, you have to leave."

Not good enough, the spokesman snarled, lunging at Jonah, slashing at him with the bottle.

Jonah easily evaded the jagged glass shard and dropped the shade with a kick to the chin that all but took his head off. As he struggled to get up, Jonah said, "Now, leave, or I'll destroy what's left of your body and you'll have to find a new one, blood magic or not."

The shade finally got to his feet. *If we can't get blood magic here, we'll just go get our own,* he said. And he led the way out the door.

Jonah sighed. He couldn't really blame them for their distrust. After all, up until a week ago, Nightshade operatives were slaughtering the people they were now supposed to be allied with. Communication continued to be a problem, and several fights had broken out already.

It's too bad, Jonah thought, that we haven't been using our resources all along to find ways to help shades instead of slaughtering them. Maybe we'd be much further ahead.

Jonah turned to Alison. "You all right? You might want to have somebody take a look at that gash."

Alison waved his concern away. "I'm okay. But this kind of thing keeps happening," she muttered. "Gabriel doesn't want us to carry weapons—he thinks that raises the chances of an incident. But the shades are getting more aggressive by the day. I wish Gabriel or Lilith would at least talk to them."

The shades were right, in a way, about the blood magic. There was a limited supply, and Lilith and her inner circle were either using it themselves or offering it to Nightshade members who had been physically declining. It made sense to try to preserve the bodies they were born into. It also made sense to win over their former enemies in that way.

Apparently, it was working. Jonah was continually ambushed by how healthy some of his comrades from Nightshade looked—better than they had within memory. Alison was the one who was most visibly transformed. She looked worlds better than she had even a few days ago. The sores that had been erupting all over her body had nearly disappeared, and she'd put on some muscle. Even her hair seemed shinier, as if she'd shed a dirty gray caul. She seemed clearheaded, less erratic than she had been.

Even as he watched, the cut on her forehead was closing, shrinking, fading until it was just a fine white line.

Gabriel had offered to supply Jonah, but he'd declined. It didn't seem right for shades to go without blood magic while seeing their former enemies blooming with health. Plus Jonah couldn't get past the source of it. That sense of justice hardwired into him—it was damned inconvenient.

So far, it was only Gabriel, Lilith, and her small cadre of lieutenants who participated in the decision-making. Jonah was on the outside, his loyalty enforced by his devotion to Kenzie. The living survivors were vastly outnumbered, though it evened up a bit if you only counted hosted shades.

"Jonah?" Alison touched his arm, pulling him back into the present.

"Don't mind me. I was . . ."

"I wanted to apologize to you." She spat it out fast, as if she wanted to avoid thinking before she spoke.

That set Jonah back on his heels. "Apologize? For what?"

"Since I've been taking the blood magic, it's like these giant holes in my memory have been filling in. I think I've said and done some things that were—that were—that I regret now."

"That's business as usual for me," Jonah said. "Don't worry about it."

"But I *am* worried about it," Alison said, her eyes clouded with remorse. "It's like I turned into this crazy, enraged person—one with no judgment at all."

"I think I can match you anytime when it comes to crazy," Jonah said.

"Why would I forget that we are friends? How could that happen?"

It's called *fading*, Jonah thought, but would never say that out loud. "I'm just glad you're feeling better," he said. "So let's call an apology truce. Okay? I still owe you for saving my butt at the bridge."

He swiveled as the door banged open, expecting more trouble. It was Charlie Dugard. Which probably *did* mean more trouble from the look on his face. Charlie had gone over to Trinity to eavesdrop on the hearing Emma had mentioned. Jonah had wanted to go and hear it for himself, but there was too much chance he'd be recognized, as would Natalie or Alison—anyone in Fault Tolerant.

"How'd it go?" Jonah asked.

Charlie met his gaze momentarily, then his eyes shifted away. "Not well," he said. "Where's Gabriel?"

"That's the question on everyone's lips," Jonah said. "I'll text him and let him know that you're back."

Charlie opened his mouth as if to protest, then closed it and nodded.

Moments later, a text came back. *Come up, and bring Charlie. I'll contact everyone else.*

You mean we *all* get to hear what Charlie says? Jonah thought. That's unusual.

Jonah led the way upstairs and down the hallway to Gabriel's office. Brendan was sitting in the outer office with Rudy, still wearing the middle-aged body he'd inhabited at that first meeting between Lilith and Gabriel. They were both staring straight ahead, bodies rigid, but Brendan stood when Jonah and the others came in.

"Hey, Jonah," Brendan said, his voice thick and a bit garbled, but understandable.

"Your speech is really improving," Jonah said.

Brendan shrugged. "Maybe you're just getting used to it," he said, but he was obviously pleased.

Alison looked from Jonah to Brendan. "You two know each other?"

"This is Brendan Wu," Jonah said. "Remember? He was at Safe Harbor with Kenzie."

"Hi, Alison," Brendan managed. "Antarctica, remember?"

"I'm sorry," Alison said, after a long pause. "This is really hard for me. I just—"

"It's all right," Brendan said. "It's hard for us all." Turning back to Jonah, he said, "Speaking of Kenzie, would it be okay if I went to see him?"

"It's fine by me," Jonah said, "but you'll have to ask Gabriel where he is, because I don't know."

Brendan tilted his head, like he thought he might have heard wrong. "What are you talking about? Why wouldn't you—?"

"Ask Gabriel," Jonah said. "It'll be interesting to see what he says."

Right then, Natalie, Mike, and Thérèse arrived. Patrick's eyes flicked over them, as if taking a count, and then he buzzed them in.

Gabriel and Lilith were in the small meeting room, sitting side by side on one of the plush couches, a laptop in front of them and several paper files spread out as well. There was an intimacy to the scene that made Jonah's skin prickle. So many times they had all sat together, setting up plans, trying to head off one disaster or another. Lilith's presence felt like an intrusion.

"So," Gabriel said, when they were all seated. "What happened at the hearing, Charlie?"

"What's this about a hearing?" Rudy asked.

Charlie shifted uncomfortably. "I went over to Trinity because we heard there was going to be a hearing about the Halloween murders, with some new evidence. The hearing was organized by a mainliner—a wizard named Rowan DeVries—the one who was rumored to be dead after the . . . after Halloween. He's alive after all."

"I guess it's good news that only three people died, instead of four," Natalie said.

"You may not think so when you hear the rest of this," Charlie said. "In a nutshell, he says it was Jonah who attacked him at McCauley's that night."

After a moment of stunned silence, Natalie said, "No. No way. That can't be right."

Charlie shrugged. "Sounds crazy, doesn't it? But he testified that Jonah tried to kill him."

It was true, then, what Emma had said at their last meeting. *Rowan DeVries is going to accuse you of murder.*

Still, even though it didn't come as a surprise, it was hard to hear when you're accused of the one thing you're not guilty of.

"He's lying," Alison said, her voice trembling. "He's lying and we all know it."

"Damn right," Rudy said. "You need to tell them that, Gabriel. Tell them there's no way Jonah could have——"

Gabriel put up his hand, as if to quell the outrage. "Did DeVries offer any proof, Charlie?"

"He claims that Emma witnessed the whole thing."

"*Emma?*" Natalie straightened. "What does *Emma* have to do with any of this?"

"All along, the police have suspected that she *was* a witness to the murders," Charlie said. "Her clothes were covered with DeVries's blood."

"But there's an explanation for that," Jonah said. "He attacked her in the gazebo and she hit him."

"DeVries also accused you of murdering his sister and Hackleford's daughter and a bunch of other wizards. He says Emma witnessed that, too."

A growl rolled through the other members of Nightshade. "Have they gone crazy over there?" Mike said.

"Maybe something got into *their* water," Thérèse said, rolling her eyes.

Jonah felt like he'd been punched in the gut. How would DeVries know Jonah was there when his sister was murdered if Emma hadn't told him?

He wants me to testify, Emma had said. *He wants me to support his story. I said I would, but I won't.*

But maybe the wizard had overheard Emma, that night by the lake. She and Jonah were talking while DeVries lay on the floor of the gazebo. Jonah struggled to remember what she'd said. It seemed like she'd accused Jonah of all kinds of crimes—crimes that he was mostly guilty of. He took a quick breath, braced himself, and looked up at Natalie, who was staring at him like she hardly recognized him. Because Natalie knew that Emma had witnessed a massacre of wizards at her father's house. Natalie was, after all, the one who'd called Jonah in for the rescue when Emma was being held prisoner at the Bratenahl house. And Natalie would remember that it was Jonah who had convinced them both to keep quiet about it.

"All I've heard is 'Emma witnessed this, Emma saw that,'" Rudy said. "What does Emma say?"

"Emma wasn't at the hearing," Charlie said. "But DeVries claims that she agreed to testify in support of his story."

"Emma agreed to set Jonah *up*?" Alison half stood, her hands gripping the arms of her chair.

Charlie nodded. "So he says. But she didn't show, and DeVries claims we've either killed her or we're holding her prisoner."

"That's bullshit," Rudy said, pulling out his phone. "Let's call her."

"Emma's gone," Jonah said without thinking.

Rudy looked up from his phone. "Gone where?"

"Away."

Everyone looked at Jonah. Nobody said anything, but Jonah shuddered under the wave of mistrust washing over him.

Jonah sighed. "Look, I told her to leave, that I was worried that something bad was going to go down, and I didn't want her caught in it."

Gabriel's eyes narrowed. "So you knew this was coming?"

"Not exactly this, but—"

"And you're sure you don't know where she is?"

"I didn't want to know."

They all looked at one another. Nobody seemed to know what to say.

"I'm calling her anyway," Rudy said, finally, and he did, putting it on speaker. They all waited while it rang, and when it went to voice mail, he stumbled over the message. "Um. This is Rudy. If you get this, please call back. Something bad's going down, and it's really urgent. Call any time, day or night." He put his phone away.

"Well," Gabriel said, massaging his temples. "Maybe we can still sort this out." He pulled out his own phone. "Let me call Mercedes, and perhaps we—"

"There's more, Gabriel," Charlie said. "DeVries is saying that *you* are the one giving the orders, that Jonah didn't act on his own. You're heading up a conspiracy of Thorn Hill survivors, bent on destroying the mainline guilds. It's supposedly headquartered here at the Anchorage."

"What?" Gabriel slammed both hands down on the table. His phone case splintered, sending shards of plastic in all directions. He pointed a shaking finger at Jonah. "This is *your* fault. What possessed you to murder mainliners in the middle of the Sanctuary, including Madison Moss's little sister? Didn't you realize that the blame would automatically fall on *us?*"

"I didn't kill anyone at McCauley's," Jonah said. "Why is it that you suspect me instead of her?" He tilted his head toward Lilith.

"Could it be because DeVries *identified* you?" Gabriel's voice rose to a shout. "Could it be because you've been arguing for so long that we should be going after wizards and not our own kind?"

Lilith looked a bit stunned at this revelation. "Is that true, Jonah?" she said.

"It's true," Jonah said, "but I did *not* propose that we go out and slaughter mainliners, regardless of guilt. My idea was that we should try to find out who was actually guilty of poisoning the wells—if that even happened at all." He turned to Gabriel. "Anyway, if we're looking at history, you said yourself that if the mainliner killings went on long enough, we would get the blame."

"It's not a matter of blame," Lilith said. "It's a matter of credit. We've been doing your job for you. We are all Thorn Hill survivors, damaged by the crime that was committed a decade ago, still paying the price for that. They murdered *all* of us, Gabriel—if we're dead, then you are, too. Don't marginalize us because *you* haven't realized it yet."

"That makes no sense at all," Gabriel said, but he lacked his usual confidence.

Lilith put her hand on Gabriel's arm. "It does make sense. It's their guilt that feeds all these conspiracy theories. It would make total sense if we took revenge on them, and they know it. And if their dying could save the lives of those they slaughtered—isn't that what we call justice?"

"No," Gabriel said. Avoiding Jonah's eyes, he added, "Perhaps we should arrange for them to question Jonah. That will give him the chance to convince them that their suspicions are misplaced."

Jonah wasn't sure what to make of that. Was Gabriel relying on Jonah's charm to save the day? Or did it mean that his mentor was willing to make a sacrifice to maintain the status quo, and that sacrifice was Jonah?

Alison must have thought the same thing, because she

stood up and said, "No. You can't give them Jonah. That's just wrong."

Gabriel looked blindsided. "It is not my intention to give them Jonah," he said irritably. "Did I say that?"

"Good," Alison said. "Because that's so not going to happen." She sat down again.

Jonah had to admit that, under treatment with blood magic, Alison was much more like her old self. The friend he remembered.

"You're not going to be able to go back to the way things were, anyway," Lilith said, "even if you give them Jonah. If we can't come up with a permanent solution, the cease-fire will be over, mainliners will continue to die, and sooner or later, the guilds will decide it's time to eliminate the problem, just like they did at Thorn Hill. What will you do once you lose your bodies? Will you drift aimlessly in the ether, or will you join the rest of us in trying to win back some of what we lost?"

"It won't be our decision to make," Charlie said. "They're coming here, and they're planning to question Jonah—and you—and search this place, whether we like it or not."

"We can't let that happen, Gabriel," Lilith said. "You know that."

"Who's coming?" Mike asked, apparently already strategizing.

"I don't know most of the people at the meeting," Charlie said. "But it sounds like the whole council is coming, including Madison Moss. You know, the one they call the Dragon."

Gabriel and Lilith looked at each other. Then back at Charlie. Gabriel weighed the battered phone in his hand. "Do you have any idea how much time we have?"

Charlie hesitated. "I don't know. DeVries wants to move now, because he thinks we're holding Emma, and we might kill her if we know they're coming after her. We'll have some warning, because McCauley is supposed to call and try to schedule a meeting. If I had to guess, I would say in the next few days."

Jonah tried to make a quick exit after the meeting with Gabriel, but of course Natalie caught up with him anyway. She planted herself in his path, a familiar fire in her eyes. "Talk to me, Jonah," she said. "What have you been up to?"

"I don't know what you—"

"Cut the bullshit; it's me you're talking to," Natalie said. "I feel like I've been lied to and set up, and I don't like it."

"We all have," Jonah said. "Gabriel—"

"Gabriel's sins are no excuse for your bad behavior," Natalie said. "I'm having a little trouble figuring out who the good guys are."

"Good luck with that," Jonah said softly. "There are no good guys." And he walked away.

ᛒ CHAPTER FORTY-ONE ᛒ
IT HURTS ME, TOO

"I thought you liked barbecue," Mickey said, scrubbing at his face with a napkin. It came away orange.

"I do like barbecue," Emma said. "I'm just not very hungry." She pushed her sandwich toward him. "You want this?"

He shook his head. "You better eat that, honey—keep your strength up."

"I don't want any more." Emma stretched her legs out, leaned back against the tree, and closed her eyes. It wasn't long before she heard the rustle of the wax paper as Mickey helped himself to her sandwich. He was not one to let food go to waste. Just like Sonny Lee. She smiled sadly.

Sometime in mid-afternoon of this long and heartbreaking day, Mickey had driven miles and miles to the nearest crossroads and brought back food. In the meantime, Emma had searched the rest of the building. She'd rooted through the small apartment with a single bed and a kitchen area, bare as a jail cell. There were closets full of clothing, cob-webby with dust. Dressy clothes, work clothes, uniforms of all kinds. Disguises. In the drawer of the nightstand, a torn photograph. It was a picture of Emma, maybe four years old, holding Tyler's hand. On her other side, somebody had been ripped away, right through their joined hands. It was like holding up a mirror to what had happened in real life.

I don't get it, Emma thought. Everybody else at Thorn Hill either died or got damaged or ended up with some odd-ball power. Everybody but me.

Why am I different? As far as I can tell, I'm just a regular person who glows. Was that what my mother intended? Or did things go wrong?

Yes, things went wrong. Things went very, very wrong.

"What are you going to do?" Mickey asked, breaking into her thoughts.

"I don't know. All I know is I can't go back there. I can't face those people." She hadn't been real specific, but when she told Mickey that Tyler had done something terrible to people who were now her friends, he hadn't seemed at all surprised.

"It wasn't you that did it," Mickey said. "It was him. You were just a little kid."

"I know, but all this time I've been all high and mighty, telling people that I wanted the truth, no matter the cost, that I hated the lie. Blaming this person and that person for my troubles, never knowing that I had no business throw-ing rocks." She'd thought she was cried out, but more tears escaped from under her lashes and ran down her face. Blot-ting at them with the backs of her hands, she said, "I just never thought that the truth would hurt this much. I don't know how I can ever turn out to be a good person, seeing who I come from."

Mickey thought about this for a while, then shook a cigarette out of the pack and lit up. He took a deep drag, released a stream of smoke, then said, "You ever notice how sometimes, in the middle of July, right downtown, you'll see a flower poking up through a crack in the asphalt. And you think, What a stupid place to set down roots. It'll get run over, or it'll dry up and blow away. But it hangs on, and it grows, and it blooms. Somehow, against the odds, it finds what it needs and it makes that place better for being there." He looked sideways at Emma. "That's you, Memphis. You're a survivor."

Emma couldn't help smiling, though there wasn't much joy in it. "Why, Mickey, who knew you were a poet?"

"I'm not a poet, but I know good when I see it, and I see it in you," Mickey said.

Emma thought about this one thing Tyler had said in the note he'd pinned to the binder of music.

I like to think that there's a little bit of me in you: a love of music and a stubborn streak a mile wide. But we're different, you and me, and I don't forget it. You're strong, and you're tough, and you tell the truth. You're a good person, Emma. I'm none of those things.

"You don't have to go back up north if you don't want to," Mickey said, breaking into her thoughts. "But I think you might want to set things straight, because that's the kind of person you are. You're a quiet one. You keep to yourself, but when you do speak up, you tell the truth: in your music and every other way."

"Maybe," Emma said. "But if I'm going to do that, I need to do it face-to-face. Not over the phone or by e-mail. They deserve the right to ask questions, or spit at me if that's what they want to do."

But there was something else. She was trying to recall what Gabriel or Natalie or somebody had said about treating the Thorn Hill survivors. That because they didn't know exactly what happened or what poison was used, it was like they were working in the dark. A spark of hope kindled within her. Maybe there was something in one of those notebooks that would help. Some clue that would help them get better, or at least hold their own. She stood, dusting off the seat of her jeans. "Can you help me carry these notebooks to the truck?"

Mickey was big in the shoulders and arms. He could carry a lot at a time, but he moved slow. There was a lot to carry, and it was dark by the time they finished. She wished she had her cell phone so she could take pictures.

Emma slept through the long drive back to Memphis, and then the two of them moved the boxes of records and notebooks from his truck to her car. It was the wee hours of the morning when they moved the last of it and stood awkwardly in the alleyway.

"Why don't you stay here tonight?" Mickey said. "I can make up the bed in that spare room, where you stayed right after Sonny Lee passed. You can get a fresh start in the morning."

Emma shook her head. "I'm going to hit the road," she said. "The sooner I get moving, the sooner I'll be there. And if I go to bed now, who knows when I'll wake up."

"You know I start early," Mickey said. "I can make sure you're up."

"You know I'm a night person," Emma said. "I like driving at night."

"You got your phone?"

She shook her head. "I left that back in Cleveland. I was afraid somebody could trace it."

"I don't like the idea of you driving that far without a phone," Mickey said.

"I drove all the way down here without a phone," Emma said.

"Well, be careful," Mickey said. "And, remember —the offer still stands. I'd be proud to have you go in with me."

❧ CHAPTER FORTY-TWO ❧
KILLER HEART

The Keep had been something of a fortress all along (hence the name), but now it was everyone's job to make it that much more impregnable. Those Nightshade members who hadn't been called in already were summoned home. Thérèse and Rudy went over every element of the digital security system, making updates and changes, destroying some electronic records and making others inaccessible. Mike and Alison went to work on the armory, making sure all weapons were edged and battle-ready.

Jonah and Charlie were assigned to shred papers and help Natalie re-label materials in the pharmacy to hide the ingredients where that seemed prudent. They also locked a vast array of drugs away in Gabriel's underground vault.

"Cheer up," Charlie said, looking sideways at Jonah. "I know this isn't the most exciting job, but—"

"It's a waste of time," Jonah said.

"Is it?" Charlie said, sliding an armload into a Dumpster. "How so?"

"We may be resistant to conjury," Jonah said, "but this place isn't." He patted the brick wall with his gloved hand. "When the building comes down on us, a new security system won't help us. We'll be just as dead. I feel like the Three Little Pigs, barring the door before the wolf blows the house down."

"Would they really do that?" Charlie kicked at a chunk of ice. "Demolish this place, right here in the middle of the city?"

"You tell me. You heard what they said."

Charlie thought a moment. "Yeah, I think some of them would, given the chance. But Madison Moss, the one they call the Dragon—she seemed to want to avoid a bloodbath."

"That's surprising," Jonah said. "Her little sister was among the dead." His phone vibrated somewhere deep in his pocket. He ignored it.

"She seemed sincere." Charlie tugged his knit cap down around his ears. "If this is a waste of time, then what do you think we should do?"

"If not for Safe Harbor, I'd say we should just leave," Jonah said. "They can't question anyone if we're not here. If it weren't for Kenzie, I'd be gone already."

"Where are we going to go? Brazil? That worked out well."

"I guess that's not an option." Jonah hesitated, then said, "Do you think if I confessed to everything and turned myself in, the mainliners would leave the Anchorage alone? I think that's what Gabriel was hoping for."

"That depends," Charlie said. "*Are* you guilty of every-thing?"

"Not everything," Jonah said, hunching his shoulders inside his leather jacket, shaking snow from his hair. "Some things."

"It might work," Charlie said, "or it might not. I think this attack has been brewing for a good long time, and I think some people are keen on it for political reasons. The thing is, if you confess to something you're not guilty of, you can't take it back if it doesn't work."

It might be worth it, Jonah thought, if I knew it would protect my friends and protect Kenzie, wherever he was. If he was still alive.

By now, Jonah's phone had gone off, several times. Now a familiar ringtone sounded. Jonah hurriedly dug out his phone and scanned the screen. It displayed a map of the campus, with a bright, pulsing light in one corner. Jonah zoomed in. The Infirmary.

"I just realized, I've got someplace I need to be," Jonah said. "I'll see you later." Spinning away, he tore down the street, weaving around pedestrians, faster than was safe on the slippery pavement.

The Infirmary! Why hadn't he thought of that? Because it was too obvious? Though it was intended for outpatient procedures, infusions, therapies, and the like, the building was linked to the medical network, and there were beds and other equipment set up for patient care. Since the student population had dwindled, there were a number of exam and observation rooms on the rear wing that were rarely if ever used.

Jonah entered the building from the rear, on the basement level, which was primarily used to store supplies and unused medical equipment. As he loped up the steps to the main floor, his phone sounded again. *You're getting warmer.*

The rear hallway was dark, and at first Jonah guessed he was in the wrong place. Until, at one end, he saw that makeshift signs had been mounted on the double doors. KEEP OUT. RADIATION DANGER. When he tried the doors, they were locked, but a second later he heard a soft click as the electronic lock disengaged.

Cautiously, Jonah stepped through A young man he'd never met sat alone at the nurse's station, head bent over his tablet, so engrossed in it that he hadn't heard Jonah come in.

Jonah scanned the unit. Only one of the rooms had a live display. All the other doors were open. That door was closed.

Jonah circled around to the closed door. Cautiously, he tried the door. Locked.

He looked down at his phone. *You'll have to get the key from Mikito. Careful. He's quick and cagy.*

Mikito *was* quick and cagy. But he was no match for Jonah. In no time, Mikito was stowed in the supply closet, and Jonah was fitting the key into the lock.

Standing to one side, Jonah pushed the door wide open and peered around the door frame. There was Kenzie, in the chair next to the bed, dressed in a sweatshirt and jeans, head-phones slung around his neck, grinning.

"Took you long enough," Kenzie said.

Jonah took a step forward, but Kenzie put up his hand to stop him. "Watch this." Gripping the arms of the chair, he planted his feet on the floor and stood.

Jonah gaped at him. His brother was obviously wobbly, gripping the back of the chair with one hand, but he was standing up.

"Okay," Kenzie said. "I just wanted to show you that. You can go now." He gestured toward the door with his free hand.

Somehow, Jonah was across the room. He wrapped his arms around his brother and pulled him close. "God. Kenzie. That—that is so—remarkable."

"I *am* pretty remarkable," Kenzie said. "Or what's that PC term they use? Exceptional? Anyway. I'm going to sit down now. Despite those years of physical therapy torture, my muscles aren't really up for this."

Jonah released his brother, and Kenzie sat down with great dignity. Jonah tried not to notice how amazingly healthy Kenzie looked. How free of medical paraphernalia. How much physical function he'd regained in a few short days. No. Not regained. Kenzie hadn't looked this good since Thorn Hill.

Jonah pulled up a chair and sat. "I assume that I'm seeing the wonders of blood magic."

"You would be right," Kenzie said. After a long pause, he added, "I guess it's kind of like eating sausage. You don't want to think about where it comes from or how it's made."

Jonah cast about for a different subject. "I can't believe they let you get online."

Kenzie pushed his tray table toward Jonah. On it was one of the handheld electronic vitals monitors. "Did you know there's a little computer inside every one of these things? It talks to all the other computers on the network."

"So I've heard," Jonah said. "I assume you've had your way with it?"

"That's why they call it *jailbreak*," Kenzie said, grinning. "It's a lot more versatile than I thought."

"Mikito didn't notice?"

"All he knows is that the damn thing isn't working. Speaking of, what's going on? Rudy's been beefing up the security system for the past few days. I can hardly find my way around anymore."

So Jonah told him. And as he did, Kenzie's expression changed, morphing from thoughtful to alarmed.

"You need to leave," Kenzie said abruptly when Jonah came to a stopping point. "Now. It's time to take care of yourself for once."

"We all need to leave," Jonah said. "But there's nowhere to go."

"There is for you." When Jonah said nothing, Kenzie went on. "If you're worried about money, I can get you some." He flexed his newly functional fingers. "I have a great future in white collar crime. I promise, I'll only target total assholes."

"I won't leave without you," Jonah said. He took a breath. "Is it—is it possible you could come with me? I mean, you look—"

"No," Kenzie said, without hesitation. "I've already written the end of that story, and it sucks. Remember the blowback the last time, when I took a single dose? If I quit cold turkey, it'll probably kill me. And I'm not going to put you in the position of either watching me die, or going after blood magic yourself."

He stopped. Took a quick breath, let it out in a disgusted sigh. Their eyes met, Kenzie shifted his eyes toward the door, and that's when Jonah knew. It was a setup, a trap, and Kenzie had just figured it out.

"Do you think they know I'm here?" Jonah asked softly.

"I don't know. I would have said it was an honest hack, but maybe I'm just that predictable. It doesn't matter. They would have brought us together eventually, so you could see just what the benefits would be if you play nice. And the price you'd pay for saying no." When Jonah opened his mouth to protest, Kenzie said, "Don't you see? If I stay and you go, somebody else has to deal with it—not you. And that's the way I want it. Now. This conversation is over. You need to leave now while you still can."

Jonah tipped his head toward the door. "They're probably waiting outside, anyway."

Kenzie shrugged. "Maybe. Maybe not."

"If I leave, what will happen to you?"

"If you're talking about Gabriel, I think he'll keep me healthy as long as he can," Kenzie said. "He has no reason not to, and I might still prove useful. If they demolish this place, obviously I'm likely to be adversely affected. As I would be if you stayed here with me."

Even though Kenzie was putting his usual spin on things, it did make sense.

"I'll think about it, I promise."

"Don't think. Go."

"All right, I'll go," Jonah snapped. "Happy now?"

Kenzie smiled. "Happy now." And he did look happy—and healthy, his hollowed-out cheeks filled in, his face clear of pain for the first time in a long time. Even his red-brown hair seemed thicker, glossier.

Is this just an illusion? Jonah wondered. Digging out his cell phone, he pulled Kenzie in close and took a selfie of the two of them, nearly cheek to cheek.

They embraced again, and it felt bittersweet, like it might be the last time.

"Let's keep in touch," Kenzie said. "Through the back door, of course."

But when Jonah walked back out onto the unit, Gabriel and Lilith were waiting for him in the deserted nursing station.

"I see you've been visiting your brother," Lilith said. "He looks fantastic, doesn't he?"

Fishing for compliments, are we? Jonah thought.

"He does look fantastic," Jonah said, folding his arms and broadening his stance. "Superbly exceptionally great."

Gabriel and Lilith looked at each other, as if they were the long-suffering parents of an unruly child.

"Please," Gabriel said, gesturing to an empty chair. "Sit. We need to talk."

"I'd love to, but I've got someplace I need to be."

Gabriel sighed, as if disappointed, and Lilith squeezed his shoulder. They seemed to have gotten past their little tiff over the mainliner murders.

"Jonah," Gabriel said, "we are facing the greatest crisis in our history since Thorn Hill. The future of the foundation hangs in the balance. We need you on our team. We can't risk your behaving like a loose cannon when this thing goes down."

Jonah raked his hair back with one hand. "Do you really think I'm responsible for the murders at McCauley's?"

"It doesn't matter what we think," Gabriel said.

"Yes, it does."

"Whether anyone here at the Anchorage is guilty of

anything, the mainliners are coming," Gabriel said. "This time we're going to be ready."

"We had hoped to have the luxury of time to consider alternatives, before taking action," Lilith said. "We'd hoped to do some preliminary testing, to see if there were a way to duplicate or otherwise maximize the beneficial effects of blood magic."

"Good idea. If it's twice as effective, you'd only have to kill half as many people."

"But these new accusations have shortened the timeline and forced our hands," Lilith continued.

"I expect they would say that ongoing murders of main-liners have forced *their* hands."

"So we think we've come up with a plan that might offer a long-term supply and minimize bloodshed."

"Good," Jonah said. "Now, if you'll excuse me, I'll—"

"You need to hear this," Lilith persisted. "You'll have a key role." She paused, and when Jonah said nothing, added, "Don't you want to save your brother's life?"

"No," Jonah said. "I don't want anything to do with you and your plans. I'm sick and tired of being used and lied to. I just want to be left alone."

"This is self-defense," Gabriel said. "This is self-preservation. This is justice. Weren't you the one who always asked why we didn't target the guilty? Well, now we are."

"If you can point out the person responsible for Thorn Hill, I'm totally on board. Otherwise, what makes us better than them?"

"Sometimes you have to make hard decisions," Gabriel began, "Sometimes—"

"Yeah, you make the hard decisions, but I'm always the one doing the hard thing," Jonah said. "When the two of you were building your perfect assassin, you should have thought to install a killer's heart."

"You're right," Gabriel said. His gaze flicked up, over Jonah's shoulder. "Fortunately, that can be remedied."

Jonah heard a light footstep behind him. Familiar. Felt a sting at his neck. Also familiar. And went down hard.

Jonah awoke to the pungent scent of alcohol and the murmur of voices. Then incendiary pain, like flame was running in rivulets down his left forearm. He struggled, trying to free his arm, and realized he was strapped down, held immobile by bonds strong enough to resist his savant strength. He looked up into Gabriel's face, his brow pebbled with sweat. The sorcerer's jaw tensed in concentration as he wielded the needle. Ink therapy, Jonah thought, then screamed as the medication seeped under his skin

"Don't worry, Jonah," a woman said. "Gabriel will fix you right up."

"I'll fix *him* up if he doesn't stop it."

"You'll feel so much better in just a little while."

Who was that, anyway? Oh. The hosted shade. Gabriel's ex. What was her name?

"Lilith. One more vial, I think," Gabriel said. "Almost done, Jonah," he promised.

"Stop it," Jonah pleaded. "Please. Stop it." Now I'm begging, he thought. Didn't I used to be tougher than that? His throat was sore, his voice raspy and strange, and he wondered how long he'd been screaming.

Must be wicked stuff, he thought. And then, mercifully, he fainted.

When he woke, the pain was, indeed, gone. And not just in his arm. He felt numb all over, as if he were encased inside some kind of impervious skin that shut out the emotional noise around him. He felt calm, focused, purposeful.

He lifted his arm, which was still tethered to the bed, but they'd given him a longer leash. The skin was still puffy and red around his new tattoo, which was just below the nightshade on his arm. A shattered heart, just above his wrist.

It was Jonah Kinlock, simplified. Without the guilt, the second-guessing, the ethical debates and conflicts that plagued him continually. It was magic—the kind of magic he'd needed for a long, long time.

They kept him locked in, and nobody came and went except Lilith, Brendan, and Gabriel. He guessed he was still in the infirmary, in one of the unused rooms. And that was confirmed when they brought Kenzie in to visit one day.

His brother looked great—he'd put on some weight, and was looking more and more like a normal fifteen-year-old and less like a frail refugee from a famine. Jonah thought it was ironic, his brother coming to visit him. Kenzie didn't seem to see the humor in it. He came and sat on the side of the bed, leaned in, and whispered, "What'd they do to you, bro?"

"Nothing," Jonah said. "I have a new tattoo." He displayed it to Kenzie.

Kenzie scowled. "What does it do?"

Jonah shrugged, barely curious. "If anything, I'd say I'm more clearheaded than before."

Planting his hands on Jonah's shoulders, Kenzie looked into his eyes. "You don't look like yourself."

"Why, because I'm happy?"

"That's just wrong," Kenzie said. "You're never happy."

"Meet the new, laid-back Jonah."

"I want the old one back," Kenzie said. Opening one of the cabinets, he pawed through medical instruments until he came up with a foil packet. Returning to Jonah's bedside, he ripped away the foil, revealing a metal file. Pinning Jonah's arm to the bed, he began scraping the file across the tattoo, as if hoping he might be able to flake it off.

"Kenzie!" Jonah gripped his brother's wrist with his gloved hand, pulled him in close, and said in a low, deadly voice, "Stop that."

With that, Gabriel and Brendan hurried in and dragged Kenzie away, with Kenzie shouting, "That's not laid back, Jonah! That's creepy!"

Later, when Gabriel and Lilith came in together and told Jonah what he needed to do to save his brother's life, it wasn't a hard choice at all.

❦ CHAPTER FORTY-THREE ❧
AIN'T GONNA STUDY WAR NO MORE

"I still can't believe that Mandrake agreed to this." Fitch stomped snow off his boots and shook like a dog before stepping from the porch into the foyer.

"You didn't think he would?" Leesha said.

Fitch shrugged, his eyes fixed on Leesha. "Nope."

"He said that he wants to clear the air and move on. That they have nothing to hide. That we are welcome to interview Jonah or anyone else."

"What about searching the place?"

"He has no problem with that, as long as we avoid destruction of property or disturbing the students. And that we do it quickly so they can get back to normal."

Fitch digested this, then said, "It seems like an odd time. Who has a meeting at five P.M. on a Sunday night?"

"Mandrake picked the time. He wants to meet at the club, so maybe that's the least-busy time. And apparently most of the students will be at an event—those who are able to go."

"Ah," Fitch said. "Who else is coming from Trinity?"

"Everyone."

"Everyone?"

"The whole council's coming, and all the members of the task force investigating the Halloween murders."

Fitch whistled. "Well, *that's* a really bad idea."

"I know," Leesha said glumly. "I'm finding democracy has its drawbacks."

"I'm fine with democracy, but having all those bigots— I mean, intense, opinionated people— there? Seems like it makes it more likely there'll be an incident."

"It'll take a lot of people to search the campus, if we want to do it quickly. We'd love to pick and choose, but everyone we'd like to keep away is determined to go."

"I could help with the search," Fitch said, "if you're short-handed. Or if you need any more help with the tech issues."

"No!" Leesha took hold of his lapels and stood on her tiptoes so they were nearly eye-to-eye. "You've already done a lot, what with setting up the handhelds for the search. So. You will drop me off, and you will wait at Cuppa Joe's until I call you. Otherwise, you are staying here. Do you understand me?"

"Alicia!" Aunt Millie called from the kitchen. "Don't you shout at that nice young man. Even if he's not our kind."

"Sorry." Leesha let go of Fitch and began winding her scarf around her neck. But then it was too tight, and she had to yank at it to loosen it.

Fitch seemed unruffled. "I may be Anaweir, but I'm not helpless. And if I were you, I'd trade that whole pit of gifted vipers on the council for three people I can trust."

"I know," Leesha said. "That's why I have to go. We need

people who haven't already made up their minds. If I don't go, and something happens that I could have prevented, I'll never forgive myself."

Fitch helped her into her coat. "I'm worried that you'll go, and something will happen that you *couldn't* have prevented, and you'll still never forgive yourself."

"This is my job," Leesha said. "Madison's going, too. That should discourage people from acting out."

"Madison?" Fitch blinked at her. "I know everybody's cooperating and all, but . . . isn't that risky? I mean, we scarcely know anything about savants, and what we do know could be wrong. We don't know what their gifts are, or how many of them there are, or whose side the zombies are on." He paused to take a breath. "We don't really know what they want, and we haven't asked the people who do know."

"Well, I guess now maybe we'll find out," Leesha said. "Look, I agree with you, but I think Madison's more worried that someone on our side will misbehave, given what's been said in the meetings. She wants to make sure everybody plays nice, and she's the only one with a big enough stick to do it."

Fitch scowled. "I don't like it. I keep thinking of those movies where somebody keeps poking at this jewel in the rock, trying to pry it out, and this beast erupts out of the ground, and it turns out they were poking a dragon in the eye."

"Well, in this case, the dragon's with us," Leesha said, forcing a smile. She dug her hands into her pockets. "It's just so hard to convince people that this might be dangerous. People are acting like they're visiting the zoo or the haunted house. The problem is, nobody's seen the zombies but a group of preschoolers and us. Nobody else knows how hard they are to stop, even though they should get a clue from the fact that mainliners have been dying for years. Wizards are used to being at the top of the magical food chain. It makes us arrogant."

"Arrogant? Wizards?" Fitch's eyes widened in mock disbelief. "Speaking of arrogant wizards, have you considered the fact that I might worry about *you*?"

Leesha pulled on her gloves, trying to come up with a response, then swatted at her pocket as her phone vibrated again. "Stop *calling* me," she growled.

"Who is it?"

"It says *Blocked*."

"Maybe you should answer it."

"I have never answered a blocked call and found somebody I actually wanted to talk to on the other end," Leesha said. "If it's somebody I know, they'll text me. Let's go."

Fitch parked two streets away from the Keep, next to Cuppa Joe's. When he turned off the engine, the cold seemed to come at them from all sides.

"You'll stay here, right?" Leesha said. "I don't have to immobilize you, do I?"

"If you don't want to bail me out of detox, you'd better not leave me immobilized in a car on a downtown street," Fitch said. "Anyway, I thought I might go into Cuppa Joe's and warm up."

"I'm sorry," Leesha said. "I just can't help worrying."

"I know," Fitch said softly. "Look, if you promise to be careful, we'll call a worry truce."

"Okay, deal," she said. "I'll be careful. I really will."

But when Leesha went to get out of the car, Fitch said, "Hang on. There's one more thing."

She turned back toward him, and he slid his arm around her, pulled her closer, tilted her chin up, and kissed her. His lips were warm and firm and not at all wizardish.

When they finally broke apart, he leaned his forehead against hers and said, "Whoa," in this really impressed voice.

Some people said that wizard kisses created a sweet buzz, like spiced rum. Others said it was kind of like sticking your tongue into an electrical outlet.

"You haven't kissed a wizard before?" Leesha said.

"I haven't kissed *you* before," Fitch said, and kissed her again. "The great part about it is that now nothing bad will happen to you."

"What do you mean?"

"My kisses are magical," Fitch said. "That's *my* gift."

"I see," Leesha said. "Then you'd better kiss me again. For luck. Because we'll need it."

What with all the magical kissing in the car, Leesha was the last to arrive at the command post, which was in a warehouse Seph had rented across the street from the Keep. That was the compromise. Madison Moss was determined to come, but a lot of people, including Seph, were worried about having her on the inside. This way, she could weigh in if needed, and coordinate things on-site while still being out of the line of fire. That was the theory, anyway.

Jack and Ellen had assumed charge of the campus-wide search, communications, and operational security. They strode around the ground floor of the warehouse like gladiators on the field of battle, looking naked without weaponry. Seph had asked them to leave their swords at home in order to present a less hostile appearance and reduce the risk of unfortunate incidents.

Too bad we can't make wizards leave their weapons at home, Ellen had said.

"Now that we're all here," Seph said, "I'll review the schedule, and cover a few logistics. Most of this information is loaded onto your PCDs."

"What do you mean, PCDs?" Morrison asked.

"Personal communication devices," Seph said. When Morrison still looked blank, he added, "Those small tablets we handed out."

Morrison dug hers out of her coat pocket. "Why don't you *call* them tablets, then?"

Seph ignored this. "They are preloaded with details about the operation, including maps of the campus, blueprints of buildings, photos of some students and staff of the Keep and the Anchorage, and lists of teams and team leaders. Foster, DeVries, Middleton, and I will do the face-to-face with Mandrake and Kinlock, and call in other people as needed. Does everyone know what team you're on, and who's in charge of that team?"

"I would prefer to be on a different team," Hackleford said.

"The assignments are final," Madison said. "We've spent a lot of time on them already."

"With all due respect," Burroughs said, "some of the rest of us have considerable experience in interrogation techniques, and might achieve better results if we were the ones to question Mandrake and Kinlock."

Madison made a quick turn, her skirts swirling around

her. "Has anyone else noticed that whenever anyone says 'with all due respect,' they're about to say something disrespectful? Anyway, it's not an interrogation; it's an interview. We're here with their permission."

Burroughs snorted. Apparently, he was a slow learner. "We'll just see how cooperative they are."

"Who made this decision?" Hackleford persisted. "About the assignments, I mean."

"The assignments were made by an executive committee," Seph said. "All people with tactical experience."

"Like who?" Hackleford demanded.

"Like people who are actually *on* the Interguild Council," Madison said.

Seph and Madison had made the final decisions, with input from Mercedes, Jack, Ellen, and Leesha. They'd been selective—okay, *biased* in their team assignments. The objective was to keep certain individuals as far as possible from the main action. Hackleford was assigned to search campus buildings with Jack. And Burroughs was assigned to the command post, where Madison and Ellen could keep an eye on him and he wouldn't come into contact with savants.

"I don't really know what you're complaining about, Hackleford," Jack said. "After all, you're on my team. That's a plum assignment."

"Do you think *I* want to be in the command post, answering phones?" Ellen said, without a trace of sympathy. "You don't hear *me* complaining."

Publicly, anyway, Leesha thought. Ellen had complained plenty at the meeting, when the assignments were made. Leesha knew that Seph had his reasons for making that assignment. He wanted a strong fighter at hand to protect Madison if anything went wrong.

"If you don't want to be part of this, Burroughs, we'll understand," Seph said. "We'll let you know how it all turns out."

"I didn't say I didn't want to be part of this," Burroughs said.

"Just pretend you're in the army," Jack said sweetly. "The army is not a democracy."

Hackleford and Burroughs exchanged a look, like they were passing nasty notes in class. Leesha shifted her gaze to DeVries, who was watching them, frowning. Uneasiness rippled through her. Maybe we should have posted them farther away. Like Indianapolis. We'll have our hands full as it is, without having to keep an eye on them.

Hackleford's daughter died, Leesha reminded herself. DeVries lost his sister. It's no wonder that they want to confront those responsible.

"Listen up, everyone who's assigned to search the peripheral buildings," Jack said. "It's go time. Hopefully, you've reviewed the building checklist, so we're all on the same page, and you have the pass codes we distributed. In each building, the first thing we do is secure the premises, so nobody goes in or out. Then we clear the place—meaning we search the building, floor by floor. If you find evidence — you've seen the list of what we're looking for, and it's on your PCD—or if you encounter somebody you think we should talk to further, call the command post and we'll send somebody to check it out. If you have questions, or need help, contact the command post. Ellen and Madison will be here to troubleshoot, allocate assets, and question any high-value personnel."

I just love it when Jack talks military, Leesha thought.

"If you find Emma Greenwood, contact the command post immediately. And remember, we're guests here. We don't want anybody hurt on either side. If you're having trouble gaining access, contact the command post. Don't destroy property in an effort to get in."

How would *we* react, Leesha thought, if savants showed up in Trinity, claiming they meant us no harm, but they were going to search the place whether we liked it or not.

"One other thing," Leesha said. "There are some savants here that have medical problems, and they may even be dangerous to get close to. They are the ones who will still be in their rooms. Those buildings are marked on your maps, too. Just leave them alone for now."

"Wouldn't that be a prime place to hide someone?" Morrison said.

"We'll get there," Leesha said. "It's just not our first priority. Jack's team will head there once they've cleared the Oxbow Building."

Hudson was flipping through photos on her phone. "You're sure these are labrats?" she murmured, frowning. "They look almost normal."

"Let me re-emphasize that nobody is to be harmed, except in self-defense," Madison said. "Nobody here has been convicted of anything. Any questions? No? Then let's go."

❧ CHAPTER FORTY-FOUR ❧
HARD TIME KILLING FLOOR BLUES

Fitch kept his word and walked straight back to Joe's, meaning to drown his worries in a dark-chocolate peppermint mocha. "Shaken, not stirred," he told the barista, but she just rolled her eyes and gave him a standard one. He ordered a cinnamon bun, too, but it tasted like cardboard. The fault was not in the bun, but in himself. Every time he loosened the leash on his mind, he saw images of Leesha buried under a mob of ragtag undead.

Hey! he'd shout. *Over here!* But they couldn't seem to hear him, intent as they were on Leesha. Just like that night in the Flats.

Who were they? And what did they have to do with Jonah Kinlock and Gabriel Mandrake and the Anchorage? Were they allies or enemies? And what about Emma? Where did she figure in?

Minutes crept by. Fitch finally decided that he might as well make use of the time. He suspected he had an online test waiting for him that he hadn't touched. He staked out his table with a large coffee and went back out to his car to get his laptop out of the trunk.

Though it wasn't quite five, it was already nearly dark—one of those short December days when the light begins to bleed away almost as soon as it arrives. As Fitch unlocked the trunk, he scanned his surroundings, squinting against the bits of ice the wind flung into his face. At first, he thought the street was deserted, but then he noticed several dark shapes passing through the circle of light from the streetlights. They were all heading in one direction—toward the Keep.

Fitch shivered. Zombies? That was his first thought, but they didn't move with the same rolling, staggering gait as the ones he'd met before. These looked more like thugs. No. Assassins. Maybe they were bouncers, heading to work in the clubs in the district.

They passed out of sight. Still uneasy, Fitch dug his computer out from under a stack of blankets. As he went to shut the trunk, he heard an unfamiliar voice coming from under the front seat. "Leesha Middleton. If you are there, and if you care about your friends, pick up the damn phone."

Fitch circled around and yanked open the driver's side door. Leesha's phone was lying on the floor between the seats, lit up like Christmas. It must have slid out of her pocket onto the floor of the car.

Fitch scooped up the phone and put it cautiously to his ear. "Who's this?"

For a moment, nothing. Then, "Who's *this*?"

Fitch almost hung up. Instead, he said, "This is Harmon Fitch, a friend of Leesha's."

"This is Kenzie Kinlock, Jonah's brother. Where's Leesha? I need to talk to her."

Why would Jonah's brother want to talk to Leesha? "She's busy right now. Can I take a message?"

Kenzie responded with an explosion of spectacularly bad language.

"Is that the message?" Fitch said, holding the phone away from his ear.

"No." Kenzie took a quick breath. "Emma told me that Leesha is one of the good guys, that she wants to prevent any more bloodshed. Tell her—tell everyone—not to come anywhere near the Keep or the Anchorage. Tell them something is seriously wrong. I don't know exactly what, but tell them it's a trap."

It was a short distance from the rented warehouse to the front door of the Keep, but Leesha couldn't help feeling like she was crossing a no-man's-land in an undeclared war. Tendrils of snow eddied around them like unquiet spirits as they picked their way across the icy bricks—Mercedes in the lead, followed by DeVries and Leesha, with Seph bringing up the rear.

A flicker of movement to her left caught Leesha's eye. She spun around in time to see several muffled-up figures disappear around a corner, but she didn't get a good look at them.

She breathed in deeply, testing the air, but it seemed as clean as it ever is in the middle of a Midwestern city in the wintertime.

"I saw them, too," Seph murmured nearly in Leesha's ear, and she about had a heart attack.

"Do you smell anything?"

He shook his head. "When it's this cold, it seems to wring all the scent out of the air." He paused. "Steady on. A lot of people live around here, and we all look like zombies in this weather."

Still, Leesha was grateful to get inside, and not just because it was freaking cold.

It seemed peculiar to be in the ticket lobby of the Keep when it wasn't swarming with people and ablaze with lights. Leesha killed time by walking around, studying the vintage concert posters that lined the walls. The others huddled together, just inside the door, shifting their feet, checking their watches, and generally acting nervous.

"Whoa," Leesha said. "Five dollars to see the Rolling Stones? Those were the days."

DeVries checked his watch for the ninety-fifth time. "Where are they?" he muttered. "I don't like this."

"Don't worry," Mercedes said. "We're on rock and roll time."

"*What?*" DeVries said sharply.

"I've been working with Gabriel Mandrake for several years now, and he's always late. You'd think the head of an international murder conspiracy would be on time." The sorcerer slid a sideways look at DeVries.

DeVries grunted. He constantly scanned his surroundings as if he anticipated an attack at any time. But who could blame him, given what happened to him on Halloween?

It seemed like they were all edgy, because a door banged open and everybody jumped.

Leesha turned to find a youngish man in the doorway. "Welcome to the Keep," he said. "I'm Patrick Murphy,

Mr. Mandrake's assistant." He didn't look much like a Patrick Murphy, with his blue hair, brown skin, and multiple piercings. He wore low-slung blue jeans, a Dragonbreath sweatshirt, and a wireless headset.

Murphy looked around the lobby a second time, then scanned the screen on his handheld. "Where are the others? I've got fourteen people on this list."

"They've gone directly to the other buildings," Seph said. "We wanted to be as efficient as possible with this so we don't inconvenience you any more than necessary. While we're talking, they'll be searching. If we finish up here, we'll join them so hopefully we can wrap this up within a couple hours."

Murphy scanned his screen again, frowning. "Mr. Mandrake expected to meet with all of you first, and then provide escorts to those who go to the other buildings."

"Damn," DeVries said. "I wish he'd said something."

"You would be Mr. DeVries, I believe," Murphy said, checking off something on his screen.

"I hope that won't be a problem," Leesha said. "I mean, the fact that they don't have escorts."

Murphy shrugged. "Probably not. As I believe you know, most of the students are off-campus tonight. And you are—?"

"I'm Alicia Middleton," Leesha said. "And this is Seph McCauley and Mercedes Foster."

Murphy thawed a bit, at least where Mercedes was concerned. "Ah, Ms. Foster, it's a pleasure to finally meet you. Mr. Mandrake thinks highly of you, as does Natalie Diaz, one of our students."

"We think highly of her," Mercedes said.

"Where is Ms. Moss?" Murphy asked. "We understood

that she would be here. Mr. Mandrake was looking forward to seeing her again."

"She'll join us later," Seph said vaguely.

"Is she with the search team?" Murphy persisted.

"She's off-site right now, handling logistics and making sure everyone has what they need."

Murphy turned away, murmuring something into his headset. He listened, murmured some more, then turned back toward them.

"Well, then," Murphy said, "if this is everyone, come with me. We're meeting in the small concert hall."

Jack surveyed his little band of warriors and sighed. It was a team of scrubs—mostly people they'd wanted to keep away from the main action. Morrison. Hudson. Hackleford. Scavuzzo. And one longtime friend and ally—Blaise Highbourne, Jack's former neighbor, and a seer on the council.

"Okay," Jack said, "I'm pairing you up. Morrison and Hackleford, Hudson and Highbourne, me and Scavuzzo. Stay with your buddy, watch each others' backs."

His tablet vibrated, and Jack said, "It's go time."

They threaded their way through twisting downtown streets and back alleys, dodging piles of slush.

They entered Oxbow through the side door, using the pass code they'd been given, which worked like a charm. Two young women with brightly dyed hair were enthralled in a video game in the first floor recreation room. They froze mid-kill and looked up at Jack and his posse.

"We're going to do a quick search," Jack said politely. "Just stay right here while we do that. Ms. Morrison and Ms. Hackleford are going to get your names and take your photos, and then you can go back to what you were doing, all right?"

The two women nodded wordlessly, their eyes large and worried.

They found nothing suspicious on the first floor—a kitchen, music practice rooms, media room. What you might expect on the first floor of any school dormitory.

Nobody was home on the second floor, so they all worked together to clear it. They were heading to the third floor when Morrison said, "Where's Hackleford?"

The wizard was no longer with them "Hackleford!" Jack called. Nothing. He pinged her on the PCD. No response. When he checked her location, her device signal was coming from the first floor. Why'd she go back down there? Was she freelancing already?

"The rest of you, clear the third floor. I'll round up Hackleford."

"Shouldn't I come with you?" Scavuzzo said eagerly. "I'm your buddy."

"Oh. Right."

They took the stairs down, two at a time, Jack in the lead. As he emerged from the stairwell, some tiny sound or warrior instinct alerted him, and he dove just as something whizzed overhead and thunked into the wall.

Craning his neck, Jack looked up and saw that it was a knife. It had struck with such force that the blade was halfway buried in the wall. Jack scrambled back into the stairwell, pulling the door shut behind him. He could hear someone moving stealthily, outside the stairwell.

"What's up?" somebody said into Jack's ear. Jack nearly throttled him before he realized that it was Scavuzzo.

"Stay back," Jack hissed, pointing to the knife sticking in the wall.

"A *knife?*" Scavuzzo said contemptuously. He pushed past Jack and was halfway out the door when Jack dragged him back.

"You may be a wizard, but all those other wizards who were killed were stabbed, cut up, or bludgeoned to death," Jack said. "Unless you're wearing armor under those clothes, I wouldn't go out there."

"We just need to let them know we have permission to be here."

"What if he or she doesn't care?" Jack hissed back. He pointed up the staircase. "Let's go up and around." That's when he heard footsteps, somebody descending the stairs toward them. Jack motioned Scavuzzo into the niche behind the staircase, putting his fingers to his lips. Waking his tablet, he hit the panic button. Above them, the footsteps accelerated to a run.

It must be one of ours, Jack thought. Cautiously, he edged his head around the step and peeked up the stairwell. The person coming toward him was dressed completely in black, down to the hooded sweatshirt and ski mask.

Okay, *not* one of ours, Jack thought. There was something else—something that nagged at him, but he had no time to work it out, because the ski-masked guy was at the bottom of the stairs, about to blow past them, when he skidded to a stop, turned toward them, and peered into the gloom under the stairwell.

He knows we're here, Jack thought, the realization rippling through him like a fever chill.

Scavuzzo stood up and said, "Excuse me. We are representatives of the Interguild Council investigating the—" That was as far as he got before the masked man shot him three times.

Time seemed to slow down. Jack saw the barrel flashes, heard the *pop-pop-pop* of the silenced handgun. At this close range, the impact of the bullets threw Scavuzzo back against the wall, eyes wide with surprise.

That's all Jack saw before he tackled the masked man at knee level, pitching him backward so that his head smashed into the concrete stairwell with a sickening crunch. Jack heard a clatter as the gun hit the wall, saw the gunman slide off the steps to the floor, where he lay motionless, facedown.

Jack scrambled to the wall and ran his hands along the floor, coming up with the gun just as the door to the stairwell eased open. Jack rolled behind the stairs and watched as another hooded figure peered through the opening. The blade man, it must be, his aura presenting an attractive target.

Were either of them Jonah? Jack considered calling his name, to see what happened, but something stopped him— something he was missing.

He took a quick glance at Scavuzzo. His buddy. Jack had done a poor job of watching his back. The wizard's aura was fading, and Jack knew he was dying or already dead.

That was it—what Jack was overlooking. The *wizard's* aura. Both of the hooded shooters were wizards, not savants. Wizards wielding guns? Teaming up with savants? Curiouser and curiouser.

Looking on the bright side, it was easier to shoot a wizard, if it came to that.

It had been a while since Jack had fired a gun. He knew his business well enough to know that there's no truly safe place to shoot a person, but he hoped for the best. Hoped he could incapacitate the blade man but keep him alive long enough to question.

Jack gripped the pistol with both hands, braced himself against the wall, took careful aim, and shot the blade man, trying not to hit anything super important.

The blade man hissed in pain and stumbled backward, out of sight, letting the door close between them. Jack debated. Should he pursue? He had some questions he really, really wanted to ask.

But he had no way of knowing who else might be out there and what other weapons they might have.

Also, why hadn't he gotten any response from the command post? He checked his tablet again. He could see everyone inside the building, but nothing from outside.

Jack didn't want to lose anyone else. He needed to find the rest of his team and get out. Then they could find out what had gone wrong.

The gunman's glow had dwindled and died as well. Jack rolled him over, stripped off the mask, and discovered that it was a dead gunwoman—Hackleford, to be specific. When he searched her body, he found two more handguns hidden in clever holsters. She was carrying a small arsenal of hand weapons, too: knives, daggers, and what looked like delivery devices for pepper spray or mace. Jack had a hunch that whatever they contained was more lethal than pepper spray. And, of course, he found Hackleford's PCD, which explained a lot.

Call me crazy, Jack thought, but I think Hackleford and friends are here to kill us.

Jack debated a moment, then stripped off Hackleford's hoodie and ski mask and put them on. He was more likely to be killed by the armed masked guys than his own team, which was unarmed. But not for long.

Jack crept up the stairs, leading with his borrowed pistol.

ᚖ CHAPTER FORTY-FIVE ᚖ
TROUBLE SO HARD

Burroughs stalked around the command post with a scowl on his face, starting at every sound, checking his phone, sneaking peeks at his watch, ignoring Madison and Ellen. He was definitely getting on Ellen's nerves. It didn't take much to get on Ellen's nerves, and it sure didn't help to have him pinballing around the room.

"Will you sit *down*?" she growled when she couldn't take it anymore. "This is supposed to be the cake assignment, but you are making me crazy."

In answer, Burroughs checked his watch again.

"Is there someplace you have to be or what?"

Madison looked up from her screen. "Are you getting a signal on your tablet?" she said, her brow furrowed. "I can't see either of the teams. It's like they've dropped off the grid."

Ellen flopped back into her chair, woke her tablet, and scanned the map, scrolling up and down so she could see the entire campus. "Huh. That's strange. I don't see them either. Maybe the buildings are blocking the signals."

"Or maybe the devices are defective," Burroughs said. "That's what we get for giving this kind of responsibility to that Anaweir boy. He looks like he belongs in jail."

"If you're talking about Fitch," Ellen said, "he's in his second year at Harvard, and a wizard when it comes to technology. Ask your wizard friends who were at the Battle of Trinity. Oh, wait, they're dead."

"Maybe we should go find the others and make sure they're okay," Maddie said.

"No!" Burroughs said.

Ellen swung around to face the wizard. She might have agreed, but there was no way she and Burroughs should be agreeing on anything. "Why don't you want us to go out there?" she demanded.

"Because that's not the plan we all agreed to," he said. "Ms. Moss is too valuable an asset to risk. There's a reason she's here and not on the interview team. I don't trust these labrats, not at all."

"If that's the case, then that's all the more reason we should make sure the others are all right," Ellen said.

"That's not the priority," Burroughs said. "We stay here until we hear from them."

Ellen took a deep breath, released it slowly. Anger management, she thought. "Why is it that the wizard in the room always thinks he's in charge?" she asked, looking up at the ceiling.

"How about this, Burroughs?" Madison said. "You stay here and hold the fort, and me and Ellen will check things out."

"Hang on," Ellen said. "I've got to get something." She sprinted across the warehouse, shoving aside bins and cabinets until she found what she was looking for, a battered marine trunk at the rear. Wrenching it open, she lifted out Waymaker, cradling the great sword in her arms as she let the trunk slam shut. She slid the blade from its scabbard, feeling the rush of connection, relishing its familiar weight in her hands.

When she returned to the others, Madison looked down at Waymaker, up at Ellen's face. "Where'd you get that?"

"I guess I must've accidentally left it here," Ellen said, shrugging innocently. "I just remembered."

Madison wavered. "I said no weapons."

Ellen slid into her baldric, did up the buckles. "What if I put a hoodie over it? Do you think anybody would notice?"

"That's nonsense," Burroughs said. "There were to be no weapons—that was the rule, for everyone's safety. Put that thing back where you got it."

"Since when have wizards ever followed the rules?" Ellen said.

Burroughs considered this. "You know, you are right," he said. "What was I thinking?" Sliding his hand inside his jacket, he pulled out a gun and pointed it at Ellen. "Drop the sword. Now."

It took Ellen a minute to find her voice. "A wizard? Packing a *gun*? Is this the end of civilization or what?"

"Don't try my patience. Ms. Moss is a valuable asset. You, on the other hand, are expendable."

Ellen released her grip on Waymaker, and the sword clattered to the ground. She flexed her hand, gazing longingly at the gun. "Aren't you afraid you'll get your hands dirty?"

"We in the Black Rose have always been practical when

it comes to weapons," Burroughs said, with a twisted smile. "It's one of the things that makes us so very effective. Our strength is in tactics."

"The Black Rose," Ellen said. "Then the rumors are true."

"What rumors?" Madison said.

"That he's part of an international syndicate of wizard assassins. That it's still around."

"Ah," Madison said. "Well, I don't get it. What's the point in this? Aren't we on the same side? Otherwise, why are you here?"

"How presumptuous, to think that we would align ourselves with you," Burroughs said. "The strong have always ruled over the weak, and the weak have always complained. We are predators, Ms. Moss, and you, my dear, are—what?—an art student?"

Madison was beginning to shimmer, a sure sign that she was losing her temper. "You must be a deaf predator, then, because I asked you a question. Why are you here?"

"Because it was too good an opportunity to pass up." He double-gripped the gun and broadened his stance as Madison spread her burning wings. "Don't try your Dragon routine on me. I'll shoot you in the leg if I have to."

"You know what," Ellen said, "that's a misconception. There's really no safe place to shoot somebody. Even a flesh wound can be fatal. The femoral artery—"

"I'll shoot *you* in the head if you don't shut up," Burroughs said. "That's *bound* to be fatal."

"I don't know what you think this will accomplish," Madison said, subsiding a little. "I won't let this slide—I can tell you that. I *will* come after you. And if I can't, the council will."

Burroughs rolled his eyes. "Do you think we didn't anticipate that? Our theory is, as long as you remain technically alive, you can continue to be the vessel for the Dragonheart. The Black Rose has some amazing poisons and potions at our disposal. We're thinking a chronic vegetative state or a twilight sleep will buy us considerable time in which to figure out how to free the stone safely."

As the wizard spoke, the blood drained from Madison's face until her freckles stood out against her skin.

"As for the council, our assassins are finishing them off as we speak. It was so helpful of you to split up. The best part is, we're using guns and daggers and other crude weapons, so the labrats will get the blame. What a tragedy: the entire council massacred by mutants, the Dragon Heir left comatose."

"You were the ones behind the killings on Halloween," Madison said, her blue eyes bright with tears and fury. "*You* murdered my little sister."

Burroughs shook his head. "Actually, no. Haven't you heard? It was Jonah Kinlock. If it had been me, DeVries would have stayed dead."

"What?" Ellen felt double-ambushed. "Isn't DeVries in on this? I thought you all were partners."

"DeVries? Please. Don't give him credit for this. He was never well-suited to take over his father's business. He's never been the man his father was." Burroughs's voice hardened. "He goes down, along with everyone else. Now, sit down, relax, and we'll wait to hear from my colleagues."

That's when Madison made her move, extending her hand toward Burroughs, marshaling her power. Calmly, Burroughs shifted his aim and shot her in the left leg. Madison screamed and went down, clutching at her thigh, blood streaming through her fingers.

Ellen dove sideways, coming up with Waymaker. "See that she doesn't bleed to death," Burroughs said curtly, waving at her with the gun.

He half turned, as somebody pounded at the door. "Ah. Here we are," he said, checking his watch. "All finished. Early, even. The Interguild Council is permanently adjourned." He backed toward the door, keeping his gun trained on Ellen. Sliding back the bolt, he hauled open the door.

And was buried under hundreds of decaying bodies.

Fitch stared at the phone, as if it might offer some clue, but the display read *Blocked*.

"Oka ay," Fitch said. "What makes you think it's a trap?"

"They've been rebuilding the security system to keep me out. They've taken my building off-network entirely." It was hard to understand him through the considerable background noise.

"Where *are* you? Why is it so noisy?"

"I'm on the roof of the infirmary," Kenzie said "It's the only place I could get a signal. What you're hearing is the wind. I'm freezing my ass off up here."

Fitch thought of the coffee waiting for him inside, said good-bye to it, and began walking toward campus. "Can you come down and meet me somewhere?"

"No can do," Kenzie said. "Gabriel's put a lot of physical barriers in my way. The bastard. The only way I could go was up."

"Why are they so intent on shutting you out? Are you really important or really dangerous?"

Kenzie snorted. "Both, I hope. It's kind of a dream of mine. Now, back on topic: where's Leesha? You've got to warn the mainliners not to come anywhere near here."

"Mainliners?"

"You know, the standard magical guilds."

"Oh. Right. But how do I know you're who you say you are?"

"Hang on." After a moment, he said, "Look at your phone."

A young boy's face had appeared on the screen, red-brown hair spilling out from under his knit cap. He looked like a pale, hollow-cheeked, younger version of Jonah Kinlock.

"How old *are* you?" Fitch blurted.

"I'm fifteen," Kenzie said defensively.

"I would've said thirteen."

"Look, we don't have time for this." Kenzie swiveled the webcam so that Fitch could see that he was, indeed, up on a roof, snowflakes swirling around him.

"That's pretty thin evidence," Fitch said, "the fact that they've changed the security on their system. Maybe they just don't want you hacking in, changing your grades or whatever."

"If you don't believe me, then why are you heading my way?"

Fitch looked at his phone, which displayed a map, pinpointing his position on it.

How is he doing that? Fitch wondered.

"Anyway, it's not just that. More important, there's something wrong with my brother."

"Something wrong? Like what?"

"Something's missing," Kenzie said. "Something's different. He's not the same person. When you look in his eyes . . ."
Kenzie's voice faltered. "Have you met my brother, Jonah?"

"Briefly," Fitch said, "when he saved my life. I can't say I
know him very well."

"In addition to being an enchanter with a killing touch,
he—"

"What?" Fitch felt like he'd been punched in the gut.
"What do you mean?"

"You *don't* know him very well, do you?" Kenzie said.
"So in addition to all that, he's an empath, meaning he's
hypersensitive to other people's feelings, he can always see
both sides of a story, he has the unlimited capacity to feel
guilty about stuff he's not even responsible for. As you can
imagine, that's a real handicap for an assassin, so—"

"An assassin? Are you saying that Rowan DeVries is telling the truth?"

"Will you shut up and *listen* to me?" Kenzie said. "Everyone Jonah kills is already dead. By most standards, anyway.
Long story short, I've never looked into Jonah's eyes and
not seen guilt, regret, empathy, and sorrow. What my friend
Emma calls the blues. Until now."

"What do you see now?"

"Nothing," Kenzie said.

"Nothing?"

"I see nothing at all. Now will you warn the mainliners?"

"They're already there," Fitch whispered.

"Where?"

"They're in the Keep, meeting with Gabriel Mandrake,
Jonah, and the others."

❧ CHAPTER FORTY-SIX ❧
ROUGH JUSTICE

The theater was set up like a nightclub, with comfortable plush seating around small tables. Sound and lighting equipment had been pushed into a corner to free up more floor space, and the chairs brought in close together. Gabriel Mandrake had done everything possible to make it less like an interrogation and more like a conversation.

Leesha was surprised to find a small group waiting for them. Gabriel Mandrake, of course. She also recognized several members of Fault Tolerant—Rudy Severino, Natalie Diaz, and Alison Shaw. There were four more people she didn't know. But no Jonah Kinlock.

"Welcome back to the Keep," Mandrake said. He embraced Mercedes; Mercedes hugged Natalie, and then introduced Leesha and the rest of them.

Leesha relaxed fractionally. It was all kumbaya so far. Maybe she'd worried for nothing.

"I was disappointed to learn that Madison Moss isn't with you," Mandrake said. "I understood that she would be coming."

"She won't be participating in the interview," Seph said. "The Halloween murders are still hard for her to talk about. But she's very much interested in the outcome of this, so she's supervising the campus search."

Mandrake's lips tightened. "Patrick tells me that a number of you have already deployed to the other buildings." He paused. "Actually, this may work out well." He motioned Patrick closer, they exchanged a few quiet words, and the assistant took his leave.

"What about Kinlock?" DeVries asked. "Will he be joining us?"

"Not immediately," Mandrake said.

"And Emma?" DeVries persisted.

"As I've said before, I don't have any idea where she is," Mandrake said. "For now, it's just us." Their eyes locked briefly.

"Who's Emma?" a woman asked, touching Mandrake's arm.

"Emma was a student here for a brief time," Mandrake said. "She may or may not have been a witness to the murders at McCauley's."

That's odd, Leesha thought. You'd think everybody here would already know that whole story. And the woman— she looked too old to be a student. Her voice was hard to understand, like someone who's had a head injury, an impression reinforced by the fact that her face was oddly devoid of expression. The hairs on the back of Leesha's neck stood up.

If Fitch were there, she would have said, *Are you thinking what I'm thinking?*

"Let me introduce those who *are* here," Mandrake said. "All of them are Thorn Hill survivors. This is Lilith Greaves," he said, touching the shoulder of the woman who'd asked about Emma. He introduced Natalie, Rudy, and Alison; then the ones Leesha hadn't met before: Mike Joplin, Charlie Dugard, Thérèse Fortenay, and Brendan Wu.

Charlie Dugard looked familiar. Where had she seen him before? And Brendan Wu was also older than the others, maybe middle-aged. If he had any Asian blood, Leesha couldn't see it. What an odd mix of people, she thought. She'd also been told that none of the Thorn Hill survivors had made it to adulthood. Mandrake hadn't said a word about their roles at the Anchorage.

It was also odd that Mandrake would want so many people present for this kind of conversation. Leesha guessed they knew what topic was on the agenda. Maybe. They seemed tense, on edge, especially the members of Fault Tolerant, who'd been present the night of the murders.

Alison, for example. She looked stylish in jeans, boots, and a brilliant teal sweater, her hair streaked with the same color. But she twitched and fidgeted, not meeting anyone's eyes, as if she wished she were someplace else.

"Please," Mandrake said, gesturing toward an array of food on the sideboard. "Help yourself to refreshments and then have a seat. We'll be here a while, so you may as well make yourselves comfortable. When your colleagues arrive, they'll be welcome to join us."

When everyone was settled, Leesha woke her tablet to bring up her list of questions. Odd. There was no Internet—

no signal at all. She would have thought that this place, of all places, would have been totally connected.

"We've developed a list of questions as a starting point," Leesha said. "I'll start, but some of the others may—" She looked up to find Mandrake shaking his head. "What? Is there a problem?"

"Let's hold off on questions for now," Mandrake said. "In the interest of efficiency, we're going to share with you the history of Thorn Hill, and how it relates to what we do here at the Keep."

Mercedes and Leesha looked at each other. "Would you care to explain?" Mercedes said.

Mandrake sat back in his chair, steepling his fingers. "Have you heard of a process known as Truth and Reconciliation?"

Seph cleared his throat. "Isn't that what was used in South Africa after the end of apartheid?"

Mandrake nodded. "It involves allowing the victims of genocide to confront those responsible and have an honest dialogue about reconciliation—which is the only way to find a way forward."

"We came here to find out the truth about what happened on Halloween," DeVries said, "and to determine who is responsible for a decade of killings. We didn't come here to talk about Thorn Hill."

"Maybe not," Greaves said, "but we did."

"I'm a little confused, Gabriel," Mercedes said. "Are you suggesting that someone here is responsible for what happened in Brazil?"

"Not directly," Gabriel said. "But indirectly, perhaps." His gaze singled out DeVries. "And in a global sense? Definitely."

"This is a waste of time," DeVries said, his voice low

and furious, flame flickering over his skin. "I agreed to this because I hoped for an honest effort to resolve this and bring the guilty parties to justice."

"We share that goal," Greaves said. Her voice was thick, and somewhat difficult to understand.

"If you think you're going to be able to use what happened at Thorn Hill to excuse the murders on Halloween, you are mistaken," DeVries said. "Madison Moss's twelve-year-old sister should not pay the price for a tragedy that was likely the result of carelessness and hubris."

"I'm afraid it's a bit more complicated than that," Mandrake said. "It's really a very interesting story. Please." He motioned toward DeVries's seat. "Sit down."

Leesha could almost see the wheels turning in the other wizard's head. If he stayed, he might learn something, and at the end of it, he'd take action, depending on what he heard.

DeVries slowly sank back down into his seat, his eyes wary.

Leesha looked at Seph, who'd been gripping the arms of his chair like he might spring out of it. She saw him relax fractionally, and guessed he might have reached a similar conclusion—that there was no harm in listening, and they might learn something.

"We'll begin with the premise that appearances can be deceiving," Mandrake said. "I introduced the others as Thorn Hill survivors—and they are. But there are differences among them. Let me explain."

Jack found what was left of his team on the fourth floor, huddled together in a laundry room—they were down to three—Morrison, Highbourne, and Hudson. Two wizards and a seer. Morrison almost brained Jack with a mop handle before they got things sorted out.

"Somebody in a ski mask shot at us down on the third floor," the wizard explained. "We've been trying to reach the command post, but it doesn't seem to be getting through. I thought we had permission to search in here." She looked betrayed.

"I thought we did, too," Jack said. "Either somebody didn't get the memo, or we've got freelancers joining in. Scavuzzo and Hackleford are both dead."

"Dead?" Morrison said, looking like this was *not* the operation she'd signed up for.

"I don't exactly know what's going on, but Hackleford killed Scavuzzo, and I killed Hackleford." He told the others what had happened.

"Wizards were trying to kill you?" Highbourne looked baffled. "That doesn't make any sense."

"What about the person who shot at you?" Jack asked. "Was he or she gifted?"

"We didn't get a good look," Highbourne said, looking embarrassed. "We ran. We came up here and hid."

"Smart move," Jack said, squeezing his shoulder. "Don't pick a fight you can't win. I don't want to lose anybody else. I'm going to pass out a few weapons that might even the odds, depending on who we're up against." He distributed the weapons he'd taken from Hackleford.

Morrison held the gun flat-handed, like it was a grenade. "I don't know anything about guns," she said. "Can't I just flame them or use a killing charm?"

"If it works, have at it," Jack said. "Should work fine on wizards. Not too sure about savants."

Morrison looked at Jack. At the gun. Lifted her chin and said grimly, "Show me."

"Short course," Jack said. "Don't point your gun at anything you don't intend to shoot. Don't put your finger on the trigger unless you're ready to shoot. Make sure of your target and what's beyond it. Shoot two-handed—one hand steadying the other." He watched as she demoed it back to him. She did reasonably well. "Okay, this is the safety. Leave it on unless you're ready to shoot. And don't shoot if any of the rest of us are in front of you." Morrison nodded, flicked the safety on, and tucked the gun into her waistband.

"All right," Jack said. "We're not going to hunt down whoever's shooting at us. I'm assuming that they know all about guns, and that puts us at a disadvantage. Remember: they are not here to defend the building. They are here to kill us. Our plan is to avoid them, get out, and get help."

Hudson was looking at the building floor plan on her tablet. "It's better to use the stairs, right? If we go right and then left, we should be able to take the stairs to the ground floor and go out through the back door."

They descended the stairs, Jack in the lead, Highbourne taking the rear, the two wizards in between. At the foot of the stairs, Jack motioned the others to the side, and tried the stairway door. Locked.

"Can't we shoot it open?" Highbourne asked.

Jack shook his head. "That works in the movies, not so much in real life. Besides, it's a steel door. The bullets will probably ricochet and kill us."

"And it'll make too much noise, right?" Morrison said, examining the hinge side of the door. "Stand back," she said. Extending her hand, she ran a thin line of wizard flame along the hinges, sweeping up and down until the metal softened, then melted, running down the side of the door until it hung loose in its frame. Jack managed to wedge his fingers into the opening and pried it open a few inches. Waited. Then pried it open farther. Nothing. Stuck his head out for a look-around. And was met by a withering volley of gunfire.

Jack jerked his head back in. Swore.

"What about those little bottles you had?" Morrison said. "What's in them?"

Jack shook his head. "I'm thinking some kind of poison. Since we don't know what it is or how to use it, we might end up poisoning ourselves."

Hudson was studying the floor plan again. "There's a side door that lets out into the alley alongside the building. Can we get out that way?"

"Depends on whether they're working with the same intel we are," Jack said. "Let's try it."

CHAPTER FORTY-SEVEN
BEFORE YOU ACCUSE ME

Leesha didn't buy *everything* Gabriel Mandrake was selling. Maybe he was a principled philanthropist, but he gave off some slick hustler vibes, like he couldn't help but present himself in the best possible light. She knew the type—she'd once been a hustler of sorts herself. He might be telling some of the truth, but he sure wasn't telling *all* of the truth.

Still, she tried to keep an open mind as she sat through his description of the founding of Thorn Hill, his claims that it wasn't a terrorist camp, that the so-called massacre couldn't have been a tragic accident since there were no toxic chemicals in use at the commune, his conclusion that it must have been a genocidal attack, carried out by someone who wouldn't hesitate to murder children. Alison talked about the "mercy killings" carried out by mainliners after the fact. Natalie shared her experiences as a healer, the ongoing heartbreak of losing family members and friends to the long-term effects of the poison.

Greaves didn't say much, but seemed intent on Rowan DeVries throughout the speeches, as DeVries grew more and more impatient. He leaned toward Leesha. "Don't you think this is just a delaying tactic?" he hissed.

Leesha shrugged. "Maybe. I guess we are learning things we didn't know before."

All this time, Seph had been listening, keeping his opinions to himself. Now he spoke up. "Isn't that uncommon— wizards using poisons?"

"Ask DeVries about his father," Greaves said. "He was very ecumenical when it came to murder. He employed sorcerers to make poisons for him."

"What do *you* know about my father?" DeVries said, obviously startled.

"I used to work for him," Greaves said.

DeVries stared at her. It seemed he had finally lost his footing. "What was your name again?"

"Back then I went by Gwyneth Hart," Greaves said. "Gwen."

"And . . . you made poisons? For my father?"

Greaves shook her head. "Actually, I worked on another project. Your father was interested in modifying Weirstones, in creating designer Weir. I worked on that—experimenting on unwilling subjects—and I hated it. I fled to Thorn Hill to get away from him. There, I became a different person. I took a new name, started a new life. I hoped your father would never find me." She paused. "Apparently, he did."

DeVries wasn't buying either. "You think the connection between you and my father proves he was responsible for Thorn Hill?"

"I think it proves that he was familiar with and a frequent

user of poisons," Greaves said. "I think it proves that he was a despicable man."

"But you *survived*?" DeVries said after a long pause. "I thought the survivors were all children."

"That depends on how you define 'survived,'" she said. She turned to Brendan Wu, who took the floor, and told them about shades.

Leesha could tell that speech came hard for him—for both Greaves and Wu. When she looked closely at him, and at Lilith Greaves, she could see the resemblance between their flat, expressionless faces and the way they moved and the zombie-like creatures who'd nearly killed her that night in the Flats.

Somehow, it was this most far-fetched claim that she found most convincing—that a sentient remnant of those who died persisted after death. Maybe it was because she'd had direct experience with what they called hosted shades the night of the attack. Or maybe Wu was just more credible than Mandrake. This was the first explanation she'd heard that made sense. Well, it was the *only* explanation she'd heard.

Not everyone was convinced.

"You expect us to believe that you"—DeVries pointed at Brendan Wu and Lilith Greaves with his first and middle fingers—"that you are actually Thorn Hill victims inhabiting stolen bodies?"

"Not victims," Greaves said. "Survivors. And whether you choose to believe it or not, it's true."

"A body is not just a costume that you put on," DeVries said. "I mean, how does that even work?"

"I don't know." Wu shrugged. "Could it be . . . *magic*? Ya think?"

Leesha smothered a smile. She could see the spirit of this boy shining through his ill-fitting body.

"Do you have any proof?" DeVries asked, looking around, like he was humoring people at a séance. "For example, are there any loose shades in here right now?"

"Not loose shades," Alison muttered, scowling. "*Free* shades."

Mandrake motioned to Severino, and he walked around, passing out small flower pendants made of silver. "Put those on, and you'll be able to see them," Mandrake said.

Leesha slid the chain over her head so that the pendant rested on her chest. When she looked up, she saw them. They were everywhere, like gossamer petticoats or spider-webs or pulsing, transparent jellyfish in the air. She couldn't help hunching down in her chair, covering her head with her arms.

"They won't hurt you," Mandrake said. "They *can't* hurt you, unless they inhabit a body. As of now, they're not strong enough to inhabit someone living—only the dead."

"I suppose this *could* be the real deal," DeVries said. "They could be restless spirits, spooks, shades, or whatever. Or this *could* be a sefa that causes hallucinations." He tapped the pendant with his forefinger.

"I, for one, believe them," Leesha said, straightening a little. "It's ironic if we as practitioners of magic can't consider the possibility that there is a kind of magic we've never seen before. Still, there's something I don't understand. I was attacked by a group of zom—hosted shades one night in the Flats. I was with two Anaweir friends, but it was clear that they were coming after me in particular. Why is that? Is it a matter of revenge?"

"Leesha's right," Seph said. "We've been talking about the connection between the mainline guilds and the disaster at Thorn Hill. Is there a connection between Thorn Hill survivors and the Weir murders?"

The Thorn Hill survivors looked at one another, as if hoping someone else would pick up the ball. Mandrake looked a little greenish, like he wished he could end the conversation right there.

Finally, Greaves spoke. "Yes," she said. "Hosted shades have been responsible for most of the killings."

This was met by shocked silence.

"There is an element of revenge in it," Greaves continued matter-of-factly, "because most Thorn Hill survivors blame mainliners for their situation. But there is an element of justice as well. The only treatment for us, the only thing that offsets the damage done to us at Thorn Hill, is blood magic."

"Blood . . . magic," DeVries said. "You mean the energy that's freed by the death of the gifted."

Greaves nodded. "Originally, shades killed in order to obtain fresh host bodies. Weir, Anaweir—it didn't matter. More recently, we've killed to obtain the blood magic that allows us to inhabit one body for an extended length of time, to fully occupy it and use it more effectively. It's also therapeutic for those of us who still have our original bodies."

Well, we wanted the truth, Leesha thought. "I was with you up until now," she said. "I'm totally sympathetic, but that's just not going to work for us going forward."

Seph McCauley's face had gone pale, his eyes blazing gold-green against the pallor. "So . . . what you're saying is, Thorn Hill survivors killed Grace Moss and two other people in my backyard in order to collect blood magic."

Wu and Greaves looked at each other. "You're talking about the killings in Trinity," Greaves said

"Jonah asked me about that, remember?" Brendan said to Greaves. "He thought we were responsible for the killings on Halloween."

"Isn't that what we're here to talk about?" Seph's voice rose. "You killed a twelve-year-old girl so you could patch yourselves up. A girl who was two when Thorn Hill happened, someone who had no idea she was even magical until two years ago."

"I'll be the first to say that I don't control more than a fraction of the Thorn Hill survivors," Greaves said. "It could have been shades that did the killings. But not anyone under my command. It wasn't us."

"This is a waste of time," DeVries said. "It wasn't zombies who attacked me on Halloween night. It was Jonah Kinlock. So where is he?"

"Yes," Alison said. "*Where is he?* What have you done with him?"

Leesha looked from Alison to Mandrake, feeling the tension that crackled between them.

"Jonah has another commitment," Mandrake said, giving Alison a look that said that she was talking out of turn.

"Like what?" Alison said. "What could be more important than this?"

Mandrake and Greaves seemed to be having trouble coming up with an answer.

Alison stood. "I have something to say," she announced, her voice trembling a little. "Ms. Greaves, you said that you left Mr. DeVries's employ because you didn't want to experiment on unwilling subjects, right?"

Greaves nodded warily. "Right."

"But when you got to Thorn Hill, you started right back in, didn't you?" Alison said. "You—and him—" She pointed at Mandrake. "You started trying to turn us into something we're not, and we never had a chance to say yes or no."

"Alison," Mandrake said, visibly shaken, "what are you doing?"

"Truth and reconciliation," Alison said. "Isn't that what this is? So here's the truth: we were experimented on without our consent."

"You're confused," Mandrake said, licking his lips, sweat beading his forehead. "You don't know what you're saying."

"Yes, I do," Alison said. "And you do, too."

"I should have known that this meeting would be too stressful for you." Mandrake looked at Natalie for help. "Natalie, can you and Rudy help Alison back to her apartment and sedate her? Once we're done here, we can—"

"No," Natalie said. "No, I can't." With that they all stood, all the younger survivors of Thorn Hill. Natalie, Rudy, Charlie, Mike, and Thérèse.

"See, we're all in this together," Rudy said. "Back then, we were too young to consent. Well, now we're older, those of us who've survived. We're old enough to decide. But you just keep on using us, don't you?"

"*Using* you? Is that what you think?"

"Your mistake was giving us the blood magic," Natalie said. "It probably seemed like a good idea at the time, to get us all on board with the new plan, to demonstrate the benefits. But there were . . . unexpected side effects. Like clearheadedness."

"Jonah had it right all along, didn't he?" Alison said.

Mandrake turned, speaking directly to Seph. "She's heavily medicated," he said. "She's been declining for some time, and has developed a paranoia that—"

"I *have* been heavily medicated," Alison said. "We all have. All those trips to the dispensary, all those therapies. You still hoped to create that perfect assassin."

"What kind of experiments?" Mercedes asked. "What was really going on at Thorn Hill?"

"They were creating magical mutants," Rudy said. "So we could defend ourselves against wizard oppression. After the massacre, Gabriel tried to carry on."

"I was trying to keep you alive!" Gabriel looked at each of them in turn, but couldn't seem to find any allies.

"But you weren't the expert on Weirstones, were you?" Natalie said. She jerked a thumb at Greaves. "Lilith Greaves was. She was always better at this than you. So your experiments weren't all that successful."

"Meanwhile, the undead survivors of Thorn Hill were causing problems," the one called Charlie said. "Making it more likely that your secrets would come out. So you sent us out to put them to rest permanently."

"Jonah caught on," Natalie said. "He kept asking questions about why we were doing what we were doing. He kept trying to get at the truth behind Thorn Hill. Worse, now shades under Lilith's command were killing the gifted, seeking blood magic."

"So you needed a scapegoat," Alison said. "You needed a sacrifice that would take the pressure off of you, so you could keep your secrets a little longer. So you set Jonah up. He was supposed to take the blame for the murders at McCauley's. The double bonus was it would shut him up. But somehow, he managed to slip through the trap you laid for him."

"Hang on," Seph said. "What are you saying?"

"You're blaming the wrong person," Alison said. "Jonah didn't kill those people on Halloween. I did." Tears pooled in her eyes, spilled over, and ran down her cheeks. "I am so very sorry."

ᏪᎥ Chapter Forty-eight ᎧᎧ
Silver Dagger

Emma spent a good part of the long drive home rehearsing what she would say. Or maybe *rehearsing* was the wrong word, because she never said the same thing twice. It was like a song where you changed the lyrics every time you sang it, but it still never quite came together. Or maybe there was just no way to turn any of this into words that were anything but ugly.

You know how your life was ruined and you lost nearly all your family when you were only six or seven years old, and you thought it was an accident? Well, it wasn't. Somebody did it on purpose.

You know how the people all around you suffered and died, and you watched it, knowing that it's going to happen to you one day? You paid the price for my mama cheating on my father.

Remember how you can't even kiss a girl or hug your brother, Kenzie, who you love most in the world? My daddy did that.

Seriously, it might be easier just to shoot herself between the eyes and leave a long apology note.

But, no. That was Tyler's way out. And they deserved better.

So she gave up and tuned the radio to a blues station, and it seemed like every one of those songs told the story much better than she ever could.

As she drove north, it got colder and colder.

Should she go talk to Mercedes first? It would help if she could bring some scrap of hope along with her. But, no. She'd be doing that more for herself, not for Jonah, Natalie, and the others. So she headed straight for the Anchorage.

She was really feeling the absence of her phone. She kept reaching for it, thinking she'd call Kenzie or Jonah or somebody, and realizing too late that it wasn't there. She decided to stop at Oxbow and pick it up.

Emma parked in her usual spot. When she got out of her truck, she was shocked at how cold it was. She tried to enter through the side door as usual, but when she put in the code, she got an error message.

Maybe they finally got around to changing the locks, she thought. She tried pounding on the door, but nobody answered. The place appeared deserted, nobody coming in or out. In fact, the whole campus seemed oddly empty of students. It was already dark, maybe just past suppertime, which usually meant a lot of coming and going.

Maybe she should go try Kenzie at Steel Wool. There was always staff on duty there, and he was one of the first people she wanted to talk to anyway.

As she turned away, she heard gunshots coming from inside the dormitory. And then what sounded like volleys of gunfire in return. Emma flattened herself against the building, next to the door, hoping that brick would stop a bullet.

Her pulse pounded in her throat as possible explanations reeled through her mind.

So at first she didn't notice when somebody materialized out of the dark and snowflakes into the pool of light around the door. He was muffled up against the cold, but had a phone pressed to his ear.

Emma shrank back, raising both hands in defense. Then lowered them slightly. "Fitch?" she said, and it came out almost as a squeak.

He stared at her as if she'd risen from the dead and tapped him on the shoulder. "Emma?" Fitch threw his arms around her, and swung her around in a happy dance. "I can't tell you how glad I am to see you. Leesha's been calling you and calling you."

The phone in his hand was crackling angrily. Raising it to his ear, Fitch said, "Kenzie! It's Emma! She's here, in front of Oxbow. And she's alive!"

There came a happy explosion of sound from the phone.

"Fitch," Emma said, grabbing hold of his lapels. "There's people shooting guns inside this building."

"Kenzie? Did you hear that?" Fitch said. "Can you get us in?"

"Why would you want to get *in* there?" Emma hissed.

"I think Jack's in there, and some others from the task force. I don't know who's shooting at them." He listened a moment, then said, "Hang on, Kenzie. I'm going to put you on speaker."

"Emma," Kenzie said, "something's happened. They've done something to Jonah. He's not himself."

Emma's heart nearly stopped. "What do you mean, they did something to him?"

"I don't know," Kenzie said, his voice husky with tears. "It's—it's like they took out his heart. I'm afraid he might hurt somebody."

"Do you think he's the one inside Oxbow?"

"No. Something's going on at the Keep. Something big. I think he's there, and it's some kind of a ruse or a trap. I know it's a lot to ask, but could you go there? If anyone can get through to him, it's you."

"It's *not* a lot to ask," Emma said, her own heart breaking. "I owe it to him—and to you. But you're the one he cares about most. Where are you? I'll come fetch you, and we'll go together."

"I'm on the roof at the dispensary. It's a long story. It'll take too long to get me down from here. Anyway, I'm going to help Fitch with this Oxbow situation."

"All right. I'm going."

"Emma?"

"Yes?"

"Use music. That's a language he understands, and that's your gift. That's your magic. You're the only one who can touch my brother. You just never figured it out."

Leesha stared at Alison and the others, feeling like she'd been turned inside out. "You?" she blurted. "You murdered a *twelve-year-old*?"

"No," DeVries said. "It was Kinlock. Not you. I don't know why you're covering for him, but—"

"I had my orders from Gabriel," Alison said. "I was supposed to kill some mainliners, and frame Jonah for it."

Mandrake slammed his hands down on the table. "If

that's what you thought I said, you were confused. I wouldn't ever—"

"No, Gabriel, I may have been sick and drugged up and—and modified to the point that I wasn't even sure who I was. But I was *crystal clear* on that. You told me how Jonah was going to betray us all to the mainliners, how he'd lost sight of the mission, how I was the best slayer of everyone, and that's why you were giving me this important job." Her body shuddered with sobs.

Natalie slid her arm around her.

"So, at the break, I put on a leather jacket and leather gloves, like Jonah always wears. When he walked out onto the grounds, I followed him. I almost walked into the gazebo, but then I heard the three of them—DeVries and Emma and Jonah—arguing. So I waited. First DeVries came out, then Emma, then finally Jonah. I followed him a little way, drugged him, then riffed the two mainliners—"

"Riffed?" Seph said, breaking out of his shell shock a little. "What's that?"

"That's the word we use to make it seem less like killing. But before I could stage everything, DeVries came sneaking along. I think he was following Jonah."

"That's not true!" DeVries said. "If anything, he was following me."

"Whatever," Alison said. "Anyway, I couldn't let you stumble across Jonah lying drugged on the ground, so I riffed you, too. Or so I thought." She paused. "Afterward, I—I smeared blood on Jonah and left my daggers beside him. To make it look like he was the killer. I was almost finished when Grace showed up and saw me. I think at first she thought it was some kind of Halloween prank. And so she—she didn't even run away." Alison's voice broke, and she mopped at her eyes with her sleeves. "I never—I didn't mean to kill Grace," she said, swallowing hard. "I knew that was unforgivable. Unforgivable. I knew that the mainliners—that Madison Moss—might execute Jonah on the spot. Still, I *betrayed* him. I left him there, and went and changed clothes and cleaned up and got back in time to hear that Jonah had already sent a text, that he'd gone home sick.

"I was scared to death. I still have no idea how he got out of that trap we set for him—how he woke up and got his head together quick enough to get out of there and be back at school so soon."

"Jonah has always been highly resistant to drugs," Natalie murmured. "Which is probably why he gave Gabriel so much trouble." She fixed her eyes on Mandrake.

"Wait just a *minute*," DeVries said. "Don't you think it's a bit premature to be issuing a general pardon for Kinlock? How do you choose one liar over another? Everyone from Thorn Hill is suspect. Maybe it *wasn't* Kinlock who did the Halloween murders, it was her." He jerked his thumb at Alison. "Or maybe he's charmed her into covering for him. He's good at that. Jonah Kinlock murdered my sister and seven other wizards. Emma was a witness, and now she's missing and I'm guessing she's dead, too."

"Actually," somebody said from the balcony, "rumors of my death have been, you know, exaggerated."

It was Emma Greenwood.

᚛ CHAPTER FORTY-NINE ᚜
EMMA (EMMALINE)

"Emma!" Leesha stood and extended her arms, like if Emma jumped, she would catch her. Or like she could give a hug across a distance. "Thank God. We've been so worried."

Emma looked down at the sea of faces. Some took her resurrection better than others. Leesha and Natalie and Rudy—they looked as if they'd just got the best present ever. Alison seemed lost, as if maybe she'd missed something. Seph was all relief, like here was finally one fire he wouldn't have to put out, while DeVries looked relieved and nervous at the same time—like he wasn't sure how this was going to play out.

Gabriel just looked wary.

And, everywhere, unhosted shades, frail tendrils of light in the recesses of the club; a choir of silent angels, looking on.

And the woman, the one called Lilith Greaves—she stared up at Emma like she'd been handed a puzzle that she couldn't work out. "Who *is* she?" Greaves said. "Who's that girl?" But nobody answered.

"How long have you been up there?" Natalie asked. "Did you hear what Alison said? About Halloween?"

Emma nodded. "I did. I heard a lot. And what Alison said matches up with what I remember. So I believe she's telling the truth."

"Emma," DeVries said. "Please. Come down here so we don't have to shout."

"I can hear you fine from here," Emma said.

"Listen to me," DeVries said, looking up at Emma, a note of pleading in his voice. "Remember how Kinlock broke into your father's house? Remember what happened to your father and my sister—and you? Just because Alison has confessed to the murders on Halloween, it doesn't change the fact that Kinlock is a killer." His voice hardened. "You need to tell them about that night in the Heights—what you saw."

"You go first," Emma said. "Tell me what you know about an old man named Sonny Lee Greenwood who died on a hot night in Memphis last summer."

And all the blood drained from DeVries's face, leaving nothing but guilt behind.

"See, you told me how the police in Memphis were hunting me on account of the fact that Sonny Lee had been murdered. That was the club you were holding over my head to get me to back up your story. But I get down to Memphis, and I find out that nobody down there has a clue that Sonny Lee was murdered. Everybody down there thinks he was an old man who fell and hit his head and died."

"Emma," DeVries said, swallowing hard. "That doesn't mean that—"

"So I'm thinking the only person who knows for sure he was murdered was the murderer himself." She paused, let a heartbeat go by. "Or herself."

Emma knew she'd nailed it when DeVries sagged, shoulders slumped, like he knew it was no good trying to deny it. "It was an accident," he said.

"An accident? How do you *accidentally* break in to somebody's shop? How do you *accidentally* knock somebody down?"

"Rachel was young and inexperienced. I never should have sent her out on her own. She was just trying to scare him, and—"

"And so she killed the person I loved most in the world. So then you turned right around and sent that same girl to my father's house. How many people died then? And then you're all guilty, so you're going to take me on as a project and set me up with a woodshop and a little house with a picket fence after I give you Jonah. So, no. You've been pretty careless with the lives of the people I care about. So I've got nothing at all to say about that night that's going to help you out."

Emma was talking to DeVries, but she was watching everybody. Gabriel was wadded up in his chair like a crumpled sheet of sandpaper, used up and useless. Greaves just kept fixed on Emma, her expression flat, unreadable, peculiar. Maybe it was because she was a hosted shade, somebody wearing a borrowed body. It stood to reason she'd look peculiar.

"Where's Jonah?" Emma demanded. "I want to talk to him."

"He's not here," Gabriel said, licking his lips, looking at Greaves.

"I can see that. So where is he? Kenzie says something's wrong—he isn't himself."

"On the contrary," Greaves said, "Jonah is finally everything he was meant to be. We've honed away those last rough edges. He is my creation, and he's perfect."

A warning pinged in Emma's head. "I like rough edges," she said. "That's what makes a person real. Now, I want to know where he is."

Leesha said, "I haven't been able to reach Ellen and Madison. I think we should go check on them." She was looking up at Emma, and Emma knew that it was some kind of warning to her. That she'd figured out the game. But Emma didn't get it.

Then Gabriel came alive enough to say, "Wait! There's something you should know."

"Shut up, Gabriel," Greaves said.

"Don't you see?" Gabriel said. "It's over. We're done. All we can do is—"

"I said, shut *up*! Everybody stays here." Then she shouted, "Brendan!"

All around the theater, doors opened and hosted shades poured in. This time, the shades didn't attack, but formed a ring around them, blocking their path to the door. And stood, as if awaiting orders. In response, Alison and the other shadeslayers scooped weapons from under their seats and formed a circle around the mainliners, pointing their weapons at the shades.

Gabriel seemed as surprised as anybody. "Lilith? What's this?" he hissed.

"You may think your life is over, but ours is just beginning," Greaves said. "We've waited a decade for this, and I'm not going to let you wimp out on me now. This is about payback for what happened to us at Thorn Hill."

McCauley was on his feet, flame flickering around his person, his eyes like twin flames in his ashy face. "*What* is payback?"

"After ten years, the only thing we've found that can restore the damaged survivors of Thorn Hill is blood magic, freed by the death of the gifted. We've been collecting it in dribs and drabs, but it's never enough to have more than a temporary effect. We're tired of bloodshed. We want to come in from the cold and salvage what's left of our lives."

"And so—?" Seph said.

"Sometimes the innocent pay a price for the sins of the guilty," Greaves said. "The Weirguilds are responsible for the massacre at Thorn Hill, so they will pay a blood price."

Somehow, Emma found her voice. "Listen to me!" she shouted. "What happened at Thorn Hill had nothing to do with the Weirguilds. It had everything to do with me and my family. If you want revenge, I'm your person."

"What do *you* know about it?" Greaves said. "Who are you?"

"My name is Emma Greenwood. My father, Tyler Greenwood, used to kill people for Andrew DeVries, Rowan's father. Tyler destroyed the commune at Thorn Hill to get revenge on my mother, who was cheating on him with *him*." She pointed at Gabriel. "I have my father's records, I have his confession, and I've been to his lab. You all have been blaming each other for something my father did. The only justice in this whole thing was that Tyler went back and killed DeVries Senior so he wouldn't come back after us."

"Tyler was the one?" Rowan looked up at her, his face a white spot of shock. "*He* killed my father?"

"Shut up, Rowan," Emma said, clean out of patience.

"You have your father's notes?" Mercedes said eagerly. "Would they tell us what was used at Thorn Hill? Where are they?"

"I've got whole boxes of files in my truck," Emma said.

"That won't help, because it's not *true*," Greaves said. "He wasn't there. Tyler was never there. He couldn't have—"

"Yes, he was," Emma said. "He was there long enough to poison the wells, and then he took me back to the States. He confessed it to me."

Greaves stared up at Emma, like she'd seen a ghost. "Claire?" she whispered.

"That's my middle name," Emma said. "I'll tell you all about it later, but right now, I need to know what you've done with Jonah."

"But I'm your mother, Claire," Lilith Greaves said.

Time seemed to stop. Emma stared down at the woman on the theater floor. "No," she said, shaking her head. "My mother was Gwen Hart."

"That's me," Greaves said. "I was Gwen Hart. When I came to Thorn Hill, I used the name Lilith Greaves so Tyler and DeVries wouldn't track me down."

"No," Emma said, digging in. "My mother died at Thorn Hill."

"My *body* died at Thorn Hill," Greaves said, "but I survived, because of the longevity manipulation we did."

"No," Emma repeated. "My mother would never experiment on her own daughter." But of course she would. That's exactly what Tyler had said.

"You don't understand," Greaves said. "You were never meant for *this*." She swept her hand, including Rudy, Natalie, Alison, and the rest. "You were never supposed to be part of Nightshade." She said it as if it were a dirty word. "You were special. It was all about music. That was your gift. In you, I was creating a savant whose music could bring light into darkness and reconnect broken spirits. Your music was designed to heal wounded souls . . . even mine."

"That's not true," Emma said, her mouth dry as sawdust.

"You used to play so beautifully," Greaves said wistfully. "You were never meant to be a weapon. You—you were a work of art. My masterpiece."

"My friends are not weapons," Emma said furiously. "They are *people*. And they don't deserve this."

"Claire," Greaves pleaded, extending her hands toward her. "Please. Try to understand. We'll talk about it. There are so many things I need to tell you."

But Emma wasn't listening. Thoughts rocketed through her head, a hundred loose ends tied up in a knot. *That's why you don't have the tattoo. That's why you can play nearly anything you pick up. It's not natural—you didn't get it the usual way, from Tyler or Sonny Lee. It got plugged into you like an amplifier or a special-effects pedal.*

"No," Emma said, backing away from the railing. "I am *not* your work of art. I refuse to let you ruin music for me, too."

"Listen to me," Greaves said. "I did it for you. It was all for you. We'll be fine, you'll see. This is perfect. After today, I can be a real mother to you. We'll make up for lost time, I promise."

"What—after you slaughter all of these people, we can go on like they never existed?"

"That's the thing," Greaves said. "It won't be necessary to kill the gifted anymore. All we need is the single, most powerful, purest source of magic available. That one sacrifice will get us a lifetime together. Maybe more than a lifetime—maybe forever."

Emma didn't get what Greaves was talking about. But Seph did.

"Maddie," Seph whispered. "No. Not Maddie. She had nothing to do with Thorn Hill. She was a kid when it happened. She didn't even know about the Weirguilds then."

Hurling flame into the crowd blocking his path, Seph tried to break through the cordon of shades, making a run for the door. One of the shades brought an iron bar down on his head, and he crumpled to the floor. Shades swarmed forward, but Rudy, Alison, and Charlie formed a wall, firing their odd weapons into the crowd until they faded back.

"No!" Greaves cried. "I told you. No more killing. We just keep them here until Jonah's finished. Then we let them go."

That's when Emma understood. "You sent *Jonah* to kill Madison Moss?" Her voice echoed throughout the hall.

Greaves nodded. "And collect the blood magic—enough to save us all. Enough to treat everyone at the Anchorage. Enough to return all of us to healthy, permanent bodies."

"No," Emma said, shaking her head. "No. You couldn't."

"It's a very pleasant death, I assure you," Greaves rushed to say. "And it's simple justice. It ends the killing for good."

"You're wrong," Emma said. "Didn't you hear a word I said? Why should Madison Moss atone for what you and Tyler did? That's. Not. Justice." She pounded on the balcony railing with every word.

"Claire," Greaves whispered. "Isn't there any thing I can do, any way I can convince you that—?"

"What you can do for me right now is to *call Jonah off*," Emma said, her voice trembling with rage. "Call him off!"

"It's too late," Greaves said. "I have no idea where he is. Besides, it's likely done by now." She extended her hands toward Emma. "We'll get past this, I promise. It's a sacrifice, I know, but worth it in the end."

"Why is it that you're always sacrificing other people?" Taking a breath, Emma let it out in a long shudder. "Let me tell you something, *Mama*," she said, pouring every bit of the pain and sorrow and guilt she'd suffered since the summer into that word. "If Jonah Kinlock kills Madison Moss, you will be dead to me in every way. *Every* way."

For a long moment, Greaves looked up at her. Stared at her as if she couldn't believe what she was hearing. Then turned and strode toward the door. The shades shifted uneasily, as if unsure whether to go or stay. Eventually, about half of them followed.

"Lilith!" Gabriel hurried after her, catching up to her by the door. He clutched her arm. "What are you doing? This whole thing was your idea. You can't leave me in the middle of this."

"Watch me," Lilith said. She jerked her arm free just as the doors to the lobby banged open and a crowd of hooded, black-clad wizards boiled in, waving guns. It was almost comical, how they skidded to a stop when they saw the shades in the way. But it quit being comical when they began firing volleys into the crowd.

Lilith must have been hit, several times, but she walked on and out the door. Gabriel Mandrake, though, stumbled back at the impact, swayed, and then toppled backward, landing flat on his back, eyes wide open. After a moment, Emma saw it, a smear of light rising from his body. It hung there for a moment, as if hoping to dive back in. Then she lost sight of it.

After that, it was bedlam. The hosted shades who were attempting to follow Lilith out of the building ran straight into the gunmen, who emptied their firearms at them with little effect. The shades were soon distracted by the scent of fresh blood magic and swarmed over the black-clad wizards.

Emma saw Leesha, crouched behind a stack of chairs. "Leesha!" she called.

Leesha squinted up at her, her eyes dark hollows in her ashen face.

"Where's Madison Moss?"

Leesha swallowed hard. "Two blocks over, redbrick warehouse, corner of Birch Alley and Stanley."

Emma turned, and ran, half-throwing herself down the staircase. But when she reached the outside doors, she found that the shooters had left a wizard there to prevent escape. A wizard with a gun.

Emma didn't have any weapons, but she just ran straight at him. Maybe she'd be lucky, and he'd miss, which wasn't a great strategy. She saw the flash of the gunman's teeth as he smiled. He raised the gun just as somebody barreled through the doors behind him, slamming him to the ground. The gun went flying. The newcomer was dressed all in black, too, but Emma recognized the shock of red-blond hair and his build. It was Jack Swift, carrying his own gun. And, right behind him, Fitch and some other faintly familiar people.

"Not a good idea to stand right inside the door," Jack said, nudging the unconscious wizard with his foot. "That's how accidents happen. Are you all right, Emma?"

"I'm all right," Emma said. "But there's a big fight going on in there. Leesha, Seph, Mercedes, and DeVries are there with a bunch of hosted shades. Seph's been hurt. Gabriel's dead. And these guys just showed up and began shooting." She pointed at the wizard on the floor.

"What about Ellen and Madison? We can't reach them. Are they in there, too?" Jack nodded toward the auditorium doors.

Emma shook her head. "Leesha said they're still at this other warehouse. And . . ." She swallowed hard. "Jonah's gone there to kill Madison."

Jack's face went pale. "What?"

"It's a long story. It's not Jonah's fault. Gabriel and—and Lilith—they've done something to him. That's where I'm heading. I have to stop him."

"I'll go on ahead," Jack said, "and see what's what." And he took off running, much faster than Emma could possibly go.

"Please don't kill him!" Emma shouted after him. Please, don't anybody else get killed, she thought. And ran after Jack.

⊗ CHAPTER FIFTY ⊗
ZOMBIE NIGHTS

For what seemed like a long time, Ellen gaped at the feeding frenzy by the door. Burroughs had completely disappeared under a pulsing mass of bodies. It was an oddly silent attack—there were no roars of rage or whoops of triumph, just the sound of bodies colliding. Some were already pulling back, realizing that they would never get a place at the table. It wouldn't be long before they noticed Ellen and Madison.

"Do you believe in zombies now, Burroughs?" Ellen murmured. Returning Waymaker to its baldric in order to free up her hands, she slid her arms under Madison's body, tilting her back against her chest.

"Hang on, Maddie," she whispered. "Don't you go into shock, now."

Madison's teeth were chattering, and her skin was pale and clammy. She'd left a puddle of blood on the floor.

"You never listen," Ellen muttered.

The zombies were between them and the door they'd come in through. Ellen carried Madison to the back of the warehouse, her long legs dangling, walking flat-footed so as not to make any noise. The only door she could find was secured by a large padlock that looked as if it had rusted in place. She'd have to put Madison down to melt it or bash it with her sword, and she wasn't sure that would even work. Not quickly enough. She continued along the back wall, seeking a refuge, a place to hide, a way out. The only thing she found was one of those large freight elevators, the ones that look like big cages. Ellen looked over her shoulder and saw that some of the undead had found the puddle of blood. They raised their heads, as if looking around or testing the air, then turned and stumbled toward Ellen and Maddie, as if following a scent.

Ellen carried Madison into the freight lift and gently set her down against the solid back wall. She drew her sword, leaning it against her hip, and tried to raise somebody on the PCD. "Come on, Jack," she muttered. "I know you want in on this." But there was no signal—it was like the Anchorage buildings were cutting off the signal in and out. She pulled out her phone. Who else could she call? Somebody in Trinity? Anyone there was too far away to be of much help before they became zombie fodder.

She called Jack's number, but it went to voice mail. "Listen up, Jack—I'm here in the warehouse. Burroughs is dead, Madison's been shot, and we're surrounded by zombies. Oh, and there's a team of assassins hunting down everybody else. I could use a little help here, if you get this."

Ellen looked up to see a crowd of undead bearing down on them. Clicking off, she set her feet and dragged the metal elevator gate closed with an awful screech. The first of them reached the elevator, bringing with them the unmistakable stench of decay. Ellen's eyes watered so badly, she could barely see what she was doing as she fumbled with the latch, trying to secure it.

Finally, it clicked into place. She stepped back as they thrust fingers through the gate, either trying to reach Ellen or muscle the gate open again and working at cross-purposes. She grabbed up Waymaker and jabbed at the groping hands, lopping off body parts whenever she connected. They scarcely seemed to notice.

"Do you smell something disgusting?" Madison made a face and struggled to sit up.

"I do," Ellen said, and punched the elevator button. The lift lurched upward with a *rattle-bang*, zombies clinging to the outside, Ellen poking at them with her sword, trying to dislodge them until the elevator entered the shaft, scraping them off. Again, there was no screaming as they fell, just the crunch of bodies hitting the floor.

Ellen debated about whether to ride all the way to the top floor, so they would be as far as possible from the mob below, or stop on the second floor, where they might reasonably force their way out a window and survive a drop to the ground. It wasn't a hard decision, though, because when they arrived at the second floor, shades were already swarming out of the stairwell. So she punched the button again, and they rattled up two more levels to the top floor. There she helped Madison out of the elevator, and sent it back down to ground level, hoping they would follow it back down. She could hope they weren't smart enough to figure out where they were.

She used Madison's scarf to wrap around the wound in her leg, pulling it tight to put pressure on it.

"Wait here," Ellen said to Madison, which was stupid, because she wasn't going anywhere. Ellen did a quick once-around the top floor of the building. It was nearly empty, save for a lot of dust, a pile of furniture pads, and a bunch of heavy barrels lined up on a pallet in one corner.

Returning to Madison, Ellen propped up her feet on a rolled-up furniture pad and covered her with another one. Then, she tipped the barrels, one by one, as quietly as she could, and rolled them to the top of the staircase.

Peering over the railing, she saw the zombie hordes boiling up the staircase. She waited until they'd crossed the landing on the floor below and were halfway up the last set of stairs, then sent the first of the barrels careening down toward them. It pretty much cleared the stairs of zombies on its way to the bottom. When it hit the concrete floor, it exploded into shards, splattering a sticky black substance everywhere. Some kind of pitch or marine oil, maybe.

The creatures were persistent, though, and they didn't seem to feel any pain. If their bodies were intact enough, they would begin dragging themselves up the stairs again, only to be trampled by those coming behind. A couple of them even made it to the top of the stairs, where Ellen used Waymaker to cut them into pieces. Sometimes, she switched off, sending flame through her blade instead. Those that had been covered in pitch went up like a torch.

Ellen had a bad feeling she would run out of barrels before she ran out of zombies.

Even worse, she heard the rattle of the elevator on its way back up. There was no way she could cover the staircase *and* the elevator. Thinking quickly, she used her sword to smash through the lid of one of the remaining barrels, then tipped it so its contents slopped down the stairs. She raked flame across it until it caught, going up with a *whoosh*, effectively blocking the staircase.

This could be a big mistake, she thought, as she charged back toward the elevator, which was just arriving. *Here's an update, Jack: now the warehouse is on fire.* Reaching the doors of the elevator, she directed a stream of flame at the latch, hoping she could fuse the doors shut before the zombies arrived. Instead, it melted and dropped away, rendering the door unlatchable.

That always works in the movies, Ellen thought. She pulled out the dagger she must've forgotten she had hidden in her boot and waited, her sword in one hand, the dagger in the other.

When the elevator arrived, she found herself face-to-face with Jonah Kinlock, pale and blood-spattered, his eyes as cold as glacial ice, a massive sword in his hand. And, all around him, the dismembered bodies of zombies. He was the only one standing.

Ellen was so startled that she nearly dropped her knife.

"Where's Madison Moss?" he said. "That's who they're after. Though you'll do, I suppose."

"What?" Ellen said stupidly.

"The shades. They're after blood magic, and she's like the mother lode. That's what drew them here."

"She's hurt, and . . . hey!" Ellen pivoted and saw that the shades had reached the top of the stairs, having broken through her wall of flame. Bringing the tip of her sword up, she sent flame ripping into them as she barreled forward, swinging Waymaker in a broad arc, neatly cleaving their heads from their bodies.

Behind her, she heard the cage door bang open, and then, moments later, an ear-shattering crash as the lift hit the floor three stories below.

He's cut the cables, Ellen thought. Why didn't I think of that?

The next thing she knew, Jonah was up next to her, whacking at the shades with his own two-handed swing. "It's better if you swing low," he said. "It really slows them down." He demonstrated, cutting through three shades at thigh level. They toppled backward, impeding the progress of those behind. "If it makes it easier, you're not really killing them; you're just evicting them from borrowed bodies."

Why would that make it easier? Ellen thought. It means I'm doing all this work for nothing. "Is there any way to, you know, permanently kill them?"

"Yes," he said, but he didn't elaborate.

Ellen stole a sideways look at Jonah's sword. "That's a named sword, isn't it?" she said.

Jonah nodded. "It's Fragarach, one of the Seven." With his other hand, he ripped off a long piece of railing, and drove it, endwise, into the oncoming shades. It seemed that anything was a weapon in Jonah's hands, and yet he hadn't demonstrated any magical powers so far—only superhuman strength and agility. And fabulous moves.

"Leesha was right," Ellen said "You're good at this."

"It's what I do," Jonah said. And it must have been true, since he dismembered corpses with deadly efficiency.

What about live people? Ellen thought. What about Halloween? It was really hard to think that about the warrior fighting next to you. The warrior with a cold, ruthless quality she hadn't seen before. A chill rippled down her spine.

Not warrior. Enchanter. Savant.

Ellen wiped sweat from her forehead with her sleeve, then drove her blade forward again, using her booted foot to free the body from her blade. "Did you let me and Jack win that day in Trinity?"

Jonah shook his head. "Warriors are better fighters than hosted shades," he said.

Eventually, the seemingly endless supply of zombies dwindled and ran out. Ellen looked down at herself. She was totally slimed, and so was Jonah. Stowing her sword, she sprinted back to where Madison lay and fell to her knees beside her. Madison's eyes were open, but her pulse was thin and fast, her skin cool and clammy.

Jonah squatted beside her. "Did she get stabbed or—?"

"Shot," Ellen said. "It's a long story, involving wizards behaving badly. I'll try Mercedes again. She'll fix her right up." She groped for her phone.

"Wait," Jonah said. He reached inside his sweatshirt, pulled out a large, stoppered bottle, and set it on the floor beside him. Then a small tubular device that he balanced on his hand.

"What's that?" Ellen asked, leaning closer. "Medicine?"

"Not exactly," Jonah said. "Here, I'll show you." Quick as thought, he gripped her arm with his gloved hand and pressed the device against her skin. Ellen felt a quick pinch, like a mosquito bite, before she yanked her arm free.

"Hey!" Ellen said, pitching herself backward, away from him. She came up holding her knife. "What did you just do?"

"What I had to," Jonah said. "That's what we all do, isn't

it?" His voice was cool, matter-of-fact, detached. "Don't worry. You'll wake up in an hour or so, with nothing more than a headache. I'm speaking from experience here."

Ellen rubbed at the tiny puncture on her arm. "But why, after fighting off the shades, would you turn on us?"

"It's nothing personal," Jonah said. "They were after blood magic. So am I. You want to keep Madison alive. I need to save my brother's life. We both can't get what we want. It's as simple as that. A clear conflict of interest."

"I was beginning to think you were one of the good guys," Ellen whispered.

"That's where you made your mistake," Jonah said. "There are no good guys."

He looked down at Madison and gently raked her damp curls off her forehead with his gloved hand. "I'm told that this doesn't hurt a bit."

Ellen lunged at him, but somehow she missed, and hit the floor instead.

❧ CHAPTER FIFTY-ONE ❧
WARRIOR VS. SAVANT

Jack was surprised to find the door to the warehouse open, with some raggedy dudes milling around in front. As he got closer, though, he began to notice a stench that grew stronger and stronger the closer he got. Like something had died. His steps slowed a little as he realized that some of the dudes were missing limbs and had bones protruding through their rotting flesh. Some of them were carrying makeshift clubs and broken bottles.

He inventoried his weapons. He had Hackleford's handgun and some concealable knives. He tried to remember what Fitch and Leesha had said in the hearing about the best defense against the walking dead.

Jonah said the best way to stop them was to take off their legs, so they can't chase after you.

His sword, Shadowslayer, was what he needed, but it was back home in Trinity. He eyed a flagpole that protruded from the warehouse, but it looked too lightweight. But the cast-iron streetlamp pole looked plausible. He ripped it free from its base, then wrenched a length of chain from a decorative railing. He coiled the chain around his shoulder and advanced, holding the pole across his body like a staff.

Three of the undead charged at him. Jack swung the pole in a broad arc, aiming at knee level, and heard the cracking of bone as he connected. They went down like kingpins, and the rest scattered.

Inside, it looked like a major battleground, with dismembered corpses lying about. Burroughs lay on his back just inside the door, an expression of abject terror frozen onto his face, a pistol by his side. He was dead. Jack checked the pistol. Its magazine was empty.

All was quiet on the first floor—Jack saw nothing alive or even undead. But he could hear voices from upstairs. He recognized one as Ellen's. He almost shouted up to her, but something stayed him. He looked for a way up. He could tell that the elevator was no longer in working order, but he climbed the outside of the elevator shaft, jockeying his body past the framework on each floor. He kept climbing until he heard the voices just above his head. Dropping to the floor, he eased up the last set of stairs from the third floor to the fourth level, picking his way through a minefield of charred bodies.

When he reached the top of the stairs, the voices had gone silent. The first thing he saw was Ellen, sprawled face-down on the wood floor nearby, Waymaker's hilt poking over her shoulder. She was covered in blood and gore. His heart shuddered, then began to beat again, painfully hard. Tears burned in his eyes. She'd gone down without even drawing her blade?

Pulling his pistol out of his waistband, he flicked the safety off and eased forward.

Across the room, he saw Madison propped against the wall, her skirts muddied with blood, eyes open, staring at him. No, staring beyond him. Her hand twitched, pointing.

Without pausing to look, Jack leaped aside just as a body glanced off him, breaking his grip on the pistol so that it pinwheeled away. Moments later, he heard it hit the floor below. Jack rolled back to his feet, and found himself facing Jonah Kinlock.

Jonah stood over Ellen's body, looking like he, too, had been the guest of honor at a bloodbath. Jonah saw no visible weapon, only some sort of small device in his hand.

"I don't want to kill you, Jack," Jonah said. "Not if I don't have to."

"I *may* want to kill you," Jack said. "I haven't decided." He recalled Emma's words. *They've done something to him. Please don't kill him.*

Yet, grief squeezed him like a vise. *Somebody* had to pay for Ellen, for that massive hole in his heart.

Jonah nudged Ellen gently with his foot. "She's not dead, if that's what you're worried about. She'll be good as new in an hour or so."

Jack broadened his stance. "And I should believe that because . . . ?"

"Because I have no reason to kill her. Or to kill you, for that matter. All I want is her." Jonah tilted his head back toward Madison.

"I'm sorry," Jack said. "That's not going to work for us."

He wondered what had happened to his metal bar. Had he dropped it somewhere?

Jonah took a step back, and another, away from Ellen, and back toward Madison. "Here," he said, gesturing toward Ellen. "Take her and go."

Jack took a step toward Ellen, then another.

Jonah nodded encouragingly.

Keeping his eyes on Jonah, Jack knelt next to Ellen. With a quick movement, he pulled Waymaker free and came back to his feet, pointing the blade at Jonah.

Jonah sighed. "Seriously?" Taking three more steps back, he reached down and came up with his own sword, still blemished with blood from the earlier battle.

Jack shrugged. "I'm a hero. What can I say?" He swept Waymaker back and forth a few times, testing the weight of it. "I don't suppose you'd like to surrender?"

"I can't," Jonah said, advancing on Jack.

At first, it was a gentle dance. They were testing each other, identifying strengths and weaknesses, those bad habits that always betray a swordfighter in the end. Unfortunately, Jonah hadn't lost any skills since the last time they'd met on the lists.

Except. It might have been Jack's imagination, but Jonah seemed less able to read him than he had in that last bout, to anticipate his moves. Unless Jack was getting better at hiding his intentions. His intentions were, of course, to drag this out as long as possible, since time was on his side. Sooner or later, the battle in the Keep would be over, and this fight would be interrupted.

It was, of course, the kind of match Jack would have enjoyed in other circumstances. The warehouse was like a three-level Ninja Warrior obstacle course with hidden hazards such as unstable railings and charred staircases that might give way at any moment.

Jack wasn't sure if he could actually win with an unfamiliar sword, but he hoped he could keep Jonah occupied long enough for help to arrive.

Leesha tried to fight down the waves of panic that washed over her as the fighting raged on, the flashbacks of the battle outside of Trinity, when Jason fell and died, and there was nothing she could do. At first, she crouched under the steps to the stage, her arms covering her head like a first grader during a tornado drill. Eventually, she forced herself to come out of cover. It was one of the hardest things she'd ever done.

She discovered that Jonah was not the only one skilled at fighting the undead. The launchers didn't work all that well against the hosted shades either, so Rudy and Alison eventually set them aside, producing swords and hatchets and other edged weapons from some other hiding place. Along with the three unfamiliar savants—Mike, Charlie, and Thérèse—they formed a perimeter around the stage, where the mainliners were huddled.

At least the arrival of the Black Rose wizards provided a new and welcome distraction for the remaining hosted shades, who saw an opportunity to collect blood magic on the spot. The wizards, for their part, couldn't seem to grasp that neither conjury nor gunfire was all that effective against hosted shades. Even direct magic had its limitations when used against creatures who don't mind getting a little charred. Some of the would-be assassins fled through the theater doors, but it sounded like there was more fighting going on outside in the lobby.

Leesha knew the breather wouldn't last long—when they'd finished off the Black Rose wizards, they would again focus on the mainliners in the middle. And there weren't that many of them. She headed backstage, looking for a possible exit. But shades encircled the building on all sides, filling the alley outside the stage door. She did find a ladder that led up to a catwalk for the lighting techs. That looked defensible, anyway.

She ran back to the front of the stage, just in time to see the lobby door open, and four more people burst into the room: Hudson, Morrison, Blaise Highbourne, and Fitch. Two wizards, a seer, and a Harvard sophomore. They hesitated just inside the door, staring at the carnage, then began to fight their way forward.

"No!" Leesha screamed, waving them back. "Run! Get out! Go!"

But it was too late. They were swarmed by shades. She saw Blaise go down, and then she couldn't see any of them.

"Blaise!" Leesha cried. She leaped off the stage and ran toward the place they'd disappeared. They were easy to locate: Hudson and Morrison were spewing flames in all direction, and Leesha all but got fried before she made it to where the newcomers were huddled.

"I guess that's what they mean by friendly fire," Fitch said, batting out sparks on his sleeve.

Leesha looked around. "Where's Blaise?"

"He—he's gone," Fitch said, shuddering. "He went down."

Leesha found herself wishing *she* could flame someone. So she yelled at Fitch instead. "Harvard! What don't you understand about 'stay away'?" she demanded. Still, she grabbed his hand and held on tight.

By now there was no chance of getting back out of the theater—there were too many shades between them and the door. More seemed to be coming in from outside, to replace the ones that left with Lilith.

"All right, everyone, head back to the stage," Leesha said. She turned to the two wizards. "You two! Keep the shades off our rear, but don't flame anything until you see what you're aiming at."

To her surprise, they obeyed. Well, she always *was* good at giving orders.

She would have said it was impossible, and yet somehow they made it to the edge of the stage, with Morrison and Hudson covering the rear, Alison, Rudy and the others keeping zombies off their flanks. Fitch climbed up first, then reached down to lift Leesha back onto the stage.

"Leesha!" Hudson called out a warning.

Leesha looked up to see a large blade descending, glittering in the stage lights. It was just like everybody said. Time slowed down, so she had time to regret the fact that she'd only kissed Fitch a few times, and now she'd never get to go to the ashram, but truth be told, she'd rather go to Belize, but who goes to Belize anymore anyway? She wondered where the shade had come from, how he'd got through to her. Her life didn't pass before her eyes, because she had no interest in revisiting most of it.

She had time to think all that, and then Fitch covered her with his body and she breathed in his scent, his hair was tickling her neck, smelling of that bargain shampoo he used, and she could hear the hiss of his breath, close to her ear, and she was crying, "No! No! No!" and then something slammed into them, hard, pitching them off the stage and onto the floor and blood spattered over her, it was everywhere in her mouth, her eyes and she was sobbing, and yelling, "Harvard! Harvard! I told you not to come!" and then somebody pulled her in close, pressing her face into a wool peacoat that stank of wet sheep and blood, and he held her tightly, and stroked her hair and murmured, "It's all right, it's all right, Leesha. We're both okay."

And it was Fitch.

She looked up at him, and his glasses were smashed and splattered with blood and dangling from one ear, but he was alive. He was alive and she thought she just might die of happiness.

But then she turned to look, and it was Alison there on the floor, limp as a rag doll, nearly cut in two where she'd intercepted the blade. The shade lay nearby, broken and still. And kneeling next to Alison, Sylvia Morrison, weeping.

As Leesha watched, she saw something rising from Alison's body, like a vapor. Or an angel. It lingered there a moment, like a spiderweb that catches the sunlight. Morrison reached her hand out toward it, eyes wide with wonder, but it rose higher and higher until Leesha couldn't see it anymore.

Somehow, Leesha resisted the urge to just sit there in Fitch's embrace. Somehow, she got back on her feet and nagged and cajoled the others onto the stage. She herded them back to the ladder and pointed. "Climb."

"Where does that go?" Hudson asked, peering up into darkness.

"Away from zombies," Fitch said. Hudson climbed.

❦ CHAPTER FIFTY-TWO ❧
SORRY ON MY MIND

On the way to the warehouse, Emma stopped and fetched the SG from the car. She felt kind of foolish, but she respected Kenzie's wisdom, especially where his brother was concerned. Anyway, she had a feeling that the outcome with Jonah would depend on something other than firepower.

She found the building with no trouble. The door stood ajar, and bodies sprawled just inside the doorway. Farther in, she realized that the building had come under attack by shades, and somebody had fought back big-time. It was a major battlefield, with dismembered corpses scattered all around. She found nobody alive on the first floor, but every once in a while, a flicker of movement told her there were free shades around. She did her best to ignore them.

The old freight elevator had been thoroughly trashed. The staircase wasn't much better—it was charred, like somebody had set it on fire but it had burned itself out. It was littered with more bodies.

Is it all over? she wondered. Am I too late? Then she heard faint sounds from upstairs.

She began to climb, testing each step with her foot before committing herself, one hand on the railing, the other hanging on to her guitar. As she climbed higher, the noises overhead grew louder: the thud of feet on the wooden floors, the hammer of steel on steel, breath rasping in and out.

The sound of fighting.

Flinging caution away, Emma flew up the stairs, her feet barely touching the treads, her guitar swinging away from her body as she made the turns.

When she reached the third floor, she saw them: Jack and Jonah, circling like gangsters in a knife fight, their swords bright flames in the fading light. Feinting, thrusting, jabbing at each other, each looking for the opening that would end the fight and break Emma's heart.

It seemed they'd been at it for some time. Sweat dripped from their bodies, staining the floor, and the walls around them were scorched here and there where jets of flame had hit. Both of them were bleeding, though neither seemed badly injured.

She saw no sign of Ellen or Madison.

Jonah's back was to Emma, so she couldn't read his expression. Jack was facing her, though. His cheeks were flushed, and he looked like he was just about done in. When he spotted Emma, standing frozen at the top of the steps, he looked up at the ceiling, then back at her, up at the ceiling again.

Emma got the message. Maddie was upstairs.

Leaving Jack and Jonah fighting was really hard, but she still did it. As she scrambled up the stairs, Jack howled a challenge and lunged forward, hard, driving Jonah away from the foot of the stairs and toward the back of the building.

As Emma turned the corner onto the next flight, she looked down and saw Jack dodge sideways just in time to avoid Jonah's questing blade.

Whatever I do, I'm too late, she thought.

Crossing the landing at the stop of the steps, she saw Ellen lying facedown on the floor. Madison was slumped against the wall nearby, her skirts and the floor around her smeared with blood.

For one terrible moment, Emma thought that they were both dead. But Madison, at least, was alive. Her blue eyes were fixed on Emma's face, and she was taking quick, shallow breaths.

Was there any way Emma could get her downstairs, past Jonah and Jack, to safety?

No. There was no way.

So Emma looked around, hoping for a hiding place, a back stairwell, something.

Nothing. Only a bunch of old barrels, a liquor crate, and some furniture pads.

At least she could make it a little harder for Jonah to find her, and buy a little precious time.

Placing a furniture pad next to Madison, she rolled Madison over onto it. Maddie moaned in pain, but Emma could tell she was trying to cooperate. Taking hold of the edge of the pad, she dragged her back into a corner, and covered her with more furniture pads. Then she rolled barrels into the opposite corner, making a little barricade, and piled pads behind it. She carried over her guitar case, unlatched the catches, and lifted it out. Sitting down on the crate, she settled the SG onto her lap and waited.

Finally, she heard someone trudging slowly up the stairs. Jack or Jonah? The question was answered when Jonah's head and shoulders appeared at the top. His hair was in disarray, and a long scratch slanted across his cheekbone. He carried his sword in one hand, a steel bar in the other. His gloves were on.

His gloves were on. That was a good sign, wasn't it?

Odd that he hadn't noticed her before now. Ordinarily, he was impossible to sneak up on.

What should she say? Emma was *not* the kind of person they'd send to talk somebody out of jumping off a ledge.

It doesn't really matter, she thought. Ellen was dead, and Jack, and Maddie maybe dying. Jonah had already leaped from the ledge and was hurtling toward the ground. There was no way she could save him. Which meant there was no way she could save herself.

But, ironwood spine and all that, she had to try.

"Hey, Jonah," Emma said.

Jonah stopped in his tracks, showing no flicker of emotion, recognition, nothing. His eyes had always been a mingling of guilt and pain and hope and humor and history—an abstract painting of the blues. Now they were flat, impenetrable, like a painted-over window or an opaque finish on an exotic wood. Now she knew exactly what Kenzie had meant.

"You need to leave now, Emma," he said finally. "I thought you'd gone away."

So he *did* recognize her. That was a start.

"I did go away," Emma said. "I went all the way to Memphis. But I came back for you."

"Well, you shouldn't have."

"Did you really have to kill Jack and Ellen?" Emma said.

"They seemed to be good people, and that's something we need more of."

For a long moment, he just stared at her, that awful blank look on his face. "They're not dead," he said finally. "I want to keep casualties to a minimum. Which is why you need to leave."

Hope thrilled through her. *Maybe it's not too late if I can keep him talking, and buy some time.* But she had no gift for persuasion.

"Um . . . didn't you worry that they might win?"

Jonah shrugged. "I cheated," he said. "They really are better than me."

"Kenzie's worried about you."

"He should be worrying about himself. Maybe now I can finally do something to help him." He looked past Emma, scanning the room, looking for Madison.

"You should at least have asked him first. I'll tell you right now, he's not willing to make that trade."

"Well, I am." A muscle worked in Jonah's jaw. "He'll get over it."

"I don't think he will," Emma said. "And I don't think you will either."

Jonah lifted his sword high, so that the light penetrated all the way to the corners. "When did you talk to Kenzie?"

"Just an hour ago. He says you're not yourself—that it's like they took out your heart."

"What they did was set me free. They did me a favor."

"What do you mean?"

"Empathy. I've been an empath all my life. As you can imagine, that's a major handicap for a killer. So they disabled it." Scraping back his sleeve, he displayed his forearm.

A second tattoo of a rendered heart had joined the familiar Nightshade flower. He snapped his fingers. "Like magic. My guilty conscience. Gone."

"It's still there," she said, trying to act confident. "Anyway, you are not a killer."

Jonah laughed, the sound a harsh clanging in Emma's ears. "Go home, Emma," he said, like she was a child. "It's not like I have a choice. Since I'm hardwired for this. I might as well embrace it."

"That's not true."

"You don't know anything about me, and you sure don't know anything about killing."

"Is that so?" Emma said. "Well, if anybody is a natural-born killer, it's me."

"Would you just go so I can get this done?"

"Nobody's stopping you," Emma said.

"Fine," he said. Striding over to Emma's barricade, he set down his weapons and began to dismantle it, lifting the barrels like they weighed nothing and tossing them aside. One of them cracked open, splattering the contents all over the floor, filling the air with the stink of petroleum.

Well, Emma thought, begging isn't working. And so, heart thudding, she began to play, running through a new improvised bridge for "You're Gonna Miss Me."

As she played, she talked. "See, you know how we thought the mainline guilds were behind what happened at Thorn Hill? I found out that the wells *were* poisoned, but not by them. It was my father, Tyler. He was mad because my mother was cheating on him with Gabriel."

"Tyler," Jonah said, wading into the nest of furniture pads, pushing them aside. "The man I killed the night we met."

"*Did* you kill him?"

Jonah wanted to say yes, Emma could tell, to prove just how low-down bad he was. Instead he said, "I still don't know."

"Lilith Greaves is my mother. Her real name is Gwen Hart."

"Lilith is your mother." He wasn't exactly asking questions, just making statements, repeating whatever it was that she said.

"That's right. So between the two of us, who's hardwired for murder, do you think?"

"It doesn't matter who poisoned the wells," Jonah said. "The end result is the same, and the fix is the same."

Emma could tell she was losing him, so she hurried it along. "You don't even know it's a fix," she growled. "Who knows what will happen if you kill her?" She jerked her chin toward Madison. "Even if you end up with blood magic, it's going to run out sooner or later. You might be worse off than before."

"We don't know if it's a fix," Jonah said, "but it buys us some time, and it's the only option we have."

"Maybe not," Emma said, licking her lips. "I've been to Tyler's lab. I have all his records, all his recipes, all his files. Don't you think Natalie or Mercedes could do something with that? Gabriel always said what we needed was more information. Now we have it."

"You may be right," Jonah said. "But I can't take the chance that you're wrong." He kicked a barrel out of his way and crossed to where Madison lay in her nest of padding.

With a grunt of satisfaction, he began to pull away the quilts.

"Jonah!" Emma said, her voice ragged with desperation, "You listen to me. If you're looking for revenge, I'm the one you should be coming after."

"This isn't about revenge," Jonah said, squatting next to Madison. "It's about doing what's necessary to save Kenzie's life."

"Really?" Emma growled. "If you want to save your brother's life, you do have a choice. Who are you going to bet on—Lilith Greaves or me?"

Jonah didn't seem to hear. Slowly, methodically, he began to strip off his gloves.

Emma recalled her mother's words. *In you, I was creating a savant whose music could bring light into darkness and reconnect broken spirits. Your music was designed to heal wounded souls . . .*

You've told so many lies, Mama, Emma thought. This time, this one time, I hope you were telling the truth.

She launched into the opening bridge for the new song she'd written on the way back from Memphis, the song that she never sang the same way twice. She began to sing

I ain't looking for forgiveness, I won't try and cop a plea,
There is no earthly reason you should take a chance on me.
I've been a loser all my life,
So this should come as no surprise
But, this time, I've got sorry on my mind.

Through the entire first stanza, she was afraid to look up, afraid Jonah would be doing what he'd come here to do. When she finally did sneak a look, he was sitting, spooky and still, bare hands resting on his knees, staring out into space. So she went on.

I'm thirty miles from Memphis and a thousand miles from home.
I've got murder on my conscience, and I'm guilty to the bone.
There's too many ways to hurt a person
With no way to make it right,
But here I am with sorry on my mind.

Now Jonah's eyes were closed, his lashes dark on his cheeks. "I don't know why you should be sorry," he whispered, swallowing hard. "None of this is your fault."

"I can't help how I feel," she said. "If you or Madison end up dead, that'll be my fault, too. That's a big load to carry around."

I was born to be a sinner, I was born to play the blues.
You were born to pain and trouble in a world you didn't choose.
My daddy was a killer,
Says my mama was to blame,
But I'm the one with sorry on my mind.

"Maybe you can help me out with this last verse," Emma said softly. "It's giving me a lot of trouble. Try as I might, I can't figure out how this song ends."

I've got no right to be here, you've made that pretty clear,
I don't like what I'm seeing when I look into the mirror.
But I just had to come here
And lay it on the line.
And tell you I've got sorry on my mind.

"Why are you doing this?" Jonah's voice shook, and tears leaked out from under his lashes. "It's like they finally gave me a drug that takes the edge off the pain, and you just keep poking at it, opening up the wound, making me feel things I don't want to feel."

"That's what makes us human," Emma said. "Feeling things—even pain. That's what music does, if it's any good: it makes you feel things. You listen to a song, and somehow you know what that person was going through when he wrote it. Or maybe it puts a name to what you're feeling. And because you can share that, you don't feel so alone."

She grabbed a breath. "You may think you can't touch anybody without hurting them, but you're wrong." Setting her guitar aside, she crossed the distance between them and dropped to her knees in front of him so they were face-to-face. Reflexively, he pulled his hands back, balling them into fists.

"You've touched me, Jonah," she said, "and I'll never be the same." Their eyes met, and, once again, she saw the Jonah she knew.

"How did you do that?" he whispered.

"I guess," she said, "I've finally figured out what my gift is. Now, please, put your gloves back on."

One heartbeat. Two. And then, with a quick movement, Jonah scooped up the gloves and slid them on.

Emma breathed a sigh of relief.

"All right," he said. "We'll do it your way. I don't know anyone I'd rather bet on."

Emma put her hands on his shoulders. "You know what I think? What you call *empathy*—that knack you have for putting yourself in somebody else's place—that's a strength, not a weakness. Never, ever give it up."

Jonah pulled her in for a fierce hug. Emma rested her

head against his chest, so she could hear the beating of his heart and breathe in his familiar scent.

"You know what *I* think?" Jonah said, after a while.

"What?"

"The ending of that song does need work."

"Maybe," she said, "we can work on it together."

CHAPTER FIFTY-THREE
INTERMEZZO

When you bring guns to downtown Cleveland and start firing them off, sooner or later the police are going to show up, and that's just what happened at the Keep that night. It was a crime scene that had everything but live suspects and a plausible explanation.

There was plenty to go on CSI could have camped there for a year, given all the evidence that needed collecting. The scene could have been a training stage for murderers—some of the victims had been hacked apart, some had been shot. There were guns all around, but everyone who had used them seemed to be dead. In fact, the vast majority of the bodies looked like they'd been dead for some time, though some were remarkably well preserved. Some of the dead were people who had been missing for months.

Madison Moss was the only seriously wounded person who was still alive. They took her to Metro, but she was out in a matter of days. Too stubborn to stay, they said.

On the night of the attack, none of the witnesses had much to say, and the perpetrators all seemed to be dead. Eventually, Ross Childers arrived, one of the rare occasions when a big-city department calls on a small-town officer for investigative help. He interviewed as many survivors as he could, and so finally, like all terrible ordeals, the long night was over.

There was a big memorial service for Gabriel Mandrake, and music superstars from all over the country showed up. It would have made sense to have had it at the Keep, in the fortress he had built, but it was closed for major cleanup. So they held it in a nearby church.

The media buzzed around Cleveland for weeks; there was plenty of fodder to keep them occupied, but when nobody would agree to an interview and the police just kept saying the investigation was ongoing, after a while they had to close up shop. Merchants and restaurateurs downtown were worried that the lurid coverage of the Carnage at the Keep, as the media called it, would deter business. In fact, the demand for zombie tours increased and the entertainment district took on a kind of edgy, dangerous appeal.

The investigation was never formally closed, but the prevailing theories seemed to be that it was either a meth-fueled turf war or it had to do with some kind of bizarre religious cult.

⊚ CHAPTER FIFTY-FOUR ℘
YOU'RE GONNA MISS ME

"**H**ow come the party always ends up at *my* house?" Kenzie said, scowling as the others filed in.

"Um, I don't know, best sound system, maybe?" Jonah said, shutting the door behind him.

"Best light show?" Emma said, setting down sacks of takeout. "Though I have to say, Kenzie, lately, the display is not up to standard."

Natalie eyed Kenzie critically. "*Hmmm.* Show me?" She extended her arms to demonstrate.

Grumbling, Kenzie stuck out his arms. They were rock steady, showing no telltale webbing of flame.

Natalie nodded, displaying grudging approval. "Mercedes and I think we can do even better with the symptoms once your Weirstone is completely healthy."

"Whatever happened to patient confidentiality?" Kenzie muttered. "Harry! Fill the ice bucket, please."

"You're not supposed to rely on Harry so much," Natalie

chided. "You're supposed to try to do more things for yourself."

"Harry likes doing it," Kenzie said. "I mean, we've been together forever. I don't want to hurt his feelings."

"How's the walking coming?" Natalie persisted.

"Are you ever off-duty?" Kenzie pulled up his sweater to reveal the T-shirt he had on underneath. Emblazoned on the front was NAG in large letters with a slash across it.

Natalie rolled her eyes.

Jonah couldn't help smiling. Just after the standoff at the Keep, when Kenzie no longer had access to blood magic, he'd hit a low point, suffering from a major rebound reaction. During that time, Jonah scarcely left his brother's bedside. Emma was there a lot, too. Sometimes they just sat and talked and held hands, Emma's grip firm and warm through the leather. An anchor. Sometimes, they brought their guitars and played until light leaked in through the windows. Like an old couple, finishing each other's musical sentences.

They were still working on the ending of that song they were writing together.

For the last few days, though, Emma had seemed distant and a bit standoffish. Jonah would catch her looking at him in this perplexed and wounded way. He wondered if it was because she was leaving for Memphis in the morning. Did she expect he'd try to talk her out of it? He would not. She deserved a chance to move on, if that's what she wanted.

Mercedes and Natalie and some of the other healers from both Trinity and the Anchorage had worked nearly round the clock on the records from Tyler's lab. Eventually, they identified the poison Tyler had used—it was a plant native to Brazil, and not one they'd have likely chanced on without help. It was largely unknown, so there wasn't much out there in the way of antidotes, but once Mercedes knew the mechanism, she had a scheme for treatment.

It was Natalie who had determined that the poison embedded itself in the Weirstone, which was what made it so difficult to find and treat. They tested Weirstones from savants who had died, and confirmed it. After research trips to Memphis, and trips to Brazil, they devised a two-step process: first, extract the poison from savant Weirstones, and second, a chelation therapy to take it out of the body.

Kenzie was the first patient, because he was totally out of options. At first, the extraction made him even sicker, but he began to improve as soon as the chelation treatment began. Now, six months later, he was putting on weight and muscle, what with his daily torture sessions with the physical therapists and his ravenous appetite. He'd probably always be slender, and he'd never be as tall as Jonah, but this time his glowing good health seemed real . . . and permanent. For the first time that Jonah could remember, it seemed safe to look forward to a future with Kenzie in it.

"Speaking of sound systems, can you get some tunes going, bro?" Jonah said.

"Harry. Favorites playlist, please." He watched as Jonah arranged beverages on the windowsill. "Did I miss somebody's birthday? Or are we celebrating something else?"

"We *are* celebrating," Natalie said. "We're waiting for a special envoy to arrive."

As the first bars of "Untouchable" blasted through the speakers, Rudy groaned. "You never get tired of that, do you? Is it going to be all Fault Tolerant, all the time, from here on in?"

"Why should I listen to inferior music?" Kenzie said. "Anyway, you were the one who was hot to make the EP."

The EP project had grown out of Kenzie's recovery. It had been on the to-do list for a while, but now they had an extra incentive to record the Kinlock catalog.

"Note to self: be careful what you wish for," Rudy said, with a mock shudder. He gave Kenzie a sideways look. "The thing is, we need more tunes."

"They're coming," Kenzie said. "The creative spirit is not like a faucet you can turn off and on. Anyway, it's not like we've had nothing to do."

"Kenzie isn't the holdup," Jonah said, easing himself into a chair. "I've got a whole lot of new material from him. It's just that the chelation therapy wears me out. As soon as I get home, I'm done."

"Welcome to our world, Superman," Rudy said. "People can live totally normal lives without leaping tall buildings at a single bound."

"If things go as expected, Jonah should keep his strength and sensory acuity," Natalie said. "What Gabriel and Lilith did changed the architecture of our stones, so some things are hardwired. If it's true that the uncontrollable toxic touch thing is really a side effect of the poison, then the removal of the stored poison should help that. As a matter of fact—"

"Has anyone else noticed that Natalie is getting harder and harder to understand?" Jonah said. "When did she stop speaking English?"

Natalie looked at Jonah, narrow-eyed, and he shifted his eyes away. Quit pressuring me, he thought.

Just then, the doorbell pinged.

"That'll be Leesha," Natalie said, leaping up and keying in the okay to enter.

"I just live here," Kenzie murmured. "Don't mind me."

It *was* Leesha, and, behind her, a tall, angular Anaweir boy with platinum hair. He looked familiar, but Jonah couldn't place him.

"Fitch!" Emma cried. She hurtled out of her chair and flung her arms around him. "I didn't know you were home. Are you back for the whole summer?"

"Unfortunately, no," Fitch said. "I have to be back in Cambridge for summer session in a couple weeks. I'm still catching up after being gone for fall term."

"I hope it's okay I brought my friend Fitch along," Leesha said to Natalie. "You'd said that Kenzie was feeling better, and we both wanted to see him again."

Fitch had been looking around the room. When his gaze lit on Kenzie, he made a beeline for him and bumped fists. "Kenzie! My man!"

"Fitch!" Kenzie grinned. "My jailbreak partner. Welcome to my lair."

Seeing Jonah's confusion, Fitch stuck his hand out. "I'm Harmon Fitch. You probably don't remember me, but you saved my life in the Flats just before Christmas."

"Ah," Jonah said. "I remember—you were at the Halloween party, too. Dancing with Leesha."

"After *you* turned me down," Leesha said.

"Make yourself at home," Kenzie said. "Lord knows, everyone else has. Drinks are over there, snacks on that table. Empty chairs there."

Leesha and Fitch fetched drinks. Leesha perched on the

edge of a chair. Fitch declined a seat, but leaned against the wall, looking just a bit awkward and ill at ease.

"Jonah and I were with Leesha in Trinity all day today, working out some legal issues," Natalie said. "I asked her if she would come answer any questions you might have about the outcome." Natalie nodded to Leesha.

"Okay, well, Mercedes and I have been working with Jonah and Natalie on a plan to put the buildings, assets, and endowment of the foundation in trust for the survivors of Thorn Hill."

"Hear, hear!" Kenzie said, and they clinked their glasses.

"So, as of today, it's a done deal. The papers are signed, the lawyers paid."

"Really?" Rudy said. "It was that easy?"

Leesha nodded. "Frankly, everyone was amazed at how well-endowed the foundation is." She paused, and repeated, "Amazed. There should be plenty of money to provide support for all Thorn Hill survivors as well as fund research into treatments for free shades, assuming that becomes a priority. So. For now, the foundation will be governed by a board of trustees that includes representatives from the Interguild Council as well as students and staff from the Anchorage. Mercedes has agreed to direct health services here, for the time being, at least, and we'll be recruiting for a school director as well. We'd prefer to hire a savant, but—" She stopped. Cleared her throat.

"But there are no adult savants, at this point," Jonah concluded. "None of us have made it to eighteen."

"But we will," Natalie said. "To the future." She raised her glass.

"What about savant representation on the Interguild Council?" Kenzie asked.

"The council has agreed to that," Leesha said. "Ironically, Hilary Hudson and Sylvia Morrison were two of your most vocal supporters. If there's anything you want to ask for, now is the time. I think I speak for everyone when I say the council would be willing to lynch any and all members of the Black Rose. It's a shame that none of them survived the incident at the Anchorage."

"A shame," Emma said solemnly, and they toasted again.

"DeVries is going along with this?" Rudy said. "From what I heard, he seemed hell-bent on convicting Jonah of something."

"Remember that thing Jonah said about starting a fight?" Emma smiled her street smile. "I don't think he wants to get into it with me. He knows he'll lose. And without my testimony, he's got nothing."

"One issue we haven't settled is what to do about shades," Leesha said. "It's been totally quiet for the last six months— ever since the standoff. The Weir killings seem to have stopped for now. We don't know if they'll continue to pose a threat to us. And we don't know anything about how to communicate with them. Or how to fight them, if we have to. That's something we hope you can help us with."

"We've talked about that, too," Emma said. "Their leaders—some of them, anyway—know now that what happened at Thorn Hill was not an attack by the Wizard Guild, but that it was a . . . a case of domestic violence and revenge." She stopped, released a long breath "My mother was the one organizing shades against mainliners. I don't know what she's thinking or planning at this point." She looked at Jonah for help, and he picked up the story.

"At least it's blown up the argument that mainliners are fair game because they caused the problem in the first place," he said. "But we really don't know what they might do. I have no desire to make war on them. They didn't deserve what happened to them. So for now, I'd advise watching and waiting. If the killings start up again, then we won't have a choice but to do something about it."

"Maybe Gabriel and Lilith are together again," Emma murmured. "They deserve each other."

"What about Madison?" Jonah said. "How is she feeling about all of this?"

Leesha stared down at her hands, as if working out what she was going to say. "Seph says that Madison is having a hard time. She blames herself for the violence over this past year—she feels like if she'd taken responsibility for her role as the Dragon, none of this would have happened. I don't think that's necessarily the case, but . . ." She shrugged. "Alison and Gabriel are dead, and they are the ones most directly responsible for Grace's death. So in that regard, justice has been done."

"I just feel bad for Alison," Rudy said. "I wish things could have been different for her. It's so unfair."

"Maybe it will be," Natalie said. "She is still out there, you know. Maybe one day we'll come up with a way to restore free shades in a permanent, ethical way."

"Would you be willing to be on the Board of Trustees, Leesha?" Natalie asked. "If we nominated you?"

"I'm willing to do whatever it takes to make sure this all

works out," Leesha said. "Just so you know, I won't be available for the month of July."

"Vacation?" Jonah asked.

Leesha smiled, stealing a look at Fitch. "I've never been to Cambridge, and Fitch has promised to give me an insider tour."

◌ Chapter Fifty-five ◌
Walking in Memphis

After Leesha left, Jonah looked at Kenzie. Kenzie looked back, poker-faced, and then they both burst out laughing.

"Amazed," Kenzie said, raising his glass.

"Amazed," Jonah said, clinking with him.

"What?" Rudy said, looking back and forth between them. "Are you Kinlocks holding out on us?"

"No, actually, Gabriel was holding out on *us*," Kenzie said.

"Explain," Emma said.

"We're talking about Gabriel's supersecret hidden padlocked offshore accounts," Kenzie said. "The ones he thought were safe from punks like me. And the U.S. government. I actually hacked in six months ago, and I installed some code to keep track of keystrokes, password and account changes and like that."

"Six months ago?" Rudy said, frowning. "That would have been right before the standoff at the Keep?"

Kenzie nodded. "Remember when I said you should never piss off a hacker? Gabriel still hasn't learned his lesson. First, he doped me up with blood magic, which rendered me *even more* clever and creative than usual. Then he locked me up in a technological desert." He smirked. "I had time on my hands, a fresh grudge, and a technical challenge. So I started knocking on digital doors. At the time, I wasn't aiming that high. My idea was to establish access to Gabriel's assets so Jonah would have some options if I could talk him into leaving. He could parley the Kinlock catalog into a rock-and-roll empire. Or he could offshore himself—just lay on a beach somewhere—one of those places where they'll bring you cold beverages when you put up your drink flag and never ask for an ID." Kenzie put up both hands to forestall a protest. "I'm sorry, bro. I've been living vicariously through you so long it's hard to get out of the habit.

"Much to my surprise, I discovered that Gabriel has been making money hand over fist from the properties in Brazil, and from the foundation itself. Gabriel was systematically looting foundation assets and offshoring the money. He recently mortgaged all the buildings to the max. I figure he'd already decided to cut his losses and split, maybe with Lilith. But before I could do anything about it, they did their Frankenstein thing on Jonah, and all that shit went down with the council and the Black Rose. Then I was totally incapacitated by blood magic withdrawal. When I'd regained my senses, I muscled in again, and simply restored the funds to their rightful owner—the foundation. And now we are flush." Kenzie rubbed his fingers together.

"To Kenzie!" they all said, and clinked glasses while he made *pshaw* sounds.

I can't believe I'm leaving now, Emma thought, with so many good things happening.

It was as if Natalie read her thoughts, because she said, "I wish you'd stay here this summer, Emma. Rudy and I are going to try to get the club going again—on a small scale, anyway. We could play some gigs there, and go back to the studio and lay down some more tracks."

"Please, Emma," Rudy said. "Help an orphan fulfill his dream of producing an LP. Maybe you could wait and go back to Memphis in the fall, when it's getting cold up here."

Emma shook her head. "Don't get me wrong, I love it here," she said, "but I've just got to be in Memphis in the summertime." She shrugged. "I guess I like it hot." Her eyes met Jonah's, her pulse quickened, and her stomach did that shimmy thing that was happening more and more often. But he looked away.

"What will you be doing down there?" Rudy asked. "Woodworking?"

Emma collected her thoughts. "My friend Mickey has a club down there. I told him I'd help him out this summer, see how I like it. I'm going to hang out my shingle and make some connections, and hopefully pick up some custom work and commissions that I can work on this winter. The shop stays here, because I'll definitely be coming back in the fall for school."

"Good," Rudy said, looking mollified. "If the shop stays here, I know you'll be coming back. Just don't be romancing any other bands while you're down there."

"You know my heart belongs to you," Emma said. "Anyway, Nat's coming to visit, right? So you and Mercedes can spend some more time at Tyler's lab?"

Natalie nodded. "We'll be in touch about dates."

"Kenzie, you and Jonah are still planning to come down in August, right?"

Kenzie grinned. "The Kinlock brothers make a road trip. I can't wait. I don't think we've ever had an actual vacation."

"Just keep working hard in therapy," Emma said. "I plan to take you into the twistiest, seediest, low-down dives in town, and they aren't always that accessible."

"Nothing motivates my little brother like twisty and seedy," Jonah said.

"I guess I'd better go now," Emma said. "I still don't have everything in the truck, and I want to get an early start tomorrow." She took Jonah's arm, gripped it tight. "Walk me back to Oxbow, Jonah?"

It was either rip his arm free or go along. So he went along.

Summer was finally taking hold on the city after fumbling several times. The street trees were blooming, and the bars had finally opened their patios for good.

I guess that's progress, Emma thought wryly. She never thought she'd see Jonah Kinlock clad only in a thin T-shirt and jeans, not even in the summertime.

They threaded their way around diners on the sidewalks, hearing bits of conversation as they passed by.

"You have Sibelius loaded on your laptop?" Jonah said.

"For the tenth time: yes, I do," Emma said. "And I have the three-ways on my calendar." Her cheeks burned as she realized how that sounded.

Jonah pretended not to notice. "Now that school's out, I'll have a couple weeks to rough out some lyrics for the tunes I already have. Meanwhile, Kenzie will be working on some more melody lines. We'll do a swap—I'll send you what I have, and you can give it the smell test."

"If it passes, I'll work on the guitar line," Emma said.

They walked a few paces more, and then Jonah returned to an old topic. "You'll let me know if there's any shade activity? Or if Lilith shows up in Memphis?"

"You'll be the first to know. I really think I'm safer there than here."

They'd gone over this before, but Jonah kept bringing it up. It was like he didn't trust any scrap of happiness that came his way. Like he worried that it would go up in flames.

They loped up the steps of Oxbow, entered the code for the elevator, and rode up, silent as two strangers trapped together for the ride.

"You think Kenzie will be good to come in August?" Emma said as they exited on her floor.

"He really, really wants to do it," Jonah said. "So I'm going to say yes."

Emma caught herself. She always talked about Kenzie when she wanted to talk about Jonah, because that topic was safer. It had fewer sharp edges, and they nearly always agreed.

When they reached her door, she said, "Come in for a minute."

"I'd better go," Jonah said. "There's still a lot of cleanup at—"

"I said, *Come in for a minute*," Emma repeated. "It's not an invitation; it's an order."

She pushed open her door and stood aside, arms folded, as he edged past her. Then closed the door behind him.

"What's this all about?" Jonah said, shifting from one foot to the other.

"Sit down," Emma said, and he eased down onto the edge of the couch, hands on his knees. She drew up a stool and sat opposite him. "Natalie says that the resident toxin in your hands is nearly gone. That it's down to a trace."

Jonah hunched his shoulders, like a kid caught out in a lie. "That's what she says. Though I don't know how she can tell for certain."

"She says she's been trying to get you to do exercises in therapy. Touch therapy. What she calls desensitization."

Color stained Jonah's cheeks. "I can't believe she told you all this. That's just wrong."

"She told me because she thinks it's safe for you to—to be more aggressive, but you run the other way."

"I don't know why she's in such a hurry about it," Jonah said. "I'll get there."

"She's not so sure," Emma said. "She thinks you have a—a phobia about it. A mental block."

"It's—it's really hard for me, all right?" he growled. "She of all people ought to understand that."

"I think she does understand that. But she's afraid that if you aren't pushed, it'll never get better."

"It's just that everything I touch . . . everything I love . . . dies. Lilith said that the poison was intended to surface at will. Well, how do I know it won't surface again, unexpectedly? How do I know I can control it? I couldn't live with myself if—if it happens again."

"Well, it's hard for *me* to watch somebody I care about torture himself. What are you going to do—have throwaway romances with people you *don't* care about?"

"No," he said through gritted teeth. "Being an enchanter, it's not fair to—"

"Oh, shut *up*, Jonah," Emma said. "I have to admit that resisting you is something I never get really good at. It's like playing the Dobro."

Jonah's head came up. "What?"

"It's like playing the Dobro. I have to keep practicing. And if I get distracted, *wham!* But that doesn't mean it can't be done. I'm not here because I'm a natural nag. I'm terrible at it, in fact. My usual policy is, let people be. I'm here because you're my friend, and I love you. We may not end up being anything more than friends, but I'll be damned if I'll let you go through life alone because you're scared to be with somebody."

She waited. He said nothing. She said, "I want you to try something with me. Will you?"

Jonah licked his lips. Looked up at the ceiling and sighed. Then looked at Emma, straight on, and said, "What *exactly* did you have in mind?"

Emma's cheeks burned again. "I'm going to hold your hands," she said. "Very easy, very low key. I won't do anything without asking. Any time you want to say whoa, say whoa." She drew up the stool until they were knee-to-knee. "Let me see your hands."

He extended his gloved hands toward her, palms up. She cradled them in her own. They sat like that for a minute, face-to-face, Jonah's hands resting in hers. "Now I'm going to take your gloves off, okay?"

He nodded, panic flickering in his eyes.

"Close your eyes if it makes it easier," Emma said. He did. "See, I used to have stage fright, believe it or not," she said as she worked his fingers free. "I was fine playing in the shop, or with one or two friends in a back room, but I would just freeze when I got up in front of people. Sonny Lee, he told me that the only cure for that was doing it. I did, and he was right, but I did my first three songs with my eyes shut."

Jonah snorted softly, but kept his eyes closed.

"Okay," she said. "Gloves are off. Are you all right?"

Jonah's nostrils flared as he took a deep breath, then released it. "I'm okay," he said faintly.

Emma could tell he was scared. His face gleamed with sweat, his T-shirt was stuck to his shoulders and arms, and he was taking quick, shallow breaths.

Gently, she pressed her thumbs into Jonah's palms and massaged them. Then she squeezed each of his fingers in turn. His nails were clipped short, and the tips of the fingers on his left hand were callused from years of guitar work. They were experienced hands, supple, capable hands, and yet, at the same time, unweathered, having been covered in gloves for most of his life.

"You can tell a lot about a person from his hands," she murmured. Taking one of his hands between her two, she worked it from wrist to fingertips, mapping how muscle, tendon, and bone fit together. Then she did the other hand.

Gradually, the tension left Jonah's body. His head tilted back, exposing his long throat, and the bunched muscles in his shoulders relaxed.

"You're doing great," Emma whispered. "You're doing just fine. And I'm fine, too. I'd like to try one more thing, if you're up for it."

"What?" he whispered.

"This," she said, and gently pressed one of his hands to her face.

His eyes sprang open, and they were looking each other in the eye, tasting each other's breath, their lips inches apart.

"Okay?" she said softly.

"Okay," he said, his eyes like oceans, his voice a little hoarse, his body rigid with tension again. He moved his hand, brushing his fingertips across her cheekbones, the bridge of her nose, sandpapering over her lips. Finally, he cupped both hands under her chin so that he held her face in his hands. He studied her intently, as if looking for any sign or symptom of damage.

"Are you all right?" he whispered.

"I'm just fine," she said.

Taking hold of his hands again, she turned her head, kissing each of his palms. Then returned both hands to him, but kept hold of them. "Good," she said. "You did good. I think that's enough for today." She stood, lifting him with her. "Well, I need to get to bed," she said. "I want to get going early tomorrow." Sliding her arms around him, she hugged him. "Keep working on that."

"Good night, Emma," Jonah said. "And thanks." He pressed her closer, one hand on her back, just at the base of her spine, the other on the back of her head, his fingers stroking her hair. "Emma," he said, after a minute. "I have a question."

"What is it?" she murmured.

"Can we do that again sometime?"

Emma blinked back tears. "In Memphis," she said. "I'll see you in Memphis this summer, and we'll write the end of that song. But be ready. You know what they say about Memphis in August."

"What?"

"It's hot. Smoking, in fact."

❧ ACKNOWLEDGMENTS ❧

The very best part of this job is getting to hang out with people who genuinely love books. This Heir Chronicles series has been nurtured, shaped, and championed by so many people over its nine-year gestation. These are some of them.

Thanks to savvy agent Christopher Schelling, who has always found a good home for my novels through good times and bad. Sometimes I feel like we're sharing a tiny raft on the turbulent seas of publishing. Though at times we get a little seasick, so far we've managed to stay afloat.

Christopher has the best laugh in the world, all *heh-heh-heh*, that comes from some well deep inside him. He also makes great use of timely silence.

Me: Wait till you read it. It's got everything— rock 'n' roll and zombies and there's this PIRATE!

Him: {silence}

Me: Um. So. Do you think it needs more cowbell?

Thanks to Chris Lotts and his team for their foreign rights expertise. He has opened the door to incomprehensible French and German tax forms and fan mail in Turkish and Portuguese.

Thank you to the legions of writers out there who share the joy and pain of this business. For better or worse, you make me feel in context.

The entire editorial team at Hyperion has been stellar. I am so fortunate to have had a home here for so long. It all began when editor Arianne Lewin chose *The Warrior Heir* to be her first acquisition. She stayed with me through five-and-a-half books in all, almost unheard of amid the comings and goings of publishing.

The wise Abby "Steamy Bits" Ranger took over when Ari left Hyperion for new opportunities. Abby has always been able to wring the very best writing out of me, and I have the bruises to prove it. She helped me find a road through a thicket of reader feedback when I returned to the Heir series with *The Enchanter Heir*.

Editor Lisa Yoskowitz ignored the rumors that I drive editors away, and stepped bravely forward when Abby moved on to new challenges. She wrestled *The Enchanter Heir* into shape, putting up some guardrails to keep readers from plunging over the cliff at the end. Now she's helped make *The Sorcerer Heir* the very best book it can be. Any errors, omissions, and em dashes are my own.

And who presides over all that talent? Editorial Director Stephanie Lurie, a giant talent who still makes me feel tall.

Elizabeth Clark designed the original Heir Trilogy cover brand, which has been called iconic. I call it GORGEOUS. These days, my covers just seem to get better and better, thanks to the talented Tyler Nevins and the genius of illustrator Larry Rostant. I can only hope that my books keep the promises the covers make.

The publicity and marketing teams at Hyperion have helped keep this series alive in the reader hive over the years. One of my earliest publishing memories is Angus Killick doing the happy dance when *The Warrior Heir* made the Lone Star list. I'm all, *What's the Lone Star list?* And he's all, *This is huge.*

Over the years, we've evolved from White Box mailings and postcards to digital advertising and social media outreach, most recently with Andrew Sansone, Holly Nagel, Seale Balleiger, the incredible, irrepressible Dina Sherman, and Mary Ann Zissimos. Thank you for building the platforms that allow me to interact with readers.

Speaking of readers, thanks to the librarians, booksellers, and teachers who've put my books into the hands of readers. And thank to the readers of all ages who've taken my characters into their hearts.

I often say that readers and writers are partners in story. I have learned so much from all of you, and I appreciate your partnering with me. Thank you all.